THE LENS OF DESIRE

L.S. TEMMER

Book Formatting by Victoria Wright

Author Photo by Nely Piper

Cover Design by German Creative

Dedication:
For Barbara T, Mickey, and Anita. Here's to the resilience of the human
spirit.

CONTENTS

SHANGHAI, AUGUST 1937

In the morning light, Shanghai, modern and bright, a European city, arises on the River Whangpoo, off the South China Sea. On the yellow water, picked clean by scavenger boats; junks, steam ships, and yachts drift past and unload their passengers and wares. Chinese coolies, stripped to the waist, work the docks and haul great loads from daybreak to dusk.

On the Bund, where the British have built their hotels and their palaces dedicated to business and banking, and in the International Settlement where they live in enormous houses, and in their smoky, whiskey and cigar filled clubs, on their cricket lawns, racecourse, and tennis courts, life moves at a slow privileged pace.

In the French Concession, which is not inhabited by the French but by Russians, stores open, bakeries display their wares, and dance hall girls and musicians crawl into bed in the early morning hours after long nights playing the clubs.

And there are things which are unspeakable, animals and people who have died on the streets at night, child prostitutes, boys, girls, and women, Chinese, Korean and white, who cater to any taste, any depravity imagined by the human race.

The gangs run the city and control the drug trade, and people come from all over the world seeking adventure and escape.

Everywhere the odor is rank and unmistakable. It is of the unwashed bodies of the poor, the stench of cooking oil that lingers in the air, the pervasive and revolting smell of shit that is inescapable; and always the damp, which crawls into each and every corner.

❦

The day was promising to be hot and sticky as Tatiana Alexeyevna Zhukova walked down the Bund. She was a slight, dark woman of twenty-five. She had designed her own costume, an asymmetrical bone colored gabardine that recalled the silhouette of the city itself. The skirt was pencil thin, hindering her stride, which was further hobbled by high heels. Her hat, a glazed straw concoction, recalled the hats of coolies who worked in the fields under the blazing sun. She was easily more stylish than any of the white women or the rich Chinese in the city, yet despite her attention to design, she had little sense of herself. She was what she was, no matter how she adorned her treacherous body. Tanya was a mix of bravado, shyness, self-criticism and ambition, yet oblivious to the effect her manner and beauty had on other people since she could not see it in herself.

She was in a rush that morning after an early office meeting with her employer, the architect, Ladislav Hrbek. She had to get to the villa of their new client, which was also in the International Settlement. The trouble was that Tanya had known him before and recognized the ball of tension welling up inside her, but that was how it had always been with him. Hellyer. George Richard Arthur Hellyer; she repeated his name.

It was not the first time she would be seeing the villa. Ladislav had taken her to see the site and the building in progress many times, and then unapprised of their past, he had sent her to see Hellyer, who was waiting, seated in a planter's chair with his legs crossed, a superior smile on his lips, amused at her discomfort, though anyone who did not know her well would not have recognized it. She had fumbled with her portfolio, but then they had sat side by side, and he had grown quiet once he had seen what she intended to do with the interior of his new house. Hellyer was decidedly coming up in the world, but she was not sure she liked it.

They had been equals in the beginning, she thought. Well, not quite equals, never that, but his status had not been as high then, and he had been somehow more approachable. I work for him now, she reasoned. I am employed by him. It put them on a different footing, and her skin began to prickle at the thought of it.

It's the heat, she said to herself, but knew it was a sense of anxiety, the same anxiety, which drove her forward; the anxiety that she felt when she thought about herself and her future, and the past. The feeling followed her because she knew she had no real place in Shanghai, that her position was precarious and depended not as much on her talent as her ability to please and get along.

Ladislav had hired her for her looks, though she did not know it and thought it was because she came cheap and was willing to put in endless hours, toiling away on ideas he would throw her way, expecting her to refine and finish them. All the credit went to him, of course. She was considered merely a pretty appendage by male clients, and perhaps they even thought Ladislav brought her along to meetings as an incentive, and that they would be able to prevail upon her after kissing her hand and saying what a charming young lady she was.

All the while, she knew what they were thinking. To them, she was another impoverished Russian, not really all that white, not European in any sense, one step up from the Chinese, one step up from being a woman they could hire.

It had been different when she was young. She still believed something would happen, or someone would come along and restore her to her rightful position, well not that, but a respectable life, a safe life where things that were too frightening wouldn't touch her. And then she had realized that she had never had a rightful position of any sort, that her father had died soon after she was born, and that her family was ruined even before the revolution

- before all their friends were, before she had had chance to taste life.

Hellyer had never promised her anything, and eventually she had stopped expecting anything from him. He wasn't like the other Englishmen who had come out to the big trading houses as griffons and aspired to become tai-pans. He had been different.

She hadn't been able to place him at first, and then after she had heard his story, that he had been born in St. Petersburg where his father had been working at the time, and that they had only been back to England for a short time only before his father had gotten ill and had to move ever southward to France and Italy for his health, had she understood that he was as rootless as she was.

But they had not been alike. He was wild and where she was afraid of things touching her, he had wanted to experience everything, to see everything in all the raw ugliness that was so terrifying to her, and it was that which stimulated him and made him feel alive.

It was all those things which had attracted her, which intrigued her, that, and his tales of places she had dreamed of in her imaginings, not just France and Italy, but Oxford where he had been educated, and Greece, and Turkey, and Arabia where he had traveled. He had lived in Africa before he had shipped out to India, before transferring to Shanghai, where there was a place for promising men with his talents and languages. She had loved those stories, and his rooms with all their collections, the African masks and Turkish carpets, the Persian tiles, the carved ivory, and Mogul miniatures.

'That kind of man is dangerous,' her landlady Natalia Ivanovna had said, eyeing him up and down once when he had stopped for a moment to collect her. But later that evening when Tanya had insisted she knew how to take care of herself, Natalia Ivanovna had lit a cigar, and letting her eternally present robe carelessly fall open to expose her soiled slip, replied, 'I'm speaking of the danger to your heart, my dear.'

And she had replied that she expected nothing, that she had had such a pinched little life, and that she liked his stories, and Natalia had just laughed, opening her mouth to reveal red lipstick smeared over her yellowed teeth.

Eventually, there had come a time in those rooms when she did come to expect something, not a declaration nor a proposal, but some show of feeling which she suspected he might have for her. When it didn't come, when he started to change, becoming more serious about his work and how he appeared to others, she had withdrawn from his life.

Stop thinking about that, Tanya commanded herself, and she did. It's just business. You will meet him once more and you will be on your way, leaving him to his own fate. She knew it was impossible to make her appointment on time and remain cool and crisp, and so she hailed a cab, which dropped her off in front of the white villa with its curving facade and linear overhangs. It was a lovely house, she thought, but she refused to speculate what might have been, though her heart had begun beating in an irregular way.

She paid the driver and walked down the drive, up two steps to the front door. She saw the door was ajar, and she opened it and stepped into the house, knowing that she shouldn't.

The new furniture hadn't yet arrived, his rugs were still rolled up, his collections were in crates, half unpacked, not yet displayed, and everything was eerie and still. She called for the servants and when no one came, she called for him by name. She went to the back of the house, stepping down into the kitchen and saw a pot of water on the stove, and fresh vegetables, and a whole fish on the chopping block. The work had been interrupted, though the stove was cold and the rear entrance closed. For a moment, she thought to run out of the house and call for help, but something propelled her up the stairs to the second floor bedrooms. Now, the only thing she heard in the stillness of the afternoon was the sound of her own blood coursing through her veins. The street was silent despite the open windows where the curtains had been pushed aside. No breeze came through, just the oppressive afternoon heat, though the fan swirling overhead made a soft whirring sound.

The unmade bed was rumpled and reminded her of a long

afternoon of love making, though she couldn't be sure why she would have that impression. Perhaps it was envy, she thought. She walked through the entire second floor, but there was nothing and no one to be seen. The open door was reason enough to be suspicious but what could it possibly mean? A crime, a robbery? She wouldn't have known if anything was missing, in any case.

She thought about calling the police but then reconsidered. Corruption was rife among the department, and who knew how they would deal with her. No, she would telephone Ladislav and ask for his advice. It would be better to let him handle it the way he saw fit. He was a rational man, and she was certain he would have a reasonable explanation. But the whole time, she knew something was terribly amiss and she was doing the wrong thing. She tried the telephone but the line was dead. It was only then that she heard the explosions. It could only mean one thing. The Japanese had arrived in Shanghai.

PART I

SHANGHAI, AUGUST 1966

L i Kong entered the shabby courtyard where he lived with his old aunt. His heart was pounding, and although he could hear the chanting and shouts of the students he had been with earlier that evening receding in the distance, he was still afraid. He didn't understand what had compelled him to retrieve the notebooks that were slated for the bonfire they had made that evening.

It had all started with a march and a raid on the house of a class enemy. He had been consumed with anger when the speeches were being made, but when they reached their destination he had been shocked. Another group of Red Guards was already present. They had overturned the contents of the house, piling books, clothing, and household items into the middle of rooms. One of the boys was shattering vases and screaming they were remnants of bourgeois culture.

'Out with the old, in with the new!' he shouted.

Li Kong had seen a girl pocket a gold watch she found when she was shaking out the dresser drawers in a bedroom and had said nothing, turning his head away. By the time the two groups were finished, the house, which had been lovely, was in shambles, and feathers from torn mattresses floated about and settled all over the floor like dirty snow.

The whole time, the woman who lived there stood on the side, guarded by a boy and a girl, saying nothing, not even when they had shattered her vases, not even when they had confiscated her photographs.

The woman was older, though of indeterminate age, and Li Kong thought her still quite lovely. She had removed herself emotionally from the scene and looked on as if it was happening to someone else. When an angry girl shouted that the woman was living in a house that could be occupied by several families, she lowered her head and looked at the floor. She couldn't be aroused in any way, though she winced when they twisted her arm and forced her to kneel.

Li Kong had wondered what would happen to her, but none of them knew. They would leave it to the authorities to decide. They had made their point. They had shown her what was expected in the new society they were building. There would be no room for the luxury she was used to. No place for her collections of vases or her scrolls. All that was obsolete and going to be swept away. And so he had followed a group of youth into the garden where they had piled her books and recordings together and made a bonfire, and he had stood there looking at it, wondering if he should throw the notebooks he had found into the fire, but he hadn't. Now he was afraid they would find him out before he had a chance to look at them thoroughly. I shouldn't have done it, he berated himself. He wondered what harm could it do. None, unless someone else found out. I'll burn them afterward, he told himself.

Li Kong had come from a provincial town to live with his aunt in Shanghai after his parents had died. He did not remember them very well, but his aunt was a kind and generous person who loved him. Sometimes he was happy to have had the opportunity to be in the city and felt guilty for thinking so, because he knew had his parents lived, he would have ended life where he had begun it.

He was a brilliant student and knew he would have more opportunities in Shanghai. He would go to university, study medicine, and perhaps become a specialist. Sometimes he daydreamed of becoming a pure researcher and finding cures for the terrible diseases that afflicted mankind. In all likelihood, he would be sent to a drab provincial town, or even worse, to a village, to administer to the people there. Perhaps he would be fortunate enough to be able to remain in Shanghai. Still, that was many years away.

His aunt was asleep, but she had left food for him in a pot. He lifted the lid but remembering the notebooks went up the ladder to the loft where he slept and slipped them under the bed. Looking around he thought he would have to find a better hiding place after he had the chance to look through them. Then I'll throw them away, he promised himself.

He climbed down and ate quietly by the dim light of a single bulb. His aunt stirred and in a half sleep murmured his name.

'I am home. All is well,' he assured her.

He glanced out the window and saw a light on in the room opposite their courtyard. The Director lived there, alone. Li Kong often wondered why this tall man with patrician bearing was living in their part of town, and after he had first come to live with his aunt he had screwed up enough courage to ask, only to be hushed. It was only after some time, overhearing the gossip of the old women, that he discovered the Director had once been a famous figure in the Shanghai film industry. His career had ended during the purges of the late nineteen- fifties when he had been accused of being a Rightist, which was compounded by the fact that he had been educated in Paris and gone to film school in the Soviet Union.

Li Kong had for a moment wondered if it could be true, that such man was still living among them, but his aunt had discouraged all conversation on the topic. Once he had overheard her saying, poor man, when speaking to her neighbor, another old woman, who sometimes brought food to the Director when she could spare it.

The Director, he knew, made his living as a cleaner now, but it was not nearly enough to sustain him. Still, Li Kong thought, the state was benevolent and even provided for those who were its enemies. He finished his meal and set the dishes and utensils to the side. His aunt would wash up in the morning. He climbed back into the loft and lighting a candle took off his jacket and trousers. Lying down, he reached for the notebooks.

The fantastical drawings, which had initially caught his eye, now sprang to life. In the first, a woman wearing a green ball gown floated amid beds of seaweed filled with cockleshells and starfish. She seemed to have the body of a jellyfish, and yet her face and hair were those of a lovely maiden. Carp, bug-eyed and curious, swam about her. In the next drawing, she floated among the stars, a winged fairy, surrounded by white moths and creatures of the night. This time her dress was flounced and littered with stars. In another, she rode a seahorse, a trident in her hand, a helmet of coral on her head. In the following, she danced wearing butterfly wings, partnered by a dove; then floated like a swan on a glistening pond that was set in a park with waterfalls and willows.

These fantasies were soft and lovely, as if the dark haired creature could not bear the world and wanted to escape far above it, dancing, floating in realms of inner space that were completely of her own making. Li Kong couldn't help but smile. He had not opened the other notebooks, and now he did so. The one he held in his hand was filled with marvelous drawings of gems that were set in clever arrangements echoing the architecture of the nineteen thirties which was prevalent throughout the city. He had never seen anything quite like them. Each finished drawing was accompanied by tiny notes in a sharp slanting script he could not make out but knew was western.

The third and fourth notebooks were written in the same hand with scratched out portions, as if the writer had gone back to revise them. On the leaf of the first book, a photographic portrait of the girl in the drawings was pasted in. She was Caucasian, dark, and very pretty. She was also holding up a starfish that was irreverently threaded through her hair. She looked at the viewer enigmatically as if to say, well, what do you think of that?

What sort of girl could she have been? Li Kong wondered, still smiling. Frivolous, no doubt, but lovely and strange. He flipped through the pages, and those of the other notebooks, hoping to see another photograph of her but there were none. He shook the books out, thinking he had missed something, and he had, because a small photograph of a man fell out. Li Kong brought it closer in order to make out the features. He was a wild looking barbarian, with short-cropped hair and high cheekbones, who looked at the camera and at the world with a supercilious expression. Li Kong tucked the photo back into the book. He looked around for a hiding place, but finding none, placed the notebooks between the wall and the bed, with the intention of borrowing some tools and loosening the floorboards the next day to create a nook for them. He knew that he should throw them away, but he just wanted to look at the enchanted drawings a few more times.

He had unsettling dreams all night long but could not recall them in the morning, though he knew they had something to do with water and finding a way to get to it. The first thing he did was to pull out the second notebook and have a look at the photograph of the man again. In the morning light, the man's expression seemed more mocking than superior, a bit amused, intelligent, and questioning. He put it up next to the portrait of the girl. She was much softer, of course, but it Li Kong thought, they are so alike it is almost as if they are of one mind. His aunt was calling him, and he rushed downstairs to wash and eat before going to school.

There was a great commotion when he arrived at the schoolyard. Banners painted in huge red characters had been hung from the gates of the building. Students, in a state of disarray, were shouting. He pushed his way through the crowd, only to see one of his teachers, Mr. Po, being hauled about with a rope about his neck. A girl Red Guard had taken off her belt and was screaming in a shrill voice that Po was a reactionary before proceeding to beat him. Students formed in a circle around the teacher and forced him to kneel. Li Kong was pushed to the back of the crowd, but he could hear them calling Po an imperialist dog and an enemy of the state. Could it be possible? Li Kong wondered. Po was one of the best and most popular teachers in his school.

'You are making a mistake,' he heard Po saying.

'Shut up, stupid shit. You have no right to speak unless we give you permission,' a husky voice that belonged to one of the worst students there, Zhang Bojing, commanded. Li Kong knew that Zhang's father was an important party functionary and that was how Zhang was able to get through school.

'The State does not make errors,' a cold shrill voice that belonged to the school's Party Secretary, Chen Aiguo, a man who had been seconded from a Shanghai shoe factory, resounded. Chen then proceeded to check off a litany of accusations against the teacher, amid the taunts and curses of the students. Po was finally given a chance to refute them, but each time he would begin to point out the logical fallacies in Chen's arguments, Chen would twist his words against him. Po was dragged away and locked in a classroom, until it was decided what to do with him.

Students were chanting party slogans and raising their fists in defiance. Li Kong overheard that classes were canceled indefinitely but that he was expected to report each day for discussions. He also saw on a list on the wall that he, along with a few other good students, was assigned to write slogans.

'How long will this last?' he asked a tall gangling boy, who had won the top prize for high school mathematics in Shanghai the previous spring. Before the boy could answer, Chen was standing next to them.

'You think a revolution can be made from inside a class room?' he demanded.

Li Kong shook his head, not certain how to respond.

'You boys are so soft and spoiled. A revolution is made from the blood of its martyrs,' Chen said. 'And we will be watching all of you to see how well you fulfill your duty to Chairman Mao.'

It was only in the days that followed, as Li Kong and the other boy toiled side by side painting huge banners and trying to come up with slogans such as, 'Scatter the old world, bring in the new!' 'Smash the Four Olds!' 'To Rebel is Justified!' that they realized Chen was illiterate and seemed to approve their banners by their size and color.

Lao Shaoqiang, the thin boy, pressed his lips together and murmured something about Chen having had a difficult life. Then he suggested that since it was not known when classes would resume, he and Li Kong might study together so as to not fall behind when it came to taking the entrance exams for university. Li Kong was honored. Lao had mentioned his father was a physicist and his mother taught languages at the university.

They were both satisfied and set about painting another sign, when several breathless girls rushed into the room.

'Have you heard the news?' they inquired.

The boys shook their heads.

'Teacher Po has hung himself.'

'This proves he was a class enemy,' Lao said. The girls seemed satisfied with his response and went on their way. Li Kong resumed writing a character poster without looking up or commenting. Teacher Po had been his favorite.

On the way home, Li Kong was silent. Lao sensed his mood. 'I heard he was taken to a cow shed. The Red Guards beat him almost every day. They say he finally confessed.'

Li Kong looked toward the sky. The day was sunny and cool.

'You have nothing to say?' Lao asked. After a while he said, 'It's better that way.' Regretting he had said too much, he swerved off to walk on his own. Li Kong was left behind, gawping after him.

When he came home, he went to the loft and took out the notebooks from under the floorboards where he had hidden them. It had become a habit, a guilty pleasure, to look at the man and the woman and the delightful drawings. I am also reactionary for finding pleasure in such frivolous and foreign things, he thought.

He knew what foreigners had done to China, exploiting her people to open up markets in Asia. I need to be rid of these, he thought, but did nothing. He knew he would do nothing until he was able to decipher the script and find out what the entries were about.

~

'What are you doing?' Li Kong asked. He had arrived at Lao's house to study chemistry at the agreed upon time.

'Nothing.' Lao had his back to Li Kong, but he was packing something into a suitcase. Li Kong stepped closer.

'My mother has been detained. I'm getting rid of her books in case the Red Guards come here.'

'What sort of books?' He asked.

'Mostly Russian language books.'

Li Kong put his hand out and picked up one of the books, 'Russian?' he asked.

'No, this one is Russian,' Lao said, handing over a thick volume.

Li Kong grew excited. Notes were written in the margins in a hand that resembled the one in his notebooks. He tried to conceal his pleasure at this discovery. 'What's it about?' he asked.

'It's about a student who kills an old pawnbroker and then feels guilty afterward.'

'It sounds revolutionary.'

'Well, it's far from that.'

'Have you read it?'

'Of course not. It is reactionary.'

'Can you read it?'

'No,' Lao said. 'Are you going to help me get rid of these?'

The boys hauled the books in the suitcase until they reached a dump. Lao looked through them once again, tearing out any pages that could link the books to his mother. While he was occupied, Li Kong pocketed the thick book about the student. He hoped that Lao would not notice the bulge in his pocket, but Lao was more concerned with ripping up the incriminating pages to shreds.

They were gone most of the day, but Lao said they would resume their studies tomorrow. Li Kong wondered what he was going to do with the book he had taken, since he could not read it. By the time he got home, he had decided to ask the Director for Russian lessons in exchange for food. It was dangerous for them both, but if anyone discovered them, he would say that he only wanted to keep his mind occupied while classes were cancelled. He wouldn't mention the notebooks to the Director, of course.

SHANGHAI, 1966

Sun Mu gazed out through the dirty windowpane across the courtyard to where that boy lived with his aunt. What had he really been after, and what could he be thinking asking for lessons in Russian in order to read a forbidden book in this highly charged political atmosphere? Sun Mu wondered. He had turned him away and rightly so. Perhaps he was merely a gauche boy, whose naivety would soon get him into trouble, but perhaps he was one of those terrible young people who ran through the streets creating chaos without moral compunction, and without compassion for the lives they were destroying. Perhaps the boy had been sent to root out those who had fallen under suspicion, those who like himself had been purged and lost their place in the world, to see whether their ideas had changed or not, because as everyone knew all the vestiges of the old must be wiped away, and the old still harbored recalcitrant ways, even if those views were hidden somewhere deep down inside of themselves.

Still, as he looked at the courtyard, he remembered the sudden thrill he had experienced at the sight of that book, which he had read when he had not been much younger than the boy. It had been years since he had spoken Russian and even longer since he had spoken

French. He glanced at the callouses on his hands and the deep cracks that gave him so much pain during the cooler months. It had been years since he had used his mind at all, that he had even thought about anything other than getting through another day.

He had believed, truly believed, in the New China, and he had not run away to Taiwan or Hong Kong like many of his contemporaries had. He had stayed, been purged in 1958, and his films had been banned and his name blacklisted. That was his life. That was all there was. Now there would be the winter to get through, and the cold wind coupled with the humidity always gave him arthritic pains. He would have to scrape together enough money to buy ointment and perhaps that would help a bit, at least with the cracks in his skin.

At least I lived my life, he said to himself, thinking of the boy and his prospects. He momentarily felt sad, and sad that he had turned the boy away, for what would he learn now in his young life, to march and write slogans on posters? There would be nothing of the beauty and refinement that had so inspired Sun Mu in his formative years. He thought back to himself as he had been then, at seventeen, at eighteen, at twenty, and remembered the things he had surrounded himself with, the ideas he had had, and the money he had squandered. All that has passed, and there is nothing more to think about, he said to himself. For the rest of the day he could not help but recall his days in Paris and his film training in Moscow, afterward. He had been adept at languages and had picked them up quite easily, like a collector, from his Russian friends in Paris and Shanghai, and from the lessons that his father had caved in and paid for, after he, the adored brilliant only son, had exhibited his temper.

Ah, he had been quite the dandy then, a friend of Cocteau and his circle, and so many others who were not quite friends but whom he had met, Picasso, and the strange Americans who were drinking themselves to death in Paris at the time. What did that boy have to look forward to, he asked once again before unscrewing the single bulb that illuminated his barren room so he would not waste it. Then he sat in the darkness until his mind was at rest and he could fall asleep.

~

Li Kong was thoroughly shaken. He had never seen anyone murdered before. But it had happened, the thing he had dreaded most and was afraid he would one day witness. An older woman had intervened when the Red Guards had dragged her husband, an oil engineer, out of his house. He had worked for the British, and the British were class enemies who had exploited his people. The man had been pulled along the streets, half stumbling, unable to use his legs, as the Red Guards beat him, forcing him to keep moving. The woman had come running after them, begging them to stop, saying he was ill, that his heart would give out, and that he needed his medicine. They had not listened, and he had fallen like an old carthorse, unable to get up, but they had kept whipping him with their thick belts. Then they had stopped. He was already dead, and the woman had fallen on her knees next to his body and rocked back and forth, and then he heard her wail, a sound that was inhuman, that had come from a terrible and far older place that was wild and uncivilized, as uncivilized as they themselves had been that day.

He had hung back as he always did, but he had seen, and the sight was terrible to him. Afterward when they had dispersed, on the empty street, empty save for the woman who was still weeping, a cold rain had fallen down in sheets, and he had been soaked through his padded jacket, through his clothes, down to his skin.

He was still shivering in his room, and he could not stop, even after his aunt had seen him looking so wild and frightened and had made him tea and forced him to drink it down. She had surmised what had happened but did not ask and turned away from him, until, not knowing what to do, he had climbed up into his loft. The images still on his mind threatened to engulf him, so he pulled out the notebooks and looked at the pictures of the enchanted girl. Each day, he thought about her more and more, and sometimes he longed to step into her world, and be done with everything that was happening within his. He had managed to acquire a Russian language primer by meticulously searching through the piles of materials they had confiscated from the houses they had raided, but it was no good, he had no facility and could not learn on his own.

The Director had turned him away, and Li Kong knew it was because of his fear and did not blame him, but he vowed not to give in so easily and to try again. Perhaps if the Director saw the drawings in the books he would relent, he reasoned.

The next day, he brought his own dinner to the Director, rapping lightly on his door, until he was admitted. The room was even poorer than theirs, shabby and moldering, dark and close. He had sat silently watching the Director eat, refusing to take anything for himself. And then he had pulled out the book with the pictures and slid it over the broken down table, over to the Director, who looked at it blankly.

'Open it, please,' Li Kong said.

The Director did as he was asked, and Li Kong saw something change in his expression but could not read what it was.

'Where did you get this?' the Director asked after a few moments.

Li Kong watched him finger the pages delicately as if he was stroking a live thing. He thought for a moment to lie to the old man, but something inside him broke and he said, 'On a raid. We came into the house of a woman. It was a beautiful house. She had so many priceless things, vases and scrolls. They were beautiful, but we shattered and slashed everything we could find. I picked this off a pile that was going into a bonfire.'

The Director stared into space, and Li Kong could not tell what he was thinking. He had been too frank, too direct, and now he was afraid of the things he had said.

'Do you know who the woman was?' the Director asked.

'No. I remember what she looked like, but who she was or what happened to her, that I don't know.'

'And the street she lived on?'

Li Kong tried to remember, but it was no use. They had marched through streets he had never seen before. It had been dark, and he had not been paying attention, swept up as he was by the speeches that had gone on beforehand.

'I can't recall,' he said.

'Who else knows about this?'

'No one. No one knows,' Li Kong assured him.

The Director looked straight at him, 'Are you sure about that?'

'Quite sure.'

'Tell me something, then. Of all the priceless objects you found so lovely, why would you save this, an old Russian notebook?'

Li Kong reached over for the book and flipped to the page where the girl was holding a starfish up to her hair. He showed it to the Director, and said, 'There's something about the girl...' but could not finish his thought.

Oh yes, the Director thought to himself, there is something about the girl, but he said nothing to Li Kong.

'Please, I must know what it says. Won't you read it to me?'

And so the Director began to read, curious about what the girl had written, all the while knowing that there were things that he would need to explain to the boy along with the reading, all the while knowing there would be things he would conceal.

TANYA'S DIARIES

Shanghai, April 1932

  Some days that begin badly, through fortuitous circumstances, can end up happily and well, and I must always remember that and never let myself despair.

  Anya had been at me for some time. Sometimes I think she genuinely wants to help and other times when I see the look she gives me, a mix of exasperation and disbelief, I really wonder if she doesn't resent me. She has taken me on, nevertheless. I am her burden, and she bears it. I can't help the way I am I want to tell her, but she'd just say that my aunt had prepared me for nothing, and that I was not capable of dealing with real life.

  This real life of Anya's is coarse and brutal, and it's filled with pettiness and grubbing for every bit of cash she can get her hands on. It's competitive and rough, and she is always ready to take it on. What value is there in a life lived like that? We are all living in reduced circumstances here, but there is still beauty, and kindness and the good things we have in ourselves that can bring joy to our fellow creatures on earth.

'She's nice,' Li Kong interrupted, 'and thoughtful.'

'Hmmm,' the Director mused. 'We'll see. Save your own thoughts for later and don't interrupt me, please. It's hard for me to translate directly. I haven't done it for a long, long time.'

'Of course. Very sorry,' Li Kong apologized. In truth, he could hardly wait to hear the rest.

Anya says I can still afford to think like that because I haven't been on the edge, that I have been cushioned, that I haven't come to the end of the line. She mocked my aunt, even on the day of her funeral, saying she was the one who put all those airy ideas into my head. I knew they weren't true, I want to tell Anya. I just didn't have the heart to point out the obvious facts to my aunt.

'No one will save you, Tanya,' Anya says, 'so look out for yourself.'

Later, Anya bought over some crepe de Chine that a man had given her, and I was able to cut two evening dresses from it.

'Is this how they pay you, nowadays?' Natalia Ivanovna, our landlady, sneered at Anya.

Natalia can't get over the fact that Anya sometimes goes with Chinese men. Natalia has a house and rents out rooms, but Anya has never had advantages.

'Mind your own business, old woman,' Anya says, and just being called old puts Natalia in a huff, so she uses a few choice words before slamming her door.

'Take one for yourself and come down to the club,' Anya says.

The club is where Anya works most nights as a dancer. She comes home dead tired and sleeps half the day away, and that life is beginning to show on her face, in the dark circles around her eyes and the downward pull of her mouth.

'No. It's okay,' I say, but she has other ideas.

'Look, you don't have to do what I do, but if you come down wearing that dress, the other girls will see what you can do and hire you to make dresses for them.' Anya knows that I have been looking for work as a dressmaker, but that no one will hire me since Chinese are willing to work so cheaply.

'All right,' I agree, hoping something else will come up, but it doesn't.

So when she comes to pick me up, I am ready, though I feel a fool in the dress, which I have cut for Anya who is tall and flat chested. Anya takes one look at me and tells me to stop tugging at the bodice, and that I look fantastic.

'I feel naked,' I say, as Natalia Ivanovna steps out on the landing to look me over. That's how it begins, her look seems to suggest.

Li Kong was already squirming. He had questions to ask, but a sharp look from the Director put a stop to his agitation, and he stopped fidgeting and settled down.

At the club, the manager, a burly Russian named Yevgeny Borisovich Golovin, takes one look at me, and kissing my hand, whisks me to his table. All night long, people approach him with various business matters, but he won't let me leave. And so I sit there and watch the program, and after that is over, Yevgeny Borisovich asks me to dance, and while we are dancing he offers me a job. When I balk, he says it will be in the chorus, and I will not have to dance with customers at all.

'Come tomorrow afternoon, and let me see what you can do,' he says, kissing my hand again.

I don't know what to do, but Anya is happy for me and says not to worry, Yevgeny Borisovich isn't the kind of man who messes about with his employees. I was so nervous, I couldn't sit at home waiting until the appointed time, so I took my pad and went out to make some sketches. I was still debating what to do, until I decided that I might as well go and see him.

Yevgeny Borisovich was busy when I got there, and directed me to sit at a table and wait. When he was finished, he called a Chinese man over to the piano and put me in front and told me to show him what I could do.

The absurdity of this hit me. I was always the worst dancer in ballet class, always moving in the opposite direction of everyone else, but my aunt wanted me to have lessons to develop poise and a good silhouette so I stuck to it. The pianist, not looking up, began a jazzy piece, so I flapped my arms a bit and did the Charleston with my feet, and Yevgeny Borisovich laughed and shook his head.

I picked up my sketchpad and was about to leave when he called me over and asked me to sit.

'What do you have there?' he asked.

I thought he must have felt bad for making fun of me, but I was a bit angry at him as well, so I shrugged and didn't say anything.

He reached over and started leafing through the pad. He paused at the portrait I had done of Anya.

'Oh, you've caught our girl, all right. Tough as leather on the outside, pure mush on the inside.'

'She has a good heart,' I said mechanically, though I did not think that was particularly true.

'I meant that if one more thing goes wrong in her life, she'll go over the edge,' he said. I was thinking about this when he stopped at my fanciful drawings. He whistled. 'Now, this is something,' he said, tapping on the one with me walking through a field of flowers, which were transforming into butterflies before soaring to the sky.

'Can you do one like this, only large scale? I'd like it as a backdrop for a number we're rehearsing.'

I said yes, though I had never done anything like that before, and he gave me money for the materials and said I could use the back room for a studio.

'Don't let it go to your head. It's just one job. He didn't even say how much he was going to pay,' Anya said.

But I didn't care. It was a job! A real job doing something I was good at!

'Oh, she's funny. And nice!' Li Kong exclaimed when the Director paused. 'And she's not a prostitute like the other.'

'Few of them were really,' the Director said. 'They were desperate to survive. They'd lost their homeland, and they had to fall back on what they had, and the only thing most of them had was their beauty, youth, and charm.'

'They could have stayed. They chose to leave Russia,' Li Kong countered. He knew a bit about what had happened to White Russians after the Revolution.

'You will have to learn that not everyone thinks alike, and besides these women would have been young girls when their parents made the decision to leave. They had nothing to do with it themselves.'

'Oh, well, I'm certain the state would have taken much better care of them had they stayed,' Li Kong said.

'Possibly,' the Director countered. 'Shall I go on?'

'Oh yes, please.'

Shanghai, May 1932

Anya has a lover. It's made her ever so much kinder. At first, she wasn't confident in him. She said she didn't want to talk about any of it, she was afraid she would jinx it. But today, she told Yevgeny Borisovich to go to hell and stormed out of the club. They were fighting because she was late to rehearse the new number. I was afraid and ran after her, but before I could reach her, she got into a big dark car. I haven't met him. All I know about him is that he is a rich Chinese who was educated in the West.

I am busy designing a new set for the club and costumes for it as well. The butterfly flowers were a success. Yevgeny Borisovich brought in a couple of Chinese girls to help me do the sewing after I cut the patterns. The girl called Mei is talented and hardworking. I think she is about fourteen years old. There are a lot of children in the family, and she says they are always hungry. I gave her some extra money out of my pay. Yevgeny Borisovich gets the girls for almost nothing, and they, themselves, seem to have few expectations of life.

I don't know what to expect either. I don't think about it much. Not the way that I did when I was young. You always believe that something magical will happen, and that your life will somehow be special. There are so many people here that fall between the cracks. I don't mean just us, the ex-military men who work as bodyguards for rich Chinese when they can, and send their women out to prostitute themselves when they can't find work. They drink to forget and have lost hope that the government at home will fall and that we will all go back. No, I mean the Chinese, who live and die on the streets of this city, as if their lives didn't count for a thing. Each morning when I go out I see bodies, and by the time I return, they are gone - someone has picked them up. Somehow, we Russians seem to survive. People I know have even started their own businesses. The baker, who was a general, remembers his servants' recipes. That's how it goes, and you do what you have to do.

Li Kong listened with a mixture of shame and vindication. He wanted to break in and say so many things, about the past and the evil that was wrought in China, and the present since Chairman Mao had changed so many things for the better, and in particular he wanted to comment on the glorious future, because he knew that everything would be different then.

The Director had been struck by the phrase, 'You always believe that something magical will happen, and that your life will somehow be special.' Yes, that's the way it is. She was quite prescient despite her youth, but the boy is too green to understand that and so immersed in his own line of thought. And so he did not comment but went on reading.

May 1932

I'm so happy! There is an Indian jeweler who wants me to design some pieces for him. He is a Sikh, and though they are not supposed to drink, this one does. He comes to the club and dances with a few of the girls. He does this very deliberately as if he is weighing the merits of each. They compete for his attentions, for it is said he is very rich. And he is handsome and tall as well. Anya showed him some of my fantasy sketches for brooches, and he thinks he can make them work if I simplify them a bit! Well maybe a lot.

Shanghai, May 1932

Sirdar Amrit Annand Singh has shown me the precious stones that I should use to make setting designs. The emeralds and rubies are beautiful, their colors so deep and pure. Amrit Singh says I choose the best ones instinctively. He says it is a talent to be able to do so, and that the power of the stones themselves will suggest the way to move forward. He is very serious at work, in the office on the second floor of his shop, and strokes his mustaches when he is thinking. He says not to rush, to take my time and it will come to me. I tell him, I know this is the way, that the best things come to you when you are not straining or overthinking, and then thoughts and images that are fully blown spring into your consciousness. He says it is those things which are divinely inspired.

Shanghai, May 1932

Amrit Singh was delighted with my designs. I worked in geometric shapes, arranging the stones, offsetting them with diamonds, which I do not like just by themselves. I looked at some of the new buildings around town for inspiration, the lines and oblongs that are so modern yet so pleasing to the eye. Then he thought about how we would make the settings and called the goldsmith in. The master craftsman looked at my drawings, and smiling, made a few corrections. Later, we tried the stones to see how they would look in the molds. I was not satisfied, but Amrit Singh said not to be impatient. Today, I am going to look at the finished product. I can hardly wait.

It was thrilling. Amrit Singh was right. I could not have imagined how stunning the finished pieces appear! He says he will show them to a few select clients. I tell him I can dress his windows to showcase his jewels, but he smiled, and shaking his head said that is not the way he operates. I wonder who will buy them. I love the brooch with the carved emerald that hangs from a pave diamond key lock design. I think it is our best piece.

'Her drawings are beautiful,' Li Kong said. 'She is so excited to be able to work.'

'Indeed,' the Director commented. 'Have you ever created anything?'

'Me? No. I'm just a student.' Li Kong paused. 'I want to be a medical researcher. I want to find a cure for a disease.'

'Any disease?'

'I don't know. Yes, any. Whatever best serves the people.' He did not say anything about his fantasies of glory: how he would receive a special commendation from Chairman Mao, or be celebrated and respected by the people he would help save.

'I see,' the Director said. 'More?'

Li Kong nodded yes.

Shanghai, May 1932

Amrit Singh sent a letter. He has sold all the pieces to a real Indian princess. He says he would like me to make more drawings. It is a good thing, because the popularity of the two musical numbers at the club has grown and Yevgeny Borisovich says he will not be changing the program for a while. I must have looked very despondent because he said he would introduce me to a friend who can help me get more work. I think he must care about me somewhat if he is willing to risk competition from another club owner.

Shanghai, June 1932

I met with Yevgeny Borisovich's friend, Mister Isfahani. He works for Victor Sassoon, one of the most important men in Shanghai. He would like me to design the backdrop for a costume party they are giving, and perhaps I might even get to do some costume designs for the Sassoons as well!

'She's so lucky!' Li Kong interjected before a sharp look from the Director shut him up.

Shanghai, June 1932

I met the princess. She is going to the party as Marie Antoinette. I suppose that for her a French queen must be as exotic as a Hindu princess is to us. She wanted help with her costume and suggest jewels to wear with it. She invited me to her house and talked quite a lot about the Sassoons and their friends, leaving me with the impression that she would like to make a good match while she is here. She seems to have money, but many such live on credit using their connections and good name. A woman friend of hers turned up in the middle of our meeting, and from their demeanor they gave me to understand they were more than friends. They both seemed so carefree.

I went home thinking about all the parties they went to and how at ease they were in the world. It didn't matter at all, I told myself. Not to me. There was my work to think of. I wanted to create something very special for the Sassoons, and not just because there would be many important people there from whom I wanted to get work. No, the work, itself, has become important to me. I have become more exacting in my demands. I can see Mei and the other girls are not always happy with me, but I will make it up to them. I am thinking of two designs for the party. One is an enchanted forest with strangely shaped trees and hanging fruit, like an odd paradise that occurs in nightmares. The other is more conventional: the Palace of Versailles, only the boisseries will be drawn free hand, black lines on white canvas and draped about the rooms.

Li Kong did not understand what the girl had meant when she had said the Princess and the other woman were more than friends and thought perhaps they were somehow related, but he felt that it was not worth interrupting the Director to ask.

Shanghai, June 1932

Mister Isfahani said that while Victor Sassoon liked my designs, he had something else in mind. I asked what that might be, and Mister Isfahani screwed up his face and said that Victor was an exacting man and he would recognize it when he saw it. God, please, never let me be in such need that I would sell my soul like that toady. I went home to think, and then it popped into my head that Victor loved horses above all things. So I drew stylized horses frolicking in the forest and meadow, and drinking at streams, and then I reversed the colors, so that the trees were pink and red, and the horses green and blue, and the skies white and yellow. I stayed up all night and rushed over the next day, but when I got there, Mister Isfahani was meeting with Victor

Sassoon's architect. He asked me into the room, though he had me wait. Then, cleverly, seemingly in passing, he introduced us, and somehow the architect, whose name is Ladislav Hrbek, stayed to look at my sketches, which I left for Victor's approval. On the way out Architect Hrbek said that he loved my color sensibilities and that he had been looking for someone who might design textiles for him. I was thrilled and said so. He said he would be in touch soon.

Shanghai, June 1932

Three exciting things. The first, Victor (I call him Victor though I have never met him) approved my horsey drawings and I am making the full size cartoons now. The second, Architect Hrbek (I could never call him Ladislav, he is so old) hired me to do fabric designs for the furniture he will be putting in a new hotel which is going up. I looked at the furniture, and I said I could do some beautiful geometric fabric designs based on the drawings of the hotel, but that I had an idea how to make the furniture itself more fitting. I clearly overstepped myself, because he said it was not as easy as it seemed. He said that anyone with a bit of talent could draw something interesting on paper, but the trick was to make it fit the human body, and to make it fit the occasion. Look at the difference between the chairs we sit in at the dining table and the chairs we sit in at a club, he said. I replied yes one is upright for eating and the other slouched for relaxing. And he smiled and said the one for relaxing is so that people will sit for a long time and order more drinks, and the upright one is so that our guests will not overstay their welcome. I said I had never thought of it just that way, but that I could see his point. And that brings me to the third thing: I got an invitation to the Sassoons' party!

Anya says I had better make the most of it, and that there will be many rich men there, but I said I didn't care about that, just the jobs I might get from them decorating their houses!

Shanghai, June 1932

I finally decided what to go as - a horsefly. I made a shirt and slim trousers of green silk shot through with gold thread, a head dress with antennae, and gossamer wings. Then I cut the mask to look like huge bug eyes. Natalia Ivanovna laughed and laughed when she saw me, but Anya said I was an idiot, and that I was squandering all my opportunities. I wanted to tell her not everyone wanted or needed a man and that I was doing all right for myself, at least I was starting to, but I knew she would read too much into that and act insulted and pout for days. Anyway, Natalia Ivanovna said my costume was young and clever and there would be nothing else like it at the party. The she started to talk about a party that she and her departed (and sainted, though she did not think so at the time!) husband Kolya went to twenty years ago, and pretty soon she was getting all maudlin, and Anya was too. Then the two of them got drunk, so I left to finish my work.

Li Kong was laughing now. He quite liked the girl. She was special and so different from the rest of the people she had described. The Director smiled only slightly and resumed reading.

Shanghai, July 1932

I was so excited about the party and so nervous, but once the designs, which I was thrilled to see in their final form, were hung, and all the flowers and food arranged in front of them- it was boring! No one even asked me about the sets. They were just focused on themselves and the impression they were making. And there was no real conversation going on. The men talked about business and sports and the women either gossiped, or spoke about gardening and food, and the endless servant problem. Really, I don't know how anyone could go on and on about a plant. If it's not thriving, pull it out and plant another in its place! I didn't know anyone, and I didn't know what to talk about, so I drank too much and got dizzy. I wanted to go home, only I couldn't manage to go that far, so I found a settee in a back hall and lay down.

I could hear conversation and music in the background, and it was all mixing pleasantly with that dreamlike place we go right before we fall asleep,

when a man walked by, and sitting down next to me, said suggestively,
'Hullo, what do we have here?'

He was dressed in the robes of an Arab sheik, so not thinking he would
understand, I muttered, 'Ibn-il-himmar, ' which means son of a donkey, and
was just about the pinnacle of the Arabic I had learned from a Muslim school
mate. Well, wouldn't you know, he understood me and, laughing, slapped his
knee and got up and walked away. I fell asleep until the end of the party
when Mister Isfahani found me and sent me home in his car.

'Ha-ha!' Li Kong laughed. The girl could see through their
pretensions, he thought, but then he wondered how she could be so
carefree and not worry about the impression she was making. And he
puzzled a bit about her lack of respect for her elders. Though the
people she described had been imperialists, they were rich and
important, yet she didn't seem to be intimidated by them at all.

Shanghai, July 1932

The princess, or Rajni Leilani, had me do flower arrangements for a
dinner party she is having. She has been very generous to me, so I wanted to
create something special for her. I made garlands, hung them from the ceiling
over the dining table, then put large bouquets in the four corners of the room
and another garland across the length of the fireplace. I was just finishing,
when the Princess received a telephone call from her girlfriend who had a
cold and was canceling.

'Oh, you must do me a favor,' the Princess said, turning to me. Seeing the
look on my face, she tried to convince me that she only had fascinating
friends, not like the Sassoons, who entertained a lot of boring English tai-
pans. 'Oh, please, the number will be uneven, you must make up the table!'
She was close to tears, so, I said I would, and she took me by the hand to an
armoire, and opening it, gave me a most beautiful white sari with a black
border.

. . .

Shanghai, July 1932

I wasn't sure how to drape the sari, so I wrapped it high at the waist, tucking in the sleeveless bodice and then tied it in front like sarong, using needle and thread to make it lay flat. I draped the sheer fabric over my shoulder and arm, loosely, like a toga, leaving a train. It was incredibly simple and impossibly chic. Crimping my hair, I parted it in the middle and tied it in a low knot at the neck. Anya and Natalia Ivanovna said it was the best I had ever looked, and Anya lent me her new silver sandals and silver evening purse, which were a gift from her lover and yet unworn. They were a little too big, but she insisted, and I must say, the whole ensemble looked rather splendid. I was so taken with myself that I forgot to be nervous. Natalia didn't want me to become soiled, so she called her friend, who is a driver for a Chinese warlord, and he came to pick me up in a fancy car. I was surprised he could use it, but he said the boss always had him wait while he visited his Russian girlfriend, since he never knew how long the evening would last due to her bad temper. He said it seemed to be going well that evening though and he'd only be sitting there all night.

I arrived a bit early to put the final touches on everything, and when the Princess came out of her room, she was pleased with my appearance. She wore a red evening gown and Indian rubies.

'I wonder if you should wear jewels?' she said, and sat me in front of her dressing table, trying things on me. After a while, she said, 'You know, it's a bit like gilding the lily.' Then she had me try a deep carmine red lipstick. 'That's all you need,' she said, and though I was looking forward to wearing the jewels, I had to admit she was right.

Her guests arrived, a mixture of sketchy aristocrats and new artists. I sipped champagne slowly, not wanting a repeat performance of the last time. I was introduced to her guests, listened, nodded, and asked leading questions. Grabbing my arm, the Princess whispered in my ear, 'Everyone loves you.' I decided then the secret to being popular was being a good listener and not saying much.

When we were about to go into dinner, a latecomer arrived. He was a tall man with high cheekbones, and at first, I thought he was a Russian. He seemed familiar, and I wracked my brain wondering where I had seen him before. I had just remembered that I had called him a son of a donkey not too

27

many days before when the Princess asked him to take me in. I took his arm and while we waited our turn, I couldn't help but turn red with embarrassment. He hadn't recognized me until then. He seemed to think it a great joke when I found myself seated to his right.

I spoke to the older gentleman on my left, or rather listened, until the Princess turned to her right, and I was forced to pay attention to that man, though I had been aware of his energy impatiently forcing itself against me the whole time. The Princess, I couldn't help overhearing, had known him in India.

She saw I was staring out in space and momentarily interrupting her dinner companion, said to me, 'Georgie, you know, was born in Russia.' Of course, that was my cue to ask all sorts of polite questions, but he needed no prompting.

I hate to admit it, but his stories were fascinating. He had been everywhere it seemed, living in Europe, Egypt, and India, and had traveled throughout East Africa. I asked him a lot of questions. His ideas are sound, and he is well read, though he is a man of adventurous nature, and for a while, I forgot how my first impression of him had led me to believe he was most high handed. I overcame my qualms and asked him more and more questions, which was fine, since the others were engrossed in their own conversation. After dinner, I was not eager to show that I was desirous of his company, but once we had moved to the drawing room, he sought me out and stood behind me, smoking. The princess said her car would take me home so I stayed last. He bid us goodnight, taking my hand. It was not until I was sitting alone in the dark, mulling over the evening, that I realized he had not asked me one question about myself.

She was describing the man in the photograph; Li Kong thought but said nothing to the Director, since he had not brought the other notebooks nor the photo itself.

Shanghai, July 1932

Flowers were sent to me today. Natalia Ivanovna announced, 'Your first bouquet,' as she brought them up. Then she stood there while I opened the card. It was signed, R. H., and I couldn't think who that was, until it occurred to me that Georgie, like most pompous Englishmen, had more than one name.

'Well?' Natalia asked, but I merely shrugged, and she closed her robe and turned on her heel, walking away.

I'd like to say that I thought nothing of it, but I couldn't help wondering what would come next, particularly since I seemed to have been saddled with some free time between projects. I went walking through the city, sketching, and when I got home, there was in invitation to lunch waiting on the hall table. It was from him.

Of course, there was panic in the house while Anya and Natalia decided what I should wear. They both thought I had outgrown my girlish wardrobe. When I suggested the beige suit I wore to meetings would do, Anya exclaimed, 'Oh, you couldn't possibly wear that. It's so drab.' I reminded her I had no time to sew anything, so she took her new white suit out of the wardrobe and handed it to me.

'I'd be too afraid to wear that,' I said.

'Take it before I change my mind,' she said. She had me try it on, and though she was so much taller, it had a sort of louche charm once I had combined it with a fedora that her lover had left behind and a pair of black suede sandals with straps.

'You need cherries,' Natalia Ivanovna said, and ran to get a brooch the late Nikolai had given her. It was all over the top, and the only thing that was missing was a handbag, but between the three of us, we managed to overhaul a clutch and put a new bow on it. They both nodded approvingly, but as I was leaving Anya called after me, 'Mind you don't spill on it!'

'They seem terribly focused on clothes,' Li Kong interjected.

'They were poor but they had pride,' the Director explained. 'And in those days, a poor but stylish girl could catch the eye of a rich man who might patronize or even marry her. Remember they had nothing but themselves to sell and their clothes were an expression of those selves, of their culture and breeding, and perhaps their uniqueness and innate individuality.'

'Oh how terrible that must have been,' Li Kong said, much to the Director's surprise.

Of course, the Director reasoned, the boy knows nothing of romantic love, or the things that pass between men and women, or how very charming and seductive those fashions had been.

Shanghai, July 1932

I was the only guest. Richard Hellyer lives on the top floor of a house and the entrance is through a gate and up the stairs to an apartment surrounded by mature trees.

Standing at the top of the landing, he watched me come up. Then he said, mockingly, 'Is that your mother's suit?'

'My grandmother's,' I replied.

The patio and the parapet were freshly whitewashed and an outdoor table was set for two in a most charming way. He held the chair out and then opening a bottle of champagne asked me if I thought I was old enough to drink sensibly.

'Insensibly, then,' I said holding out my glass.

'What will your mother think?' he asked.

I hated banter like that; it was so false. I thought to say I was alone in the world, and I'd been left as a child once for a year in an orphanage in the east before my uncle remembered that I was alive and came and got me. But who knew what a man like that was capable of once he knew there was no family and no one to care if he overstepped himself, so I said, 'My mother is dead, and I hate cheap talk like that.'

He suddenly sobered up, and said, 'I do too, really.' Then he poured the wine.

Once that had been cleared up, I sort of sat there, sipping the wine, and looking at the trees. The wind had turned and the leaves in the canopy above us rustled a bit before settling down. 'It's so peaceful here,' I commented, for something to say, and, truth be told, I was getting a bit sleepy.

He started to talk about a great many things, the goings on in the city, business and the economy, but I didn't really understand him or why he wanted to speak of such ordinary things when he had had such an extraordinary life.

'I'd rather hear about your exotic adventures,' I said, and saw he was a bit taken aback.

'Have you traveled much?' he asked.

'I really haven't been anywhere or done anything yet.' Then I got a little nervous since he was looking at me in a strange way, so I said, 'In real life, that is. In my mind, I travel a lot.'

'Where do you go?' he asked.

'I move around in time, to the places I have read about, then sometimes I think about traveling through space or under the sea.' Seeing that he was still taken aback, I quickly added, 'It helps me with my work.'

I could see I had lost him, so I explained. 'When I made the backdrops for Victor Sassoon's party, I was thinking of his love of horses, but I didn't want a common racetrack theme, so I thought about my grandfather's estate. I can recall it, you know, the meadows and the forest, and his horses. It took me a while, because I couldn't think how to make it stand out, until it occurred to me to reverse the colors.' I was a little nervous, talking about myself and wondering what impression those drawings had made on him, or on anyone, since no one had ever said anything. I went on talking. 'When I did the flowers for the Rajni's party, I was picturing her in an Indian garden overhung with flora and green everywhere.'

He smiled broadly, and I said, 'Of course, it is the India of my dreams that I pictured.'

'Have those been your only commissions?' he asked. So I told him about the club and Amrit Singh and Ladislav Hrbek.

A Chinese houseman brought lunch out, and we spoke about art and particularly about Italy, where he had lived. His descriptions were wonderfully vivid, and I could see the works he admired in my mind's eye.

The time passed easily.

'I have collected a few African and Chinese pieces, if you'd care to see them,' he said.

I must have looked like a frightened rabbit, because he laughed and said I would be safe.

We went into the house. There were tribal carpets from Arabia and the

Caucasus strewn about the floor and over large divans. Precious ivories and jades were displayed on shelves and tables. Most arresting were his collections of African masks and statuary. It was an extraordinary place to be, so personal, and quite artistic. I was gawking at him as if he were some sort of god, and he seemed both amused and pleased. He told his man that we would take coffee in there.

I was still smiling and looking around when he said he would give me a penny for my thoughts.

'I'm so happy I had the opportunity to see this. I think I could really do something with the African theme for the club.'

He laughed and said he was glad the afternoon had been educational for me. 'I didn't mean it like that,' I explained, 'and you are a wonderful storyteller.' Of course, that only made it worse, as if I thought of him as my tutor.

'You're awfully young, aren't you?' he said.

'I can't help that.'

'No, and you shouldn't have to.' Then he said he would be going away for a while, but if I wanted to look at the collections or his art books for inspiration, the houseman would admit me. Then he wanted to pay for my cab, but I was offended to be dismissed like that, so I said I wanted to walk and look at the neighborhood for a bit, and that the new houses were of interest to me.

Li Kong had listened with a mixture of curiosity and revulsion, and thought the man had been terribly disrespectful toward the girl. It is not how I would treat her, he thought.

'Shall we break and resume tomorrow?' the Director asked. 'I'm a little tired.'

Li Kong wanted him to go on reading, but he saw that the old man looked worn out and nodded.

'It would be better if you left the book here, since there are always prying eyes about,' the Director said. 'From now on, you will come with food when they are busy with dinner, so that they will be preoccupied. If anyone asks, you might say you are helping me with political thought to aid my rehabilitation. But it is better if you do not come each day.'

Li Kong was about to balk at being separated from the book, after all it was the one with the drawings and the photograph of the girl. He wondered whether to tell the Director that there were more books. He didn't want to give them to the old man, and yet for a moment he considered that he might be better off doing so. If anyone ever found out he had the notebooks it would mean nothing but trouble and endless questions. He immediately felt guilty for being so selfish and realized that, in fact, he didn't know what to do. Everything could happen in reverse. The Red Guards might even begin seeking out those who had already been purged.

'What if the Red Guards come to see you?' he asked. 'Surely it would be better that I hold on to the book. I will put it in my coat pocket when I bring food. No one will see it, and I have an exemplary record. They wouldn't suspect me.'

'Perhaps it is better to do as you say, at least for a while until you see how things will unfold for you,' Sun Mu replied.

Li Kong nodded and picking up the book put it in his pocket. He took the pail and nodding to the Director said, 'I'll be back in a couple of days.'

On the way across the courtyard, he was tormented by the dawning realization of what the Director had meant when he had said: *until you see how things will unfold for you.* Does he think I will get into trouble over this? Surely, I could explain it if it ever came to light. I could claim I was curious and just wanted to learn what had happened here in the old days. That way, I can understand the roots of corruption and everything that needs to be dug up and cast aside. Yes, that is what I will say. Li Kong tried to convince himself that it would work. The whole time he knew he should either bring all the diaries to the Director or discard them in a dump and keep himself pure for the sake of the revolution.

The Director had been anticipating the boy and when he arrived with a pail of food two days later, they both were ready to sit down to begin reading immediately. This time Li Kong did not interrupt but listened intently to the girl's account.

Shanghai, August 1932

I have been working on the fabrics for Architect Hrbek's furniture collection, and I got a new commission for the club. I quickly sketched up the sets with an African theme and told Yevgeny Borisovich I could make African masks for the dancers of paper mache, and he liked the idea. I was tempted to go back and look at RH's collection a million times, but then I'd think, what if had returned and I was intruding. He might not want to see me, and, anyway, I wasn't certain how serious his invitation had been.

Shanghai, August 1932

Packages have been arriving a couple of times a week- all books. The first were catalogues of exhibits of African art in Paris, then a monograph on Picasso, and one on Matisse. Later still, some beautiful books containing reproductions of Renaissance paintings arrived, another on Turner, and one Rembrandt. Never a note, never an inscription.

'A-ya,' Anya mocked me, 'now he wants to be your teacher,' she said suggestively.

'I don't suppose it ever occurred to you than a man and a woman could just be intellectual companions?' I said, and she and Natalia Ivanovna laughed hysterically. I stormed out of Natalia's shabby sitting room and went upstairs to my own. Soon, Anya was scratching at my door. She came and sat on my bed.

'Look at this place,' she said grabbing the worn bedspread. 'It's disgusting. The wallpaper is peeling and so is the paint. There's mold everywhere. I wipe it off and it's back the next day. And it all smells. Natalia cooks her greasy stinking food and the whole place is permeated with it. I swear it's coming out of the walls.'

'What do you want from her, Anya? She cleans every day. She's doing the best she can.'

'Don't you want to get out of here? To have clean white sheets and sit on furniture that doesn't sag or smell of sweaty bodies?'

'Of course I do.'

'Well you are getting your chance.'

'You presume too much.'

'Get your head out of the clouds,' she shouted. 'You think your Richard wants an intellectual companion? He's grooming you, you fool. He found a little girl and now he's going to make her in the image that he desires. What do you think comes next?'

'All right, Anya,' I said trying to calm her down. 'What if you are right and he wants me for a mistress, what I am I supposed to do? Manipulate him into giving me gifts? An income? An apartment? I'm not sure he has that kind of money. Or do you think I should fall pregnant and shame him into a wedding? There's no guarantee he'd do the honorable thing, then I'd be stuck with a kid to provide for.'

'You could use him as a stepping stone, Tanya. Englishmen are easy. They have never met women like us. Do you see their women? They are like ice. They don't know how to dress, they don't know how to cook, and I'm sure they know nothing of love.'

'Ah, well, we are a romantic race,' I said, but I could see what she was angling at. 'I promise, if he invites me anywhere, I'll introduce you as well.'

She put her head on my shoulder. 'Shi-shi loves me, I can feel he does, but how will it ever work?' I hated when she called her Chinese lover that, it made him sound like a Pekingese dog, but I knew he would have to contend with his family. They were rich, and he was depending on them to set him up in business.

'So you're giving up on him?' I asked.

'I need to be wise and keep my options open,' she said. 'I'm six years older than you are, and I need to use my charms while I still have them.'

'I promise, but we might be speculating for no reason. Richard might not ever turn up again.'

'Oh he will, and when he does, I would like you to be prepared. Do you know what to do?'

'I'm not interested in any of that.'

'But someday you will be,' she said and explained what I could expect and how to avoid falling pregnant.

Shanghai, August 1932

Anya was right, Richard did turn up to the opening of the new number at the club. It had been advertised all over town and many people attended, Chinese and European. The stage curtain was cut in strips to imitate vines, and the girls, in their masks, peeked out between them before coming out to dance to drums, each in turn, suggestive of a wild African festival. Tamara Andreyevna, the great ballerina, was in town and danced the lead role, in a jazzy, modern, though balletic way that brought the house down. She got so many bouquets and when she took her bows she called us all out there with her. I was so excited, I didn't see Richard at all, but afterward, he sent a waiter to call me, and I went to his table to say hello and thank him for the books.

He wanted to talk, but it was so loud- the band was playing and people were talking and shouting, so I told him I couldn't really hear and it was impossible. He suggested we go for a quiet dinner, but I was tired and told him so. He seemed a bit surprised, but took it with good grace, and said perhaps some other time.

Shanghai, August 1932

I was at the stables with Mister Isfahani today. Victor wanted new colors for his jockeys, and I went to measure them. Mister Isfahani knows I love horses and took me to see them and so that I could get a good match on the colors. While we were there, we ran into RH. He was with a tall and stunningly beautiful Eurasian woman of about thirty-five. He stopped to chat. Apparently, he and Isfahani know each other. She was incredibly disdainful toward us. Of course, to her, we are just hired help. She was very attentive to RH, though, and apparently desirous of his exclusive company, though he did not seem to notice that, and kept chatting. I became anxious *and reminded Mister Isfahani we had a job to finish. When they were out of earshot, I asked if he knew her.*

'Oh, yes,' he replied. 'Her family is very rich, have their hand in just about everything; land, finance, construction. He would do well to make that match.'

'And he isn't rich?' I asked, innocently.

'No, my dear, he has had to make his own way. Though what he is doing in the business world, few could say.'

'What do you mean? He doesn't seem stupid.'

'No. Of course, he has a fine education and languages to recommend him, but you know that is not the same thing. And some say,' Mister Isfahani lowered his voice, 'Some say he really is here to keep an eye on things.'

I must have looked blank. 'For the British government,' he explained. 'We are living in uncertain times, my dear, the world being what it is.'

I didn't know what he meant, but seeing he assumed I was wiser than I was, I nodded and said something like, 'Mmmmhmm.'

We looked at the horses, which were truly magnificent, and I said I'd have something ready in a couple of days.

Shanghai, August 1932

The woman we met at the stables telephoned for me. She wants me to see her new villa and to suggest some interior schemes. Natalia answered the phone since it is in her sitting room and is her prized new possession.

'I said I was your aunt,' Natalia said nervously after I hung up. The Liu family owns the entire world, it seems, and she didn't want the woman to think I lived in a boarding house.

'You're such a snob,' I told her. 'I'm sure she doesn't know or care how her help lives.'

I went to her house the next afternoon. It is in the new art deco style with extensive grounds in the best part of the French Concession. I was taken inside by a houseman and ushered into an almost empty room. The houseman bade me sit on a sofa, the only piece of furniture there. Three-quarters of an hour later, Madam Liu made an appearance and ordered tea.

She was dressed as if she had just finished riding, but the materials were exquisite and perfectly made.

'Well, what do you think of my house?' she asked.

'I think it suits you to perfection,' and then added, 'It's modern but has clean classical lines. The materials and design are of the finest quality. Its placement is extraordinarily well thought out from what I can see, and the doors and windows are positioned to catch both the light and the breezes.'

She seemed pleased and a bit surprised. 'And what suggestions might you have to furnish it?' she asked.

'I was sitting here, thinking, and I believe it would be a mistake to overfill it. I keep envisioning a curved sofa, here, looking out the windows, in dove grey velvet and a pair of barrel shaped armchairs with walnut curving around the sides and backs. Here, like this,' I took out my pad, sketching for her.

'Yes,' she said, nodding.

'I keep seeing silver framed mirrors, but square and quite austere, between the windows, and above the fireplace, and sconces to light the place, and a chandelier here. I once saw something in a Hollywood movie, where the house had been kept locked and had mesh nets over the chandeliers and white muslin over the furniture, and I'd like to have an airy, pale elegance throughout. Perhaps we could drape the beds in muslin...'

'Yes, I see.' She laughed. 'I love it. Let's have tea, then I'll show you the rest of the house, and we'll talk about the possibilities.'

When we were done, she walked me through the house and ideas kept coming like magic; a stone Buddha on the staircase landing, silver backed glass tile in the baths, white, grey and lavender in the bedrooms.

'How soon can you do the sketches?' she asked when we were back in the drawing room.

'Right away,' I replied.

She took a checkbook out of her handbag.

'No, afterward,' I said.

She took a long look at me. 'You know, I have a confession to make. The other day when we met you at the stables, Richard talked a lot about you, and I was a little jealous. I thought I'd call you and show you up. But you are really a nice person, and you aren't interested in Richard at all, are you?'

I wondered if that was her condition for hiring me, so I decided to tell her straight up I was poor and what I was really interested in was getting work. Then she said, 'Oh, you're not poor at all. You have a great talent. And once this house in done, you won't be lacking for work, I assure you.'

'Then you want me to move forward?' I asked.

'Oh, yes,' she replied.

Shanghai, September 1932

I've had a terrible disappointment. Everything was moving forward so beautifully with Madam Liu. We had even found craftsmen who could make the furniture I had designed. Then, I got a call to come to the villa. Madam Liu was in a terrible rush. Her servants were packing her clothes and the rest of her belongings.

'I'm so sorry, Tanya. My family has ordered me back to Hong Kong. I don't know when I'll be back.'

I saw my brilliant career shattered to pieces before my very eyes. 'But, how, why?' I stammered.

'It's complicated. I really can't explain. One day, I'll be back and we'll create the most beautiful house ever.' She took an envelope full of cash out of her bag and gave it to me. 'It's not enough,' she said to herself and removed the heavy gold and jade bracelets she always wore and put them on my wrists. I actually started crying then.

'You'll take care of yourself, and you will take care of Richard for me,' she said.

'I don't want to take care of Richard. I just want to be with you and in the world we are creating.' I can't imagine what she thought of me or of what I was saying. It wasn't that she was just sophisticated and somehow innately... superior, without the pettiness and base desires that consumed other people. And it wasn't only because she was rich and that elevated her from all the disgusting struggles the rest of us had to bear. Over the past few weeks, I had grown attached to her and her kindness and encouragement. She believed in me and she pushed me to go that extra step, to refine my work and myself. Her chilliness was something that was up front, something that she exhibited with other people, a defense, perhaps because she was of mixed race and

didn't fit in the word either. I knew she didn't like to touch people, but she held me, let me blubber on her beautiful suit, and then wiped my snot with her lace handkerchief.

'Go now. I'll come back, don't worry.'

So I left.

'Shall we stop for the present?' the Director asked.

'Yes. All right,' Li Kong agreed. He didn't want the girl's story to end, yet he wanted time to think about what he had just heard. He was less interested in nightclubs and dance hall girls, and even the specter of the man (a real spy!) whose expression had so intrigued him, paled in comparison with the questions he had about Madam Liu. He had heard foreigners had looked down upon Chinese, but this girl had looked up to the older woman, understood, admired, and perhaps had even loved her. He was moved by her honesty and by the fact that she never sought to aggrandize herself, or to save face, but was direct in her speech and thought. That was something unusual, uncommon to his own people, and though he found it alien, he decided he quite liked it.

'Any questions?' the Director asked.

Li Kong shook his head.

'Then until next time.'

'Until next time, 'Li Kong repeated. He liked that phrase. It gave him a sense of continuity and purpose.

Sun Mu was ill and had lain on his pallet covered with a thin blanket, his only one, shivering and drifting in and out of sleep. He had missed work, but no one had missed him, and no one came around to check on him. The boy had not been to see him either, and Sun Mu wondered what had happened, but to his relief he heard a knocking at the door, and opening it, ushered the boy in. This time he fell on the food the boy had brought. He realized had had nothing to eat since the day before.

'Where have you been?' he asked between mouthfuls.

'They kept us overnight at school. We're having political meetings almost around the clock. They've asked us to write a critique analyzing our own faults. I've been working on mine, but I don't know what to say,' Li Kong explained. 'You see it's the book. I know we shouldn't be reading it. I know it's wrong, and yet, I can't help myself.'

Sun Mu put his bowl down and looked directly at the boy. 'Say nothing about it. When they ask where you need to improve, you should say that you are always striving to become better and to understand and apply the writings of Chairman Mao in all situations.'

'I don't know if that will be enough,' Li Kong replied.

'You are a clever young man, and I am sure you will think of something to say-something humble, yet nothing which would get you into trouble.'

Li Kong nodded his head, but in fact, he was worried about what it was that he was actually supposed to write.

'Shall we?' the Director asked, indicating the diary.

'Yes, of course.'

The Director began reading:

Shanghai, September 1932

Shi-shi's friend took some photographs of me today. I wasn't desperate for work yet. I was frugal and the money Madam Liu gave me could be stretched for some time. But I thought it would be good to make as many contacts as I could. Shi-shi was investing in films, Shanghai made. His friend is a cinematographer at Shanghai Film Studios but is very interested in photography as well. He had first asked Anya to pose and had gotten some shots of her that were quite interesting. On film, she projects the cool aura of a statue, and he photographed her in a sort of surreal manner, half alive, almost inanimate, dreaming in a garden that was patently false and manmade. But when he wanted something livelier, more comedic neither she nor the Chinese girls who normally posed for him could quite get the hang of what he was looking for.

A sharp rap at the door interrupted the Director's reading. The Director looked up, startled, and rapidly rising, slid the book under his pallet. He went to the door and opened it. Li Kong's aunt stuck her head through.

'Your friend came looking for you. An important meeting at school has been called. Your presence is required. Right now,' she emphasized, seeing the boy was hesitant. She only remembered to nod in Sun Mu's direction once Li Kong was through the door.

When they were out of sight and the courtyard had quieted down, Sun Mu took the diary out and began to read.

Anya asked me if I would do it, since she claims I am always making faces, and I agreed. Anya has led me to understand that the cinematographer is homosexual and that his dealings with women are chaste. I went to the studio and was promptly issued in by a pert, wisecracking Chinese girl. She made me feel comfortable right away. While I waited, I looked over the props he used. There were giant plaster casts of feet and hands, and of horses' heads. He kept collections of animal skeletons, seashells, driftwood, stuffed birds, and found things, like bed springs and bicycle wheels. I was looking into a big silver mirror he had hanging on the wall and putting a starfish up to my hair, thinking perhaps I could make a hat in that shape, when he came in.

'Hold that pose,' he said, just like that. I did and we made some pictures together. I can hardly wait to see them. The longer we went on, the more fanciful my ideas got-and he fed into them.

He's a strange man, really. Not what Anya led me to expect. He is very tall with a long, melancholic face and a phlegmatic disposition. He smokes almost constantly. There is something indefinable in his manner though, as if he is open to anything. We tried everything I suggested, and he was so patient. Even if he thought it wouldn't work, he never said so directly. I really liked him, even though we barely talked about anything.

. . .

It had been the first time the Director had seen Tanya, and it was the first time he would see her unexpurgated thoughts of their affair. He had been shocked when the boy had come around with the diary; shocked at the sudden unexpectedness of it, and of the incredible coincidence, though lately he had begun to think, in his old age, that all things come back around in life and have their purpose and that there are no real coincidences, only long journeys which turn out unexpectedly and bring with them terrible and profound lessons.

He recalled that first encounter with a mix of sadness and delight. She had been ravishingly beautiful and so unaware of that beauty. And she had been so kittenish and playful, almost like a child. Almost, but with a terrible underlying sadness, almost as if she was a will-o-the - wisp that needed to be anchored to earth. She had certainly enchanted him. She had seemed so winsome then, and it was only that he later recognized she had a will of iron. I was not as phlegmatic nor as complaint as you believed Tanya, he thought. I was only afraid you would disappear, and I'd never see you again, and so I was constrained that day about saying or doing the wrong thing.

She had hurt him terribly, and perhaps it was because of her beauty, which had so enthralled him, that he had forgiven her and continued to love her. After the war, when he had seen photographic portraits of the actress Vivien Leigh, he had been struck at the resemblance between the two, though after studying them closely, he had concluded that perhaps Tanya's profile had been sharper, particularly about the nose and cheekbones, giving her a slightly more exotic look, which he had always associated with the Russians. Certainly, her figure, particularly later, had been more lush and womanly than Miss Leigh's.

The memory of her had stayed with him for years, but he would deny all knowledge of that to the boy, and the fact that he had looked for her after the war. It wouldn't be difficult. He had changed his name in Yunnan and then again after he had been purged. He had been someone once, though these days, he had almost forgotten it.

He skimmed ahead to see which portions he would keep to himself. And then he began to read more slowly remembering the events themselves.

Shanghai, September 1932

The photos were done, so I went to see them. They were quite delightful, and we agreed to make some more together. The Cinematographer invited me to dinner and I went. Now that he wasn't working, he was livelier, and he had a lot to talk about. He was educated in Paris and knew many Russians there. We didn't just talk about existing art and films, but how we would like to craft our own vision. I think the Cinematographer would like to be a film director. He says cinema will be the greatest art form of our century. He spoke about his ideas, and about adapting Japanese and Russian literature for Chinese audiences. We spoke of our favorite books and stories. He explained how he would film Chekhov. I described what the sets would look like, and how I would costume his productions. He spoke of lighting and effects, and so on.

The evening flew by. There was a common bond between us. We spoke the same language, and I feel that he could be a real friend, an artistic collaborator, someone who really understands me. His name is Fang Shirong.

Shanghai, September 1932

Fang Shirong told me that in Paris his friends called him Sasha and that he would like me to use that name with him. We have been spending a lot time together mainly talking about the work we would like to do in the future. I realize that I have been hoping to get jobs, and that I have been lucky to get jobs, but that I have no plan, no vision or concept what the future might look like for me.

Sasha and I were eating dinner at a wonderful restaurant with potted palms and overhead fans, where the breezes come through the dark window slats, the sort of place that arrests time, the sort of place that makes you feel introspective. I was toying with my hair, really coiling it between my fingers tightly, as I do when I'm thinking, and Sasha asked, 'What is it, Tanya?'

'I don't know,' I said. 'Maybe I don't think too far ahead or have plans because I'm too afraid to think. Oh Sasha, I'm one step away from the street. If I miss one job, I'm doomed. And if I should ever become ill or disabled, there is no one to take care of me.' I don't know why that thought came into my mind at that moment. The young never think anything bad will ever touch them, but recently there have been ever so many beggars on the street. Some are maimed and disfigured. You walk past these people, averting your eyes. You hope someone will take pity and feed them. They are coming from in country and there are more and more of them. Mei got married. She hardly knows him. 'Too many people in the house,' she said.

Sasha took my hand, 'I will take care of you. I promise.'

'Sasha, in what capacity? What are you thinking?'

Sasha looked uncomfortable, and a bit dismayed. We've never spoken about his personal life. I've never asked any questions. Sometimes his friends come to his apartment unannounced; all beautiful young men and he seems a bit anxious. I'm not sure then if he wants to be rid of me or if he really cares about what I think. I always excuse myself and quickly leave, no matter how they might protest. I really don't mind. I prefer it. It allows us to be friends, without complications.

I didn't want him to feel bad, so I said, 'I know you won't let me fall through the cracks.' We didn't say any more and didn't talk while eating the lobster. Then we went for a walk, and Sasha began to talk about other things like Paris and architecture. It was all fine because I do like to listen to him.

The Director thought it odd she had skipped a few dates. Perhaps she thought nothing of interest was happening in her life, and maybe it hadn't been, though they had seen each other almost every day. Clearly, she had regarded him as a friend only while his infatuation had been growing daily. He tried to remember why he had allowed her to meet his friends. Perhaps he had sensed she had not been ready to get involved with a man. He had wanted to keep her near him without frightening her away, the way that Hellyer had done with his show of direct interest.

That evening, at the restaurant with the dark shutters, she had touched him with her vulnerability. She had no one to fall back on, and her fear had triggered a powerful and protective response in him. He had spoken without thinking things through, directly from his heart. Later, when he had had time to reflect, he had liked the fact that she had not jumped at his offer as so many women in her position would have, although it had stung him momentarily to be disregarded as a man.

In truth, though he had never told her, he had had numerous women both in China and in Paris, but was at an age then when neither messy emotional entanglements nor prostitutes particularly appealed to him. Not that men's emotions were not messy, he thought, but somehow he had always been more than able to dismiss them.

Shanghai, October 1932

Sasha and I have been fighting. He hired me to work on a set, actually more than one, since they shoot movies here quickly, but it is not working out. For all our plans and ideas about working together, we are not a good match. I suppose I assumed we would prove outstanding collaborators when we were making photos. But here in the movie studio he wants things the way he wants them and tells me I do not understand how the camera works.

It was true, the Director remembered, they had been fighting. It was at a stage when he had wanted her near him all the time, when he could not stand to be away from her. But Tanya had been an individualist. She could not take direction well, nor could she tolerate criticism and worked best alone when she was free to dream and take her time. The pace had put her off and the fact that she had become his subordinate and had to take orders from him. But she had not considered she was a beginner at the job, a hireling and not an equal, not a collaborator. He had tried to explain to her what needed doing and what she had to learn, but she had chafed under his direction and had no patience or forbearance.

. . .

Shanghai, October 1932

Sasha came by and apologized. It had just rained and we went out for a long walk in the French Concession. The streets were slick and shiny and the leaves beginning to yellow and fall. I didn't say anything about coming back to work at the studio and he didn't either. We had just turned the corner on a dark residential street; I never can remember names of the streets, when he took my hand. It seemed very natural and I didn't object. His hand was dry and cool. We kept walking. There was an overgrowth of plants spilling down a wall and he stopped and leaned me into it. We kissed for a very long time. I suppose that in China some men have it both ways.

It was pleasant. Then he walked me home.

When we got back, he picked the leaves very gently from my hair. I asked if I should come back to work and he said, of course I should. Anya was waiting on the landing for me. 'Well, well,' was all she said.

He remembered that evening as well as if it happened only months ago-the slick wet night, the street lights reflecting on the pavement, his nervousness and desire, the throbbing of his pulse, and the sound of his blood coursing through his veins. He had wanted to dismiss her from her job, and then decided to talk to her once more and see if he could make her see reason. But when he had gotten to the house and saw her framed in the doorway, her hair freshly washed and waving in the damp air, and saw how the dull light in the hall illuminated her body through her cheap house dress, transparent from many washings, he had stopped himself.

He had stood near her while she put on her shoes and inhaled her scent, which was redolent of chamomile, and roses, and innocence, and he had felt a mixture of love, pity, and desire. She had considered they had many things of which to speak, but he had only thought of filling the lacuna between his imagination and her presence with the things she wanted to hear.

He had taken her hand, and when he found her responsive, he had stopped and kissed her and kept kissing her for a long time, because he could not get enough. And she had followed his lead as if they were engaged in a long slow dance.

Shanghai, October 1932

The fall racing season has begun. Sasha took me to the opening. The Sassoons and the Keswicks and all sorts of so- called important people were there. I was wearing a man's trouser suit, very similar to Sasha's, that a friend of his lent me. It was a bit of a sensation. The older women looked at me disapprovingly, but the men seemed to like it. Sasha went to place our bets. I didn't really know how to calculate the odds, so I told him I would go with my gut and put money on one of Sassoon's horses just because his name appealed to me. He laughed and shook his head, but agreed.

While he was gone, a man approached and stood quite close to me. That sometimes happens, and if you ignore them, they go away. I didn't look up until he said, 'First your grandmother's suit and now your brother's.' I didn't have to see him to know that it was Hellyer.

I don't know why he always has to be so condescending when he speaks to me and it made me irritable, so I said, 'Richard, I'm poor, if you hadn't noticed, and I have to make do. Besides, I thought it was clever.'

He was about to say something when Sasha returned. I introduced them. Sasha was standing quite close to me and there could be no mistaking the nature of our relationship. Richard took his leave but shot me a look that seemed to say, so this how you make do?

Sasha asked how I knew Richard, and I told him about Madam Liu, which seemed to satisfy him. I was a little upset that I hadn't thought to ask Richard about her. I wanted to write to her so very often but was afraid that she would think that I was in need of money, and anyway I didn't have her address in Hong Kong.

Funny, the Director though, how she recalled every conversation she had had with Hellyer, but only spoke of 'her' Sasha in the most general terms. There were times in the past when he had thought about her lack of love for him, and wondered if it was not because he was of a different race and she had not seen him in the same light as she did Hellyer, or if perhaps his affairs with men had been too off putting for her, and yet she had not seemed to harbor any prejudices of the sort. Since then he had occasionally wondered what was it that made us love some people and not others.

Shanghai, November 1932

The days are moving along quite pleasantly. I work at the studio most days and have done some more designs for a German client of Sirdar Singh's. Sasha and I are too tired at the end of the day to do anything much except eat- which we usually do at Chinese restaurants. They are making socially conscious films here now. We are working on one about a prostitute and another about a family that has lost its rice crop. The work is not bad, steady, but watching the crews film has ruined the magic of cinema for me. It's just not the same anymore. I keep seeing the machinations behind it, and I can't get that wonder back at all.

Sometimes I miss my freedom, days when I could just wander. Everything moves so quickly in the studio, and my schedule is rigorous. I have so little time to think and create on my own and must do what Sasha says.

He is working so hard now. He is trying to move up and get a script of his own to direct. He has a friend who is a writer. He is a communist, and he looks it-a theoretician-skinny, pale, nervous with round glasses, the kind blind men wear. Sasha thinks he is quite brilliant. I'm not inclined to see him that way-rather rigid and single minded, but Sasha says my background is responsible for my judgment. I think the script writer and I resent each other. When he comes over, he seems very prickly and I leave. I tell Sasha not to confuse art with social responsibility, one is one and the other the other. But Sasha is swayed by this man. He talks in a different way now, full of rhetoric. Those are not his words, not his thoughts.

Ah yes, the Director thought, the choices we make that take us down life's byways. If we only had a looking glass to see ourselves reflected

49

as we are and not as we choose to think of ourselves. If I only had a glass that could see into the future and predict the consequences of those paths, I might have chosen differently or acted differently. And though I resented you for saying that art and social responsibility should not be mixed, and thought you were a shallow girl because of it, you were right about Ming Gui and my association with him.

Shanghai, December 1932

Something so exciting has happened. Sasha is going to direct a film! Shi-shi put up the money with a few investors. Sasha wants to take me out to celebrate. I asked him if we could wait a couple of days until I made something to wear, and he said he would buy me anything I wanted. I said just the material, and he laughed and said he could wait.

I had narrowed it to three choices, one was a green lame shot through with silver, one was white satin that I thought I might trim with black, and the last, a black net with beading. I couldn't decide and the sales woman kept saying white would be most appropriate for my age, and then perhaps the green, but I kept lingering over the net. I could see it in my mind's eye, demure in front and gathered at the hip creating a train, but completely backless. I decide to buy it and then immediately regretted it, because it was quite the most outrageously expensive thing I have ever had. Even so, I bought a roll of black velvet to make a cloak to wear over it.

Then I went to the Sikh perfumers, and asked them to mix up something just for me, a rose, lily, and jasmine blend, and we worked on it all day before we got it right.

Saturday morning

The dress is spectacular. I have black satin pumps and a black diamante bag to go with. Anya rolled my hair up in back, and left a waved lock to fall over my left eye. When I stepped into the dress, Anya and Natalia Ivanovna were floored. Natalia whistled and said that I looked like a real woman and then added, finally. It made me self-conscious as if I was trying to be something that I am not, but I don't care, the dress is the most utterly sophisticated and beautiful thing ever and I love it so.

I must have Sasha make some photographs of me wearing it!

How silly, and yet how delightful she had been, he thought-and how young we both were then.

Shanghai, December 1932

I don't really know what happened. The evening started out so well. I told Sasha I would meet him at the club, because I rather wanted to make an entrance and surprise him. He was waiting in the lobby, and we went to the cloakroom together to check our coats. After I took off the black cloak, I turned all the way around slowly. Sasha's eyes got a little wider, and he just said, 'Oh, Tanya,' and smiled.

'Does that mean you like it?' I asked, perhaps a bit too coyly.

'I love it, and I love you in it.' He put his hand on my bare back to guide me, and I shivered.

We had dinner and danced, and Sasha held me quite closely the whole time we were dancing. The champagne had gone to my head in a very pleasant way, and I didn't really care what people thought. Sasha whispered in my ear, and I said yes, I thought I was ready.

He held my hand in the cab and we went to his place. It's so vivid in my mind, his hand on the light switch, the almost Japanese simplicity of his apartments, the single flower arrangement on the shelf, the sconces throwing light up on the walls. Sasha took my cloak, and then he kissed my neck and stroked my back before he took the pins out of my hair.

I never said, but Sasha has a musical voice, not the sing song of people here or the soft shr-shring of the northern Chinese, but a little bit deeper, and mostly we speak French to each other, though now he said in Russian, 'I want this to be good for you.' I was shaking all over, as if a nervous hum had begun somewhere in the core of my body and wouldn't stop. Sasha said not to be afraid, and that he would stop if I said so.

He undid my dress and sat on the sofa. As I stood in front of him in my underwear he stroked my skin very softly with a light, gentle touch.

He took the rest of my clothing off, leaving on my stockings and shoes, and looked at me for a while from all sides. Then he did something men do when they really like a woman or are very perverted, according to Anya. It was very soft and a bit ticklish but to tell the truth it really didn't feel like much at all. At least I didn't feel anything, though Anya has mentioned that this is her favorite thing of all. He took me by the hand to the bedroom and removing his clothes, sat next to me and touched me in many ways. It took a while for him to get everything open enough and then he got on top of me. I really didn't know what to do, so I lay there with my arms around him trying to understand what I was supposed to be feeling and mostly wondering why people make such a big deal about sex. After a while, he shuddered and rolled off. I didn't know if I was supposed to go to the bathroom to wash myself, or if I should say something, or keep still.

'It takes time with young women, before they get warmed up,' he said. 'Go and wash.' I did as he said. When I got back, he was asleep. I slid into bed next to him, but of course, I was wide awake and everything felt tender and raw.

In the morning, we tried again but it was no better. I borrowed trousers and a shirt, rolled up the sleeves and legs, and went home.

Oh, she had been so young and stiff. Too young and too inexperienced to know how to play-act, too nervous to relax and allow herself to feel pleasure. But he had wanted to possess her beauty, and beyond that beauty, her essence and its spark. And he had wanted to be the first, the last and only, though it had not transpired that way, and though he had never felt that way again or held it to be of much importance before or since.

Next day

Sasha sent flowers. Later he called, and we went out to eat. If he was disappointed in me, he didn't show it. He said he wanted to go slow and teach me, and that I would grow to enjoy it in time. I said I was willing. Then he said he was going to be very busy with the new film but that I shouldn't worry if he wasn't as attentive. It wouldn't mean anything bad was going on between us, just that he had to concentrate because this was his great opportunity to make a name for himself.

I said I totally understood, that I knew it would be a beautiful film, and he was the most talented and brilliant man I knew. Then he said that Ming Gui, his communist friend, was finished with the script. My heart sank when I heard this, because I now knew what kind of film it would be. I couldn't read Chinese very well, so I asked him to tell me the storyline. Sasha began to talk about it, and when he saw I was dismayed, he asked me what I was thinking.

I didn't want to lie to him, though in retrospect, I probably should have. I said, 'Sasha, that script isn't about the things that are inside you at all. You love beauty and the things that are eternal, like painting and music. When you talk about the way you see life, the words that come out of you are pure poetry. Your view of life is so subtle, so delicate - the nuances, the details, the juxtapositions that you notice are about the beauty, sadness, and loss that is associated with ephemera. You're shortchanging yourself by making a film that is not true to you or who you are.'

He grew very quiet and withdrew into himself. I reached for his hand, but he didn't put back any pressure on mine.

'You know, Tanya, you're such a child. Take a look around you. What do you see? Beauty? I see starvation. I see poverty. I see China being exploited by its enemies and rotting from within.'

'But don't you want to bring your vision into their lives?' I asked, very stupidly.

'The people I am talking about can't afford the price of a movie ticket, and what use is there for beauty when you don't have bread? My duty now is to bring awareness to the people who can do something about it.'

I was flabbergasted. I thought, well, if they aren't stirred by the human misery they see all around them what makes you think they'll respond to sentiment? But I knew the answer already, and I knew that people like Ming Gui wouldn't hesitate to use heavy handed imagery to galvanize the public into making a bloody revolution.

'Look,' he said, 'don't worry. Eisenstein made films that were socially conscious but full of beauty and ground breaking imagery. I can do the same.' Sasha proceeded to explain how he would film some scenes, and I understood that his days of surreal imagery and faded gardens were over. I wondered how Ming Gui had had time to corrupt Sasha's mind with those ideas, even as I understand that his vision had deepened and that it was broader and more powerful. I was torn, and in the end, I let him convince me he was doing the right thing.

Funny how he didn't remember that conversation at all, though he did recall his blinding ambition, not only to make films, but to change the world. He had really believed then, and for a short time in Yunnan, that art could affect life and raise consciousness. Perhaps in a sense that was true, because most people were so easily led that you could turn their heads with a mere slogan or a poster, and they would believe anything, such was their innocence.

He wondered what she had seen in him. That night, he had thought his flirtation with surrealism, a borrowed form, reflected what she had wanted to believe and not what was inside of him at all. When she spoke of subtleties and sadness, she spoke of herself, and yet, he had said those things and had felt them at one time. Later in life, he had been so blunted by the hardships he had endured when the regime turned on him, he had almost forgotten who he had been altogether.

'There is beauty in the passing world of illusions, Tanya,' he said turning the pages of the diary to her graven image, 'but so much suffering.'

Would he have done things differently if he could turn back time? Would he have listened to her words of warning? Or would he, like many men, have disregarded them and kept pursuing her, flattering her, paying her attentions? He had been wounded by her words so she had seemed less worthy in his eyes afterward.

. . .

Shanghai, December 1932

I broke it off with Sasha. Anya says I am crazy to let go of a man who clearly loves me and is going places. I said, 'These days he is consumed by politics'. She asked why I should care, that grown people could disagree about things and still be friends. I said I didn't know why, just that I felt that I couldn't stand the way things were going. She said that was an excuse, that I was selfish and destructive.

I expected I would miss him and feel sad, but I don't feel a thing.

But he had felt it, eventually, the loss of her presence and her blithe spirit, the loss of her words and the deep silence that confronted him in the solitary evenings when he realized he was all alone. He had shut his emotions off and thrown himself into his work. What would he tell that gauche boy, he wondered, the truth? It was all too personal, too close, despite the years that had gone by. He decided he would describe things in the vaguest details and if the boy noted a resemblance between himself and who he once had been, he would say, 'I knew him, but not well.'

SHANGHAI, 1966

Li Kong was exhausted by the rounds of self-criticism sessions and the grueling meetings at school. Teachers were marched out before the student body and often forced to their knees in the airplane position with their arms tied in upward and behind them, often for hours on end, until they confessed to their purported crimes. It frightened him to see such brutality, and later when he had a chance to sit down with the Director, he just wanted to escape for a while into that other world. The Director read from where they had left off, glossing over the things he deemed the boy needn't know and emphasizing the things he did. Li Kong, in turn, was too tired to argue about Tanya's stance on social responsibility and let it go with a mild protest remembering the Director's warning that some people thought of events differently than he would do.

Shanghai, January 1933

There are no jobs to be had. Isfahani says nothing for now, Architect Hrbek said he might have something for me in the near future, Yevgeny Borisovitch is still using the old sets, and Sirdar Singh says, maybe soon. I don't want to call Sasha, even though I know I was at fault. Perhaps he is happy to have me off the set for now. Anya and Shi-shi think it is up to me to apologize and that Sasha will take me back, but I can't bring myself to dial the phone.

Shanghai, February 1933

    A few days ago, Natalia Ivanovna came home and taking off her too tight shoes-I really don't know why she wants to pretend she has small feet- sat heavily. I knew she wanted a foot rub, and though I hate touching people's feet, I gritted my teeth and did it for her, since I could see she has trouble reaching over her fat belly.

    'Tanya, I am back from seeing Masha Alexandrovna,' she said. Masha is a friend of hers of long standing who has done very well investing other peoples' money and keeps her finger on the pulse of everything that is going on in town. 'She says they need someone in the dress department at The Sunshine Globe. I mentioned you needed a job, and she said she would recommend you.'

    It was not the kind of job I wanted, but I also knew I had no choice. I told Natalia I was interested and that she should set it up.

Shanghai, February 1933

    This is the most soul crushing thing I have ever done. I get up early, wash, and put on my clothes, which I have laid out the night before, as I did when I was at school. I have to recycle the same things over and over again and make them look fresh and interesting because I must set a standard where I work, catering, as I do, to rich women all day long.

    It is ugly and sycophantic and I hate it. I couldn't do anything with my first paycheck except pay my overdue rent to Natalia and buy materials for new clothes. I made some solid color dresses, cut on the bias and past the knee, one in deep purple, one green, one burgundy, certainly chicer than anything they have for sale there. I'm not even looking forward to wearing them, that's how much I hate my life.

. . .

Shanghai, March 1933

Something great and interesting happened today. The head of the department asked me up to his office. He said that reports had come back to him that customers were asking to buy the dresses I was wearing. He asked me a lot of questions, where I had ordered the patterns from and so on. He didn't believe me when I said I had drawn them up myself from ideas I had. So he had me show him. I had been thinking up things for a while since it is so excruciatingly boring here when no one is around - and time passes so slowly. So I asked for paper and pen and drew some ideas I had for dresses, gowns, coats, and shoes and hats. He asked if I could make patterns up for his seamstresses. I said I only made dresses for myself and my friend Anya, and I would just drape them, then sew them up; I didn't know how to make patterns. He said never mind, he had a talented seamstress who could think things through from my designs, and we could work together if I was interested. I said, was I ever! And he laughed at my enthusiasm. Then I negotiated a salary increase, though I would have done the job for free, if I hadn't needed the money. I then asked if Mei could come work for his team. He was going to say no, but I talked her up so much that he finally relented.

He said to finish work, and we would start in the morning. Afterward I went to Mei's house and waited for her to come back from the factory. It's an awful place, dark, dingy, and reeking of cooking. Her mother-in-law couldn't understand what I was doing there. She seems like such a mean little woman, and I think she gives Mei a lot of grief.

Mei came home, and when I told her that I would make her my right hand she cried and couldn't stop. She never said anything, but I think her life is much worse now that she is married.

Shanghai, March 1933

Hong Zongying is the cleverest woman. She is the head of the seamstresses and the one assigned to cut the patterns. She can tell what can and can't be done from the drawings I have done. She also knows how the cut will need to be altered for Europeans and for Chinese women. She is in her forties and very stern, but I think I will learn a lot from her.

. . .

Shanghai, March 1933

We work day and night here. Hong Zongying cut the first of the patterns, and we sewed the dresses up. She is so disciplined, and she demands excellence from the seamstresses. They don't complement each other in this country, but I can tell she is pleased with Mei's work. She grunts a little when she inspects it.

I don't know what she thinks about having to work with me. She is older and so talented, and she has been doing this since she was a girl. I feel that I have had unusual good luck in my life so far. I told Hong not to hesitate when she thought something was not right with my sketches and to point it out. She took this very literally! And so she dissected my designs down to the last detail, and pointed out the flaws in the purple dress I was wearing. I was a bit wounded and silent at first, but I realized she was right. Then I said, 'We will do as you say.'

She seemed pleased.

Li Kong thought the girl's luck was remarkable, and he was pleased by how much she valued Hong and Mei. He had been so shaken during the last meeting at school that he had wanted to come home, burn the diaries and absolve himself of the guilt of having them and wanting to know what was in them. Now he felt as if his interest in the diaries and the girl had been justified. He said nothing to the Director, not wanting to interrupt the flow of his reading.

Shanghai, April 1933

We finished working on the spring and summer collection now, and it will premier as soon as possible, since we are late for the season. I convinced the Boss to do an event-a sort of grand opening for it, and to publicize it. I told him I had spoken to the Rajni and that she promised to bring all her smart friends, and he finally agreed to spend the money. Chinese people are frugal, but they are also pragmatic. He could see the wisdom of spending some money to make even more. I think by the time I was done talking it up, he thought we could rival the great Wing On's, which is the chicest, most wonderful department store in Shanghai.

Hong is working almost round the clock. Sometimes the seamstresses even sleep here. She really is the driving force, and now that my work has tapered off, I am rearranging the dress salon to look more upscale and inviting.

Shanghai, April 1933

I got Anya a job modeling clothes for the opening! I think we might be able to keep her on afterward if she does a good job. She wears them so well, with such an attitude. And she is so regal- tall, cool and blond. Hong Zongying brought in a few exquisitely beautiful Chinese girls to model at the opening as well. I am very excited.

The Boss didn't give me much of a decorating budget, so I had to think of what would work to give a sense of both splendor and intimacy. We painted the walls celadon green and the trim dark green. I found a red lintel and some old carved doors, quite magnificent, that someone building a new villa was going to toss out. The carpenters put them up, respectively, at the entrance and as a back drop. I then bought a few potted palms and a ton of orchids. Anya and I went to the market and bought a bunch of caged birds that we will release after the show. Anya is so sentimental about them and is the one who cares for them. I think, that, along with some of the overhead fans and the little gold chairs we have rented, will set the tone. We have also gotten a caterer who will serve champagne and canapes.

Sasha has called several times. I told Natalia Ivanovna to tell him I was working around the clock to make the opening a success. She did, but now she says she won't lie for me anymore. I don't know what is wrong with me. Sasha is such a good man, better than I deserve, but I just don't feel like talking to him, or anyone else for that matter.

'I don't understand her,' Li Kong remarked. 'She says he is a good man, but she doesn't want him.'

The Director sighed. 'Perhaps if he had made a legitimate offer of marriage instead of offering to keep her, she would have taken him seriously. The way things stood, she would have to live at his whim and pleasure, and an arrangement like that could end at any time. Where would she have found herself then? No, it was better for young women, if they had talent and ambition, to develop their own careers and be self-reliant.

'It will seem odd to you, but really, these young women were breaking new ground. They had the chance to show the world what they were made of and what they could be. And some were just as good or better at their jobs than men, since they were trying so much harder.'

'Yes, I see that now that you've explained it,' Li Kong replied.

Shanghai, May 1933

The opening was spectacular. Everyone came, rich Chinese women, all of The Rajni's smart set, the French, German, and younger Englishwomen as well. We got a ton of orders, and now we will be filling them. The Boss is happy. Hong Zongying seemed a bit overwhelmed by all the hoopla, but then her innate sense of discipline took over and she organized everything, the orders, the appointments for the measurements, and the fittings. She's quite the thing, and she was incredibly elegant in grey qipao she made for herself with a black border and a pale pink lining. I wore a black dress with a high collar, long sleeved, past the knee, but very fitted and close to the body. Sirdar Singh lent me the brooch I had designed in the shape of a stylized bow, with the large emerald center piece set off by paved diamonds and blue sapphires. I was so very nervous about it, though he assured me it was insured.

It is so very funny, but the clients want to look like me! My dress got the most orders, and then they really oohed and aahed when they found out I had designed my jewels too. I think it is only because Anya and the Chinese models are so perfectly beautiful and that their look is unattainable for ordinary people. In any case, I think I will be doing more work for Sirdar Singh very soon!

. . .

Shanghai, July 1933

I'm swamped with work. Just as I predicted, Sirdar Singh commissioned me for a whole new batch of jewelry designs. We are doing brisk business at the store, and I am starting to design the fall collection. I'm excited about it. I've learned so much about cutting clothes from Hong and it reflects in my designs. They are not as fanciful, but clean and elegant. I love the team and my work. Sometimes, I daydream that one day I'll be as famous as Coco Chanel or Elsa Schiaparelli, and living in Paris. Oh, but that's a long way off!

August 1933

Sasha's movie premiered. I went with Shi-shi and Anya. I sat through it and clapped at the end. The public loved it. It was all about a poor family, who evicted by their cruel landlord were forced to live on the streets, and the daughter had to prostitute herself, and so on. The Chinese were weeping. They love drama and sentiment just as much as Russians do. It was heavy handed, but it looks like it is going to be a success, and maybe it will give Sasha the freedom to do what he should be doing. I say that, though I do not think it will happen, not at least, until Ming Gui lets go of his hold over Sasha.

Sasha is so changed. He is even more serious and melancholic now, and he has taken to wearing those dreadful blind man's glasses as well. He has gotten so thin, I thought he might be ill and was worried, but Shi-shi said it was just that he had been working so hard cutting the movie.

We went to congratulate him afterward and had to fight our way through a throng of fans and reporters. He seemed surprised to see me there and smiled. It was terribly awkward, and I wanted to say so many things, that I was foolish and so very sorry for the way I had behaved. I never got the chance because he was distracted by reporters.

Afterward, Shi-shi insisted that I go to the party he was giving for Sasha, so I agreed because I still wanted to say those things to him. But when we got there, Sasha was with his leading lady, Anita Cheng. Shi-shi says they are contracted for four more films. I asked if they were romantically involved, and Shi-shi didn't want to say, but Anya replied, 'Well, what did you expect Tanya? He couldn't wait for you forever.'

I suppose it's what I deserve. Anita looks very Western with crimped hair and round eyes and is quite voluptuous. Everyone says she is going to be a big star. I was feeling terribly sad and left without saying goodbye to anyone. All the way home, I cried.

Both men were silent as Sun Mu closed the final page of the notebook.

'Did you know Fang Shirong?' the boy asked.

'Not well, but I saw him often before he disappeared during the war.'

'I think he was right in making those films. Consciousness needed to be raised,' Li Kong said.

'Yes. I too, thought so.'

'What kinds of films did you make?'

'Films very much in the same vein.'

'She was mistaken about that, but I think she did care for him,' Li Kong said, thinking a bit.

'Perhaps. Perhaps she was only sad because he had moved on and she was left behind,' the Director said.

'She doesn't seem the type!' the boy exclaimed, defending Tanya.

'We will never know, will we?'

'There are three more diaries. I have them,' Li Kong unburdened himself.

'Ah, I see,' the Director said. 'Then, until next time.'

'Until next time,' Li Kong smiled.

When Li Kong left, the Director lay down on his pallet remembering that evening, though he did not recall Tanya being there. He remembered the premier, the party, and Anita, of course. Mostly he thought back on that first endeavor with embarrassment. He had worked so hard, had struggled with the work which had not come easily at first. And he had fought with Ming Gui over the script, which resulted in constant rewriting. Anita had been difficult as well, vain, silly, and demanding, but beautiful.

Tanya, you were right about that film, he thought. It was pure kitsch.

PART II

SHANGHAI, AUTUMN 1966

'What is it?' the Director asked, noting Li Kong's heavy mood. He had been waiting several days for the boy to come back with the second dairy but when he had not shown up at the appointed hour the Director assumed more unavoidable meetings had been scheduled at school. Still, he had anxiously kept looking out toward the courtyard until he remembered Li Kong said that sometimes the sessions dragged on for days and often students were detained overnight. When he heard the boy's light knock, he had been elated until he had seen the look on Li Kong's face.

'Has something gone wrong?'

'Not for me. It's my friend. His mother, really.'

'Sit down. Tell me what has happened,' the Director said, holding a stool out for the boy.

'I'm not sure. His mother was detained weeks ago. She's a professor at the university,' he explained.

'And your friend is worried?'

'Yes. But it's not that. He says his father wants to divorce her so that he can go on working.'

'Ah then, she's been purged,' the Director said.

'Worse. Her students tortured her, calling her a snake demon. And then some girls threw boiling water on her.'

The Director was shocked. 'What was she accused of ?' he managed to ask after a few moments.

'Those girls are from the provinces. They say she is a snake who turned herself into a beautiful woman and hypnotized her husband.' Li Kong took a deep breath, 'In truth, she taught languages.'

'I see,' the Director said.

'Do you? Because it gets even worse. My friend will also have to cut his ties to her if he is to have a future.'

'Where is she now?'

'They released her but she has to report back, soon. My friend was shocked when she came to the door. She is so changed. He says she seems so much older and that she has lost all her confidence and optimism.'

Oh, yes the Director thought. That's how it goes. They work on you until they break you and you no longer have any sense of yourself. Eventually you believe they were right, all along.

'Tell me, do you think that is a choice you would consider, cutting ties to your own mother?'

'I don't have to. My parents are dead.' Li Kong seemed about to say something but then changed his mind. 'I don't want to think about it anymore. Please, let's just read.'

'All right,' the Director agreed.

SECOND NOTEBOOK

Shanghai, January 1934

I suppose I thought I was too old to write a journal any more, and really looking back at my first journal, I think I was such a child, but I'm keeping it, primarily because of the sketches contained within, and because of something Natalia Ivanovna said. Sometimes when she has been drinking alone, and I come home late and find her sitting in the dark, she'll get testy, as if she resents me for the span of years that separate us. Sometimes, she's quite maudlin, and bitter, in turn, and other times she is like one of those idiot-savants, who says just the right thing at the right time.

She was sitting there, no light on, and I thought she had fallen asleep. Her cigarette was burning in the ashtray to a dull red, and I thought to put it out. She said, 'Leave it, Tanya. I'm wide awake.' There was something so heavy about her voice, and I knew it was not just the alcohol speaking, so I sat down quietly next to her, as I sometimes do just so that she can unburden herself.

Sometimes, afterward, she is kind and attentive to me as if she is grateful I am here to hear her thoughts. Sometimes, she'll be distant, and even cruel in the morning, as if she can't bear that anyone has heard her thoughts.

She said it seemed to her that her life was over as a woman. Love had gone out of her life, and with it, her ability to feel and give, and now she would only have a protracted old age to look forward to with none of the things that would make it bearable; security, children, and grandchildren.

'What would you have changed about the past?' I asked her, and she replied it was useless to think like that. Then she added, 'I wish I had taken my diaries with me when I left Russia. I can't even remember who I was before I lost myself.'

I didn't even know she had kept diaries. She doesn't seem the type, rough as she is.

She said, 'Oh, you should have seen me then, a willowy girl, full of hopes and dreams.'

'What did you hope for, Natalia?' I asked, and that's the thing, because she replied, 'That's what I can't seem to remember.'

It was a scene straight out of Chekhov, and I would have started laughing if she had not been so very sad.

After I left her, I thought that I'd keep my old notebook, but that is not why I have started this new one. This one is to help me think, and to help me quell my anxiety, because this is the time of Richard, and everything I seem to do, and think, is about Richard and for Richard.

I wish I had started it earlier, the recording, because now it is difficult to remember, and those first sweet moments are somehow becoming compacted into one long extended summer's day when I found myself falling, as if from a pleasure boat, into the depths of a murky lake.

It was, perhaps really on a lake that it happened, for that is how I see it, in my mind's eye. Me in white, with a parasol, trailing my hand languidly in the green water. Richard is rowing, looking at me while he is rowing, and I suddenly think, I can't do without him.

Or, perhaps, it is the night when we are dancing, without music, under the stars, on the balcony, barely moving, and he is holding me so closely, with his large warm hand on my back, when I feel so safe, and I think, please never let me go.

Maybe, it is when he is asleep next to me, and I am sitting up in bed listening to the rain fall against windowpanes and over the roof, when I feel something welling up in me, which expands from my heart and fills me, and is love, for him, and myself, and everything in that pale grey room, and for the rain on the rooftop, and the slick green leaves on the trees- and this feeling moves beyond the garden to encompass the city, and the whole, wide world. And I want to hold that moment forever, unchanging. Unchangeable.

Or perhaps it is when the sheets are damp in the late afternoon, and the fan is swirling overhead, and I am holding on to the sheet, gripping it, bunching it in my fist, because Richard is infusing his essence into me, the whole of it, and his mouth is on mine, and he cups the small of my back to bring me upward and even closer, that I feel a fusion with him and connected to all things.

Or maybe it is in the morning, a lazy Sunday, when the houseman is off, when I make breakfast in the kitchen, and the light permeates everything around me and makes it golden, that I think, what if this could be made permanent and last forever?

But I never know with Richard, what he is thinking, or if he loves me, or if this is just the way he goes through the world, taking his pleasure until he grows weary of the novelty because he never says a thing, not about tomorrow, and certainly not about forever. So I am left, always a little devastated afterward, always uncertain, in a half dread when I am away from him, anxiously expecting his next call, anticipating his next move, afraid that each time will be the last.

'So, she fell in love with a man she disliked initially,' Li Kong said. 'I don't understand.'

'I am not certain what to tell you, but sometimes things can happen between a man and woman that cannot be explained rationally,' Sun Mu replied.

'Like sex?'

'Yes, like sex.'

'The Red Guards would not approve of such goings on. They are ascetic in their outlook towards those things.'

'You mean like accusing a professor of languages of being a snake demon?' the Director asked.

'They are not all like those girls. Some are truly dedicated to changing society for the better,' Li Kong said.

'A society based on hardship and violence, without love? Now what kind of society is that?' the Director mused, but noticed that the boy was lost in his own thoughts. He sighed deeply and continued reading.

Shanghai, January 1934

I went to Anya and Shi-shi's. They live together now that his father has died, and he is his own man. They have a splendid apartment in the French concession, very lovely and feminine, very much to Anya's taste.

'I can't stand you like this,' Anya said to me. She was fussing with tea.

'Like what?' I asked.

'You remind me of one of those pathetic street dogs that's been so maltreated, it doesn't know where to run to save itself.'

'That good?' I asked, and she laughed. But then she put down the teapot and sat close to me, taking my hands in hers.

'You've got to get hold of yourself before you make yourself crazy.'

I asked her what she would suggest, and she said to give Richard up, only that is impossible, and I told her so. She listened to me blather on about how I felt, and then sipping her tea slowly said, 'You must have something of your own to thoroughly engage you.'

'I have my work at the store,' I retorted.

'No,' she said. 'It doesn't animate you the way it used to, and you know that Hong is the one really in charge now.'

I had to agree, and I was feeling so miserable, so nervous, that I asked, 'Well, what then?'

She said she had been listening to me talk about Richard and how he made me feel, and what she heard over and over again were the words connected and expansive. 'What else makes you feel that way?'

I thought about it and said I was most happy when I was creating something new, something that would take me outside of myself and give me a feeling that I was in the stream of, well, I don't know, Being, maybe.

'You want to feel alive?' she asked.

'More than that, Anushka. It's so much more than that.'

I could see she really didn't know what I meant, but she said, 'You need to find that thing, and you need to do it and keep doing it.'

I promised I would think about it, and we had tea and talked about small things, her little complaints about Shi-shi, which were good natured and a sign of her devotion to him.

On the way home, I was so melancholic. They had the comfort of each other's domesticity, and I only had uncertainty.

Shanghai, January 1934

I have begun painting in oils. I think I hate it. I can barely concentrate and the results are not up to snuff.

Natalia has given me a little pantry to use as a studio. She says Anya is quite right, and if Richard was around all the time, I would soon tire of him and seek my out my own peace. 'You're that type, Tanya. You would never be happy with cozy domesticity.'

I wonder how can she say that, or think it all, when she knows what it is like to be displaced and without real moorings. I've never had the benefit of a real home, not even in childhood, because after my father died, my mother and I were dependent on the good will of relatives. I suppose the closest I came was my grandfather's house in the country, with the land and the horses, but even that seems like a faraway dream, and anyway it is gone and lost forever.

I don't know what I want. Richard has not called for days.

. . .

Li Kong nodded. He knew how the girl felt. He thought, we are similar. I am rootless, I have no one but my aunt, and Shanghai has never felt like home to me, especially now.

Shanghai, January 1934

He wrote. He needs to go away on business. He is not sure how long he will be away. I think it will be good for me. I will stabilize and get hold of myself.

Shanghai, January 1934

I can't think at all. I can't function. I go to work, but I am not even there. My every thought is of Richard, and not just the memories I have of him.

I imagine us on safari, in Paris, and in India, and in all these fantasies we are united, and there is no fear of abandonment, and no shame about the expression of real emotions, instead of the continuous pretense that I find all this fun, that I am fine alone, and I am strong and only interested in the pleasure our fleeting encounters bring to us both.

Shanghai, January 1934

Anya and Shi-shi took me to dinner. I felt even more alone. Shi-shi has actually grown a pot belly since Anya has taken charge of the domestic arrangements. She cooks him rich Russian dishes to show her love, but he is not used them, and he has never been a man to take exercise. Still they are striking. Anya is still as thin as a worm, and so very fashionable. Shi-shi is shorter, of course, with the look of portly prosperity that happiness bestows upon men.

Shi-shi is having a lot of success in business. He is still invested in film, among other projects - mainly construction and building management. He talked about Sasha and Sasha's career as a film director, which is flourishing. Sasha was engaged to that leading lady of his, but now they've broken it off.

'He can pick and choose now,' Shi-shi said, and Anya gave him a withering look, and said, 'He didn't mean it that way, Tanya.'

I shrugged. It's all in the past. I ate my food mechanically, almost wolfing it down, until I saw that Anya was staring at me. She's quite the lady now, and disapproves of bad manners.

When Shi-shi excused himself to go to the gents', she said, 'Tanya, get hold of yourself. You dress like a widow, and you look even worse. Rub some rouge on your cheeks and put on something with color. Get out there and have some fun, go to a nightclub, dance, remember who you were before that stupid man came into your life.'

I must have looked even more sullen, because she continued, 'You're not a plant waiting for the sun to shine on you, remember that.'

After dinner, we went dancing at the Paramount. Anya made Shi-shi take me out on the floor, but I only felt worse for wear.

'Should we stop for now?' the Director asked.

'No, please go on, just a bit longer. I don't want to go just yet,' Li Kong said.

He seemed like a very small boy who didn't want to be sent to bed, and so the Director went on reading.

Shanghai, January 1934

I went to the park today. People were strolling about, since the temperature was a bit warmer than normal. It was still brisk, but I felt refreshed by the wind and the beauty all around me. Everything seemed intensified, the clouds passing over the span of the sky, the tree line against the blue, and the water, which was still. I felt that it was all so fleeting, so imbued with sadness, and that eventually everything would pass and the lovers would part, the children would soon be adult, and everyone present would grow old and die, and their ashes would be carried away on the wind, or they would lie in the cold earth, and no one would remember them, nor their joys or sorrows.

I went to my studio-pantry afterward and stared at a blank canvas. I

*thought, what if Richard is with another woman, someone sophisticated like
Madam Liu, who I could not compete with, or one of those Egyptian, or
Indian, women he had had, who knew a thousand tricks to hold a man and
keep him satisfied. What did I have but my dog like devotion and endless,
annoying, cloying love to give? The only thing I could think to paint was a
woman, mourning, holding on to a dead horse.*

Shanghai, January 1934

    *I sketched the woman, nude, with her hair half hanging over her face, the
head of dying horse in her lap. I worked all day on it, without stopping.
Natalia was worried about me, and when she came to check that I had
presumably not hung myself in her house, she said, 'Whew, Tanechka, I think
you might have something there.'*

    I stepped back to assess my work, and asked, 'Do you think it's good?'

    *And she said, quite honestly, 'I'm not sure if it's good, but it's you, a true
expression of yourself.' Then she said, 'I'll make you a sandwich. Keep
working.'*

    *At midnight, she came in again and then once more in the morning. She
was carrying a wooden box. 'I've reconsidered. Oils aren't for you. They're
too harsh. This was Kolya's. I want you to have it,' she said, handing over a
wooden box. I opened it and found it was filled with a full spectrum of oil
pastels. 'Toss the canvas out. Go to sleep. I'll go out and buy paper, and then
you can start again,' she added.*

    I was so surprised and so tired that I did exactly as she said.

Shanghai, January 1934

    *It turned out well. I changed the sketch from the maudlin and heavy
handed symbolism of the dead horse, and sketched a woman, perhaps
sometime in the medieval past, in Russia, pensive, and sitting at the banks of
a river, three sorrel horses lapping the quiet water around her. The landscape
was autumnal and still, the trees gold and orange, reflected on the water, and
everything was muted and enveloped in a soft violet mist. Natalia was*

rhapsodic over it, so I gave it to her, and she is having it framed under glass so that she can hang it in her sitting room.

Shanghai, January 1934

I've been working on variations of the same theme, women, horses, the nature of the north, cool and clean. The pastel I gave Natalia is hanging up in the living room and looks quite impressive. I'll have to stop soon and draw up a new collection for the store, but I think the loose robes on the women and the draping has given me some new ideas for evening and lounge wear.

Shanghai, February 1934

Hong and I are working on the new collection, lots of mauves and pale greens, flowing robes to be worn over slinky trousers and blouses, and silk evening dresses. When I get home, I quickly eat and go to the studio where I get busy and everything seems to flow. I never get to bed until past two or three o'clock, but it is all right because I am not expected in early. Hong has everything under control. It's really her show, once the sketches have been finalized.

Shanghai, February 1934

I think I have something really good here. My technique has improved, but the themes have not gone anywhere until a day or so ago. I was fixated on women and their emotions, but once I let go of that, it all seemed to come together, and I arrived at something altogether different.

It is a re-imagining of my grandfather's farm. The horses were in the meadow, beyond them a copse of trees, and in the distance the refection of the setting sun, but it was so flat and not right, so I added some hills, shining pink and golden in the late afternoon, and then it was as it should be.

Natalia got all misty and said it was the best one yet. I was so pleased, though I don't know why I trust her in this matter since she has terrible taste otherwise!

. . .

'She was able to discipline herself and channel her passion for that man into art!' Li Kong exclaimed.

'Yes.'

'And you, have you done the same?'

The Director thought how to answer the boy. In the end, he thought it best to say what he really thought. 'I think sometimes when human relationships fail and prove utterly disappointing, art is the only refuge and the only thing that can give meaning to our lives. Everything passes. Fashions change. Social movements wax and wane. Even art is not eternal, and sometimes it is not even worthy of the name. But that process, the process of creation, awakens something within the heart of man, something greater than himself, which makes life worth living and makes one eager to get up in the mornings and face the world.'

'Even if you are purged for it?'

'Even if you end up on the dung heap, you are still able to say, I created something. It came from me and it challenged me to become something greater than my own small self.'

'Yes. That is something. It's late. I'll go now. Until next time, then.'

'Until next time,' the Director said. He shut the door and lay on his pallet for a few minutes before getting up to go to work, thinking if what he had said to the boy was really true and wondering if he would have made the same choices again.

Over the next few days, Li Kong considered what Director had said as he painted characters posters. He wondered if he should try painting but then reasoned he had no money for materials and if he took paper and paint from school he could get into trouble, be accused of self-aggrandizement and selfish thought. They would ask what need was there for a boy like him to create art. And what shape would art take in the new world they were creating, in any case? The Red Guards had smashed and destroyed so many beautiful and irreplaceable things- furniture, paintings, scrolls, statues, and pottery. They had no eye for beauty and no respect for those who were able to create it. And yet, they were right in their aims in wanting to deliver social justice, he thought, until he remembered their savage cruelty. An idea formed in his mind: They are drunk with power and taking revenge against their elders. He immediately stopped himself from reasoning further. It was dangerous to think that way, and yet he could not help repeating that phrase over and over, despite his best intentions.

~

Li Kong did not discuss his thoughts with the Director. They settled into their routine. Li Kong brought food over, the Director would eat quickly, and they would begin reading.

Shanghai, February 1934

Richard is back. He stopped by to tell me himself just after he returned. I was thrilled to be able to show him the new work, thinking he would be enthusiastic and happy for me. He was looking at the framed pastel in Natalia's sitting room with his head cocked, a slight smile playing around his lips. I thought, surely he'll say something, but he just murmured and asked me out to dinner. I was deflated and didn't bother showing him the rest of my output. Natalia was out, so he waited while I got ready.

I thought of what I could wear to please and delight him, and I put on a black qipao with an emerald lining and went downstairs. I had a matching velvet cloak with a darker green silk lining over my arm and he said, 'Well, well.' as if that was supposed to mean something.

Throughout dinner, I kept waiting for him to speak words of love, to tell me that he missed me and that he realized he loved me and couldn't wait to get back to me, because he longed for me as I had for him. But Richard talked of only small things, his new enthusiasm for some obscure artifact he had run across on his travels that meant nothing to me whatsoever. I wished he would be quiet, stop talking about things I had no interest in, and take me in his arms and hold me. Then I actually began to feel tears coming on, so I checked myself using an old trick, looking upward until the flow stopped. I became even sadder and quieter, but he never noticed at all.

Afterward, I thought, now he'll want to take me home and we'll make love all night, but he didn't. He put me in a cab and sent me home. I was so miserable, I poured myself some of Natalia's cheap brandy and made myself drunk with it. She heard me shuffling around in the dark, and came in. I asked her to read my cards, and she tied her robe tighter, poured herself a drink, lit a cigar, and sat down with her deck.

It was all doom, heartbreak and misery, so I made her do it again, only it was as bad the second time. I asked her to read them again, but she said it didn't work that way. Then I forgot my pride and that she had warned me against Richard, and I put my hands over my face and sobbed. And even Natalia, with her gruff ways, broke down and held me like a mother bear, until I was too weak to cry any more. She put me to bed and tucked me in, and said, 'Sleep, Tanya. Everything will look better in the morning.'

When I woke up, it was the first time I felt that Richard was disassociated from me. Viscerally, physically. It was if I had never been involved with him at all. I thought, now I'll be able to manage this horrible anxiety, and I will be in control of my situation and myself.

Natalia and I made ourselves busy baking, and cleaned up afterward. She packed her cakes in a basket and went to visit friends. I was alone and decided I would straighten out my room. It all began well. Then, of course, I could not bear the silence any more, and began to wonder what Richard was thinking, and where this all would lead in the end. I was tormenting myself, and though I knew I shouldn't have, I telephoned him. I only wanted to know where I stood with him, but afraid of hearing the answer, I was afraid to ask the question.

He was cheerful, polite, non-committal, and I merely thanked him for dinner and asked if he would be traveling again soon. He was silent for a while and said, 'Let's go to Hong Kong for a few days, just the two of us. We'll make it a honeymoon of sorts, if you can manage to take off work.'

I said it was no problem and we set a departure date.

· · ·

'He disrespected her art and still she would go with him?' Li Kong said.

'As she disrespected Sasha's work?'

'She did not disrespect him. In fact, she thought so highly of him that she expected him to do great things.'

'How do you know he didn't do great things? You are neither familiar with his career nor his films,' the Director said sharply.

'I did not say that. I said she expected greater things of him at the time.'

'Perhaps he produced what he was capable of at the time.'

'Perhaps he was afraid of doing something real and searching within himself. Perhaps he took the easy route,' Li Kong said. He could not understand why he was being so belligerent toward the old man, or even if he meant what he was saying.

The Director looked at him with new respect. The boy is not as foolish as he initially seemed. Perhaps there is hope for him yet. 'Let's continue,' he said.

'Yes. Let's,' Li Kong said.

Hong Kong, February 1934

I dreamt Madam Liu was in the house. We are in the hills, in a new villa, which belongs to Richard's friends who have gone to England to visit family. Richard said he had it all planned, a private hideaway, and no hotel, not even the new Peninsula, with its prying eyes, would give us that feeling. I wondered what he could mean by that. Who was he hiding our relationship from, and why should they care? Perhaps he is ashamed of me; perhaps he wants a fling with no questions asked by his peers, and no reminders afterward. I was stung by it and brooded while we were on the ship going south, though I didn't let him see how I really felt and was charming and flirtatious. How false I am, like a dog eager to please its master so that it will be fed.

When we arrived, I found the house to be lovely, white and clean, nestled in the green hills with louvered doors and shutters, letting in the breezes, overlooking the bay.

We have an automobile at our disposal, and after unpacking, we went on a drive. The bay below with its pleasure boats and junks was a magnificent sight from the hills, the vistas breathtaking.

It began to rain, and we went home and made love all afternoon, as if we were newly acquainted, slowly and hesitantly, because I was resistant and stiff at first.

I fell asleep and took one of those long afternoon naps that leave one disoriented and melancholy afterward. I had the feeling that something terrible was happening that I could not control and woke up with a dreadful feeling of anxiety. I lie there trying to think what could have upset me so, and then I remembered I had been dreaming, and that in the dream Madam Liu had been in the house.

When I came down, Richard was lying on the sofa, in his robe, reading. I was still half asleep and said, 'Has Madam Liu been in the house?' Richard looked up at me, with that right brow of his rising, as it does when he annoyed or surprised.

'I dreamt she was here,' I said, sounding petulant, even to myself.

'Silly Darling, come here,' Richard said, and took me in his arms. We were lying so closely together on the sofa when he added, 'That was nothing, Tanya. You needn't worry.'

Had I been brave I would have asked if he considered the thing we have to be something, but I wasn't brave. I merely said, 'I liked her so. Could we see her while we are here?' He was silent for a moment and said, 'I heard some time ago that her family sent her to Singapore.'

'Why would they have?' I asked.

'Oh they have interests all over Asia, and she is a capable business woman. They need her to oversee things there.'

'So you have had no contact with her, at all, since Shanghai?' I asked.

'None,' he replied. 'Perhaps I never say enough to you, but a woman like that, as charming as she is, holds little charm for me. You see I'm quite as jaded as she.'

'But with me, everything is all fresh and new, because I'm newly minted and dewy eyed?'

Richard laughed but didn't deny it.

'Wonderful, Richard. You know, in time, you'll feel the same about me. What charm will grownup Tanya hold for you then?'

'Ah, you're still younger than springtime and have a long way to go,' he replied.

'So, I'm gauche, to boot.'

'No.'

'What then,' I asked.

'Just, no,' he said with finality.

Of course, I had always known he would tire of me eventually and that made me even angrier with myself and sadder about the fact that I would have to give him up whenever he decided he had had enough.

'Let's dress and go somewhere for dinner,' he said.

I had brought with me a red evening gown that Hong had made for a client who had never claimed it. She had given it to me because I had the same measurements. I had never worn it before, because I couldn't stand the sight of myself in it, brazen and bold, almost whorish, but when I was packing, I had thought, that is what I am.

Richard's eyes popped when he saw me, and he said, 'Tanya is growing up quickly.'

I was so self-conscious, I put my hand up to my throat nervously and asked if it was over the top, because I could change in a minute, but Richard said it was just right.

We drove seemingly forever through the night before we arrived at a secluded restaurant that was almost empty. I thought, of course, he doesn't want anyone he knows to see us together and that is why we are here. We had made small talk on the drive, but now having run out of things to talk about, I asked about his work and what he had planned for the future.

'Don't ask me about my work, Dearest,' he said. 'I don't want to think about that or anything serious now. As for the future, who knows what it may bring? The Japanese have installed a puppet government in Manchuria, the communists and the Kuomintang are fighting a civil war, there is chaos in the north and eventually it will sweep southward, if it is not stopped. The Japanese have always had designs on China and its resources. God knows where it will end.'

I felt a bolt a fear shoot through me, but managed to contain it and said, 'Ah, Richard, but then you'll have England to return to, a safe haven.'

'And who would want to live there?' he asked rhetorically. I thought it was dreadfully insensitive considering I had a worthless passport and no home country of my own to return to.

'Where would you want to go after Shanghai?' I asked.

'Well, the plan was to amass enough money to buy a spread in Kenya.'

'And what would you do there?' I asked, becoming more and more dismayed as the conversation progressed.

'Do? I suppose the idea was to be my own man.'

'Marriage, children?' I asked.

'I've never wanted a conventional life and having children doesn't particularly appeal.'

'I see,' I said.

'And what about Tanya? What does she long for?' he asked.

I wanted to tell him to stop being so blind, that I loved him, that I would go wherever he went, sacrifice whatever I was, or would become, just to have the chance. 'I don't know. Everything has moved so quickly, my work, life. I never had a chance to think or really plan anything.'

'That comes in time, you'll see. After you've seen a bit of the world, you can decide,' he assured me, and I thought, well I suppose you think you are in my life to give me a taste of that world.

When we left the restaurant, he walked several steps ahead of me, and I thought, why can't you ever take hold of my open hand?

Hong Kong, February 1934

In the morning, Richard said he had to see someone on business but that he would drop me off in Victoria so that I could see the sights and do some shopping. We scheduled a time and place for a rendezvous later in the day.

As we drove down from the hills, I steeled myself and thought, you might as well pretend you are here alone and do what you would do if you were alone. I bid him good-bye and began strolling through the arcades, looking at shops, wondering what I should see next, when I heard a young man's voice calling, 'Oh, I say, aren't you the insect girl?'

I turned to look at him. He was one of those cheerful, string bean types that the British produce in quantity, so seemingly light and carefree that you wonder if there is anything of substance inside of them at all.

It appeared we had met at the Sassoons' party, though I had no recollection of it. He on the other hand, remembered me. 'Frightfully clever costume,' he said.

We made some inane banter for a while, and I lied to him, saying I was visiting friends but was on my own for the day.

'Oh, I say, what a stroke of luck,' he said, mentioning that he too was at loose ends, and wouldn't it be fun if we wandered and saw the sights together. I thought why not? Why shouldn't I let myself be picked up by a stranger like this? Why shouldn't I experience something new, rather than the heaviness that always seems to permeate everything in me and around me?

We walked through the center of town and the wide white streets, down to the waterfront, and took a pedicab when we grew tired, and laughed and took shelter in the rain at a restaurant where we had lunch. When the rain cleared, we walked through the crowded Chinese sector, where life is lived on the streets. We watched children play, old women cook, barbers give hair-cuts, and looked in the dark dingy shops at oddities and dried bits of things, mushrooms and animals parts which are used medicinally.

In the late afternoon, I had to go back, but we promised to write.

His name is David, he has been here many times before, and now he will be saying on, since he has a job at the Bank of Hong Kong. I liked that he never once asked me to tell him my sad stories, not of Russia, not of Shanghai. He talked and listened, as if I was a person with worthwhile opinions, and he liked and often agreed with my observations, of the city, and of people.

Hong Kong, February 1934

Richard was preoccupied all evening, and after a light supper, shut himself in the study, saying he had some paperwork to take care of. I found a few books on the shelves worth reading and went to bed early.

In the morning, we made love, but it was not as intense. Perhaps it is the time of day, when things are just awakening, that makes the transition a bit softer, and everything a bit dreamier. I was feeling sleepy, contented, and consoled. After breakfast, he got a telegram and said we had to cut our trip short, because he was needed at the office.

I said nothing, neither then nor on the return trip, but when the car dropped me off, I couldn't look at him. I was ready to say don't call again, when he grabbed my arm. 'I know you are disappointed, as am I, but it couldn't be helped. I promise to make it up to you,' he said. I wrenched my arm away and didn't look back.

The following afternoon, one of the smaller pieces I had designed for Sirdar Singh was hand delivered, with a note that just read R. I took it up to Natalia and showed it to her. 'It means he is serious,' she said.

'Maybe it means he is buying my affections, Natalia. I think I should send it back.'

Natalia stuck out her lower lip and shrugged a bit, as she does when she is thinking. 'I think if that were true, he would have sent any piece of jewelry. And yet he didn't. He picked out something he knew you would want for yourself, and what is more he picked out something of your own design.'

'But what am I supposed to do, just sit there, until he is ready to pay attention to me again, whenever he wants to, regardless of my own need to be with him? I'm not allowed to need anything, or feel anything, or ask for anything!'

'Oh my dear, that's the age old lament of women,' Natalia said. 'We are required to wait while they live their lives in the world.'

'Well, these are modern times, Natalia,' I sniffed.

'So they are, and that is why you have your own career.'

'The worst part of it is I don't know how long it will last, or what I am sinking my time into.' I was angry, miserable, and heart-sick.

'Then you need to think long and hard about what you really want and where you are headed.'

'I don't know,' I said. 'All I know is that I want to be with him all the time.'

'Then be with him now and leave the rest in God's hands.'

I went upstairs and wrote Richard a thank you note, saying I would treasure his gift, and God knows what else. It was all so maudlin and *melodramatic that I am almost ashamed on my own behalf as I read over this entry.*

Shanghai, March 1934

Life seems to have settled into a pattern. I go to work, come home, and draw. Richard and I see each other beginning late Saturday afternoon, unless he has work to do, spend the night together into late morning Sunday. He needs to the rest of the day free to rest, and I understand that. It is fine because I am full of him and filled by him until I am alone again. Monday rolls around, work keeps me busy, but always there is the terrible longing, the anticipation of seeing him again, the fear that he will never call, and the horrible anxiety as I am getting ready. I worry about getting there on time, of being somehow waylaid, and of something bad happening to Richard. It's all so exhausting, but no matter how much I try, I can't take my mind out of this loop. The only time I seem to be able to forget is when I am in the studio.

'Perhaps, she desires him so because he is so elusive,' Li Kong commented.

'Ah, yes. It is human nature to want what we can't have and to spurn what comes easily, isn't it.'

'Were you ever in love with anyone?' Li Kong asked.

'Hmmm. I often wonder what that term means. If we are to understand it in terms of the Western romantic tradition, as Tanya does, with all its attendant anxieties and woes that keep the couple apart, then, yes, more than once. Have I ever truly loved anyone, spent years with them, cared for them in illness and old age, had a family, then no. That love was reserved for my career.'

'Your art, you mean?'

'Maybe, maybe my art, but perhaps I loved the thought of being a film director even more than I did the creations at the end of it.'

'But that contradicts everything you said before!' Li Kong protested.

'Does it? Well perhaps I am reflecting on my failures now.'

'I wish I could see your films.'

'There is little chance of that now,' the Director replied.

'But you could tell me about them. At least your favorites, and you could tell me what it was like to make them.'

'What is prompting your sudden interest?' the Director asked.

'I don't know. Maybe I'm thinking of writing something. I keep thinking of my grandparents' village, how green it was, and how every day seemed to stretch on forever, and how life seemed aligned with the rhythms of nature- the rising and setting of the sun, the sowing and reaping of crops, the great silences, birdsong in the morning, and the croaking of frogs at night. I know life was harsh there but compared to this,' Li Kong motioned with his hand, 'it seemed so peaceful.'

The Director listened to the boy's poetry and said, 'You have vision. Develop it and we will refine it together.'

'I'm not sure how,' Li Kong said.

'Begin by writing down what you just said.'

'And then?'

'It will come to you of its own accord. Perhaps not at once, perhaps it will happen in fits and starts, but it will eventually flow.'

'Maybe. If I have time. I must study as well. I can't afford to fall behind.'

Ah, the Director thought, so he realizes that this latest political aberration will end and he will have to move forward somehow. 'There's time enough. Why don't we break now and you can work on it a bit while it's fresh in your mind. We'll get back to Tanya tomorrow.'

'Yes, I'd like that. See you tomorrow.'

'Well?' the Director asked.

'I'm working on it,' Li Kong smiled.

'Should we read then?'

'Yes.'

. . .

Shanghai, March 1934

A big commission came from Sirdar Singh for a special client he won't name. I have to say the designs this time around are magnificent. Comparing them to what I did before made the old ones look quite simple and childlike.

I told Singh I wanted to do something different this time, with turquoise, malachite and coral, and he agreed once he had seen the drawings. He calls my style art deco, and says it is the rage in Europe. I wish I could see other people's work, so often it can be an inspiration, but Singh seems to think my designs are first class.

Shanghai, March 1934

More work. They've asked me to do perfume bottles for the store with atomizers, evening bags, cigarette cases, compacts, and such. Everything is in the art deco style, some of it inlaid with semi-precious stones.

Hong and I are working on some very intricate evening dresses with beading in deco motifs. The most beautiful one is in a nude silk georgette with a handkerchief hem and embroidered with silvery-gold sequins. It is so delicate and subtle, not in the least vulgar, as some sequined gowns can be. I wish I could afford it myself. Alas!

Shanghai, March 1934

The Rajni is back from a protracted visit back home, and organizing a dinner party. Richard and I both received invitations, but of course, no one knows we are a couple, least of all the Princess. I thought that it would be a great opportunity to come out and said so, but Richard said that he didn't want anyone to know about us. We were in the room with the African masks and moments before had been sitting together on the sofa looking at a book, when his houseman brought the invitation.

'Why is that?' I finally asked. 'Are you ashamed of me?'

'No,' he answered.

'Then tell me!' I insisted, jumping up.

'Leave it alone, Tanya. Stop pressing,' he answered.

'Fine then. I'll be happy to leave you alone, and I'm not going to her stupid party!' I shouted, and picking up my handbag I stormed out.

My heart was thundering on the landing, and I was so unfocused I almost stumbled down the stairs. I was hoping that he would come after me, but of course, he didn't.

I was in such a rage on the way home that I decided never to see him again. In the morning, I was going to send my regrets to the Rajni, but then reconsidered. I decided to make him sorry for his behavior.

When I went store, I told Hong that I wanted to borrow the silver dress for one evening. It was a sample and not intended for anyone yet. She fought me, saying that it might be ruined but finally relented, muttering a torrent of nasty Chinese invectives.

'Please, Hong, don't be angry,' I said and must have looked quite desperate, because she said, 'You are like a bitch in heat,' before stalking away.

I took the dress anyway.

Shanghai, April 1934

I wore the dress to the Rajni's, but it held no joy for me. I knew I only wanted Richard to see me in it and think: this is what I am letting go of.

Of course, Richard never turned up. My eyes were on the door all evening long, and I couldn't concentrate or enjoy myself. It was a small party and somehow the talk turned to politics and talk of the situation in Germany and Hitler's rise to power. A few of the Rajni's guests were German, and they seemed to admire the man tremendously. Knowing nothing of events, I had nothing to contribute. I listened to them bicker back and forth. There was an older man present who strenuously objected to Hitler's intimidation tactics of the past few years and the havoc his Sturmabteilung had caused brawling in the streets with the communists. The conversation turned towards economics, so I couldn't follow it at all. Each person there seemed to make sense to me, until the older gentleman said how Hitler's men hated and harassed the Jews.

There were many Jewish people who had fled Russia and were living in Shanghai, and I found them to be a kind and gentle race, who were hard working and long suffering. I said so, and they all laughed at my naiveté, except for the older gentleman who said, 'Bravo, Miss Zhukova.'

Emboldened, and remembering what Richard had said about the Japanese, I asked what they thought would happen to Shanghai in the long run. That sparked an intense debate, but the consensuses was that they wouldn't dare touch Europeans no matter what happened.

At the end of the evening, the older gentleman kissed my hand and said I was an intelligent young lady. I replied that I really was quite empty headed, and he objected in a most charming and enthusiastic manner.

I was feeling better about myself and decided to drop in on Richard, thinking I would repair things between us, since I had behaved so badly. It was getting quite late, but I was determined to see him. I wished I had something to give him, a book or a bottle of wine, but I didn't and set off as I was.

When I arrived at his house, I saw the lights were still on, and although I had misgivings, I decided to go up anyway. I peeked in the window and saw him engaged in a conversation with his houseman, Zhang, except they were both sitting at the table and discussing something in a heated manner. Zhang was quite altered, and seemed to be angry with Richard. He looked up, and suddenly resumed the attitude of a servant, quietly gliding toward the door and opening it.

'Miss Tatiana, please enter,' he said.

Richard half stood, smiling. He seemed quite tired. 'Zhang and I were arguing over household expenses. It seems that I have been overspending myself, haven't I, Zhang?'

Zhang stood silently as was his manner until Richard dismissed him, and I put the episode out of my mind entirely.

'Did you have a nice time at the Rajni's?' Richard asked.

I told him I had had a horrible time. That I was miserable without him, and that I had waited all night for him to walk through the door.

'Poor silly darling,' he said, embracing me.

'I wore this dress just for you Richard,' I said, sounding like an idiotic child, even to myself.

'It's a lovely dress,' he said. 'Why don't we take it off?'

I did as he said, and thought it was strange that before he had ever made *love to me, I had control over my feelings. Afterward, I had none, and was dependent on his moods and his physical presence entirely.*

Afterward, when we were lying in the dark, I listened to the rise and fall of his breath and knew he was still awake.

'Richard, about your work - a long time ago, Isfahani told me that you were some sort of British agent.'

Richard laughed. 'Is that what they say?' he mused.

'Are you?' I asked.

'A very long time ago, when I was young and adventurous, I did some work for the government, but no longer. I do suppose rumors and speculations follow one, though.'

'You never tell me anything personal. I know about your travels and interests, your observations of people and places, but I don't really know how you feel about anything, or about your childhood, or what you could be thinking.'

'It's because those things don't matter.'

'Tell me anyway,' I said.

'My father preferred to live the life of an invalid. My mother was old fashioned and spent her life coddling him. I was sent to school very early on, and though I am grateful to them for providing a fine education, I think I shaped myself through the travels you mentioned. As for feelings, I don't express them easily, but it doesn't necessarily mean I don't experience them.

'Tanya, you're inexperienced, but I can assure you if you were privy to all my thoughts and feelings, you'd soon tire of both them and me.'

I decided to steel myself and asked, 'Do you see any future for us, together, I mean?'

Richard sighed, 'I'm not a marrying man, Tanya.'

'I see,' I said. I rolled away from him, and though he put his hand on my hip, I pretended to fall asleep.

'It amazes me that she can put aside the concerns of the world and only think of her love affair,' Li Kong mused aloud.

'Ah, that's how it is. Historically, we remember those times as turbulent but really life went on with all its little permutations.'

'Go on.'

Shanghai, April 1934

The next day, Richard and I acted as if nothing untoward had happened. It was Sunday, so we followed our routine and had a leisurely breakfast. Afterward, he read over some papers and worked on a report. I approached him, and we kissed, but I could see he was busy and so I said I would go home. I didn't even say, 'See you next Saturday,' and though I was torn up about it, I vowed not to be so accessible in the future.

Shanghai, April 1934

Something has changed. It all began after that evening when I burst in on Richard.

Afterward, I had Natalia field his calls and say I was busy at work designing a line of accessories. Each time the phone rang, my heart would beat frantically, and I would die a thousand deaths, longing as I did to rush to the phone just to hear his voice. I made myself hard hearted except I wasn't and would shake from head to toe for a quarter of an hour afterward.

He finally came to the store and asked to see me. I knew he was hoping I would not make a scene. The Boss was gone, and I took Richard into his office where we would have privacy.

'What's this all about, Tanya?' he asked.

I had anticipated this encounter, only because I knew that a man like Richard could not go without understanding why he was being dismissed. I thought I would tell him everything I hated about him, his egotism, his lack of care and empathy for me; that I could not be so easily bought off with a jewel...

That is not how things transpired, however. I sank into a chair and putting my head into my hands, began to cry silently. I knew he was uncomfortable with this display of emotion, so I cut myself short, and said, 'There, that's enough.'

He held out a handkerchief and asked what it was, and I said plainly, that I could never stand not knowing from day to day if I would ever see him again, that I was so lonely, and that I ached for him from Sunday to Saturday. It was too long and too empty for me to go without him, despite his occasional telephone call during the week.

'I had no idea that was the problem,' he said. 'But what do you think will happen during the week? We have a steady regime. I always call you midweek to arrange it. I have no other women in my life, nor am I interested in anyone else.'

'I have no assurances,' I said softly.

'You'd have no assurances even if we were married, Tanya. You very well know that most of the married men in this colony have mistresses or outside interests. I choose to be with you.'

'When you say,' I replied.

He thought for a while and said, 'Look, what if we started having dinner Wednesday evenings as well? We could make it an adventure, explore all kinds of places. What say you to that?

And of course, I said yes, and gave him a thousand kisses.

'Poor girl. Well perhaps he did love her after all,' the Director said, before continuing on, and yet he felt his heart beginning to beat erratically when he read the next section though he did not censor it for the sake of the boy.

Shanghai, May 1934

Richard and I see more of each other now. Our weekends are longer. I stay until late evening Sunday, sometimes even until Monday morning, and we see each other on Wednesday nights as well.

I am able to breathe again, and notice the small things around me, which bring me joy. Each Wednesday, there is something new. Richard seems to know every nook of this city, and even though I have walked past all these things a thousand times, he will point out a nuance, a detail on a building, a tree, a sign, and I'll see them for the first time.

Last night we went to a place I had been with Sasha before, though I did not say so, and had loved. It's the restaurant with the dark wood, and the shutters, and the overhead fans, and the potted palms. Inside, once seated, you feel a world away from the city, as if you were on a plantation in Indochina, or perhaps it's Indonesia I'm thinking of. At the far table, hidden from view, you feel like you are on your own, in a private world, just the two of you. And as your white hand with a fresh manicure in the new style, red nails and pale half-moons, reaches across the heavy white tablecloth for the starched and intricately folded napkin, his hand, heavy and warm, intercepts it, and twines its fingers around yours. You feel the flow of his life mingling with yours, and you think it is like a river, wide and dark, that will flow endlessly.

You talk, you eat, and you watch Richard, with his long elegant fingers, handling his knife and fork. You notice the cuff of his jacket, the edge of shirtsleeve, the cuff links you had made for him, and then you think how beautiful his arm is when it is bare. You know every golden hair on it; you love the wrist and the carpal bone, the blue veining on the inside, the throb of its pulse.

You don't look into his eyes, because they are always mocking, and you are afraid he'll see in yours how desperately you love him and be frightened away. You look at his mouth, full on the bottom, a tiny mole above it, and you can't wait for the next two days to pass, for him to strip off your clothes, and put his mouth on yours.

You think about the last time, when he carried you naked to his bed, and putting you down, looked at you from all angles. Then you think about the way he touched you, so softly, and how light his fingers were along the expanse of your skin. You think about soft whirling of the fan overhead, of the light spring rain and the greyness of the sky, and the leaves in bud, yet to flower on the trees. You feel his mouth between your legs, and how, when he senses your tension he grabs your hand, holding it tightly until you finish. You see yourself lying in a crumpled, shattered heap, unable to recover. And then you think how he reaches for you, and holds you, so closely, before bringing his mouth to yours. You think about the flick of his tongue on your lips, his tongue in your mouth, and his lips about yours, as he sucks them bit by bit.

You think about his kisses on your throat and your breasts, and you remember the moment he kneels before your outspread form, and parting your legs, strokes your inner lips before entering your flesh. You then feel the *pleasure that shoots through the entirety of your body, and picture the colors that you have seen, and think how you wish it would never end.*

And then you think about the pleasure you can give him and all the tricks you have learned. You hold him in your mouth until his strength returns and afterward you touch all the scars on his body, aware of all that he experienced before you came along. Yet you are never jealous because all that has passed is a part of his being.

You look at yourself in the mirror when he is asleep and there are dark circles around your eyes, and your dark hair is tangled about your pale bloodless face because you are weary and exhausted with love.

And so you listen to him talk in the darkened restaurant, but you are not hearing his words because you are thinking of what will happen only two days hence. When you are alone in your bed and only then, in the darkness, do you think about the meaning of his words and are frightened the day will come when you run out of things to say to each other. And you think- there is nothing to hold us together, nothing binding, nothing legal.

Then you keep yourself busy through your Thursday and your Friday, even though time moves so slowly, and you watch the clock, its hands ticking, the face barely changing, and you can hardly wait until Saturday comes round.

And you plan what you will wear to make him think you are beautiful and not the pathetic creature who only lives for the moment when he will open the door when you walk past the threshold and everything you have been waiting for begins, once again.

So when the evening at the beautiful restaurant is over and you step into the night, and he puts you in a cab, and kisses you goodnight, you are forlorn. And you stare out the window at the night and the lights and the life all around you which is now quieting down as the car drives through the city and emerges in the French Concession, and you pass Avenue Joffre, in Little Russia, where you are still living in Natalia's shitty house, because Richard Hellyer won't take you out of there and bring you to live with him in his eternally clean and solitary space.

. . .

'Let's stop for now. I need to get some rest before I leave for work,' the Director said.

'Yes, all right,' Li Kong replied. In truth, he had been shaken by the girl's words and felt a mixture of revulsion and desire rising up within him. He had experienced nothing like it and could not imagine the girls he knew ever behaving or even thinking in that way. He wanted to think about what she had written and its implications, and he wanted to be alone, imagining her and what it would be like to be with her.

After Li Kong left, the Director did not rest, but read the section over again. 'What was it Hellyer awoke in you, Tanya. And why did he affect you so profoundly?' the Director asked aloud. 'Later you changed, toward me and toward the world, but then every event, every trauma, leaves it scars upon us.'

'I have something,' Li Kong said, handinga piece of paper to the Director.

'Read it to me, I want to hear it in your own voice,' the Director said.

'All right,' Li Kong was nervous and cleared his throat. He started, and stumbling, began over:

> *A winter moon lights up my room exposing its bareness.*
> *I look at the dark sky, vast and empty, save the moon*
> *And feel the chill of the room, and think of my green home*
> *in the countryside, the pines on the hills, the scent of freshness*
>   *and rain*
> *and new shoots arising from the rich earth.*
> *Birds fly overhead, and moss grows over the stones on the*
>   *trodden path.*
> *It is empty here too, but perfect, and free of man's burdens.*

The Director listened and thought, it is, of course, derivative of the ancient poets, but still lovely. It did not surprise him that Li Kong had chosen to write of an unpeopled landscape. He sensed the boy was appalled by human behavior and felt very alone and alienated from the things he was witnessing. The Director praised the boy and urged him to continue writing.

'You think it's good? I mean, I'm not wasting my time with it, am I?' Li Kong asked, but really he was wondering what he was going to do with his life. His dreams of becoming a scientist were now deemed bourgeois and writing poetry would be censured if anyone found out. He would be publicly humiliated and pressured to conform.

'It's fine. Keep going. You will find it gets easier with practice. Shall we?' the Director asked, indicating Tanya's diary.

'Of course,' Li Kong replied.

Shanghai, May 1934

Richard and I took an excursion to Soochow to see the Chinese gardens. They have been developed over a thousand years, and some were created as early as the 10th century. There are pavilions and pagodas nestled between the greenery and footbridges that take you over slow green sluggish ponds and streams choked with water lilies.

Though I most love the round moon gates that give you a different perspective of the world, all the gardens were tranquil and pleasing to the eye. And the best part is that we were a couple, just like any other, who see each other day in and day out. Interestingly, our tastes are similar; our eyes catch the same things. I was so happy with him, so happy to have him to myself, even though I know I got on his nerves and even though I know the more nervous I became, the more I could not stop my endless babbling and attention seeking.

Shanghai, June 1934

Richard has been called back to England. His brother is gravely ill, perhaps dying, and there are so many things he must see to. Interestingly, his brother, who is older, has never married. He has a government position, and I think must have inherited whatever it was that Richard's parents left. A house, certainly, somewhere in Somerset. The way Richard describes it makes it sound so lovely and green, with rolling hills and thatched cottages. He talks about Bath and Glastonbury with pride, though he claims it is dull there, yet I think that was perhaps the feeling he had as a young man when he set out to see the world. Now he might have second thoughts about the place and what the future might look like.

I behaved well when he told me he was leaving, no scenes or tears. Though I would have loved to go with him, I know there is no place for me there now.

I'm still harping on about it, at least in my own mind, though I say nothing to him. He thinks an ordinary life, one that focuses on the mundane, drains the joy from every relationship. He thinks this way love will always be like a short unexpected holiday that leaves you refreshed and longing to tackle worldly cares again.

Shanghai, July 1934

Dreadful news at work. We are a smaller store, boutique, with a rather exclusive and chic clientele, at least once Hong and I had begun to work together.

The Boss called us in today. We are operating in the red, far above budget. It seems that Hong and I, in wanting to create the best, have caused problems. But I think that perhaps we are to be scapegoated for the bad business decisions of the higher ups. They will try to keep the store open, but they are cutting our department.

Hong and I have talked it over and we will approach Sun Sun, Sincere, Wing On, and Da Sun, the most exclusive department stores in Shanghai. We feel confident that they will find a place for us.

No news from Richard but perhaps the post travels slowly all the way from England.

Shanghai, July 1934

We've been to every store on Nanking Road. They smile, look at our drawings and samples and say, it is impractical, impossible. We then went to Moulmien Road and Cardinal Mercier where the Russians have their boutiques, but of course, we were dreaming. They couldn't afford us, even if they did sing our praises. We've been talking about setting up in business together, but neither one of us has any capital, or collateral for a loan. I will see Mister Isfahani and Sirdar Singh about obtaining alternative loans or perhaps I can convince them to become silent partners. At least they could advise me.

Shanghai, July 1934

Sirdar Singh was brutally honest, though he is kind. He explained to me the real in's and out's of running a business, what it would take, the knowledge I would have to have. He said I would be best off apprenticing with someone who had a small business, or even a flourishing one, and learn the money side of it first. Then he said, 'Miss Tatiana, forgive me for being so bold, but you are a creative artist. That is your gift, and it would be crushed if you had to concentrate on money matters.'

I replied, 'Forgive me, Sirdar Singh, but Miss Tatiana has to keep body and soul together.'

He smiled and commissioned a set of new jewelry designs. I said that I didn't want his charity, and he replied that he made far more money off my work than I did. Well, at least, that will tide me over for a bit.

Shanghai, August 1934

Hong has found work. It's with the Hongbang Cai Feng (Red Group Tailors). She is the first woman they have hired. It is a great honor, and she will learn much about men's tailoring, which is challenging in its own way. She says our own salon is a pipe dream, and she can't hold out financially or live on dreams. I gave her a hug and wished her well. We both cried a little, and although I didn't expect it from her, she said I should always remember that we had done great things together. I hope we keep in touch, but people never do, do they?

Nothing from Richard, but I can barely stand think about any of that. It is too overwhelming.

Shanghai, August 1934

Mister Isfahani took me to lunch at the Cathay. Victor Sassoon owns it, of course, like he does so many properties. Mister Isfahani is such a kind man to take time to listen to my troubles. He agreed with Sirdar Singh about my lack of business experience but assured me that he would make inquiries and get back to me in a few days. I asked him what he might be thinking of specifically, but he put me off saying he had to look into the matter first. I must have looked so forlorn that he felt compelled to add that Victor was doing a lot of building these days and might require someone with my design talents. I decided to trust him, went home, and worked on the designs for Sirdar Singh.

Shanghai, September 1934

I have a job, not on spec, but full time with Architect Hrbek. I know he liked my work before, but this time I will have more serious duties, and Mister Isfahani intimated that Hrbek would teach me something about business as well.

'She is unbelievably lucky,' Li Kong said, admiringly.

'So you've said before. But do not forget how beautiful she was. In those days men were willing to step up and help lovely young women, even if it didn't lead anywhere.'

'A few more minutes and then I must go to another session,' Li Kong said.

'Did you ever write your self-criticism?'

'Yes. That was a while ago.'

'Ah, you never said anything. How was it received?'

'I don't know. They have us doing one thing, then it gets dropped, then they tell us to do something else.' Li Kong sighed.

'What about your friend?'

'He's a pariah now because of his mother. He is always upset and bristling and won't speak to me anymore.'

'He'll get over it in time, you'll see.'

Li Kong shrugged, 'I don't expect he will, but he may still have to denounce her to save himself. The way things are going they'll pick him apart like a flock of crows. Read, please.'

'Let's stop for now, shall we? You might be late otherwise and it wouldn't do to draw attention to yourself.'

'Yes, that is true. Until next time then.'

'Until next time,' the Director said, but when Li Kong left, he continued reading.

Shanghai, November 1934

I haven't been writing. I've been so busy. I've had to learn so many new things at work. It's interesting but not easy. The part I find most difficult is dealing with other employees, and well, not being in control any more. I now realize how much I loved working with Hong. It was wonderful, liberating, creative, and I was free.

Architect Hrbek says he'll be taking me along to client meetings now that I have learned a bit about the business. He has given me specific instructions, what to say and not to say, as if I was a schoolgirl. I'm shrugging it off. At least, I will be meeting people and learning new things.

Shanghai, November 1934

I ran into Sasha today. It was lovely and spontaneous. We were happy to see each other and began chatting right in the street as if nothing had ever gone wrong between us. We realized we were blocking the street, so we went to Huxinting Teahouse in the Huangpu. I always loved it there, so serene on the green water and so warm, red, and enveloping inside, perfect on a dreary day.

We talked and talked, about his work and the things he was doing. He has broken with Ming Gui, who he said had been too heavy handed with the scripts and too difficult to deal with. Now he is trying to blend his own sensibilities with social responsibility. I suppose he wants to capture things as they are but tell some profoundly human stories with themes that are not just specific to China. He says he is working on a couple of scripts and hopes the results will be good.

I told him all about my work at the store, and what had happened, and that I was now working for Ladislav Hrbek. We paused, and I knew we were thinking the same thing and if we should ask it of each other, so I finally took the initiative. He said there was no one special, a few actresses he saw from time to time. They seemed to come and go out of his life, but really he was too busy with work and had no time to invest in a serious relationship.

I said I had been seeing a man who had gone back to England for a while or perhaps for good. I told him no details, pretended to shrug it off, as if it had not been important, so that he would not be hurt by the fact that I had loved someone else and not him.

He said, 'Tanya, with her icy heart. One day you'll fall in love.'

I wanted to tell him everything then, all about Richard and how miserable I have been and still am. But I didn't.

After we parted, I thought about what a good man he was and why it was that I had fallen for Richard instead of him. I couldn't explain it.

Sun Mu remembered that day. The clouds had been heavy and hanging over the city. He had been walking aimlessly because he had been frustrated that his new script was not developing in the direction he had wanted it to go. Sometime before, he had realized letting things go often seemed to help him with his creativity. Solutions seemingly presented themselves after he had stepped away for a while.

And then he had seen her from a distance, coming toward him, and had felt his heart leap and then constrict with anxiety. She was changed, he realized, but her face was even more beautiful than it had been and had taken on more character, losing its babyish softness. Whatever suffering she had gone through was reflected on upon it.

She had been overjoyed to see him and couldn't stop talking, which was unlike her, since she always preferred to listen. And though he had been chafing to return to work, he saw she was lonely and felt pity for her. So he had suggested the teahouse and she had gladly accepted.

Even now, he could not explain why he had not taken the risk and asked her out once again when she had told him the man she was seeing had gone back to England. He wondered if he been protecting his heart or his ego. But perhaps he had been right not to do so, since her story with Richard had not been over and had to end naturally of its own accord.

Shanghai, December 1934

Winter, dreary and cold. I went to Anya's. She is planning a big Christmas party, Russian style. She is excited thinking about menus and the invitation list. I promised to help her decorate. We had a little spat over Natalia Ivanovna, who she wanted to exclude, claiming she was coarse and could behave badly if she drank too much. I reminded her how good Natalia had been to us and to her when she couldn't pay the rent, keeping her on, and she finally relented.

Then she said something, which made my stomach feel as if it had flipped over. I can't exactly recall what she said, but it seems Richard is back and has been for some weeks.

From my expression, she saw that I had no idea of that fact, and then said, 'Tanyusha, all that time, he never wrote once. You must have known it was over.'

I knew, but I didn't want to admit it to myself. 'I kept hoping,' was all I could manage to say.

'Even the busiest of men could find an opportunity to pen a few lines. Surely you see that,' she said.

'I see it now, Anya,' I replied.

She felt terribly sorry for me and wouldn't let me go home. I stayed for dinner and both she and Shi-shi tried to cheer me up, but it was no use.

. . .

Shi-shi had loved Anya, the Director thought, worshiped her, in fact. What a kind and good man he had been. What a good friend. And to end up as he did, shot by the Japanese, who confiscated everything he had built. It was his own fault, really, the Director thought, anyone with common sense and money had gotten out on time. *My poor friend, what a waste.*

Shanghai, December 1934

Richard called! It was awkward at first because I was so surprised. He said I sounded strange and I blurted out that in all this time he had never written, and I had not known whether he was dead or alive.

'But I did write in the beginning,' he said. 'When I got no reply, I thought you had forgotten about me.'

'I could never forget, Richard. Never,' I said. I felt warm, relaxed, and happy. We talked for a while, and made a date for Saturday, as usual, at his house.

The Director was surprised at how naive she had been and how willing to believe Richard's lies. How convenient for him to have her at his beck and call like a trained dog. *I never lied to you, Tanya. I was always honest and true, but you loved your drama and you loved your Richard, the way only a snob could love, despising your own kind, and mine, as something less worthy and not worth having.*

He was almost at the end of the notebook and kept reading. He reasoned he would read it to the boy more quickly when next he saw him.

Shanghai, December 1934

It was odd to be with Richard again. He is changed. A bit older and wearier. He is preoccupied with all the work he will have to make up. Regaining his position is paramount in his mind. I could tell he was happy to see me, but his passion has cooled, and I felt it even before he told me that now he would be spending more time at the office.

I wanted to talk about the time he had spent at home, his brother, and everything that had happened to him. But he said it was painful for him to revisit those experiences and merely commented that his brother had probably not suffered greatly. As for the house, he says it is sadly neglected and needs a great deal of work to repair it to a habitable condition, adding he has to concentrate on earning money in order to do that.

I said I could certainly understand, considering what I had gone through over the last six months. He listened and said, 'Tanushka is like a cat that always lands on its feet.'

He is right, but it is only because I've had to be.

Shanghai, January 1935

I have seen little of Richard. It is difficult for him to focus his attention on me, and he is often too exhausted to make love. Sometimes, I'll stay over at his house, and sit and read quietly, while he is working, but it is hard for me, and I am restless. It seems that even when we are together these days, I feel more alone than I ever did.

Yes. That's how things end, more with a whimper than a bang, the Director concluded.

Shanghai, January 1935

Hrbek has asked me to accompany him to Hong Kong where he will be working on the interiors of a new hotel. I was frightened at first, thinking he wanted to have some sort of adventure at my expense, but I have heard that he is completely enthralled by his wife, a formidable German who rules the roost.

I asked Richard what he thought, and he said I should go, that it would be good for my career, and that he had always thought I could do bigger things than designing costumes and sewing little bits of cloth.

. . .

Ah, Richard, how could you not see those bits of cloth were her life, the source of her pride and independence from the likes of us, the Director mouthed silently.

Hong Kong, February 1935

I love it here. It is so white and shining. The pace is slower than Shanghai, the hills are greener, the bays always changing, sapphire, aquamarine, cerulean, and bleu marine in turn. When I have time, I paint in water colors, trying to capture the lush stillness of this yet unspoiled world.

They are putting us up at the hotel. I needn't have worried because Frau Architekt Hrbek came along with us. She is a formidable woman, tall and stout, with the energy of a typhoon that disturbs everyone. She is brash, outspoken, often saying the most outlandish and out of place things, as if whatever is on her mind must pass her lips. I don't know how she feels about me, but I have had to ingratiate myself to her. I can see that Hrbek is totally in her thrall, and she could make my position precarious or even redundant if she choose to.

I miss Richard terribly, know that the work here might drag on for months, and wonder if I should contact David, the young Englishman I met the first time I was here.

Hong Kong, March 1935

Tennis parties, cocktail parties, swimming parties. Postcards to Richard and letters, with only brief, hastily penned replies. The Hrbeks have gone to Shanghai, leaving me to oversee the details of the paneling. It's a great step up for me. I go everywhere with David, who is perennially a good egg, as he would put it. I know it's bad of me, but sometimes I wonder if he ever thinks of sex.

Hong Kong, March 1935

I wrote to Richard asking if he might come down to spend a few days, and he replied he wishes he could, but he is too occupied with work. I do understand that, but his letter was so terse almost as if he was brushing off an annoying pet.

As far as work goes, I am having trouble with the master builder, a coarse German, who, it seems, dislikes taking direction from a woman. I don't know how to behave with him; harsh and demanding and he'll defy me, soft and sweet and he'll take advantage. I have no one to ask what to do, and if I turn to Hrbek for help he'll think I am not up to the job. We are behind schedule because of this man and his high-jinks. He disappears for hours at a time, and the workers have no direction and make terrible and costly mistakes. I don't know if he drinks or if he is doing this because he has taken an active dislike to me and wants to cause me trouble.

I told David about him, but David thinks everything will always work out for the best because, I don't know, if wishes were horses, or something of the sort. Lately it's occurred to me that the German detests me because I am a Russian.

Hong Kong, April 1935

I did something terrible. I can't even excuse alcohol, because I was sober enough to know what I was doing, but it didn't stop me. I decided for no reason at all that it would be a good idea to seduce David, and I did.

He was astounded, then thrilled. It was over in minutes, before anything actually ever happened. Afterward, he put his head on my shoulder. I felt wretched and got dressed before he could try again. I don't know how to tell him it was a mistake and that I never want it to happen again. He is so dear and deserves better.

Hong Kong, April 1935

I sent Hrbek a telegram, saying I was in trouble and things were going very wrong on the job. I have been avoiding David. I don't know what to do or say.

. . .

Hong Kong, May 1935

Hrbek arrived, and in essence blamed me for everything that had gone wrong. In his mind, the German is an exemplary worker and always has delivered the finest results. I was not even allowed to protest or tell my side of the story. I am being demoted and sent back to Shanghai.

I went to dinner with David and told him what had happened. He was very sorry things had gone as they did, but then brightly said, it was no matter, we would see each other on holidays. I let it go and said I would write. Everything is a mess in my life.

Shanghai, June 1935

Richard has been offered a position in Singapore. He would be heading up a rubber exporting concern at a rather high increase in pay. It's an opportunity he can't turn down. Of course, he will not be taking me with him, though he says he wants us to continue to see each other when we can.

I said, yes, of course, but I have given up hope. In the next weeks, he will be packing house, while I am stuck in the office, doing tedious and detailed drawings as punishment for my transgressions.

Shanghai, July 1935

Today was our last day. I called in sick to the office and went to see Richard. The walls of his house are barren, everything is packed into trunks, and sometime in the middle of the day, Zhang organized a group of coolies to take them to the dock where Richard's ship was sailing from.

We had an indoor picnic, of sorts, since there was no furniture left and nowhere to sit. He made jokes, laughed, and was kind but didn't touch me and only gave me a brief kiss, hello. It would be too difficult to part after making love, he said, and besides this wasn't goodbye. We would be seeing each other as soon as he was settled and I could take time off. Richard, I think, is a very poor liar.

I wanted to go down to the ship with him, but he said no, tears and parting embraces wouldn't do. When I got up to leave, he spontaneously took hold of me and kissed me so savagely, so intensely, that I thought I would not recover from it.

This is the hardest day of my life. This is the end of my diary.

But you went on Tanya, you went on, and despite the circumstances, or because of them, you returned to me, and we began our dance of death and even that was to end in time, the Director said to himself.

PART III

SHANGHAI, FEBRUARY 1967

Li Kong and the Director watched the events of the January Revolution of 1967 unravel at a rapid pace. Red Guard factions attacked municipal buildings, then faced opposition from workers' parties, which then fractured themselves. Everyone seemed to be fighting each other. Zhang Chunqiao was called in to restore order and established a peoples' commune for a short while.

The boy could not always understand the events or put them into context, and sometimes reverted to the sloganeering of the Red Guards, but the Director had known Zhang as a writer in Shanghai in the 1930's and later in Yunnan, known his complexities, his comedic nature, his ambition, his bourgeois background, and had understood both his idealism and his fanaticism. He, too, had slightly known Madam Mao when she had been a homely but highly ambitious third rate actress in Shanghai.

The Director explained that Mao, in the early part of the decade, had opined that Chinese performing arts were still classical in nature, focusing on, 'Emperors, kings, general, chancellors, literati and beauties', instead of the struggles faced and lessons taught by revolutionary workers, peasants and soldiers. Mao's request for a new revolutionary national art allowed Jiang Qing, his fourth wife, to begin imposing her particular vision on the arts. In 1963, she started with the revision of a number of operas, first The Story of the Red Lamp and Shajia Village, followed by Taking Tiger Mountain by Strategy, and Raid on the White Tiger Regiment. In the summer of 1964, these model works were performed at the Opera Festival in Shanghai.

'This is a good thing!' Li Kong exclaimed.

'But it is a lie,' the Director explained. 'Fat, happy peasants? Think about it. Our peasants are neither. In fact, they starved during the Great Famine. And what about the quality of the work itself? It is kitsch all around and laughable. Madame Mao seeks to impose her vision on the arts but that vision is based on the most melodramatic lowbrow fare that ever came out of Hollywood. Art can be revolutionary, but artists must not lapse either into gross sentimentality, nor sloppiness, nor caricature.'

'But that is what Tanya accuses Sasha of doing, and you yourself said your own films were made in much the same vein.'

'Ah, that was in the very beginning, over thirty years ago, when we were struggling for a new cinematic language. Later, I assure you, the films became quite sophisticated in their use of montage, though the context was lost on Tanya due to her background.'

'Please explain what is meant by montage,' Li Kong said.

'It is a theory postulated by the Russian filmmaker Sergei Eisenstein that states when two or more symbolically conflicting images are rapidly added together to form a sequence, they create a visceral, or emotional, impact on the viewer, thus exposing him to ideas that are much more powerful than a single image could convey. One of Eisenstein's most famous scenes was the Odessa Steps sequence from the film Battleship Potemkin, in which he elongated time by stretching out the surge of the crowd down the steps. However, that in itself is not the point. The point is that real art is created through the implementation of a thoughtful process. You see, art offers us aesthetic pleasure, as well, and can sometimes transport us into the realm of the sublime. Kitsch is an imitation of life, easy to consume and digest, appealing to the lowest common denominator, and here, used by a regime to manipulate the masses.'

'But who decides what kitsch is and what is art?' Li Kong asked.

'Ah, now that is the question. When you raided that woman's house where you found the diaries, you were distressed that works of exquisite beauty were being destroyed. How did you recognize that beauty for what it was when the other Red Guards were only seeking to destroy the Four Olds? How did you recognize the beauty and whimsy of Tanya's drawings, which could have easily crossed the border into kitsch? Your eye is untrained, and no one taught you to despise popular forms. I believe this is something innate that a vulgar person like Comrade Jiang Quing does not have and so cannot recognize.'

'These are dangerous things to say,' Li Kong muttered.

'So they are. But to whom will you repeat them? They would compromise both of us, if you did. No, I think it would be best if I opened your eyes during the time we have together.'

'To what end? Look at how you have ended up,' Li Kong said.

'True enough,' the Director acknowledged. 'But we never know where life will lead us, do we?'

'As long it does not lead to a cow shed. Do you know that a few weeks ago I saw one of the most prominent physics professors at the university being lead through the streets with a dunce cap on his head and placard around his neck denouncing him? Later I heard the guards kicked him to death.'

'And so, do you want to be part of that rabble?'

'I can see the malicious joy on their faces, even now.'

'Of course, you can. It is great fun to skip classes and travel around the country, without censure, overthrowing the old Confucian order, beating and tormenting one's elders, whom one should respect.'

'How are you not afraid to say such things?' Li Kong asked.

'I am Sun Mu, already less than nothing. Everything has been taken from me, my work, my home, my output. What else can they take, my life? I have already lived it and I am prepared to lose it. But my mind is intact and I can see the truth for what it is.'

'Please, let us resume reading now, 'Li Kong said, thinking, it is easy for you to be noble when you only go abroad at night when everyone else is asleep. You don't have to face the Red Guards or think about how you will reply to their questions, or whom you will have to denounce or interrogate to keep yourself from falling under suspicion and perhaps being annihilated. You have lived, but I haven't and I want to do something with my life.

'All right. Let's.'

NOTEBOOK THREE

Shanghai, April 1936

I can't claim that anything much has happened in my life in the last year. Office life is much the same, though I am working with clients, sometimes even on my own, without Ladislav's interference. He says I am very good with the wives, who he has no patience for, since he seems to think their whims annoying and their tastes changeable. I never say that if he had listened to their desires initially without imposing his own will upon them, there would be no issues or misunderstandings. Mostly I work in the luxury high rise apartments on the Bund. These are truly incredible, with all sorts of amenities unheard of in China previously. Lifts propel you skyward in no time, servants and ready-made meals are a telephone call away, and some buildings even have shops and theaters within.

I design jewelry for Sirdar Singh on occasion and it gives me joy to work with him, since unlike Ladislav, he always sings my praises. Sometimes, I still go into my pantry and sketch a little, but it's no good any more. I don't do it often enough, and I have nothing to say.

Natalia and I live like an old couple, spending evenings together, but I think that is about to change. Her friend, the driver for the warlord, has been widowed, and lately, he has been turning up, hair pomaded, carrying bouquets. Last night I caught them in fooling around in the dark when I came into the sitting room. When I turned on the light, they jumped away from each other. Natalia was flushed and laughing, while he was embarrassed. I made my excuses and went out.

Anya and Shi-shi are still together, still happy, and he is fatter than ever.

We go out together. I am the third wheel, but they have gotten used to dragging me along wherever they go.

The Rajni is engaged to a German industrialist. Hong is doing well, and we have tea together from time to time. Mei left her marriage and ran off. No one knows where for certain, but her sister suspects that she might have joined the communists. Yevgeny Borisovich is now heading up the Majestic and booking great artists. Sasha is famous. His films are very good, perhaps one day they will be great. We had dinner not too long ago and caught up.

For me life is flat, but in Shanghai, life is an endless whirl of parties, clubs, dancing, sex, and prosperity. The rest of world is in a great depression, but here no one thinks of anything but money and fun.

I don't even know why I am writing this. I feel nothing, I think of nothing, I am neither happy nor sad, I have no expectations, nor do I have dreams.

'So she changed her mind about Sasha's films!' Li Kong exclaimed.

The Director raised his brows, 'Yes, if I recall correctly some thought that was his best period, prior to the war.'

'Go on.'

Shanghai, May 1936

Natalia's friend, Igor Andreyevich, has moved in. I feel that my existence is even more circumscribed. I get out of the way, so that they can live their life in peace.

I gave up my pantry so that he could have his wood shop in there. He makes quite nice things, carvings of horses and such, not artistic or inspired, but he seems to enjoy it. I stick mainly to my room, but feel out of place. To think of moving is difficult for me, because I have come to depend on Natalia's camaraderie, and after all, this has been my home for ever so long.

Shanghai, June 1936

I moved. It was all due to Anya, who prevailed upon Shi-shi to let me a small apartment in one of his buildings for a song. I know he objected, because he is so frugal, but she must have nagged him to death until he finally relented. I would have normally objected to charity, but he is rich enough.

It's small but in a much chicer area in the French quarter than Little Russia. Most of the buildings are new, art deco, and lovely. It's a visual feast to walk down these streets. And in the evening, when darkness falls, it is so quiet and still. Even the air seems fresher.

I love my space. It is three floors up without a lift, but I do not care. There is a main room, and through French doors, a tiny space, which can serve as a study. Down the corridor is a bedroom, a bath and opposite, a galley kitchen. I painted everything lavender grey and went to the Chinese shops to furnish it, because it is so much cheaper than the things that Ladislav produces. It turned out to be quite chic in the end.

I placed potted palms in white pots at the ends of the big room, and have two large Chinese daybeds with amethyst cushions and gold and purple pillows between them. That makes up the main sitting room, and I bought, or rather am paying Ladislav, for the shagreen table that sits between them. I put a pier glass between the windows and a long, slim, though rather plain, Chinese table at the opposite end of the windows. It holds flower arrangements, which I change, and some pottery. The room couldn't stand my own artwork, which is too rough and colorful, so I framed the black and white photos Sasha had given me of the harbor and of found objects. In the small study, I placed a large Chinese table which I use as a desk, but which can double as dining table when I have guests. I had shelves made for my books, and it looks cozy and inviting compared to the coolness of the main room.

In the bedroom, I have a Chinese canopy bed, of rosewood, with minimal carvings, and lavender and celadon bedding. I have hung some Chinese scrolls that are old and faded and depict nature- mountains, misty and mystic, but left the rest of the room bare. It seems so airy that way.

The kitchen and bath are white and tiled with black and white squares. There is nothing to do there, a few green plants and that is it.

It's so wonderful, so private, so clean, and quiet. Except at night when it can get quite lonely.

. . .

Shanghai, July 1936

Anya and Shi-shi came to dinner. They loved the way I decorated the place. I made fish in black bean sauce with varieties of green vegetables and rice. Then I served a Russian pastry. Something for everyone. It was fun and lighthearted. Perhaps I will have a party soon.

Shanghai July 1936

Great news, Ladislav is going to give me more duties with a new client, and for the first time I'll have a free hand with the interiors. Well, almost, since Ladislav wants to approve my designs. It won't happen for a while. Ladislav is working on completing the villa first, which was begun by another firm and almost finished before they bankrupted.

When I asked who the client was, Ladislav said, someone who was moving up in the world and has a place close to the window at the Shanghai Club's long bar. When I heard that, my heart sank a bit, because it would mean he was going to be a tai-pan soon, and would be decorating in a conformist manner to please his English friends.

After exhausting myself the worst possible scenarios, I decided to brace myself and take on the challenge. I just hope Ladislav won't change his mind about letting me have control of the interiors. I keep thinking about what happened with Madam Liu and how it all went wrong, and then that awful scenario in Hong Kong with the German builder.

It took a long time to redeem myself in Ladislav's eyes. I think it helped that the German's drinking got worse, and Ladislav finally saw the truth and fired him. For a moment, I believed that there might be some justice in the world.

Shanghai, August 1936

Ladislav took me to see the villa in progress. It is in the International Settlement, and very lovely, with an art deco facade and a rounded bay with curved glass windows. There is a balcony off the second floor and French *doors leading to it. The whole house is clad in limestone, and is white and peaceful. Although some of the windows have been etched with geometric designs, there is much light inside. Ladislav reminded me that I would need to use curtains on the curved windows, because it is the nature of such glass to throw strange reflections at night.*

I have already begun to design the interiors, with myself in mind! Of course, I will need to meet with the client, to understand his needs and tastes, before I can do the real work.

'They lived so extravagantly while people were starving,' Li Kong said.

'Yes, they carved out quite a pleasant niche for themselves, but those houses and buildings are still there and are still beautiful,' the Director replied, though many were becoming sadly neglected. At night, while he cleaned the streets, he often looked at them with a sense of wonder and nostalgia for the Shanghai that had once been so vibrant and pulsing with life despite its horrors. He recalled many buildings as they were being constructed. That time seemed far-away and yet so eerily close, particularly since they had begun reading the diaries.

Shanghai, August 1936

I had a party. I invited a few colleagues from the office and their girlfriends, the Hrbeks, Anya and Shi-shi, and Natalia and Igor Andryevich.

Natalia and Frau Hrbek hated each other right away and it was both comical and embarrassing the way they tried to outdo each other. Frau Hrbek expounded on the superiority of German culture, and particularly of music, which she knows nothing about, while Natalia drowned her out in a booming voice, saying that apart from Goethe and Schiller, the Germans were a nation of illiterates. Then she sang praises to Pushkin and Lermontov, Goncharev and Turgenev, Dostoevsky, Chekhov, Bulgakov, Gogol and Tolstoy. She quoted from Akhmatova and Mandelstam. Anya's mouth was hanging open. She couldn't believe what she was hearing, especially since she always considered Natalia to be a vulgar woman. I remembered what

Natalia had said to me one evening how she had been a girl with stars in her eyes and a pure soul. Well, perhaps she had been.

Frau Hrbek huffed her way into the kitchen, where she took charge of the food, and pity on me, since she obviously felt sorry, that, in her words, 'Your party was ruined by that horrible woman.'

My Chinese friends thought it was all a very good time, gorged themselves, and laughed for days afterward. When the older folks left, we pushed the furniture toward the walls, turned on the phonograph, and danced all night. I quite enjoyed it, aside from the cleaning up.

'Do you know those writers?'

'Yes, most of them.'

'Would you recount their stories to me some day?'

'Yes. When we finish reading the diaries, we can begin lessons in Russian, and someday you will read those works yourself,' the Director said, since he had quite gotten used to the boy and their evenings together and wanted them to continue. But the boy thought, I'll never read those books. The Guards have burned them in the university library and only the charred remains are left. So many books lost, so much knowledge lost, and nothing to think about but smashing the Four Olds and rooting out class enemies.

'It's getting late.'

'A little more,' Li Kong pleaded.

'All right, just a little.'

Shanghai, September 1936

I've started going to dance lessons again, at Madame Denisova's studio. This, after many years, but she remembered me as the worst pupil she had ever had, and laughed. I told her I was feeling stiff from sitting hunched over a drawing board all the time and needed regular exercise. She finally gave in.

When I thought it was all settled, she said, 'But how are you really, my dear? You might have been the worst dancer, but you were so full of life and had such strange and lovely ideas. You seem drained now, like a different person.' I hadn't spent much time around Russians in the past few years and so had forgotten how direct they can be.

'I feel flat, not out of sorts, but a nothingness pervades my life. I go to work, and I'm grateful to have it, but it's all meaningless in the end.'

'Oh, you modern young people, always depressed and with such heavy thoughts!' she exclaimed. 'What you need is a little romance in your life.'

I made small protesting noises and said I was uninterested.

'Ah, Tanyushka, don't knock it until you've tried it. And I have the perfect boy for you. Tall gorgeous, educated and Russian.'

'Please Madame Denisova, anything but Russian,' I said.

'Ach, no my dushka, she said, 'This one is special. Well paid, with a car and driver, and his own apartment.'

'So what does he do, this paragon?' I asked.

'A musician. Tip-top.'

'No musicians,' I said, 'Thanks, but no.'

'He headlines at the French Club,' she said. 'Just go and see him.'

I declined once again. 'Besides,' I added, 'when would he have time for a woman in his life?'

On the way home, I thought about my time with Richard and how alive I had felt, despite my anxiety. I wondered why it was that I needed a man to make me feel that way and why I couldn't reach that state on my own. And then I recriminated myself for wasting that precious time, with worry and with fear, and with my desire to make it permanent. I should have enjoyed it for what it was.

Shanghai, September 1936

Anya and I are going to dance class together now. When she heard I had started up again, she laughed, but then reconsidered, saying she was getting out of shape and should try it too. She looks as thin as a worm to me, but she said, even so, she was flabby and out of shape.

It's fun. We like it and have tea together afterwards. I told her about my strange lack of feeling, and after listening, she said we would go meditate at the temple with the monks.

'Would they allow it?' I asked, and she replied, that, yes, some of them were quite modern in their outlook and gave how-to lessons.

'I was there, you know,' Li Kong said.

'Where?'

'At Rong Hua temple when the Red Guards tore it down. They said it was the center of the four obsolete vestiges: obsolete culture, traditions, habits and morality. Then they beat the monks and called the nuns whores, and worse. There was a huge crowd. They were cheering the guards on as they pulled down the statue of the Buddha.'

'What did you do when you saw that?'

'What I usually do. Nothing at all. Please, go on.'

'It's late.'

'Please, just a bit more.'

Shanghai, October 1936

I meditate regularly in the mornings and at night before bed. Nothing special, just a few minutes, sitting quietly and breathing, emptying my mind of troubles. It gives me purpose and relief and makes the time go by, and evenings alone easier to bear.

Anya is tired of listening to me and my nihilism, as she calls it. She told me to get a dog, because I needed something to love and care for besides myself.

She has two little yipping ones that trail her everywhere. I pointed out that she was home all day, while I was away and that it wouldn't be fair to the dog to be all cooped up. She argued with me that would be better than being out on the streets, like the animals here are. I replied that I never wanted to love anything that deeply again, because I couldn't stand it or the loss afterward.

'What did that man do to you that made you act crazy like this?' she asked, quite bitterly.

'Maybe he didn't do anything, and I was always like this, Anya,' I said. 'Depressed, anxious, and depressing.'

. . .

'It would be nice to have a dog, but you know the party says it is a filthy and degenerate Western import. How can it be bad to love such a good and intelligent creature? How can people eat them?' Li Kong exclaimed.

'I suppose the logic is that our people have so little and to allocate resources to an animal rather than a human is wrong.'

'It's all repulsive. Killing, eating, brutality. I hate it.'

'Yes, but the whole universe consumes itself.'

'The monks thought there is no death, only the ever turning wheel of suffering and desire.'

'But Lao-tse said that people have a free will to act and could return to harmony with the Tao and be in the stream of it. In that way, the stream itself is the creative force which moves through us,' the Director countered.

'Yes, I understand! I feel it when I am writing. Sometimes the thing seems to compose itself!'

'So, you've been writing. Is it anything you would care to show me?'

'Soon.'

'All right. Good. Let's stop for now.'

'Until next time, then.'

'Yes, until then.'

SHANGHAI, 1967

The woman stood on the dais with her head bowed. Li Kong crept into the auditorium but hung back. He did not want to see but was frightened of being accused of being anti-revolutionary. He looked up past the rows of black hair to the woman herself and realized that one half of her head had been shaved, in the yin-yang cut that the Red Guards administered. It meant, he knew, she was considered a demon, no longer human. It meant they could do anything to her.

A tall and powerfully built Red Guard pushed the woman to her knees, and along with another guard, hoisted her arms back and up into the airplane position. Li Kong knew that this was terribly painful and unendurable, since he had tried it on with a few boys to see what it felt like. He could not see the woman's facial expression, but even at that distance he could sense that she had been broken. Still, the woman protested in pain at the Guards' brutal handling.

'Shut it or I'll smash your dog's head in,' the tall Guard snarled. The woman shook with terror.

Li Kong shut his eyes but opened them when he heard the shrill tones of his classmate, Lao Shaoqiang, denouncing the woman as being a class enemy, educated in the West, who had hypnotized his otherwise incorruptible father. Li Kong pushed his way through the crowd to get closer.

The woman raised her head to look at her son. Her expression was one of incredulity and shock, which then passed into sorrow, then compassion. Surely, she must have anticipated it, Li Kong thought, and but when it had finally occurred, she could hardly believe it. Yet, he could see in her expression that she was going to forgive her son.

Li Kong waited until they were through and she was hauled away before he left. Two days later when he heard that she had been driven away from the auditorium in a truck and shot along with a group other people, he began to retch violently in the schoolyard and went home sick.

He never wanted to see Lao Shaoqiang again or to recall that horrific scene. He went to the Director's room when he was finally able to crawl out of bed, but said nothing other than he had had a virus of some sort, and asked the Director to begin reading again.

Shanghai, October 1936

Madame Denisova invited Anya and me for tea. Naturally, her young man was there. I had to admit, he was quite handsome, charming, well-educated, well read, and knew an awful lot about music. Anya was taken with him and couldn't stop flirting. I sat there like a bump on a log, sipping tea, and listening to them chat about Stravinsky and jazz. I know very little about either aside from the fact that I don't like that music very much. His name is Ivan Mikhailovich Cherkasov.

Shanghai, October 1936

Ivan Mikhailovich asked me to the gardens. He said he is tired of clubs, and crowds, and smoke, and craved some air. We had a nice walk, and afterward went to a tea house. He grew up in Harbin, where his father was an engineer on the railroad. He said that from an early age he knew he only wanted to play music, and his parents had had him classically trained as a pianist, though now, of course, there was money to be made in jazz and dance clubs.

I talked a bit about my work and all the things I had done previously, and he said he admired my drive. He said he doesn't have much time, playing at night as he does, and sleeping through the day, but that he did want to see me again. I agreed. He is a good conversationalist with a light, pleasing manner, hardly Russian at all!

Shanghai, November 1936

I've been seeing Ivan Mikhailovich on and off. We talk about books and music. He doesn't have much feeling for the visual arts and no interest in painting at all. His apartment is quite plain, though not in particularly good taste, but I can also see that is not important to him at all. We go there to listen to records, and I have gone to the French Club to hear his band. He is a year younger than I am, and I think, much younger for his age. It's nice, but I can tell that it won't go anywhere between us.

Shanghai, November 1936

Ivan declared his love for me tonight. We were sitting in his apartment, listening to music, like we usually do. Everything was going well, until he suddenly got on all fours. I thought he had dropped something under the sofa. He then pressed his face to my knees and started spouting poetry and told me he adored me. I felt embarrassed for him and quite bad about it. I told him to stop, that he was idealizing me, and that I really liked him but that my feelings didn't go beyond friendship. He seemed stunned to hear that. I felt horrible to have to tell him the truth, but I thought it was better than stringing him along.

He asked me to leave and I did.

I don't think I'll ever feel about anyone the way I did about Richard. Later I thought that perhaps Ivan Mikhailovich merely desired the convenience of having a wife.

. . .

Shanghai November 1936

David came to town for a week. We hadn't seen each other since Hong Kong, and only sent a few postcards each way since. His are always funny and light; some odd street scene he knows will make me laugh, or wonder at the life that is led here, the dichotomy of the rich and the poor, the English and the natives.

If he ever thought about that awful evening again, he never mentioned it, and was a perfect gentleman. We went out almost every night: Ciro's The Majestic, the Paramount. I've never danced so much, and it had been such a very long time since I had taken out my evening dresses and worn them.

Anya said I was being a fool not to try to land him, because he was clearly interested, but I am not entirely certain of that.

'I think he just wants to have fun, and I'm probably the only woman he knows in Shanghai,' I said.

Anya looked at me as if I were crazy and said, 'Tanya, there are a thousand places where a man could have a lot more fun in Shanghai than he could with you.'

I knew she meant the sex clubs where you can buy anything and anyone, European or Oriental, and have as many women or boys as you wanted, performing any sort of sex act, often on each other.

'He's better than that,' I replied, and she said I would be surprised if I knew what went on behind the polite facades that men wore in public. Then she added that I should wise up and start to think clearly about my future.

Anya has been telling me the same thing for years now, and I hardly listen to her when she starts in on me now.

Li Kong laughed, then he asked, 'Do you ever think about it, sex, I mean?' He had been thinking how pleasant and peaceful it all seemed, despite Tanya's infatuation and self-created suffering over Richard. Even the mention of sex workers did not disturb him the way it would have not too long ago.

'At my age, rarely. Mostly I feel loneliness. Sometimes I miss human touch, and warmth, but sex itself, not so much.'

'I don't think this is anything I will ever get a chance to experience,' Li Kong said. 'My generation is consumed with politics and there is no room for anything else. The girls all want to prove how tough they are and act like men.'

'Surely not all?'

'Mostly.'

'Is there anyone who appeals to you?' The Director asked.

'Not at all. And mostly I'm too tired to think about it- political study sessions, self-criticism sessions, criticism sessions, raids, denunciations, it's endless. I have given up even the pretense of studying. This is the best part of my day. The only good part, really.'

'Mine too. Shall we stop until tomorrow?'

'Yes. I'm so tired still.'

~

The boy had not turned up for a couple of days and though anxious, Sun Mu, anticipating what was to come, read ahead in the diary.

Shanghai, December 1936

Today I almost died. The new client with the deco villa is coming to town to meet with us. Even before I read his letter, my eye went to the signature. It was nothing but a scrawl, but I knew it was Richard's writing, even from a distance, even before Ladislav handed it over to me.

My heart began to gallop, and I could only observe it without being able to stop and control myself. I must have looked peculiar because Ladislav asked me if I was ill, and though I said no, perhaps a touch of indigestion, he made me sit down and brought me a glass of water to drink.

When I was sufficiently recovered, he told me we would be meeting with the client first thing Monday morning. Ladislav will accompany us on a walkthrough of the now completed villa and then we will be left alone to discuss furnishings, finishes and fabrics.

My head was throbbing the rest of the day, and I couldn't concentrate on work at all. I didn't want to be alone that evening, but of course, just when you need someone to unburden yourself to no one is available.

I never went to church except on Easter, and not even then, but I had an urge to seek solace, somewhere peaceful and clean. Night was beginning, life was starting all around me, couples were getting ready to go to the cinema or dancing, and I could think of no such place. The two spacious Orthodox churches that have been newly built are not yet consecrated, and I wanted to be some place where I would not be crushed by the crowd.

Walking home, I had an impulse to buy a packet of cigarettes. I had never smoked before, but my anxiety was becoming intolerable. I opened the pack immediately and lit it one, and smoked it right there, like a streetwalker. I found it incredibly soothing and smoked another on the way to my apartment.

It then occurred to me that I could go into the back alleys into an opium den and smoke a pipe, and slip into oblivion, or become so detached from it all that nothing could touch me. I was headed that way, but turned on my heel, throwing the cigarettes to the ground. I knew that a beggar would pick them up within minutes and be grateful for them.

I went home, had a bath, and sat down to meditate. After a while, I was suffused with golden light and felt calmed and peaceful. I went to bed but had restless dreams. When I awoke, I could only remember a part of the dream sequence: I had had a letter from Richard saying that he had always been looking for a warm, loving woman like me to rescue him from his solitude. I couldn't make out the writing very well and was distracted by the fact that someone was stealing large pieces of furniture from my apartment. I was upset because I had to stop him though I was desperate to get back to the letter. I thought about what that could mean and finally came to the conclusion that, in fact, I had been desperate for Richard to rescue me.

It was Saturday morning, and I had two long days before Monday to fill. I got out my sketch pad and drew up several ideas in case Richard wanted to see what my thoughts were on furnishing the villa. Of course, it helped that I knew his collections and was fairly certain that regardless of how he wanted to portray himself in the future, he would not easily let go of them. They would merely add to his mystique among his colleagues.

I sketched some designs for materials that I thought we could put in the study along with his African masks that were geometric and reminiscent of kimono, in aubergine, cerise and gold. The seating was plush and clubby, a deep maroon leather Chesterfield with chairs clad in purple and russet. I added a rug that echoed the colors and had a simple design in the four corners. In the salon, I kept the colors to pale mushroom and gray. I kept the bedrooms light and airy to offset his collections of oriental art.

By the time I finished it was late afternoon. I wasn't due at Anya's until evening, so I combed through my clothes, combining them, until I thought I had arrived at a perfect costume that said, I am professional, chic, independent, but original, and very Russian. The skirt is longish, pale green, with a front kick pleat, and the matching jacket has exaggerated Bishop sleeves with an embroidered kosovorotka collar, and is cinched at the waist with a wide belt. The hat was nothing but a circle worn to one side, with a kokoshnik fanning out on top. I thought about wearing his pin, just to see what effect it had on him but then decided he would think I still harbored feelings for him, so I chose an amethyst pendant brooch that my aunt had left me, in that deep Russian purple so prized by collectors.

I set my hair, dressed in my red gown, and decided to dance until dawn.

Shanghai, December 1936

Tuesday evening. I survived both the day and Richard.

I had pampered myself all afternoon Sunday: manicure, pedicure, facial, long bath, waxing and plucking. I dressed with care, and, ahead of the scheduled time, went straight to the villa where I was to meet with Ladislav and Richard.

Ladislav was waiting outside, and we went to the front door together. A servant, not Zhang, answered and took us to the conservatory, where Richard was seated in a planter's chair, absorbed, writing in a leather-bound notebook. He looked up and recognizing me, lifted his brow. I shot him a flat look that he understood immediately. He stood as Ladislav made the introductions, pretending, as did I, that we were meeting for the first time.

I was terribly anxious, but did not show it. Certainly, Ladislav did not spot my discomfort as he took us on a tour of the completed house. Richard was satisfied aside from some minor details, which they discussed. Then Ladislav took his leave, and Richard and I went back into the conservatory.

Richard was looking at me in that superior, amused way he has, as if to say, what now? I decided to be perfectly honest with him, and said, 'Richard, you hurt me but I've recovered. I need this job badly, so let's let go of the past and get on with it.'

Richard, tipped his head slightly, as if this was a novel proposition, and pulled out a chair for me at the table. I fumbled with my portfolio and removed the sketches, saying these were only ideas and that I was sure he had his own, which we would shape and refine together.

He looked through them, and finally said, 'It's not what I had in mind, but I can see that they are good. We will begin working from scratch, if that doesn't offend you.'

'Not at all. It is what I am here for,' I said, coolly.

'Why don't we meet in a few days from now, when I'll have some ideas written up,' he said.

'That will be fine. I'm at your disposal.' I immediately wished I hadn't said it, because I could tell he was laughing at me. He reached for my hand, but I pulled it away.

'Strictly professional,' he said.

'That's right,' I replied.

'At least allow me to take you to lunch when we next meet.'

I told him that would be all right and we scheduled a time and place.

I seemed to be in a daze all the way back to the office, replaying the conversation in my mind. Before I sat down at my desk, I spontaneously telephoned Sasha. It was the wrong thing to do, to use him to take my mind off Richard, but I did it anyway. He answered straight away, and, although we hadn't seen each other for a long time, he seemed glad to hear from me. I asked him to dinner and he agreed.

I went to his place straight after work, and when he opened the door, he laughed at my outfit.

'That bad?' I asked.

'Not at all. It's delightful,' he said.

'How would you like to take it off?' I asked, not quite knowing what had gotten into me.

He went to the bar to mix drinks for us. It was a while before he said, 'Tanya, you can't just breeze in and out of my life.'

'I know that,' I replied. 'Would you like to make it a regular thing again?'

He took a sip of his drink, and said, 'I don't know. Let's see how it goes tonight.'

I took off my clothes, and faced him squarely, straddling him as he sat. I expected the kind gentle lover I had remembered, but Sasha was quite brutal with me, yanking my hair, and then pushing me on to the floor before taking me from the back.

It was so unexpected and forceful and his thrusts so vigorous that I finished in minutes. Sasha turned me over and then put his organ in my mouth and moved it until he climaxed. We fell away from each other, panting, and lay on the floor for a long while.

'Well,' Sasha finally said.

'Well, what, Sasha? Are you surprised?' I asked.

Sasha exhaled a bit.

'Surprised that I'm not one of those soft empty headed babyish women you Chinese seem to prize.'

'You presume far too much,' he said wearily.

'So, should we go to dinner?' I asked.

'Let's stay in,' he said.

I didn't leave that night.

The Director remembered that night, but it was steeped with his later memories and now they seemed to be jumbled together. I stopped loving you Tanya, and I stopped caring what you thought. I was able to be that way with you because of it, no longer tender or loving. But you preferred it that way, didn't you? You chased after Richard, despite the agonies you suffered from his continual rejection, and you kept coming back to me to be brutalized. What made you that way? Perhaps it was something in your Russian soul that made you seek heightened sensation and create passion where none existed. After a while, I realized you were using me, but by then I didn't care and decided to use you as well.

Shanghai, December 1936

Friday

Richard was staying at the Cathay while he was in town, and called last minute, changing our plans, saying we could meet for tea at the Jasmine Lounge at the hotel. I agreed. I had always loved the Cathay, Victor Sassoon's hotel, particularly the spectacular atrium and all the art deco details. In fact, I loved all of its splendor and decadent luxury.

I went home to change into something more appropriate. I decide on a suit that I had designed some time before when Hong and I had created the collection inspired by medieval fashions. The jacket was long, cut like a robe, dark green, tied to the side, and worn over a matching skirt. I paired it with a black cloche, grey silk scarf, gloves, a black handbag and shoes. It was simple and elegant.

On the way over to the Cathay, I reasoned that since I was Richard's decorator, he would not hesitate to be seen with me in public. A wave of revulsion spread over me, and I could feel myself flushing with shame. I thought, I gave myself so easily, too easily for him to respect me, and now that there is nothing physical between us, he has lost his power over me. I felt no fear, and, for once was quite calm.

I arrived a few minutes late and could see he was waiting impatiently, and it gave me a small thrill to observe it. The waiter ushered me over to the table. I could see Richard's eyes widen as he stood to greet me, and I knew he liked what he saw. We ordered, and got down to the business at hand.

Richard had done a fair sketch of the salon, with two seating areas, a long sofa along the far wall with two occasional chairs, and two sofas in an L-shape around the fireplace. It gave the room an airy, wide open look.

I took out my pad and moved the two sofas wider apart, and added low slim tables in front of each. Richard liked it.

'Let's add some lamps and a desk here behind the short leg of the L,' I said. The room was beginning to take shape, and I could see what he had in mind.

'Your collections?' I asked.

'Not in this room. I want to keep it light. I have two pictures I would like to hang here. Modern,' he added.

I asked what the dominant colors in the paintings were and he said, 'Black, camel and aqua, but I want the fabrics kept light and the walls white.'

I colored in the sofas in camel and off white.

'No. It's dead like this,' he said.

I thought for a while. 'It's the walls. Perhaps a light shade of robin's egg blue. It would make everything stand out, and it looks lovely with camels and browns.' I colored it in for him, and he was delighted with the suggestion. I added that I would make watercolor sketches for him so that he could visualize it more fully, along with fabric samples before we actually did any work.

We talked a bit about the feeling tones he wanted for the other rooms, and I told him about what I had been thinking of for the library- his horned chairs, his African collections and ivory, set off by bronzes and modernist paintings with a leopard fabric on a settee. He seemed enthralled by the description, so I said I would get that done as well by the next meeting.

We finished tea and the waiter came to clear up. When he left, Richard asked me to dinner the next evening. I said I was seeing someone now and couldn't, which was true. He was expressionless, and we set a date for the next meeting at the Cathay room on Monday for lunch.

Shanghai, December 1936

Sasha and I were together on Saturday. At one point, when I was lying on the floor naked, he said he wanted to make some pictures and I said, no, I thought it was disgusting to be seen that way, like a common slut.

He explained that he would pose me discretely and nothing would be vulgar or obvious. He took a series of photos and developed them right away in the small darkroom he had in the apartment. They were what he said they would be, and my body took on an abstract shape, like a plant unfolding or driftwood left on the beach for a very long time. Often my face was obscured in the nude shots, but when he did focus on it, I was shocked to see how little it resembled my imaginings of what I looked like. I seemed so hard and hollow.

. . .

Ah, yes, the Director thought, those had been masterworks, lost in the war, never to be seen again. He had thought nothing of it at the time, but now regretted treating his work so cavalierly. We made art together, he thought. You and I, Tanya. The camera loved you so, your expressions, and the way you were able to unfold before it. You should have been in films, but in a sense you were, since you formed the basis of many of my heroines, though you yourself did not know it. A mix of pathos and bravado came along with that beauty; your brashness, your naiveté, your winsomeness and that whiff of tragedy that always followed you about and promised that somehow, someday, something terrible would happen to you and that you would come to a bad end.

Shanghai, December 1936

I worked all day Sunday on the watercolors, and they turned out spectacularly well. I added barrel shaped club chairs with wood veneer on the sides and backs to the study and had inserted some cubist paintings of my own, aping Braque and Picasso, amidst the African art. The salon remained cool and blue as we first conceived it.

I was tired of picking out my wardrobe to make him gawk and settled on something I had made up recently, a high waisted grey skirt and unstructured tulip jacket with a Mandarin collar and a three quarter sleeve. I added a simple black blouse, a small hat, and shoes and gloves.

At the Cathay Room we started with martinis, and Richard was about to order for me until I stopped him.

'You're your own woman now,' he said.

'Yes, Richard, I'm all grown up, something you always dreaded happening,' I said.

'On the contrary,' he started to say, but knew I detested that sort of banter and stopped himself.

I pulled out the sketches. I could tell he was quite impressed. He gave me the go ahead, pending approval of the fabrics.

During lunch, I asked him what he had in mind for the dining room and bedrooms, and we discussed some ideas and scheduled another meeting to see what I would come up with. Richard said it would be our last meeting before he had to return to Singapore, and I said it was not a problem, and that I would have several options ready for him from which to choose. He asked if we could meet at the house and I said yes, of course, if it would help him to visualize things.

I went home and began work immediately. I sketched out a circular plan of the dining room with a blond wood table with black inlay, matching chairs, a geometric carpet, parchment paper on the walls and a gilded ceiling with a bronze pendant chandelier hanging from it. I then made an alternative plan, carrying over the robin's egg blue from the salon, but deepening it, and used silver gilt on the ceiling, an added a crystal chandelier and cerulean velvet on the chairs.

I knew Richard's habits well, and had no trouble laying out his bedroom and dressing room. I did one sketch in an Islamic style, with a raised canopied bed, blue green tiles, vases, and arches, since I remembered Richard had said that he had slept in such a place once and it had been the most magnificent bedroom he had ever seen. I did another in the deco style, with lots of brass, that I was sure he would dislike, and then the last in Balinese style. I would wait until he chose one and take my cue from it before I worked out the remaining bedrooms. I was pleased and thought it was good that I would have a few more days to refine my ideas before we met.

Saturday, December 1936

Richard canceled our Wednesday appointment, saying he had to go to a meeting with the higher ups. He called me at home Friday, just as I was getting ready to go out with Anya and Shi-shi. Sasha was working late at the studio almost every night now, and so I had fallen back on their company.

Richard asked me to come to his suite at the Cathay. I was known to the staff as a decorator, so there would be no misinterpretation of why I was there. I tossed a wrap over my evening dress and grabbed my portfolio, thinking I would later leave it in Shi-shi's car since it would be easier for me to meet them in town directly afterward.

Richard greeted me at the door and took my wrap.

'Good evening,' he said, standing back to look at me.

Anya and I had been experimenting with twisting and tying fabrics and recently I had made several dresses for us. The one I had on consisted of nothing but a halter blouson made from one black and one white scarf, sewn together, with a matching scarf wrapped around the hips and tied together in front, over a long white skirt.

'I'm going out for the evening when we finish.' I said, in case he was wondering why I was dressed up.

'Is it your creation?' he asked.

'Yes, of course it is,' I said, almost adding, where would I have the money to buy ready-made evening clothes?

'You're getting better and better. Simplicity suits.'

'Thank you, Richard. Will the table do?' I asked, opening my portfolio and laying out the sketches.

Richard made two martinis and stood over me as I sat.

He approved of the designs as they were, aside from the bedrooms, saying they were too fanciful and ornate.

'What do you have in mind then?' I asked.

Richard put his hand on my shoulder, and I almost jumped out of my skin at his touch.

'Don't,' I said, shaking off his hand.

'Why, does it still mean something to you?' he asked, mockingly.

I sighed. 'Richard, it meant more to me than anything in the world. I would have died for your love. Just one word from you acknowledging that you had the smallest amount of feeling toward me, even if it was a fraction of what I felt for you.' I didn't look up at him when I said this but sat at the table still, with my shoulders hunched over, as if that position would protect my heart.

After a while he said, 'I'm sorry, Tanya. I'm sorry I hurt you so deeply.' He seemed about to say something else, but I cut him short.

'Perhaps it would be best if you worked with someone else from now on.' I said.

'No,' he replied. 'This will be a significant career achievement for you. Let's carry on.'

I said nothing. We discussed some plainer ideas for the bedrooms, and when we were finished, he said he would be in touch from Singapore, and that I should send the preliminary sketches.

We said goodnight in a civil manner but on the way out I thought, you cold hearted bastard, I was a fool for wasting myself on you.

I met Anya and Shi-shi, got rip-roaring drunk, and danced all night.

Shanghai, February 1937

Richard went back to Singapore, and we corresponded officially until the bedroom designs were completed. He said he would be back this summer, and I promised all the furnishings would be completed by then. We have our own craftsmen, so there will be no delays since the final designs were agreed upon.

I feel that I am over him, finally, but something has happened to my psyche. The deeper I go with Sasha, the more perverse our games become. I don't know if it is a substitute for genuine passion, but it seems like neither of us can get enough.

Ever since that night, the first night of utter callousness, we have repeated that performance over and over, escalating the violence to be able to feel something, anything at all. It all began with a slap, or perhaps it began just before that.

I had been wearing pajama trousers, and he suddenly pulled them off, and doubling me over, began to spank me. I was shocked, but he had me pinned down, and I couldn't get away. When he let go, I slapped his face, once, then again. He grabbed my hands, holding them over my head and pushed me on top of the bed, biting my lips and breasts before he penetrated me. I can't understand why this excites us as much as it does; it really is unfathomable.

Sometimes I am bruised from the way he handles me and must be careful not to wear anything too revealing. Sometimes, afterward, we fall apart, and I lie there, feeling more alone and empty than ever. I know Sasha can sense this, and I know it bothers him. When I become too still and quiet, he becomes more intense, as if he is trying to penetrate the heart of me, as if he thinks something will burst and I will become human again.

Anya saw the new photographs he made of me and said I looked like one of those vampiric women from Weimar Germany, all lustmord and under eye circles. Maybe it's true, maybe death is at the other end of sex. Oh, really, I don't even know what I am trying to say!

How strange, the Director thought, while the Japanese were encircling China, we saw nothing but ourselves.

SHANGHAI, 1967

Sun Mu rarely saw people from his past. Since he had been labeled a rightist and punished, he had stayed away from the artists he had known, more for their sake than his own. His loss of face had been less hard to bear than the loss of his work and though he had changed his name to reflect that he was less than nothing, he had known that he had been labeled such to meet a quota handed down from Beijing. Who better could they have picked to sacrifice? He had met all the criteria, educated in the West and therefore infected, skeptical of Mao's understanding of economics.

He later learned that tens of millions had died of starvation in Mao's insane bid to collectivize farms and industrialize China during that time. While the peasantry was diverted to melting every piece of metal they owned in backyard furnaces to comply with Mao's directive, crops were left to rot in the fields. Mao, with his paranoid distrust of intellectuals and specialists, failed to realize that high quality steel could never be produced from scrap metal.

What Sun Mu had not known was that Mao, in encouraging criticism during The Hundred Flowers Campaign that preceded The Great Leap Forward, was in fact readying to conduct a purge, which would root out thousands of intellectuals who were critical of the regime. After the Anti-Rightist campaign, you silenced us all, he said to himself, and we could not help anyone, not even ourselves.

Sun Mu could only speculate what Mao's motivations were in unleashing the Cultural Revolution. He thought Mao a good warrior, but an inept peacetime leader, one who was completely divorced from reality. However, he could see through his conversations with the boy that indoctrination and propaganda had worked to deify Mao and make him a cult figure as elevated as emperors had been in the past. The boy was beginning to question the aims of the Red Guards and workers' brigades, but he never questioned Mao himself. Mao was a god to the younger generation and whatever they might privately find suspect, they never suspected Mao, only those around him. Mao must not be aware of what was happening, the boy had said on many occasions, and the Director had not challenged him on it. Not yet, anyway, he thought.

The Director dressed carefully in his one good grey padded jacket and trousers. Though most people now dressed similarly, the Director, with his height and lean figure, wore it with particular grace. He had run into an old friend, a set designer, while he had been at the market the other day, and through whispered conversation, he had understood that Madame Mao was conducting a purge of her own which targeted people who had either snubbed her, or of whom she had been envious, during her stint as an actress thirty years before. That's a very long time to hold grudges, the Director had said, until his friend reminded him that absolute power corrupts absolutely.

Today he was going to visit his old friends Anita Cheng and her husband, the writer, Gong Wei. Anita had never been political and had sailed through much of the turbulence that had rocked China since 1949. She had been legendary for her affairs but indulged by the regime nevertheless, since she had charmed the top leaders with her stage performances in Yunnan. She had retained her position and privileges and had married Gong, who was ten years younger, in the nineteen-fifties. Intuitively she had seen to it that he keep his head down, producing scripts that focused on proletarian themes sanctioned by the regime. So very like Anita in all ways, he thought.

He walked to their apartment in an art deco building in the former French Quarter. Anita came to the door when he rang the bell.

'Oh it's you!' she exclaimed. 'Well, well, all my old friends are turning up, which must mean I am in big trouble. Come in,' she added, leading the way into the red salon. The Director followed, noting, that while he had gotten old Anita had managed to maintain her youthful good looks. If anything, he thought, her figure was better than when she had been a plump young actress.

Anita bade him sit and rang for tea. In the characteristically frank way, which he had always found disarming, she said, 'Now let me take a good look at you. Better, you're looking better, handsome even, in a geriatric sort of way.'

The Director threw his head back and laughed. The maid brought tea and he sipped it thinking it had been a long while since he had made polite chit-chat when Anita said, 'So you heard about my troubles, and you came to cheer ole Anita up?'

The Director raised his eyebrows slightly in acknowledgment.

'The Blue Apple is behind it, of course,' Anita said, referring to Madame Mao's stage name. 'That slut wants all traces of her promiscuity erased and is willing to annihilate human beings to that end. Anyone who remembers her, anyone who has wronged her, anyone with whom she was competing, will fall. You know that she posed nude for Liu Haisu back in her early days in Shanghai, long before she ever played her Nora on stage. She'll have him cleaning toilets in the institute he founded before long, mark my words. It's bad enough that Rotten Apple has us listening to her demented model operas all day long, but now she is going too far.'

Anita's temper flared, but the Director doubted whether she was aware of the full implication Madame Mao's persecution might have on her life. Anita read his expression.

'What?'

'It might be graver than you think,' he said. 'I've managed to adapt, but you, Anita-'

'Let me cut you short. I know you've always thought of me as a frivolous woman, spoiled and willful. Stupid even. Let me tell you something, rich boy, we all used to look at you in your bespoke suits and think your tailoring bill could have paid all our salaries. If you could adapt, then so can I. I came up from the same layer of filth as Rotten Apple, and I can go back there if necessary.' She was defiant.

'Anita, you're a woman who has always been proud of her beauty. What do you think a prison sentence will do to you?'

Anita slumped. 'It's not me I am worried about. It's Gong Wei. I know I'm old and crazy, but I love him passionately. If anything was to happen to him...' she trailed off. 'Do you know what I think about? If I get out of prison alive, I'll be a ruin. He'll not want me then, will he?'

The Director sighed deeply.

'You know, you're lucky to be alone. You don't have to stay up nights fearing for anyone's life, tormenting yourself with the darkest thoughts imaginable.'

'Am I? Perhaps I missed out on a great deal, being as I am, and not loving anyone.'

'Ah, I didn't say that. You loved that girl, the Russian one, didn't you?'

'Did I? So long ago, it's hard to remember what I felt or thought.'

'No, I'm sure of it. Thank God, you never felt that way about me. I might have ended up stuck with you.'

Sun Mu laughed again. That was the thing about Anita; she was such a mixture of the vulgar and sublime that never failed to make him smile.

'Whatever happened to her?' Anita asked.

'I don't know.'

'Hmmmm,' she mused sipping her tea. 'I seem to remember you went to Manchuria to look for her after the war.'

'I had forgotten about your legendary memory.'

'Don't evade the question,' Anita said playfully.

'I was never able to trace her. Perhaps she died unnamed, falling by the roadside and was thrown into an open grave. Or perhaps she followed the Red Army and disappeared into one of Stalin's camps, like so many of them did.'

'You were quite despondent as I recall.'

'Was I?'

'Indeed. I remember thinking, why couldn't he have loved me like that?'

'Oh Anita! I hurt you. I'm so sorry.'

'Don't be absurd. Who would want an old goat like you, anyway?'

'I did love you.'

'But not enough.' Anita held out her thumb and forefinger to demonstrate how little. 'Tell me what do you do with yourself these days when our glorious Red Guards have banished such bourgeois pursuits as chess and tea houses?'

The Director shrugged.

'Really you might take your camera out and take a few photos of the revolution. Save them for posterity, why don't you, just in case anyone ever wonders what went on here.'

'I have no camera.'

'Really? I'll give you mine.'

'No need.'

'You're such a coward, you know that? Afraid to love, afraid to say what you really thought. You're afraid now.'

'I seem to remember getting into a lot of trouble for saying what I thought.'

'You didn't go far enough. None of you did.'

'And you did?' the Director waved his hand about to indicate Anita's material comforts.

'Let's not quarrel, shall we? '

'All right.'

'Gong Wei will be home soon. He'll be happy to see you.'

'I should go. I have another appointment.'

'Suit yourself.'

The Director rose and Anita accompanied him to the door. She gripped his arm and looked up at him. Her irreverent expression suddenly changed and he saw her true face, which was that of a frightened old woman.

'Fang Shirong!' she cried.

'What is it?' he asked, but her mask was in place once again.

'You might come over for a meal every now and then you know.'

'Yes, of course I will.' He gently pried her hand off his arm.

'No, you won't.' Her eyes were hard. 'Who knows what will become of us. Goodbye, Fang Shirong.'

He had an impulse to reach out to her and hold her for a moment, but the moment passed and he bid her goodbye and walked the long way home though his rheumatism had flared and he felt excruciatingly tired.

Li Kong had been absent for days and when he finally turned up, he said nothing other than he had been detained in a long struggle session. They sat down and the Director began to read.

Shanghai, March 1937

Spring has arrived and with it the rain. Sasha is filming on location at Peach Blossom Lake in Hangchow. The script is a muddle, warlords, kidnappings, landlords, and romance. I'm certain it will be a hit.

He wants me to come and visit later in the month when the peach trees actually blossom. There are temples and lovely things to be seen there, according to him. I have never been. I don't know whether to go. I am not certain what we are doing is good for us.

Hong Kong, March 1937

End of March, spring, flowers, greenery. I never went to Hangchow. Ladislav is unwell, a liver ailment, and the senior architects are working on a new hotel, so I have been sent to oversee the interior decoration of a new villa for a rich English couple. He is older, staid, and a bit dull. She is much younger, very pretty, and flighty. I don't think she has had much hardship in her life. They are newly married as she has just recently come out East. She talks and talks, asks a lot of questions, and answers them herself on your behalf. Her name is Vivienne. His is Frederick Fox-Pitt. I almost laughed aloud when I first heard it.

There is a great deal of building here now, and Ladislav may send me here permanently if I don't make a mess of things like I did last time, which I am determined not to do.

Hong Kong, April 1937

The Fox-Pitts are having a party. It is in their old place, a last farewell to his bachelor life. They have invited me, along with David. Vivienne and he get along famously, as she is fond of saying, since they have friends in common at home which gives them plenty of things to talk about.

Vivienne is quite a clothes horse, so I will have to come up with something nice to wear since, as she says, everyone will be there. I suppose if we were in England they would make me come through the back door, but here everyone is bored stiff, and consequently, friendly.

Hong Kong, April 1937

I made the most sensational dress ever. White silk, cap sleeves, bateau neckline, seemingly modest and yet fitted like a second skin. No jewelry, just silver shoes, and a small silver clutch. I can hardly wait to see what Vivienne will be wearing.

Li Kong made a small grunting noise.

'What is it?' the Director asked.

'Oh, it's nothing really. I just remembered the time the Guards caught a young woman on the street. She was wearing a qipao and had a flower in her hair. She seemed so lovely and feminine. They slashed her dress right there and then. They humiliated her and broke her pride. Yet she had done nothing other than made herself look pretty. By the time they were finished, she was no longer that. I would have liked to have seen those dresses Tanya describes.'

'Yes, I know. Shall I go on?

Li Kong nodded yes.

Hong Kong, April 1937

Last night, David came for me in his car. I waited for him at the window of the house I am renting and ran directly to the car with a rain cloak on, lifting up my dress so that it would not get wet. I was worried it would be ruined by the rain but it went unscathed. As always, David was cheerful, and we chatted about nothing and everything on the way.

By the time we got there, we were in good spirits and ready to have fun. We were among the first to arrive. Vivienne hadn't come down yet, but Fox-Pitt was there to greet us, and when my cloak came off his eyes popped. David laughed and said I was a naughty thing. We got drinks, and after chatting with Fredrick, began to mingle.

Sometime mid-way through the evening, when David and I were dancing, I noticed a striking woman had approached the circle of by-standers and was looking intently at me. I recognized her as Madam Liu, and when the dance ended, rushed to greet her.

She seemed genuinely pleased, and hugged me, saying she couldn't believe that little Tanya had grown up. I laughed and introduced David, and while he went to get drinks, we sat in a corner and caught up, chatting about her time in Singapore and the fact that she was back in Hong Kong now. She was happy to hear that I was decorating the new house for our hosts.

Then she said, 'Of course, Richard told me you were doing up his house, so I already knew you had become the success I always hoped you would be.'

'I imagine you saw quite a bit of him in Singapore,' I said for something to say.

'Yes, quite a bit. He always sings your praises, you know,' she replied.

'Really? He never tells me so,' I said lightly.

'Why don't you and your young man come to lunch tomorrow and Richard can tell you himself.'

I was surprised but managed to conceal it. 'I'd love to,' I said, 'but I must ask David.'

Of course, by then David had returned with our drinks and was keen to accept.

I must get ready now, he'll be here shortly.

'I didn't think it was over between them,' Li Kong interjected.

'Nor did I.'

'Go on.'

Hong Kong, April 1937

Madam Liu's family house was not as I expected. She lives there alone apparently, but it is dark with heavy draperies and wall hangings, European in decor but Chinese in feel. She was charming and elegant in a grey quipu, dressed appropriately for entertaining at home. I was experiencing that awful feeling of anxiety that I always have before meeting Richard, but the drinks she served were having a calming effect on me and soon I was, if not relaxed, at least not ready to jump out of my skin.

Richard arrived shortly before lunch while we were still chatting in the main salon. As always, he looked like a wild man whose energy could rip the room apart, though he was well dressed and groomed.

The introductions were made and presently we went into lunch.

Madame Liu had taken charge of David, who, it seemed, she regarded as a slightly backward boy she had to guide. David was enjoying it. He was the youngest of four children, and my impression is that he had never been mothered enough.

They walked ahead and left me with Richard.

'Liqiu tells me your gown was quite a sensation last night,' Richard said. 'In fact, she says the gentlemen present were quite delighted to see every aspect of you through it.'

'Good that you missed it since you are so prudish, all of a sudden,' I retorted.

'I merely want to help you not make a fool of yourself,' he said.

'You're neither my father nor my husband, and I have no need of your advice. Aside from Madam Liu, I was quite the chicest woman there, I assure you, regardless what you heard.'

He never had a chance to reply since we had arrived at the table.

The whole time I dreaded what he would say to David, to show him up or try to make a fool of him. David is quite sensitive, though he tries to conceal it, and I hated to think what Richard would do if a black mood overcame him.

I needn't have worried. Madame Liu carried the conversation, and with her, everything is always appropriate and thoughtful. I wondered why I wasn't jealous of her, but I wasn't, and I don't think I ever could be.

Afterward, we promised to see each other again.

Hong Kong, April 1937

A supper party and cards last night at Madame Liu's, just David, Richard, she and I.

I really can't fathom the nature of their relationship. Are they lovers or friends? It's hard to tell. Neither of them is particularly affectionate or even seemingly interested in the other, and yet they are so familiar and seem to know each other well.

Perhaps they think the same of us.

I have been seeing a lot of David and think he is perhaps the best man I have ever known. In the beginning I dismissed him as being too young and boyish, but perhaps I see things more clearly now, and he has grown up a lot in the last couple of years, as have I.

Sometimes, I wonder what life would be like if I was married to him. I would have security and his companionship, but when I think of the endless tennis and cocktail parties with the same old people all the time without the solace of my work and its challenges, I think we are better off as we are.

Last night, as we were playing, Madam Liu really was asking David a lot of questions about his work at the bank, detailed ones, like how money was transferred and deposited, accounts and things like that. I was surprised how knowledgeable he was and how very serious and considered his answers.

She then began to speak of politics, the situation in Germany, seemingly gauging David's reaction. At one point, tired of her probing, Richard said, 'For pity's sale Liqui, keep your mind on the game.'

He seemed quite irritated by her.

David, on the other hand, doesn't seem to mind at all. He finds her quite fascinating and, I think, is a little in awe of her and flattered by her attentions. She is still very beautiful, if anything even more beautiful than when she was younger. Her face has an almost spiritual aspect to it. One thing I have noticed, it is a tad asymmetrical. One side is the face of a highborn classic Chinese beauty, the other half is older, sadder, the face of someone who has suffered greatly or been badly disappointed in life. I asked to make some sketches of her, but she just laughed it off. She seems to have no vanity at all.

She said something so odd the other day when we were shopping in town. I stopped to give money to a particularly ragged group of children- I could never stand seeing that sort of thing-and she stood by the side, head cocked, seemingly lost in thought. When I joined her, she said in a very strange, almost choked voice, 'It will take so much more than that.'

I suddenly felt quite ashamed of myself. For so long I've been all about my clothes, my designs, my parties, my stupid and perpetual whining about Richard that I close my eyes to the things around me, the beggars, the children, the dogs. If I look, really look, it becomes unbearable. And it frightens me, because I am not insulated, the way Liu is by virtue of her money, or the way David is, because he is part of a race which assumes its superiority, or even the way Richard is, because he can find beauty in the hideous and believes suffering just a part of the great wheel of life that turns endlessly.

'What ever happened to David, I wonder? He sounds so nice,' Li Kong said.

'If I had to venture a guess-'

'You think he died?'

'So many died of starvation or disease during the Japanese occupation of Hong Kong. Over seven thousand British soldiers and civilians were kept in prisoner of war or internment camps, and the civilians, at least, had gotten used to soft living. Who knows, maybe he survived.' The Director shrugged. 'Should we stop?'

'No. read one more entry.'

Hong Kong, May 1937

I made a terrible mistake today, and now I am frightened by the repercussions it might have. I assumed Vivienne was so modern, so free, but she is not. Not at all.

I invited both her and Liu to lunch at my house. It was a particularly beautiful day, and I set the table outside, amidst the lushness of the garden. I thought they would get along, both so chic, so lovely. But I was mistaken.

The minute Vivienne saw Liu she immediately became brittle. Liu sensed it of course, the race prejudice, and was polite, but cold as could be, during lunch. She excused herself almost immediately afterward saying she had another appointment.

I escorted her to the door, and she gave me a light kiss on the cheek. I could feel tears coming on, of sadness, and of rage, and I felt so terribly sorry for her and so terribly sorry I had exposed her to that.

She held my chin up and said, 'None of that. I'm quite used to it.'

'I don't understand. She had you to her party,' I said.

'Not she, Tanya, her husband did.'

She pressed my hand and said we would see each other soon. I hope she is not just saying it.

I went back to the garden. Vivienne was lighting a cigarette, and I sat down dumbly.

'I hate them you know,' she said, 'their filth, their cooking, the way they live on the streets like animals. It's all quite disgusting.'

I was shocked. Perhaps that is what the British all think of us, but they are usually too well-mannered to express it.

'You're surprised?' she asked.

'No Vivienne, I just thought you two might like each other,' I replied.

'A woman like that is even worse. Their women are so calculating. Butter wouldn't melt in their mouths. And the way they manipulate men!'

I remembered what Liu had said about the party invitation and wondered if perhaps she hadn't been involved with Fredrick at some point. Perhaps Vivienne had found out.

I was disappointed by Vivienne's behavior but then reasoned that if that was true, she might have reason to be jealous, even though it had transpired before her marriage.

'Your husband adores you,' I said. 'I have never seen a more beloved wife.'

This seemed to put her in good humor, and I kept flattering her, all the while feeling I had betrayed Liu and was acting falsely because I wanted to keep my job.

'We have more pride now and we have come so far. Europeans won't be able to disregard us in the future,' Li Kong said.

'Possibly, but more because of our great number than our accomplishments.'

Li Kong wanted to argue with the Director but felt himself fading. 'I'm tired. Let's leave off until next time, shall we?'

'Yes. Go home and sleep. I'll see you soon,' the Director replied.

~

SHANGHAI, 1967

As Sun Mu awoke, the bad news he had heard rose up at the tail end of his dream, and he remembered that Anita had been arrested and put in jail. He must have been dreaming about her. It was strange that she had remembered Tanya after all these years, he thought, but women had uncanny intuition about these things. She had certainly sensed he had loved Tanya, but had Anita known that the heroines she had brought to life in his films had been based on Tanya? Anita had been able to capture perfectly that blend of gamine winsomeness and humor that were characteristic of Tanya. That was what was lacking in the diaries, he realized. She had been awfully droll and fun to be around. She often had a habit of rolling up her eyes when she was delivering a particularly ponderous statement, which made you think she wasn't quite serious -and yet she was.

It suddenly occurred to him that he had loved Anita best when she was playing Tanya, and when she would revert to being Anita, he would be disturbed by it and withdraw his affection. That was an awful thing to have done to a woman who had been quite amazing in her own right. But then, he reasoned, he had made Anita a star and that was some compensation for what he had put her through emotionally. And she had endured far longer than he had. Still, for the rest of the day, he kept thinking about it. Eventually he understood that his sense of guilt would take him to see Anita's husband and urge him to write to Beijing to see what could be done to secure Anita's release. He had always considered Zhou Enlai to be a saner man than Mao, but then who knew what position he would take in these times? Perhaps, he too, is worried about saving his own skin, the Director thought. Nevertheless, it was worth a try. Yet the letter had to come from Gong Wei, who had never been in trouble with the regime and not from himself.

Li Kong showed up on time that evening. Classes were still suspended; teachers knew not what to teach since all texts were now considered bourgeois, and there was little to do other than sloganeer when criticism sessions were not scheduled.

They sat down to read and picked up where they left off.

Hong Kong, May 1937

Something happened last night. The evening began at the house of some of Liu's rich friends, a modern Chinese couple. It was a lovely night, and they had decked the outdoor garden, which was sizable, with Chinese lanterns and had swung open all the doors to the house. A band was playing, and they had set up the dance floor in the room off the patio. Chinese waiters were serving champagne, and there was a buffet with crab, lobster, and other assorted seafood.

Liu and David had gone out on the dance floor and were dancing dance after dance. I didn't mind. Richard was talking to some of the older men present, and then disappeared. I danced with several young blades in turn, and then, feeling a bit overheated, went into the garden to take some air.

I'd taken off my sandals to feel the grass under my feet, and was enjoying it, that, and listening to the music which was now being carried off in the breeze.

Even from the bottom of the garden, from his mannerisms, I could tell that the man who had come outdoors to smoke was Richard. I made my self still, hoping he wouldn't see me, but I had the white dress on and it caught the moonlight.

He came over and stood slightly to the side of the bench where I was sitting.

'It seems that Liqiu has stolen your young man,' he said to provoke me.

'He's not my young man. He's my friend. And if she wants to have a bit of fun, she's certainly entitled to it,' I said.

'It's never just fun with her,' Richard said. 'Have you thought about the impact it might make on him?'

'He needs it, Richard. She'll be good for him.'

'You're remarkably democratic, Tanyushka,' he said.

'Well perhaps you are envious of the fun they are having,' I said, slipping on my sandals.

'Yes, I am. Won't you dance with me?' he asked.

'What for? I'm going back in,' I said, standing.

'You're never going to forgive me, are you?' he asked, flicking away his cigarette.

In one of Sasha's melodramas, I would have fallen into his arms, and we would have declared our undying love, while the sunset faded and sickeningly sweet Chinese music played in the background.

'The memory of you is fading, and after your house is finished, I will never have to see you again.'

I started to walk away but could hear him laughing at me, and I had the urge to hurt him. I wanted to tell him about Sasha, about our sex, to make him understand that he had not been all that but that I had been young and foolish enough to think so. I didn't of course.

I knew David wanted to be with Liu, and I knew they might not recapture the moment if he had to drive me home, so I said, 'Let's leave them to their games. Take me home, I'll make my excuses tomorrow.'

He didn't say anything and led the way to the car.

On the way, I looked out the window at the darkness. We didn't speak until we stopped in the driveway of my house.

'Let me in Tanya,' he said.

'No, Richard, I don't think so.'

'Why not? Are you afraid of me?' He asked, mockingly.

'No, I'm afraid of myself,' I leaned over to kiss him but couldn't stop myself from biting his lip, hard.

He pulled away and brought his hand to his mouth. There was a bit of blood on it. He looked surprised but then began to laugh.

'Come in then, Richard. If you really want to,' I said opening the car door by myself.

He followed me up the walk, and taking the key from my hand, opened the front door.

'Don't turn on the light,' he said.

'All right,' I replied. 'You like the romance of the moonlight? Do you want music, a drink? Do you want to make love to me in the dark?'

'I want you to stop talking and be still.' He walked over to the picture window and drew the drapes. I thought for a moment he was looking outside, and I asked, 'Is this the part where the man with the gun follows us?'

'This is the part where I take off your dress, but I don't care for anyone else to see.'

I wondered whom he suspected of hiding in the bushes, but said nothing, and turned on the phonograph. I had been listening to Chopin's nocturnes earlier and that is what I played now.

'It's too sad, Tanya.'

'Could it be you have a heart, after all, Richard? I like this recording,' I added.

As he made his way toward me, I kept stepping back, teasing him, until I found myself cornered against the wall next to the bookshelves. I could only make out his silhouette, and as he came near, I raised my hand to slap him. He caught my arm in the air, and held it over my head.

'I hate you, Richard,' I said.

'Be still, Tanya,' he said quietly.

His whole body was pressed into mine. The closeness of it, the smell of him, the darkness and the hardness of the wall was too unbearable. I was choking.

'No,' I said, but I couldn't shake him off. He didn't move, and I could feel the sweat beginning between my legs and knew I had begun to stink with desire, like an animal.

'Do it then. What are you waiting for?' I asked.

I expected a brutal assault, but I was mistaken. Richard took my hand

and brought me over to the sofa, and gently pushed me down. I sat forward, tensely, anticipating what he might do.

Richard knelt in front of me, placing his face between my breasts. I couldn't breathe, and my heart was about to leap through my skin. I began stroking his hair and kissing it, then his face and mouth. All the time, I was murmuring in Russian, saying all kinds of insane things: dorogoy moy, radost moya, nemogu zhit bes tebya, ya budu vsegda lyubit tebya- all the things I would have been ashamed and too constricted to say had he understood me.

Richard suddenly grasped my upper arms and pushed me away from him.

'It's too much Tanya,' he said.

'How can it be too much, Richard? You seem to think love can be parceled out in small servings like pie. How can I contain what I feel and why should I have to?'

'Because I can't,' he said. 'Do you understand me?'

'No,' I began uncontrollably shaking.

'I must go,' he said, rising to his feet.

'Stay, just this once, and never again.'

'No. It was a mistake to come here,' he said. 'I'm sorry.'

'Fine,' I said, 'Go back to your sterile English world where you all worship money, gin and tennis, and are terrified of feelings or displays of emotion. And when you amass enough money to get to Kenya, I hope you will find what you are looking for. Only the Japanese are gobbling up China, and they might spoil your plans.'

Richard looked back at me once, but said nothing, and left.

The following morning, Madam Liu telephoned. It seemed that she and David had been worried about my disappearance. I told her I had felt I was going to be sick and didn't want to spoil their fun, and that Richard had been kind enough to see me home.

'Are you all right, now?' she asked with concern.

'I feel a bit shaky still,' I said, because it was true.

'I thought that crab was off,' she said. 'I should have warned you.'

'It's all right. I'll be fine. I'm sorry to have caused you worry,' I said.

'I call later to check on you,' she said.

'Thank you,' I said. I wanted to add that I hoped her evening had been pleasant otherwise but did not want to intimate that I suspected she had spent the night with David.

I suddenly felt horribly alone and made my way to the garden where I fell into a chair and sat in the sun for hours, like one of those small lizards that can remain immobile all day, only to scurry off when a shadow falls.

I had a full day scheduled on Monday and would be spending it with the Fox-Pitts at their new villa. Vivienne had never mentioned that lunch again, and I was glad of it.

Hong Kong, May 1937

Liu, true to her word, telephoned later that afternoon and asked me to have dinner with her, just the two of us. I didn't want to be alone with my thoughts, which had turned obsessive and unpleasant, and agreed. She sent her driver to take me to her house, where she said she would have cook prepare something light.

When I arrived, she greeted me at the door. I must have looked terribly drained and exhausted, because she put her arm around me and escorted me in. She started to chat about something or other to distract me, but I wasn't listening, or rather I couldn't. I wanted to tell her all about Richard, to confess, to hear some words of advice, but I couldn't manage to say anything.

As if she could read my mind, she said, 'Richard is going back to Singapore tomorrow. Did he mention that to you last night?' she asked.

'No, he didn't say a thing,' I replied. 'Though he was kind enough to take me home.' I remembered I had, of course, told her that earlier.

'Richard is never kind, my dear,' she said.

'No, he isn't, is he?' I said.

'He's an omnivore, Tanya, and your heart is too pure.'

'Ah, Liqui, how can you say that? I'm selfish, and frivolous, and very, very foolish.'

'You're young, and you've had a hard struggle. But your soul is untouched by that. Don't ever be afraid to love. There are few who can, the way you do, you know.'

'So, it's that obvious,' I said.

'Perhaps not. It may be that I am the only one who noticed.'

'How did you meet him?' I asked, curious now that she seemed to be finally opening up.

'A long time ago, when I was a student in Paris.'

'Did you love him at all?' I asked.

'Not love, Tanyush. I would say it was more of a grand obsession on my part. And I undertook a great effort to get him to notice me. It was all in vain of course. He was his own sun and moon and stars, always.'

'Yet, you are not bitter. And you have remained friends.'

'Yes, and looking back, I must say, he caused me to, perhaps, become a little bit of what I am today.'

'Did he ever love anyone, do you think?' I asked.

'I'm sure he has taken great pains to avoid it,' she replied.

Before I had a chance to ask her what she meant, dinner was announced, and the moment had passed. We talked of other things, and neither of us mentioned Richard again.

I was so busy today with the Fox-Pitts that I had no time to brood, nor to think of Richard's departure. I'll be done with their house in about a month and be back in Shanghai and will have to face Richard again.

Li Kong sighed deeply. He was exasperated by the emotional turbulence to which Tanya subjected herself.

'What is it?' the Director asked.

'Nothing. Go on, please.'

Hong Kong, June 1937

It is clear that Liu and David are involved. They don't mean to exclude me, and she is always at pains to make little dates where the two of us do something together, even if it is just having tea or taking a stroll. He seems awkward around me, though I am happy for them both, and would tell them only neither has confided in me, so of course, I can't say a thing.

I'm lonelier than ever, and since I am not seeing David, the invitations have stopped, aside from the Fox-Pitts. I do my work, read a lot, and sketch a bit. I feel dull and am looking forward to getting back to Shanghai, where I have a few real friends.

Shanghai, July 10, 1937

Fighting broke out near Peking between the Japanese and Chinese. The Japanese have expanded their troops along the railways, far more than any foreign power is allowed to have. Tensions have escalated, and here no one is really certain what is going on. The British are convinced no one can touch them or their enclaves regardless what happens to China, itself. The Japanese, it seems, are dependent on imported petroleum and are at great pains not to offend either the British or the Americans, who supply them. In any case, sporadic fighting has been going on for years: the Communists, the warlords, the Kuomintang, the Japanese. Maybe this will amount to nothing after all.

Shanghai, August 1937

Richard will be coming to Shanghai soon. The house is completed. I am arranging the furniture. All that is left for him to do is move in his personal things.

I dread seeing him again after that last evening. And I dread not seeing him even more. I can't stop myself. Each day I think, what is the purpose of living without him? Sometimes I feel that I can't go on any longer, that without him, I am a shell of a human being, going through the motions of life.

Sometimes I wonder if his spell over me would be broken had we had remained together. Would we live like the countless married couples I see day in and day out, who, while dining have nothing to say to each other? Would I resent him in time? Would I find him dull? I'll never know.

I rush to get the post each day at the office hoping to receive word of his immanent arrival, like an idiot schoolgirl.

Shanghai, August 1937

Dinner with Sasha. The place with the fans. He has missed me. Sasha

talks, but I am not with him. I am thinking of how I will walk past Richard's
threshold and how he will be sitting in the planter's chair, looking the way he
always does, amused at my discomfort, and then I look back at Sasha who
cares for me, who wants me, and who I do not love, although I cannot fathom
why, because he is a thousand more times deserving than Richard.

'Ah, so she is well aware that Sasha is the better man,' Li Kong said.

'Yes, but it didn't make a bit of difference, did it? the Director replied.

Li Kong shook his head and indicated the Director should continue.

Shanghai, August 1937

Dinner with Anya and Shi-shi, who is afraid of the Japanese, who loathes
the Communists and the intellectuals, and who believes Chang is utterly
corrupt.

Anya sees nothing other than her small pleasures and joys. Her new
armchair, her new dress, a trip with Shi-shi, new collars for her dogs. She is
like me, a foolish woman, and a weakling.

I don't let on about my internal life. I won't bore them with my eternal
suffering, over love, which amounts to nothing, such a silly thing in this
world where people die on the streets so others can have more than they can
ever use up in their lifetime.

Shi-shi says Chang wants war. If it happens, everything will change.

My father died in the Great War. When I was a little girl, I thought he
was a glorious hero fighting for freedom and for Slavic unity. Later I
discovered he had died of the typhoid somewhere in a primitive field hospital
on the Eastern front.

I can't remember the entirety of our house, only some rooms, and some
scenes: the heavy dark furniture, the lace curtains, the clock on the mantle,
and hiding underneath the dining room table and wondering about its
carved legs with animal claws. I remember Masha, our maid, and how she
always smelled of starch and dough. And I remember her carrying me to bed

when my mother received the news of Father's death. Mother was wailing, locked in her grief, and Masha picked me up, though I was kicking and screaming, and carried me to my room. I knew the truth about father even though I was very small. I went limp all over, and she stayed with me to comfort me.

Soon the house in St. Petersburg was gone and there were debts to be paid, and Mother wouldn't hear of living in Grandfather's house because he had never approved of her, though I begged and begged.

We went to her relatives in Moscow instead. They were a mean petty people who counted every morsel we ate and weighed it against us. She knew we couldn't stay. We did go to Grandfather's in the end, but she couldn't bear him and took offense at every word he said.

When the revolution broke out, she began moving us eastward. In Vladivostok, she died, a lingering aliment of the lungs, perhaps an old case of tuberculosis, previously hidden, returned. I spent a year in an orphanage. All I can recall is the stink of piss on the sheets, the bleakness of the days, the regimentation and the utter hopelessness, the feeling of total abandonment, and the knowledge that nothing would be right ever again, not that it had ever been with her, for she had been hysterical and given to impulse, always.

Then months after her death, a letter from my father's brother, inquiring after me, and more waiting, waiting for him to come, to fetch me, to take me away.

In the end, Shanghai. Nikolai Nikolayevitch, Anna Kirilova, the Zhukovs, and Tatiana Alexeyevna, a readymade child, a replacement for their son who had died fighting the Reds. They did love me, they loved me, but they died, first he then she, separated by a few years. Hard years to be sure, but the first security I had known since the day the telegram came for my mother and the world as we knew it ended.

Love is hard to come by and loss is even harder. It is easy for me to understand myself in light of my past, particularly in relation to my love for Richard, who touched my heart and whose heart I had hoped to find a home in.

The Director could see that the boy, being orphaned himself, was moved deeply by this entry, but he said nothing and continued reading.

Shanghai, August 1937

Richard will be in Shanghai soon. He asked to meet with Ladislav to walk through the house one last time before he moves in. No mention of me, of course.

Shanghai, August 1937

Sasha and I spent the night together. It was different this time. None of the mad violence was left in us; we were like friends, like old lovers reuniting, like people who are full of kindness and understanding for each other. And there was real tenderness and affection between us. And beauty. Though I have never said it before, he is beautiful. When he lets go of his sadness, there is always a little smile about his lips. The lower is fuller, the upper a bow, below a slender mustache. His chin is firm, almost cleft, which is not considered attractive in China, but I do love it. His nose is straight, his eyes oval, and a bit puffy, always. He is tall, his body hairless, golden, and beautifully proportioned in all ways.

After we made love, we talked for hours, like we did in the beginning, of things that are real and eternal, of the soul, and the cycles of life and death, and the passing of all things.

I felt calm, sleepy and relaxed in his bed.

I think everything may change for us, and perhaps we might face the future together.

There was a catch in the Director's throat and found himself experiencing conflicting emotions; those of nostalgia and longing, though he did not think it was wise to think of the past and of how things might have been had the war not broken out. He had always thought himself second best in her eyes, but now understood that friendship, kindness and respect outweighed passion in the end, and understood that perhaps she had had to live, to have the experience of a grand passion before she could comprehend that herself. He said nothing of this to the boy.

'We'll start the fourth diary tomorrow, shall we?' was his only comment.

'Yes, of course,' Li Kong replied, and standing up, crossed the courtyard and went up the stairs where he fell into his bed and dreamt troubled dreams in which his parents still seemed to be alive though he knew they were dead even within the dream. He wondered how that could be as they ushered him into their house, which was much grander and more traditional than it had been in life. He walked past the carved gate and past the lions at the door and entered a dark and intricately carved room where his mother was waiting to serve him a meal. He realized that his parents wanted him to stay on and take care of them, but he was filled with a dreadful anxiety that he would be stuck in that place forever and unable to live according to his own choices. He felt terribly guilty over his lack of filial piety, and yet he knew he had to break out and rush past the door into the green hills and valleys that beckoned him. After he awoke, he wondered what the meaning of the dream had been, and toward the end of the day, he experienced an awakening when it occurred to him that the family house was a symbol for China itself.

PART IV

SHANGHAI, 1967

'Gong Wei!' the Director shouted, exasperated at Gong's listlessness. He had gone to Anita's and knocked on the door until Gong, disheveled and puffy eyed, had finally come to the door and let him in. Gong shuffled through the corridor like a man who had just awoken from a long and restless sleep, and perhaps he had, the Director thought, given his rumpled appearance.

Gong sank onto the sofa, appearing insensible to the Director's suggestion that he write direct appeal to Zhou Enlai. Anita has indulged him so much that he is not even capable of behaving as a man would, the Director thought

'Gong Wei, have you heard anything I said?' he asked.

'I heard, but it won't do any good,' Gong said at last. 'You are not the only person who has had this idea, you know. Others have tried to get the release of their loved ones, but you know all it takes is one false accusation based on envy or a grudge from the past to denounce someone and have them jailed. If anyone in Beijing cared, this would not be allowed to happen. People have gone insane, do you see that?' Gong ran his hand through his hair, pressing hard on his flesh.

The Director saw that he was both terrified and without hope. 'Do you want to help Anita?' he asked.

'Yes,' Gong said, but his voice wavered.

'Then get a pen and paper and I'll tell you what to write.'

'Do you think the local committees would let the letter through to Beijing? It might never go through the proper channels or get to its destination,' Gong said bitterly.

'Then you must take it there yourself,' the Director said simply.

'Fang Shirong, I know what you endured during the Anti-rightist campaign. You are brave, but I am not.'

'Let's start and then you can decide what to do afterward.'

'All right,' Gong Wei said, but even as he dictated, the Director realized that Gong Wei would not have the strength to carry the plan forward.

All the way home, he felt depressed. His mood lightened when he saw Li Kong crossing the courtyard and he put his thoughts of Anita to the side at least for a while.

Hong Kong, September 1937

The past weeks have been hellish. Negotiations failed, and the Japanese have invaded Shanghai. Chang and his troops are fighting in the streets, and terrible events have affected civilians, most notably the dreadful incident in the International Settlement when Chinese pilots, aiming for Japanese warships, released bombs that landed on Avenue Edward VII killing thousands of refugees.

I am safe at Madam Liu's thanks to Sasha, but I am sick with worry about all who stayed behind that I can only manage to fall asleep in the mornings after I thoroughly exhaust myself. I'm not complaining. I will live through this. It is the others I am frightened for.

I was caught unaware, as I usually am, it seems, while I walk through life like a somnambulist, living in my mind and my fantasies. I was going to meet Richard at his house for the final inspection, simply because Ladislav was otherwise occupied.

I remember I was late and was rushing to get there on time. I took a cab, but when I arrived at the house the front door was ajar, and the glass surrounding it had been shattered. At first I thought, they were moving

Richard's things in and had been clumsy. But when I rang the bell and no one answered, I went into the house.

The rest of it is like a dream. I can recall walking through the rooms, but there was an eerie and unearthly silence there, as if the world had ended and I was the only remaining person alive. I only recall thinking, something untoward has happened, and the entire household has left. Later it occurred to me that Richard had never arrived, and that his servants had fled. At the time I thought it strange, but the more I brood about it, the more convinced I am that one of them had heard the Japanese were coming.

Then there were explosions. I tried to telephone the office, but the lines were dead. I came out of the house and wandered down the street, since there were no cabs to be seen. One of Richard's neighbors, who recognized me, was in his car and decided it would be noble to rescue me and drive me home.

I don't know what he made of my disjointed story, but once we heard the mortars going off, we both hunkered down and concentrated on the road. It wasn't crowded the way it would be later in the day, nor indeed as it would be when all of Shanghai was scrambling to either get out of the city or find a safe haven to hole up in.

He is a kind man, perhaps eccentric the way only the English can be, since he dropped me off with a cheerio. I hope he is unhurt. I can't remember the rest of day well, only that I paced a great deal and tried to calm myself, thinking, it will be as it was in 1932 when the Chinese and Japanese fought for a month in Shanghai, though outside the foreign concessions. The League of Nations forced the Japanese to negotiate then, and it will do so again. I told myself that, but all along, I was afraid because a real war was being fought in the north now, and the Japanese were hoping to expand their influence beyond Manchuria.

Anya telephoned that afternoon to tell me that Shi-shi had said the Chinese were going on the offensive. Ladislav phoned to tell me to stay at home. The fighting was localized to Chapei, nowhere near us, and so I thought perhaps they were overreacting, as was I.

I also thought it would make sense that Richard's boat couldn't dock in light of events, and that he was probably heading toward a safe harbor. It then occurred to me to worry about Sasha. I waited until I knew Sasha would be home to telephone him, but when I did, there was no answer. I continued to ring him late into evening.

Over the next days, the fighting continued in the Chinese sections since those are the areas the Japanese are eager to subdue. Life for us remained the same until the August 14 debacle when over three thousand civilians were killed by the bombs that fell on Nanking Road and The Great World Entertainment Center. Afterward the face of the city changed, Chinese refugees streamed in, barbed wire and sandbags were constructed throughout town.

When Sasha finally turned up at my door, he was a changed man. He seemed determined and impassioned, without his habitual detachment. He was adamant I should go to Hong Kong for the duration of the fighting. I refused, saying I had not the means. He gave me money and insisted.

'But you are staying, Sasha?' I asked.

'China is my country,' he said simply. 'I cannot go.'

'You are not a soldier,' I said.

'No,' he replied, 'but my words and images can make a difference.'

'Sasha, you think the Japanese will let you make propaganda films at their expense?' I asked.

'Tanya, I am not a fool, but I have some ideas how I can be useful.'

He wouldn't tell me what he meant, though I goaded him. Finally, he said, 'Humor me, if there is a ceasefire you can come back and we'll resume where we left off. If not, wherever I am, I will have peace of mind knowing you are safe.'

I knew that other intellectuals were going to join the Communists in Yunnan, and I asked if that was what he had in mind.

'No,' he said, but would not explain further. I now torment myself with the thought that he might have lied to me, and then console myself with the idea that perhaps he will be safer outside of Shanghai.

I arrived in Hong Kong, and when Liu heard I was here, she insisted I stay with her for the duration.

. . .

Hong Kong, September 1937

    I have my own quarters, a bedroom, small sitting room, and bath. Liu is happy to have me near, I think, but she is terribly preoccupied with news of the war, and spends endless hours speaking to her friends about it. I feel a little like a ghost, wandering about, with no discernible purpose at all.

    I told her what happened at Richard's house, and she listened carefully before dismissing my concerns, readily agreeing it might be just as I speculated, that Richard's boat never arrived, and that the servants fled in a panic. She said she had that it was likely they had returned to the safety of the house and would make do until the end of the fighting. Really, she claimed, they would be safest there. As for Richard, she was certain that he was fine, no doubt having returned to the safety of Singapore, and that we would hear good news sooner or later. She was so reassuring that she managed to quell all my doubts.

    I wonder if she and David are still together, because I have neither seen nor heard from him and am embarrassed to ask. I have never told her about Sasha. I don't know why, perhaps fearing what she might think of me, since she knew of my love for Richard. I have no one to unburden myself to, and so I am writing this because sketching is no good.

Hong Kong, September 1937

    I went to bed early, as is my custom, because I don't want to incommode Liu. I was already in bed when I heard male voices in the house. I should have ignored them, but curiosity got the better of me, and slipping on my robe, I went quietly downstairs, making sure I was unobserved, to, I suppose, spy on Liu.

    I heard Chinese, and listened for a while, but could not make out muffled sounds. Even had I been able to, the dialect is quite different here, and I'm not always certain I understand the nuances. I stood on the staircase for some time and then withdrew. My bedroom faces the back of the house, so I could not see them leaving. I eventually fell asleep.

    In the morning at breakfast, I asked Liu, very innocently, if she had had guests the previous evening, adding I thought I had heard voices. She was preoccupied reading some letters, and without looking up, told me I must have been dreaming. I was silent, astounded for a moment that she would tell such a blatant untruth, but then reasoned she must have her reasons.

Still I couldn't help wondering about it all day.

Hong Kong, September 1937

Liu must have felt badly, and seeing how I am moping about, finally consented to let me sketch her. She was good enough to sit very still for the duration, though I am certain it caused her a bit of hardship, since she is a very energetic person, though disciplined. Sometimes watching her eat tiny morsels of food to keep her figure, I wonder how she can stand it. But it is that way with the Chinese. They seem to have as much capacity for suffering as Russians, only they are more determined, and as I said, more disciplined.

I gave her the sketch and she really loved it. I did it in the Chinese style, very painterly, soft, misty, and almost mystical.

'Oh!' she exclaimed. 'How exquisite, I look like a lady from the Tang Dynasty.'

'Only more beautiful,' I replied.

She laughed.

Later, I was almost sorry that I had given her the drawing, because it was so very fine. When I retired to my room, I made a reproduction, here in this notebook, because I have no photos to remember her by. Once, I mustered up the courage to ask her for one, but she just laughed it off, saying I was being maudlin and silly, and I would have no need to remember her since we would always be friends.

Li Kong asked to see the sketch. 'It's her, definitely, the woman whose house we raided. She is older but not that changed.'

'Has she been arrested?'

'I don't know.' Li Kong replied. He said nothing to the Director but thought: I must get back to her house and ask about Tanya, that is, if she hasn't been arrested. Though he had been avoiding them, pleading illness, he knew that the Red Guards made multiple raids on houses where the inhabitants were deemed class enemies. A few well-placed questions and he could discover where she lived, but he would have to be careful not to trigger another incident. Yes, he decided, I will find her.

'Go on, please,' he said.

Hong Kong, September 1937

I've been doing a lot of sketching now. Mostly of Liu. I spend so much time with her, I can do them from memory. I think the one of her walking is particularly fine, I've caught the way she holds herself. Her stance is so straight, but her bearing is different from what we think of as pride. It's somehow ... unflinching, as if she is ready to face anything.

There's another that I particularly love. She's bent over some flowers, that look of meditative peace on her face, as if the flowers are the only thing that are holding her attention in this world.

I've drawn Sasha as well, the way I love him best, his fedora tipped rakishly to one side, obscuring his eyes, casting a shadow over his face, and then the light, hitting his fine nose, and his smile, which is full of warmth and humor.

Each day, I chastise myself for not loving him more, and for not loving him better. God knows what has happened to him or if we will ever see each other again.

'Ah,' Li Kong commented.

'Ah, indeed. She was probably feeling lonely.'

'Maybe, but it's possible you aren't giving her enough credit.'

The Director shrugged, 'Shall I go on?'

'Please.'

Hong Kong, September 1937

Men come to the house each night. I pretend to hear nothing, withdrawing to my room before they arrive. Liu knows I know and says nothing. We both pretend. Whatever she is doing, be it resistance or not, she clearly does not want my involvement in it.

Liu loves China, that much I know. Whatever it is, it will be for the good of the country.

Once she asked me how I felt about it, China, that is, and I didn't know what to say. I love Hong Kong, and Shanghai has been my home all these years. But I have always felt homeless there, and remembering my real home, or rather, my grandfather's estate, the firs, the starry sky, the coldness of the wind, I cannot say that I love Shanghai as I should, or as some seem to do.

I think about it, and think how little I have seen of China, and how what I have seen outside the pleasant foreign enclaves has terrified me. The poverty and the suffering of the Chinese is enormous and all consuming.

Liu says she has heard hunger among refugees in Shanghai now is terrible and that each day dead babies are found stuffed in trash cans as if they were never human at all.

People here carry on as before. I don't go anywhere out of respect for Liu. The war has affected her deeply, and it would be unseemly for me to gad about as if nothing was happening.

'Were you there?' Li Kong asked.

'No. I went to Yunnan right away.'

'So you saw Sasha there?'

'Yes, but that was long ago.'

'What was it like?'

'A golden time, where everyone believed in the dream that a new society was being born, and everything that was wretched and backward about China would be swept away and justice and equality would prevail.'

Li Kong was thoughtful. 'But that is not how things have turned out to be.'

'No. Some are more equal than others, as you may have noticed.'

'Yes. I see the children of the party cadres have more privileges and more opportunities than the rest of us. They look down on us, you know.'

'We wanted to usher in a new age but that cannot be done by force. Human nature seems to be immutable. People themselves must be open to change. Still radical changes were made, though at a high price and much suffering.'

'Tanya knew that. She did not trust them.'

'No, she did not, and perhaps she was not such a foolish girl-' the Director cut his sentence short. He had been about to say, as I once thought her to be. 'Shall I finish? There is not much more here.'

'Yes, please.'

Hong Kong, October 1937

Something strange, a letter for Liu from Richard. I saw it on a tray in the hall before her servant picked it up. I waited for Liu to say something to me about it, where Richard was or what he was doing, but she didn't mention it at all. I have been brooding whether to broach the subject with her but can't understand why she wouldn't say anything to me knowing of my past with him and how bewildered I was by his disappearance, or lack of appearance, I should say.

It's horrible really, because all those feelings of anxiety came rushing back, and despite the war and all the awful events in Shanghai, I keep wondering why he wouldn't or couldn't love me.

I wish I had serious work to occupy me, and I wish I had news of Ladislav and the office. I don't know what I am going to do if I have to remain in Hong Kong. I'll run out of money eventually, and I can't be Liu's guest forever.

Why won't Liu say anything?!

Hong Kong, October 1937

I woke up late, something unusual for me. I had bad dreams all night long and kept waking, then unable to sleep, lay in the dark for a long time with a horrible presentiment that my life was about to derail and that I would never see Shanghai or any of the people I love again. I fell asleep towards morning, and had another dreadful dream that I was searching for something amidst the bombed out rubble of an unrecognizable city. I kept hoping to find it, whatever it was, and was aware that I would know it when I saw it. Yet I had a feeling of overwhelming sadness that somehow I would miss the very thing I was searching for, even though it was right under my nose.

Sometime between the waking and the dream, a voice said, 'The steps of your life will be traced over the cobblestones. The remainder of your days...' Before I could hear the rest, I awoke with a jerking spasm.

I was thoroughly shaken and remembered how my mother would always tell me about her dreams, believing if she could decipher their meaning, the path forward would be clear. But she could not see that the road's end would lead to a narrow white hospital bed, and neither did she see the red basin where she coughed up her lungs, nor the child who would be left behind after her death.

I couldn't breathe, and jumping up, threw on my robe and went downstairs. Liu was not in the house, and her servants said that they did not know where she had gone nor when she would return. I wanted to call David, just to hear a human voice, but reconsidered, thinking Liu might have gone to see him.

I began to brood about Richard's letter again, and as shameful as the idea was, I wanted to break into Liu's locked desk where I knew she kept her private things, just to see what had happened to him, just so that I would have some peace of mind, though I did not believe anything in there would be for me. Of course, I did not do that but had a bath and dressed myself. I went for a long walk and found the greenery soothing and my anxiety dissipating.

That feeling did not last, and as soon as I returned, I began to dwell on the letter again, not that it had ever been out of my mind for a moment. From her perfume, I knew that Liu was in the house, and I went into the sitting room, where I knew I would find her. She was sitting on the sofa, a horrible overstuffed patterned thing that was as oppressive as the rest of that dark room. She had put aside a pile of papers and was staring into space.

She seemed startled by my appearance, but returning from her reverie, smiled at me. I came over to the sofa and sat very close to her.

'What is it Tanyush?' she asked.

'Liqui, I must ask, only because I find it unbearable not to know,' I said.

'Yes?' she replied.

'I couldn't help but see that a letter arrived from Richard for you the other day. You don't need to tell me anything important, though I must know if he is safe.'

She said nothing, and I imagined the very worst.

I thought about what I was going to say carefully. 'I'm not blind, Liqui. You and Richard are close, but it's not a love affair, therefore I can surmise that you have some sort of working relationship. He wouldn't have written to you otherwise. I also know of the men that come and go from here in the night and that you hold meetings with them. I have also heard that Richard has worked for his government in an intelligence capacity, and I assume that kind of work doesn't end because one merely wants it to end. You are not an average woman, so I know you won't insult my intelligence by behaving like one.'

'All right Tanya, I won't. The nature of our work is sensitive and related to resisting the Japanese occupation of China. I know you are trustworthy, but for your own sake, that is all I can tell you.'

'Liqui, the British, I think, are not greatly interested in resisting Japan's occupation of China. They seem much more concerned with appeasement.'

She looked at me with an odd expression, as if she had not considered that I might be aware of the facts.

'The truth is that our British friends prefer to keep their options open. They will go with the side they think will be of most use to them. In the past, they were quite pleased that Japan was blocking Soviet expansion in northern China. That situation has changed, now that the Japanese have made their intentions clear and threaten Britain's economic interests in Shanghai, and elsewhere, in the south. However, the British are also preoccupied with German rearmament and the rumblings of Herr Hitler in Europe, which is much closer to home. Nevertheless, they will want to keep their markets open in the Orient and will do whatever is necessary to accomplish that end,' she said.

'So, in essence, you are saying that while you serve China and Richard does Britain, you are united in your efforts.'

'If China is to fight the Japanese wholescale, we will need help from the British and the Americans.'

'Now, Liqui, you must answer this, is Richard close to the battlefield?'

'Richard hardly informs me of his movements, Tanyush, but to be fair, I imagine if he is not at present he will be at some time in the near future.'

'Did he mention me at all in his letter?'

Liqui thought about what she might say next and paused before she said it, 'He's no good for you, Tanya. You are beautiful and young and have your whole life ahead of you. There are many men who would be happy to have you and to love you.'

'And who might they be?' I asked mockingly.

'Our young friend David for one,' she said.

'But I thought...'

Liu's laughter interrupted me, 'Ah, Tanyush, he is not for the likes of me. But listen to me carefully now, Richard seems fascinating to you because of the life he has lived. Believe me, it is not quite as glamorous as he makes out. Heat, flies, lonely outposts where nothing at all happens and nothing will ever occur - that has been his life. He is much older than you are, and while he seems worldly compared to a younger man, he will be old while you are still vital and young. His fortunes may decline, while someone like David, who has the right background and connections, can only rise and in time grow into himself.'

'There is only the problem of his soul. It didn't quite touch mine.'

'Soul, soul. You Russians!' she said, affectionately. 'Forget that and be more pragmatic.'

'Liqui, I asked you a question, and you did not answer it,' I said.

She sighed and with some resignation in her expression, went over to her desk. Unlocking it, she pulled out an envelope and from it a small enclosed note, which had evidently accompanied the letter.

'He asked me to give you this if anything happened to him, but I see that you will have no rest until you have read it,' she said, handing me the paper.

My hands were shaking, and at first glance, I couldn't make out what struck me about it. Then I realized it was in Russian. I was momentarily astonished, but then the thought occurred to me that Richard could have asked any number of Russians to write the text for him.

'Have you read this?' I asked her.

*'No, Tanyush. English and French only. I'll leave you alone,' she added
withdrawing from the room.*

- For Tatiana:
The swallows in the morning light, alight
And the rustling of rowan trees in the gloam
speak of your small hands
that intelligently crafted all sorts of things:
Artifacts and loving webs that danced in the sunlight,
    now faded.
In my remembrance, your light is the only warmth I've
    known.
And if you thought I was indifferent, you were mistaken
For it is your touch I will carry to whatever bitterness
    awaits.
Death or victory, neither is painless
It is only your love that remains.
-R

*I read Richard's poem three times over before I literally felt my heart open
as if it was in flower. He had loved me and he did still. I didn't understand
why he had had it written in Russian, but perhaps he thought I might find it
preferable, the intimacy of the language, the words that did not convey the
same meaning as they did in English. I did not have to read it over to
understand.*

*The swallows, I knew, mated for life, yet in Russian, swallow is another
word for spy. The rowan is ryabina, and in the folk song the slender rowan
longs to cross the stream to be with the mighty oak, whom she loves, and yet
she cannot ever join him.*

*I crafted a web of love, but in battle Russians would form a spider's web
around enemy forces, surrounding them and seizing control territory. The
sunshine has faded, solnechnyy svet, but svet also meant the world. So the
world had faded and my luminescence was the only one that had warmed
him. It was my touch, with the dual meaning of my concern, which he would*

carry with him. And finally, the sun coupled with the birds symbolized freedom.

It read: I am a spy. No matter how much you long for it, you may not join me. I am building a web around enemy forces in their territory. Your world warmed me and it is your concern that I will carry with me whatever awaits.

Richard had known all this, and so the poem had originated with him, and perhaps he even knew the language, remembered from his earliest beginnings. But why had he not told me that before?

I put the poem in my pocket and went to look for Liu.

I found her in the garden where she was cutting flowers, examining them, holding them up to the light, before snipping away at them with surgical precision.

'Where is he?' I asked.

She did not look at me; she did not want to give me an answer. Then she took a perfect rose and crushed its petals in her hand. 'This is what happens to everything good and true,' she said.

'You must tell me, Liqiu.'

'He's in Manchuria, Tanya, where is he is liaising between already active pockets of resistance.'

I felt the earth fall out from under my feet and remembered my dream with trepidation.

Evening

Manchuria, Manchuko, as the Chinese called it, had been taken over by the Japanese in 1931. They had installed the last emperor of the Manchu Dynasty, Puyi, as the nominal head, but really, they were in control, and now they were going to use it as a base for invading the rest of China. The British have always been more afraid of Russia expanding into the area than they were of the Japanese, but now all that has changed.

I took out the poem once more. I wasn't sure where I was going or what I was going to do, but I knew that I could not bear to go on living if I did not see Richard once again.

'She followed him!' Li Kong exclaimed.

'So it seems.'

'And now we'll never know what happened to her.' Li Kong was despondent.

'Yes, that's the way it sometimes goes in life, but remember how many were lost, how many families were separated and never reunited.'

'I know but her story isn't complete-'

'Though you may never know the truth of it, her story is complete, but yours is just beginning. You've learned new things while we have been reading Tanya's dairies. How will you apply them?' the Director asked.

'How will I apply them?' Li Kong was incredulous. 'You seem to be unaware of what is happening here. I can't apply a thing. Every moment is controlled, and my thoughts are policed. I constantly have to evaluate my own shortcomings as well as those of others in criticism sessions. Only it's all lie, because that's not how I think at all.'

'That's right. So what have you learned?'

Li Kong was silent. 'I don't know,' he finally said.

'You've learned to keep your thoughts private, and you've learned that there are entire worlds contained in books that can transport you and change you, if you allow it. And that is a beginning.'

'What about now? I've gotten used to our sessions. It's the only thing I look forward to.'

'I as well. Bring the Russian book you took from your friend. We'll read from that and begin lessons as well.'

'Yes, all right,' Li Kong agreed but he was not satisfied. I must find the older woman he thought. I must find out what happened to Tanya.

SHANGHAI, 1967

Li Kong rang the bell and waited, hoping the woman was still living in the house. It had taken some doing but he had been able to extract the information from a very stupid girl who was a Red Guard leader. He had framed his questions in such a way as to put all the focus on her revolutionary activities, her dedication to Chairman Mao, and her impeccable class credentials. And she had been responsive. Perhaps she even fancied he was sweet on her, he thought with a shudder.

When there was no answer, he rang twice in succession, impatiently. He heard someone's footfall beyond the door and sensed hesitation.

'Open the door. Don't worry I'm not a guard. It's not a raid.'

The woman opened the door and stood aside to let him in to the vestibule. 'You are wearing the Red Guard armband,' she said quietly. She was dressed simply in a grey jacket and trousers but Li Kong noticed the fabric and cut were of superb quality. Her hair had also gone grey since he had last seen her, but it only made her appear more beautiful and he thought that somehow she appeared more spiritual as if all superfluity had been stripped away from her.

'Madam Liu?'

She seemed shocked to be addressed as such. 'Yes. I once was.'

'I'd like to speak to you. You see, the day we first raided your house, I found the diaries. Tanya Zhukova's dairies, I mean,' he stammered nervously.

'What is this about?' The woman was afraid, though she sought to conceal it.

'No, don't worry, it's nothing like that. You see I read them, and I, well, I was wondering if you knew what happened to her after she left for Manchuria.'

The woman's expression was one of incredulity. 'Well, then, perhaps you should come in,' she said after a moment, noting his impatience.

'Tanya always had an effect on men, so I shouldn't be surprised that her words could affect you even from the grave.' She led the way to the salon, which was now stripped bare save a sitting arrangement that included a plain Chinese daybed and two inferior Ming style chairs.

'You say she's dead?' Li Kong had been expecting it but was crestfallen, nevertheless.

'Yes, sadly, ' the woman replied, motioning him to sit. He took one of the chairs while she sat on the daybed. 'But you said you read the diaries.'

'No, not I. An older neighbor who speaks Russian read them to me.'

'Then you probably know more than I ever did. I don't read Russian,' she explained.

'I know her words from the time her aunt died to the point where she read Richard Hellyer's letter to her at your house in Hong Kong, nothing more.'

'Ah, that accursed letter. I never saw her again after she left Hong Kong. In her haste, she forgot the notebooks, and that was why I had them in my possession. I could not destroy them. They were part of her, and I could not forget her that way. Nor could I forget my guilt, because I never should have told her, and I never should have given her Richard's note.'

Li Kong was taken aback by the woman's openness. 'She loved you as well,' he blurted.

'Yes. I know. Funny how we love some people so deeply. There's really no explanation for it, is there? The Buddhists believe in the transmigration of souls, perhaps that could account for it,' her voice trailed off, and she seemed lost in her own thoughts.

'But what happened to her there? Did she see Richard again? How did she die?'

'Ah young man, she did see him again, and she died in the worst way imaginable. He was despondent for months afterward. He was a leading force in the trials in the east, such as they were, though the perpetrators went unpunished for the most part,' Madam Liu's lip curled in disgust.

'I don't understand, which trials? What do you mean?' Li Kong said.

'Ah, yes, you young people were never taught that part of our history. For some reason it seems to have disappeared from public consciousness.'

Li Kong shook his head, still not comprehending.

'You have to understand the nature of the Japanese, you see,' she explained. 'They always believed themselves to be superior, and during the Imperial period that belief was encouraged and instilled into them. They thought they had the right to take over Korea and China, to exploit us for cheap labor, and our territory for material resources. They thought of other people as cattle and they behaved accordingly.

'You see, we all knew what happened in Nanjing, but we did not know about the atrocities perpetrated in Manchuria until afterward. There was a place, a terrible place, where things went on which were utterly unimaginable.' She stopped, unable to go on.

'What kinds of things?'

'Experiments. Experiments on human beings,' she spat.

'What kind of experiments?' Li Kong asked, though he dreaded to hear.

'Ghastly things done in the name of science, but really they were only sanctioned torture.'

'Sanctioned by whom?'

'Tokyo, of course. All the results of these horrible experiments were transmitted back to research labs in Tokyo, and then later bought by the Americans, or so the Russians claimed.'

'What was this place?'

'It was called Unit 731,' she said. 'Whoever entered, be they Chinese, Korean, or Russian, never came out. The Japanese called their victims, maruta. It means logs. You see they were not even human to them.'

'But what did they do to these people?'

'Ah, what didn't they do!' she exclaimed. 'They infected pregnant women will syphilis to see the results on their babies. They performed vivisections without anesthesia on human beings. They infected people with smallpox, typhoid, plague, cholera -all sorts of diseases and observed the progress. They did horrendous experiments in cryogenics, particularly on the Russians, freezing their limbs then shattering them with sticks. They did amputations on healthy people to study blood loss. They allowed limbs to become gangrenous. What didn't they do!' she repeated.

Li Kong felt ill. 'But why her? Was it because of her association with Richard?'

'Ah, that we will never know. He would not tell me what happened between them. But usually quotas were met in round-ups by the Kempeitai, the Japanese secret police. Thirty percent of their victims were Russian. You see they were particularly desirable, able to withstand the cold as they were.'

Li Kong exhaled. He felt shattered by what she had told him.

'Perhaps now you wish you had never come here?' Madame Liu said.

'No. Part of me had to know the truth. But you said the trials? The British held trials in the east after the war?'

'Ah, you mean Richard. No, dear boy. You see, Richard was born in Russia. He knew he was different from his father and brother from a

179

young age, but it was only his mother's death bed confession that confirmed what he had always suspected. His real father was Russian and a Bolshevik, though he was from quite a good family.'

'Like yourself?'

'Yes. Richard and I were comrades from our days in Paris. Tanya never knew, of course.'

'No. You were good at concealing it from her.'

'Ah, well, that was the nature of our business, wasn't it?'

'What happened to him, afterward?'

'An apartment in Moscow, a desk job in intelligence, a wife, two children, forced retirement, a dacha in the country. That is all I know.'

'Did he love her, do you think?'

'Only he could answer that question, not I.'

The room had grown dark as the day waned, and he was only able to see the outline of Madame Liu's form and wondered why she did not turn on the light.

'What was she like, really?' he asked after a few moments.

Madame Liu thought for a moment before replying. 'She was incandescent, truly, and much of her charm lie in the fact that she was not aware of her own luminosity. You cannot imagine the type, because it doesn't exist in this world of shadows. She was so filled with optimism and so very loving. I never met anyone with such an open heart who was so willing to give of herself to everyone she met. She could make you feel like you were the only person in the room and that your words, your deeds, and your very presence were the only things that mattered. She was mutable, self-effacing and yet strong, though she was not aware of that either. And she was talented. I always regretted not being able to see what she would have grown into and how her aesthetic sensibilities would have developed had she lived.'

'You are a collector of beautiful things and perhaps of beautiful people too?' Li Kong observed.

'You are very astute, hardly anything like the usual wearer of that armband.'

Li Kong shook his head. 'Do you still believe?'

'In the Revolution? I do, but not in the people who are leading us now.'

Li Kong looked around the empty room. 'Did they give you a very bad time?'

'Ah, so far, I have gotten off more lightly than others,' she said.

'But, it's not over,' he observed.

'No. If I can weather it, I will. If not, if all my friends abandon me, if I am arrested, tortured and killed, then so be it.'

'You seem remarkably calm!' Li Kong exclaimed.

'I am prepared and reconciled to my fate, though I may not agree with it.'

'You are a remarkable woman, ' Li Kong said.

'No. Merely an old one, who has lived life. It is your generation that I am worried about. What will become of you?

'I have no answers,' Li Kong replied. He felt completely depleted.

'I despair for your education and level of culture,' she said continuing her train of thought.

'Yes, I as well. I'll be going. Thank you for seeing me, Madame Liu.'

'I have not been Liu for a long time. I became Dongfang Hong during the war.' She rose and accompanied Li Kong to the door.

'Good luck,' she said.

'What about the diaries?' he asked.

'Keep them. I suspect they will be of more use to you than they would be to me.'

'Yes, perhaps. Goodbye,' he said.

PART V

SHANGHAI, 1967

Sun Mu was thoroughly shaken. He had gone to check up on Gong Wei, less because he was concerned with Gong himself than Anita. And he couldn't rest until he knew whether Gong had followed up with the letter to Zhou Enlai.

As he approached Anita's apartment block, he saw a parade of Red Guards, chanting and bearing banners with slogans painted on them. He knew it was best to move out of the way, but he stood riveted to the spot for they were leading a man wearing a dunce cap, whose face was blackened. A sign was hung about his neck. As they drew nearer, he saw that the man was utterly exhausted. As he stumbled, the guards shouted at him that he was faking and that he must keep moving. Noticing something familiar about the man, Sun Mu moved closer. His heart began beating erratically when he realized the man was Gong Wei. He drew back and watched as the parade progressed. He thought, perhaps it was inevitable that they would single out Gong because of his association with Anita, or because of some unknown personal vendetta, though Gong had always been supportive of the party in his writings. He knew that even the most innocuous statement could be misinterpreted by the overzealous guards and they would use it to condemn innocent people to endless torment. He wondered if Gong had gone to the authorities with the letter and how he, himself, might be implicated if that was the case.

He turned towards home, the whole time wondering what Anita was experiencing in prison and what he was willing to do about it. It would no doubt be a futile gesture on his part, and he had to evaluate the consequences before he decided to act.

When he entered the empty courtyard, he saw Li Kong was waiting for him. The boy seemed unusually agitated, but Sun Mu signaled for him to wait. Li Kong understood and went into his aunt's house. It was dusk when he emerged again and knocking on Sun Mu's door, went in.

They had not seen each other for several weeks, but anticipating the boy's return Sun Mu had traded in his collected Balzac for a Russian language primer. He put it in front of Li Kong with a smile. It would take both their minds off unpleasant events, he thought.

'Oh,' Li Kong said, 'Thanks, but that's not why I had to see you.'

'Why, what has happened?' He was not yet in tune with the boy's moods and though he had seen Li Kong's agitation earlier that day, he now noted the boy seemed quite subdued.

'I found out where Madam Liu lives. I saw her earlier today.'

'Oh?'

'She knew. It was horrible. The more I think about it, the more horrified I am.'

Li Kong was not making sense, the Director thought. 'Knew what? I don't understand.'

'How Tanya died, of course!'

'Ah, I see. So she died in the war after all.'

'It is worse, much worse than that.'

The Director inhaled deeply, preparing himself to hear what Li Kong would tell him. 'Did she suffer?'

'I think she must have. Madame Liu said she ended life in Unit 731. Do you know about that place?'

Li Kong watched as the Director's habitually phlegmatic expression changed, registering bewilderment, and then utter horror which turned into something that was beyond sadness and despair. His shoulders slumped.

'Then you know what happened there?'

'Yes, I knew, though it was never broadcast by the leadership after the war. I thought she had died, of course, but not like that. Not like that!' he repeated angrily, raising his head. After a moment, he asked, 'But does Madam Liu know this for a fact? It might be false information. It was so difficult to trace people in those days.'

'She seems to have gotten the information directly from Hellyer. You see, according to her, he was a Russian agent. Both of them had ties to the party from their days as students in Paris. He was active in the trials of war criminals after the war.'

'I suspected as much. Well, I'm sorry, terribly sorry.'

'I'll come back another day. We can begin lessons then. Thank you for this, ' Li Kong said, indicating the primer.

'I'll look forward to that,' the Director said.

When Li Kong left, the Director sat at the table. His whole body ached and he felt too weary to move. Darkness fell all around him. He felt as if he was falling asleep in his rickety chair. Now, he thought, get up now. With a swift energetic motion, he pushed himself away from the table. He pulled away his bed and felt for the panel he had built where he had hidden his special things. He had not looked at them for years, not since he had been purged. A small cache, too small to reflect the work of a life time, containing a few of his favorite photographs, three scripts which he considered his best work, a roll of film, his final work, and Tanya's last diary, the one he had extracted from the people who had been living at her former flat in Harbin for the price of a few pieces of gold. Why had he hung on to that of all things? He couldn't answer. By then his love for Tanya had waned to a small residue of what it had been. But perhaps he had sensed that the revolution was not going to move in the direction he had hoped for and he would need a memento from the old days to remind him of her and the period of his life she had become entangled in. When he had been expelled from his apartment, he had taken it on impulse with him, though he had not read it for years. Ah, well, he thought, perhaps I am lying to myself and you really were the love of my cold, selfish life, Tanya. My most human love and my inspiration, and that is why I held on to it despite its contents.

He lay on his cot and began to read, though the single overhead bulb was weak and he was straining his eyes.

Harbin, May 1938

Yesterday, I thought I saw Sasha walking down the street. I was convinced it was him, and I began to skip toward him with a look of joy on my face which was departure from my usual gloom. I finally came close enough to see that it was not Sasha, but a Japanese, unusually tall for his race. He was wearing his hat rakishly over one eye the way Sasha always had, and his lips and smile were so similar that I couldn't believe it was not the same person. He touched his hat lightly acknowledging me and then was amused by my embarrassment when he realized there had been a case of mistaken identity. He looked after me for a long while as I walked, and I only know that because I was so confused that I turned back to catch sight of him once more.

I don't know what to make of these people. The fighting was terrible in Shanghai with heavy losses for

Chang to be sure, but those were military operations. There have been dreadful reports from Nanking, though, where Japanese troops ran rampant slaughtering tens of thousands of civilians and committing terrible acts, violations of women, girls, even babies, killing and desecrating them afterwards. I have never heard of such brutality. And yet some of them seem so kind and gentle. I can't reconcile the two aspects. It seems so abnormal.

I am very alone here, and life is so different for me that it was in Shanghai or Hong Kong. This is a Russian town. The buildings are Russian, the churches are Russian, the theater is Russian, but the Japanese are in charge, and the Russians are all leaving to go south, to places that are more conducive to life, Shanghai and smaller towns.

It's strange here. The Japanese distinguish between us, the Whites and the Reds, and we Whites are better in their eyes than the Bolsheviks, and freer from regulations and oversight. But there are terrible people among us as well, Russian blackshirts, fascists, who despise the Jewish settlers and sometimes harass them. I don't know why people are so cruel to each other. It's completely inexplicable. I'll never understand it.

After I left Liu, I went back to Shanghai, only to find that Ladislav had fled the city and had gone to Macao. I was out of a job until he returned. Shanghai was now bleak, no longer vibrant, or fun. Chang lost the battle at the end of November 1937 and has withdrawn his troops to Wuhan. There is a new municipal government in Shanghai, nominally Chinese, but really the city is under Japanese occupation.

It was probably a mistake to leave, but the entire time I carried Richard's poem in a pocket near my heart and kept thinking I did not want to go on with life without him. I felt so bereft without him, and I was always terrified he would be killed. The only thing that occupied my mind was the thought of seeing him again. Those thoughts were very raw, and I know Richard would not have approved of them. My heaviness, the weight of my love, had been all too much for him, and yet that poem!

But I have skipped ahead of myself. After the fighting stopped, I left Liu, though she wanted me to stay with her. When I got back to Shanghai, my first thought was to see Sasha, Anya and Shi-shi, then Natalia, Hong, and of course to get my job back with Ladislav.

I went to Anya straight from the boat with my suitcases in hand, not just because of sentiment but also to see whether my apartment was still available. She was overjoyed to see me, said that it was, just as she had promised it would be when I left for Hong Kong. And yet she and Shi-shi were in turmoil themselves, not knowing if they should remain in the city. They had been talking about marriage before the fighting had broken out, and perhaps, they both still wanted it, though I could see Anya's mind was working, and she knew that the Japanese were not going to spare the Chinese anything. I think Shi-shi was worried that in his businesses and properties would be confiscated, and Anya was worried about her destiny and his being intertwined. She said nothing specifically to me about this, but I knew her and from her vague commentary -such as 'Shi-shi thinks the Japanese might confiscate his businesses or his buildings,' I knew what that furrow on her perfect brow meant.

I was worried about her, and all of us, but as she served tea along with the biscuits I had brought, I asked, 'Anya, what about Sasha. Is he in town?'

Anya sank into a chair, though she managed to remain perfectly upright. 'Oh Tanya, you must have known where his sympathies lie.'

'Is he in prison?' I asked suspecting the worst. My anxiety was so great, that I felt my skin burning and prickling.

'Tanya, he went to Yunnan with the communists as soon as he could. All of them left. Writers, poets, film directors, even actors.'

'God knows what he'll find there,' I said.

'I don't know, Tanyushka. I suppose like -minded people,' she said absently.

I must have made some sort of sound indicating a degree of cynicism, because Anya continued, 'They'll need to put aside their differences now, the Communists and Chang, and fight the common enemy.'

'Is that what Shi-shi says?' I asked. 'Because it will be as it was with us in the last war. They'll fight the enemy, and then they'll fall to slaughtering each other. I'm no fan of Chang, but if the other side wins, we'll have to get out of China somehow.'

Anya stared at me wide-eyed as if she never suspected that I could harbor a rational thought, let alone articulate it. 'I know,' was all she said.

'Where will you and Shi-shi go afterward? I mean where in the west can you go with a mixed marriage, Anya? Have you considered that? Will you want him if he is poor? How about when he is old and sick?' Liu's words about Richard were still going around in my mind and provoked me to say the things I did. 'And what will you do? You are not so young anymore, and too old to be a taxi dancer.'

She looked at me blearily before she said, 'Well, you have changed. Now you cut like a knife. I think I liked you better the old way.'

'You always thought I was an idiot,' I said.

She sipped her tea. 'I was envious. You had you aunt and uncle, lessons, love, your art...I had no one, and no talents that I could use. And I knew if I was to ever get anything from life, I would have to get it using my body.'

'It's still a beautiful body,' I joked, and Anya laughed, but I could see she was haunted by all that I had said.

I went to my apartment afterward. A thick layer of dust had settled all over the furniture and the water ran brackish under the tap. I unpacked, bathed and began to clean up. I wondered if I should go to the film studio to see if I could get definitive word on Sasha, perhaps someone would know more than Anya or Shi-shi did. And I wondered if I should check on Richard's house. It was a ridiculous thought, really. His servants, if they were there, would know nothing.

After I cleaned up a bit, I decided to pay a visit to Natalia. I dressed, and taking a small gift of coffee from Hong Kong, made my way there. I arrived at her door, but when she answered, I got a bit of shock, because in the midst of war and suffering Natalia had been transformed by love. She was happy, no longer fat and frumpy but had a fine hour glass figure, and with her hair newly dyed to a rich brown, she looked ten years younger.

'Tanyechka, Tanyeychka!' she fussed over me. I must have looked like death to her, because she looked at me worriedly. She ushered me into her sitting room, made hot herbal tea, and forced me drink it. Her Igor was out playing with a newly formed band.

She thought I was ill and probed me, but soon she surmised that the cause beneath it was Richard.

'Tanya, don't be crazy, people are leaving Manchuko each day, not going there,' she said when she heard where Richard was. I didn't hide much of the truth from her and said he was there to help the Resistance, such as it was.

'The Japanese are both here and there. So what difference will it make where I am?' I asked.

'Tanya, you speak like a child, really,' she said. 'Let's say you go to Harbin. Of course, it's really the only place one can live in Manchuko, how do you think you will find him? If he is working with resistance forces then he is underground. What are you going to do, ask around? Oh, hello, where is Richard?'

'No, but I thought, if I was closer, I would have a better chance of finding him.'

'Manchuria is a big place, Tanya. And while you speak Shanghainese well, it is not intelligible in the north.'

'I know enough to be able to pick it up easily. I've always had a facility for languages.'

'True,' she mused.

'Natalia, I have no work here, and you know the heady days of Shanghai aren't coming back. Stage sets, jewels, clothes-that's done for now. I need a job and I know you have a lot of friends in Harbin still.'

'Tanyechka, it's madness and I won't do it,' she replied, crossing her arms over her ample chest.

But in the end, I wore her down so greatly that she sent a note to her friends who ran a French school in Harbin and they hired me as a teacher. I have Japanese pupils in my class. They are, as I said, a strange mixture, kind one moment but with an air of total superiority the next. They really believe they are a superior race. I don't know how they came to that conclusion. The Chinese are more cultured, have more feeling, and physically are better shaped, taller, and beautiful, yet the Island Dwarves, as the Chinese call the Japanese, treat them with disdain. There is a young girl in my class, who is called Yukiko and is about fourteen years old. She seems different from the rest. They are all invariably diligent, but the rest travel in packs and think the same thoughts. Yukiko is a poet. The other day she very shyly approached my desk after class, as she often does, to ask a question or two, or to ask if she can walk home with me. She said she had translated some of her poems to French, and asked if it would it be too terribly intrusive if I would look them over and correct them. I told her I would be happy to do so.

We walked home together, and she was happy, but not in the manner of ordinary girls. She looks at clouds and leaves silhouetted against the sky and sees patterns there. She is quiet most of the time, then says things like, 'Look teacher, do you see it?' and indicates a flight of birds, or a flowering bush, things which would normally escape my notice. We said goodbye, and I went home, and this is another joke on me, when I think of my beautiful flat in Shanghai, but more of that later.

I undressed and took out my papers, and of course Yukiko's poems. I have to say that I was pleasantly surprised at how mature and full of sorrow they were. All her feelings were tied to nature, the passing of the seasons, and to death and mourning. I wondered who had died that had been close to her and made a mental note to ask her about it. I thought the poems good, but mostly I thought, there is hope for the human race, after all, when it can produce a girl like this.

. . .

189

L.S. TEMMER

Harbin, June 1938

 Something extraordinary happened today when I was at the market. I was picking vegetables when I looked over and saw a woman I thought I recognized. My first impulse was to think it was a case of mistaken identity, just as it had been with the tall Japanese man, but when I looked more closely I saw that it was Mei.

 She glanced over and when she recognized me, her expression became fearful. I surmised at once that it was because she was still with the communists. You often see that look on their faces because they know the Kempetai, the dreaded Japanese secret police, would be the first to arrest them and subject them to horrendous interrogations or execution. I nodded my head very discretely and could see her exhale with relief. I moved on to the next stall, but lingered, allowing her to approach me in a natural fashion. This she did, asking whether the Tai-tai would like some help carrying her purchases home. I agreed and handed over my basket and parcel.

 We walked rapidly, and the whole time I was thinking that if she was a communist she might have word of Sasha. We came to the building where I live, in a drab and dark flat, and went up the stairs. Immediately she looked to see if there was a back staircase off my flat. Seeing there was, she put her finger to her lips, pointed toward it and went out the front door. I thought she would return shortly but when she didn't I made dinner and sat down to grade papers. As I was getting ready for bed, it was quite dark now, I heard a scratching at the back door. I opened it immediately and let her in. She put her finger to her mouth again. I nodded my head and brought a plate from the kitchen with the food I had saved from dinner, surmising that she might return at some point. She looked at me gratefully and fell upon it.

 We waited until the building was utterly still, and then sitting very closely together, we began to talk in whispered voices. She spoke of the Long March of the Red Army in almost mythic terms and I could not really ascertain if she had participated in it herself or had heard the stories second hand, because it was so paramount in her mind that it had acquired an aura of religiosity. She then spoke of their activities in Yunnan and how they were using culture to bring enlightenment to the people through drama, dance, music, literature, and painting. I immediately asked after Sasha using his Chinese name, Fang Shirong, but she shook her head. I knew the Chinese

190

*often changed their names to reflect the changing phases of their lives, so I
described him, adding that he had been a famous film director in Shanghai.
She said she knew of him and had seen him several times, and that he was
well, and beloved by the people for his dramas which reflected the struggles
and endless suffering of the Chinese peasants. I sighed, and said I was happy
to hear he was well.*

*It was only then that I articulated the thought that had been burning in
my mind; if Mei was here in Manchuria, they had sent her for a reason, and
that reason was that she had something to do with the resistance. I had to be
careful not to frighten her, so I asked very carefully, 'Mei, I have a friend, an
Englishman who left Shanghai to organize the pockets of rebels here. Have
you seen or heard of him at all?' I knew she would not want to endanger
herself or her mission, so I added, 'I love him Mei and I thought once he and I
would be married. I came to look for him months ago, but have heard nothing
and know nothing.'*

*Mei looked at me blankly, and I wondered if she had not been convinced
that marriage was something archaic that should be tossed out along with the
rest of the corrupt bourgeois institutions I knew her comrades despised. I then
described what Richard looked like.*

*I had always thought of Mei as the young girl she had been in Shanghai
and so the manner in which she replied surprised me.*

*'Tani, we all knew of your love for this man, all of us in the shop, but this
love of yours was like a sickness.'*

*I must have looked shocked, but she continued. 'You were always so blind
to the things around you. But we loved you, anyway. You were different from
the whites in Shanghai, even the ones who go with Chinese men. It was as if
you were a real person, and you were so good to me and the others. I never
will forget that, and so I will tell you things that I shouldn't.*

*'This man you speak of is not an Englishman but a Russian who has been
sent from Moscow to help us.'*

'I think you must be mistaken,' was my immediate reply.

'No Tani, it is you who are mistaken as you have always been.'

*'What is this man's name?' I asked thinking there had been another mix-
up with identities.*

'He calls himself Rostik, but many call him by his first name, Yuri.'

I felt myself sinking. There was no mistake. Rostik was Russian for Richard and Yuri was George. It took me several minutes to come to my senses, but then I thought, of course, he is an English agent and had infiltrated their cells under the guise of a Russian. It would, of course, make the resistance trust him. I felt calmer instantaneously.

'I see,' I said.

'Do you?' Mei asked. 'Because if, as you say, you have come all this way for him, then I must tell you Comrade Yuri is on a mission in Manchuria. He can't come running here to fulfill your girlish, romantic notions. You are doing nothing for him by being here, and it would only put him in danger to drop his guard if he knew you were pining for him, close by.'

'Mei, how close by?' I asked, but Mei shook her head. 'Please, Mei, anything could happen in wartime. Please tell him about me.'

'This I will not do,' she said. I could see she would not be moved by my pleading.

'Then tell me this. Is he well?' I asked.

'Well enough; as well as can be expected.'

I did not know what this meant and suspected a disease, but she said, 'We all have dysentery and are often ill. The countryside does not agree with city folk.'

I thought carefully to what I might say next. 'If he is ever in trouble or hurt, will you tell him then?' I would have given her a note or a letter under normal circumstances, but knew if she was caught and had it on her person, it would compromise all of us.

'I will tell him then, but I am not always in contact with him, you must know that, and you must know that I am often not aware of everything that is happening with any of us.'

'All right, ' I said. 'That is good enough,' thinking it is not enough at all. 'What can I do for you now? Food, warm clothes? Tell me what you need.'

'Money would be best if you can spare it. That way I can buy what I need as I go along.'

'Of course,' I said, and gave her what I had on hand from the sock in the drawer where I kept my savings.

'Tani,' she said following me, 'that's a very bad hiding place.'

'Well, there won't be anything left, so it's not a problem,' I said.

Mei laughed. 'You were always so generous.' She gave me a hug goodbye. 'If anything happens, I'll tell him. Don't worry.'

When she left I felt loneliness and anxiety threaten to overwhelm me again, even though I knew Richard was alive, as was Sasha.

Harbin, June 1938

There are rumors of something terrible happening here, and I don't know whether to give them credence or not. It is said that the Japanese are rounding up Korean and Chinese civilians against their will to exploit in their brothels.

In Shanghai, since 1932, the Japanese have had such services for their soldiers, but I, and everyone else, had heard that those women were there of their own free will, and well paid, even though they had to service many men per day. The Japanese name for them is Comfort Women. Ever since Nanking, I can't think of their military as anything but barbaric.

I try never to show this attitude towards my pupils. It would be dangerous to do so, but I am often afraid I might somehow inadvertently slip up. Yukiko wants to spend more and more time with me. I think it is normal for a young girl to have a small crush on a sympathetic older woman she admires. After all, that is the way I felt about Liqui. I try always to keep an open mind and an open heart towards her. She is so sensitive and dear. Her father is in Manchuria in some sort of administrative capacity and, I think, though she is not very direct about it, her mother is dead. It would account for her melancholic sensibility.

Yesterday, we went to the park to sketch. She imitates me in all ways, but I have told her to be herself. I don't think she knows what this means, and she seems to see herself in relation to other people only. I told her not to copy my style of drawing but to draw what she sees, and she said that she did not know how to see.

'It is just like all the times you show me the things you notice: leaves, berries, pods, clouds, the things you see as being extraordinary. It is like the things you write about.'

She, then, in a very painstaking way, tried to tell me that Japanese poetry is based on long established convention. I replied that was so, but did she not use those phrases and subtle feelings to convey moods of her very own? She thought about this seriously for a while and then made a sketch of me. I must say I have a very long nose in her eyes! I didn't want to laugh because that would discourage her and so I praised it to the skies.

Afterward when we were walking home, she very shyly indicated that she always wondered what the inside of a Russian church might look like. I knew that she wanted me to take her inside, but I asked, 'What would your father think of that? Would you need his permission?'

Her eyes grew wide and she said, 'My father knows you are my most honored teacher and is well pleased by the progress I am making.'

That was lovely to hear. Perhaps he is one of the ones who is building this place into an industrial powerhouse and not one who rounds up women for sexual slavery, or Chinese peasants to toil in the mines and opium fields. Either way, the Japanese serve themselves only. I wonder if Yukiko sees that. I wonder if she too will change as she grows up.

Harbin, June 1938

I never described how I live here or the school where I teach. In the past, it seemed silly to me to describe things I was already familiar with, but there are older people living here in this building with whom I sometimes speak, and I can tell their memories are often muddled. Time seems to shift for them and they get mixed up. Some events seem very close in their minds and others far away, and besides there are huge gaps in their memories. In my rush to pack, I left all my diaries of the old days with Liu. I hope I'll see both her and them once more. I think those heady days will never return, and I would like to remember them and have my sketches with me.

The building where I live is a Russian neo-Baroque confection, and I mean that in the most complimentary way. It always reminds me of golden slabs of cake, layered between thick cream. Juliette balconies front the building, and frosting and curlicues top it off. I walk up two flights of stairs - wide, enormous, marbled, and cracked, to my flat. Inside it is spacious with tall ceilings, and thus will be hard to keep warm in winter, no doubt. To this end, the windows are narrow and tall, and I often feel there is not enough light, just the stuff which falls in thin shafts in the afternoon and morning. I am renting it furnished from a woman who has married an Australian and is living in Macao at present. It's oppressive due to her taste. The hard furniture is heavy, Russian, burled, and dark. The sofas are scratchy horse hair. It is not enough that the light is poor, but she has further blocked it by adding damask curtains and lace sheers. I have packed her doilies, antimacassars, and horrid little statuettes away safely. Still there is the ever present vitrine, filled not with books but with repellent china - worsted and gilded, unusable, and for decoration only. I miss my things but then remind myself that I am here to find Richard.

Outside, now, I hear the clomping of horses pulling carts though there are trams and automobiles here, and all sorts of modern things. This summer, the Russian girls wore such short shorts for sunbathing at the Sungari River and on Taiyang Islet that even I was surprised. They are tall, well developed, and often very blond. Japanese men seem obsessed with them. I suppose it is because of the novelty of long straight legs, pale skin, and yellow hair. I see them walking out together, Japanese and Russians, sometimes. It's not always for money. I don't know if I ever could. They are our occupiers.

Harbin, July 1938

Something has happened. Yukiko had not been coming to school, and I had not had word of her. Finally, I went to the director, a Japanese, who has taken over the helmsmanship from its Russian founders, to ask if he had any news of her.

You really don't know what these people are trying to say unless they are barking orders. He was so circumspect that I began to read double meanings into his assurances that she was only out with a cold. But there was something about his expression that suggested it was more than that.

I knew that at Yukiko's house they would probably consider me rude for stopping by without an invitation, but of course, I could get away with it simply because I was a barbarian in their eyes. I knew where she lived, and I packed her lessons and went over there.

When I arrived at the house, a free standing villa, the servant wanted to bar my entry despite my explanation of who I was. As I was protesting,

Yukiko's father came to the door. One word from him, the servant backed off, and I was past the threshold.

Yukiko's father, Tanaka Hiro, knew who I was immediately and introduced himself. He addressed me in Russian, and I surmised that he must have been in the diplomatic service. He insisted I stay to tea and led the way through the hall to the salon. The house was not at all Oriental, neither architecturally nor in terms of decor, yet it is sparely furnished with exquisite pieces of furniture - Russian and French with Chinese art and sculpture. Somehow, it all seemed to hold together beautifully, and I thought he must be a man of rare taste and sensibility.

When he opened the doors to the salon and waited for me to pass, I knew he was international in his way of thinking, since the Japanese do not have that custom, but generally rush past women to get through doors first. The salon was furnished very formally in the second empire style. A tall man was sitting at the edge of an ornate desk, smoking. I thought it very un -Japanese and was surprised until he came forward to shake hands with me, and I realized it was the same man I had mistaken for Sasha on the street.

Tanaka introduced him, this time in French, as Tamura Nobuaki. It was clear that though Tanaka, a short energetic bull necked man, was in command, Tamura had the, I hate to say this, class and elegance Tanaka lacked. I suddenly wondered who was responsible for furnishing the villa. Surely not Tanaka. It was a lingering conceit of mine, after all, it had been my profession, and I had always thought that houses were expressions of the self.

Tanaka rang for tea, and indicated I should take my place on a settee. Tamura joined me- he has a very louche way of moving, and sat in a swan chair opposite. He made no secret of his interest in me, but it was framed in a most ironic way, as if he was making light of it, and of himself. Tanaka, of course, ignored this.

I said nothing of my suspicions concerning Yukiko's illness and made polite conversation taking Tamura's lead. Eventually, I mentioned that I had brought some French books for Yukiko, just to stimulate her while she was recovering and so that she would not fall behind in class. Her father thanked me profusely for this, and so, knowing it was wrong, I said that I would stop by from time to time to deliver more papers until she was ready to return to school.

'Of course, you must,' Tamura backed me, and her father agreed with a curt nod of his head.

When tea was over I thanked my host, conveyed my best wishes for the recovery of his daughter's health and left. No sooner was I out the front gate than I heard steps behind me. It was Tamura, grinning like the proverbial Cheshire cat. He had decided to accompany me home, and since it was a pleasant day outside, we began walking.

Since he seemed so modern, or at least had pretensions to it, I decided to risk saying what I really thought instead of playing their social game.

'I am afraid that Miss Yukiko may have more than just a summer cold,' I said.

Tamura instantly sobered up, 'I am afraid it might be so, Miss Zhukova. Her father says nothing, but I think he may be worried. His wife died of tuberculosis and it has always haunted him.'

'I see,' I said, but the thing I saw was that I liked him this way when he was not playing the rake, and I had a very comfortable feeling, one of camaraderie, just walking alongside him. I could tell that he sensed it as well, though he said nothing, and we continued to walk silently side by side.

I finally said, 'Do you think he would mind if I keep bringing lessons for the little girl?'

Tamura considered and replied, 'I will speak to him, and I am sure it will be very good for the girl. She is so terribly lonely here, you see.'

I thought to say, as I am, but then I would have to say more about myself, of Shanghai, and perhaps he would ask me why I was here, and I would be forced to lie that a job had come up and I had to take it since I was out of work.

He accompanied me to my apartment building and then said he would like to take me to tea. Before I knew it I had accepted, and we set the date for the following afternoon.

Harbin, July 1938

It was raining and Tamura came for me in a car. I asked where we were going, and he said it was his favorite place and that he hoped I would like it as well. We drove for a while and then arrived at a round garden gate. He opened it and we went through a Japanese garden with ornamental shrubs and raked pebbles that mimicked the earth and nature in a most charming and intimate way. We came to a true Japanese teahouse and while he slid open the shoshi screen, I slipped off my shoes. The house consisted of only the one room, and since it was still warm outside, he left the door open to frame the garden view.

I knelt as I had seen them do, but he said I should make myself comfortable, so I brought my legs from underneath and sat as demurely as I could. There was one painting hanging on the wall opposite, and one shelf below it with an ancient Korean vase holding a single flower. While I admired this, a testament to his exquisite Japanese refinement, Tamura made tea the traditional way, as if it was an art form. Normally I would have sneered inwardly at the pretense of this high culture while the Japanese had shown themselves to be nothing but the basest of brutes, but Tamura carried it off beautifully, with such practiced perfection that I lost myself in it; the view of the garden and the softly falling rain. In fact, I had never felt so at peace.

Somehow, I had begun to think of him as a friend, so I said, 'It's strange but when I first saw you on the street, I assumed you were Chinese.'

Tamura smiled and said, 'I have had Chinese ancestresses. In the olden days they married into my family.'

'Ah, then,' I said, 'You are from an important family, except here in Manchuria, you are your own man?'

'Something like that,' he said.

'What did you want to do in life before this all began?' I asked.

'I wanted to be an art dealer,' he said.

'Really?' I laughed, and spoke about my work in Shanghai.

'Why did you come here, after all that?' he asked.

I was going to tell him how the office had been closed and I needed to find work, but then I found myself saying, 'I fell in love with a man. He left me. I heard he was in Harbin, and I followed him, but I have not been able to find him, and perhaps he does not want to be found.'

'You said that with such sadness,' he commented.

'Did I?' I think then I became a bit frightened that he would ask me about the man I had followed and I would be forced to evade his questions. I don't know if my mood shifted or if he sensed my thoughts, but he said, quite frankly, 'You know, we don't always need to talk.'

Oh no, I thought, now he'll try to make love to me. Instead, he said, 'Sometimes words are not important. It is just pleasant to be in someone's company and to be still.'

I thought he was absolutely right. We drank tea in silence and watched the garden in the rain.

Harbin, July 1938

I have been going to drop lessons off at Yukiko's house for two weeks now, but they have not allowed me to see her. It is strange to be without her, I have no connection to my other pupils and do not like them very much.

I have seen much of Tamura since the time in the teahouse. I feel strange about it, but then I have been so very lonely here. I seem to have little connection to the Russians. I am afraid of their intimacy and of confiding in them about Richard, and mostly I am afraid of their gossipy betrayal afterward.

I asked Tamura why he seemed so different from the rest of them, and why they were so harsh. He said it was the way of Bushido, the samurai code of honor that was being perverted in modern Japan and twisted for militaristic purposes.

'It is all about death now,' Tamura said sadly. He seemed not to want to dwell on it, and so I asked no more questions not wanting to upset him.

Tamura is both modern, in the European sense, but very steeped in Japanese tradition, and the way he talks about things makes them sound so pure and lovely, particularly about the way of the artist and how long one has to practice to reach those states where material will flow from one's pen or one's brush. We have gone back to the tea house several times, but he has never invited me to his house. It makes me wonder what he may be hiding. Perhaps I am being unreasonably suspicious and only suspect him because I am hiding things myself.

· · ·

199

Harbin, August 1938

Today, as usual, I brought Yukiko's lessons to her. I am always ushered into the hallway by the servant who takes the material and reports on her condition, and I believe, is always instructed to say that she is improving.

Today when I arrived, the servant had me wait until Tanaka came out to greet me. He seemed eager to speak to me and ushered me into his study. He told me then that Yukiko's condition was not as good as he had hoped and that he would be sending her back to Japan for treatment. This was all reported in the most matter of fact way, as if we were dealing with a minor ailment.

He then asked if I would like to see Yukiko, since she had expressed that wish herself. I replied that of course I would be happy to see her and to wish her a bon voyage. In fact, I dreaded to think in what state I might find her.

Tanaka ushered me upstairs to the last room off the landing and held the door open. There was a faint odor of tar in the air that immediately recalled the hospital my mother had died in. The room was deliberately kept dark, and a nurse who was sitting at Yukiko's bedside immediately rose, and throwing a towel over a bloody basin, removed it from the room.

Yukiko was small, frail, and yellow against the bed sheets. She had lost much weight and appeared to be sinking into the bed itself. I took the nurse's chair and reached for her hand. It was so small and weak, but she managed to return a bit of pressure when she heard my voice. Tanaka stood to the side of the bed, while I talked to her of small things, what was happening at school, and of the things we had done together, and how much I missed her companionship. Then I began to lie and tell her all the things we would do when she recovered, the Orthodox church, trips to the beach, and to the park to sketch. I told her of the things we would see there, and then I quoted her poems back to her, because I had memorized them, and told her I was looking at the world through her eyes now.

She was very quiet and at last, she said, 'Arigato, Tani-san.'

I knew she would never make the voyage to Japan, and she knew it as well. I leaned over and gave her a kiss on the forehead. Tanaka led the way out of the room. He was moved but terribly constrained. I said nothing fearing that he might show me his true face, and perhaps begin to weep, which would embarrass both of us.

'Thank you for this, Miss Zhukova,' he said at the door.

'Good-bye Mr. Tanaka,' I said, not knowing whether to say more.

He closed the heavy door behind me, but the heaviness I felt followed me. Her life had been too short, too fleeting, and was going to end before she had really lived.

Harbin, August 1938

Yukiko was cremated in a Buddhist ceremony. Tamura informed me afterward saying that it had been a small and private event. Then he gave me an exquisite scroll inscribed with a sutra that read: In death, she has become the Buddha. He said it was a gift from Tanaka.

All the feelings I had been repressing suddenly washed over me, and I began to cry silently. I knew the Japanese disliked public displays of emotion, but I could not staunch my tears. Tamura stood very close to me and said, 'Please Tani-san, don't grieve. There is no death, only the passage from one state to another.'

'Oh, Tamura-san, I am crying selfishly for the loss of the girl and my own loneliness.'

'Tani-chan, you needn't be alone,' he said. And now he was standing very close to me.

'I can't,' I said simply, and I do not know how he interpreted that, whether he thought it was because of the man I still loved, or because of the fact that he was who he was, a Japanese, but he simply said, 'I want to show you my house. I think you will like it.'

'Now?' I asked.

'Yes, I think now would be a good time.'

'All right. Yes,' I agreed.

We drove the usual route, and I said, 'But this is the way to the tea house.'

'Wait,' he replied.

Instead of the usual garden gate in the rural alee that we would always go through, we drove around an enormous park and through a formal wrought iron gate. I knew from the gate itself that the house would be quite grand. I was not disappointed. It was a lovely house, the kind that had been built on Russian estates, Palladian and palatial.

'The owners have gone to America,' he said, reading my mind. 'I bought the house from them.'

'It's beautiful,' I said.

'Yes, I think so too. I rarely bring people here,' he said.

'I'm honored.'

He parked in the circular drive and led the way into the house. The staircase was majestic but had been left barren of furnishings and color. Somehow, that emptiness made it seemed all the more ethereal.

'Come through,' he said. 'I want you to see the cupola.'

The walls beneath it were white, but the dome had been painted in that elusive shade of blue common to the north, and decorated with trompe l'oeil reliefs. It was lovely, charming, and incredibly soothing all at once.

'I love this, and the blue!' I said.

'I do as well. Let's go to the loggia, we can see the garden from there. '

I followed him, noting the house had not yet been furnished. 'What will you do to the house?' I asked.

'I was thinking about filling it with all sorts of things, one day one way, the next another. But really I think I like it as is, a blank canvas.'

'Yes, I know what you mean,' I said. 'That way, you can always keep redoing it in your mind.'

'Yes,' he agreed, but I wondered if he hadn't considered that Japan would one day lose Manchuko.

We emerged into the loggia, and as he said, the open arches looked outward to the lawn and gardens, now overgrown and romantic in their rusticity. He had placed simple oriental style divans and low tables in the loggia, and as always, his taste was impeccable, the cushions, oyster white shot silk, and the pillows, the subtlest shade of pink. There were flowering orange trees in the corners of the loggia and the effect was romantic and charming.

Then he said something odd. 'Tani-san, I can sense how you feel about Japanese, but we are not all the same. And I think you loved the little girl.'

'Tamura-san, I'm getting to know you,' I replied.

'Yes, that is all that can be expected,' he said.

'You talk of the things that interest you, but you never talk about yourself,' I said.

'Neither do you,' he replied. 'Tani-chan, it is not always so important to know everything about a person, or to spill one's guts as you Europeans are so fond of doing. The only thing that is important is the feeling tone and the happiness we experience when we are together.'

There was a lull before I asked, 'Are you married?'

'Yes, but we have lived apart for some time. She is in Japan,' he replied.

'Children?'

'Two, a boy and a girl. My wife's family is very powerful, very rich. My children live with them.'

'And what did you do to merit that?' I asked.

'Many things, none of which I want to be reminded of.'

'Why me, Tamura? Why am I here?'

'Because you are different too. And you are beautiful.'

I started to laugh. 'Well, I know you generally have excellent taste.'

He laughed with me. 'And you, Tani-san?'

I knew he wanted me to say something about the way I felt about him. I wanted to say I felt peaceful and relaxed whenever we were together, but instead, inexplicably, I said, 'You look like a man I know.'

'The one you are looking for?'

'No. This is someone else.'

'Ah,' he said lifting his brow and smiling.

'He is Chinese and a film director. I haven't seen him since the invasion of Shanghai.'

'You loved him a little, Tani-chan?'

'I loved him too little, Tamura-san, though he is the better man of the two.'

'Oh, Tani, the human heart is inexplicable, isn't it?'

'Yes, I suppose it is.'

Just then, a silent manservant came out with a fruity cocktail. It was so delicious and refreshing that I slurped it down straight away. Tamura laughed and said he admired my appetite. I knew the way Japanese women ate, always taking tiny ladylike servings, always pretending not to be hungry, but I didn't care.

'Stay for dinner, Tani-chan,' he said.

'Yes, of course,' I replied.

A table had been set in a small room off the loggia with splendid china and silver that I suspected had come with the house. The room was painted pale green but was otherwise bare save a pier glass between the windows, a statue of the Bodhisattva, and two potted trees that were encircled by purple orchids.

His cook served a formal Chinese meal, complete with Peking duck. While we waited for it to be brought to the table, Tamura asked, 'The man you love, what is he like?'

I did not want to say he was English, for how would I explain his presence in Manchuria, but my own people had examples of the type, so I said, 'He is a man out of Pushkin, out of Lermontov.'

'A Byronic hero who rejected your love. Tatiana,' he said, referring to Pushkin's heroine.

'You know them?'

'I love those books, Onegin and Hero of our Time.'

'And you perhaps identify with them?' I asked.

Tamura laughed but said nothing more.

'I am not so disciplined as that Tatiana,' I said, musing aloud. 'She had the capacity to love but the strength to let go.'

'You were made for love, Tani-chan. Anyone with eyes can see that.'

'But I am rather luckier at cards, Tamura-san.'

'Ha-ha,' he laughed, 'As am I.'

We finished dinner and his driver took me home.

Harbin, September 1938

Nothingness, bleak as could be. School and pupils dull. Nothing to do. No word from Tamura after that lovely dinner. Well, what can be said about that? Perhaps it is better that way. What am I supposed to do in any case, drift from man to man? It's all too absurd. Yet, I am too alone, and I miss his company. Oh, I do not want to allow myself to think this way!

. . .

Harbin, September 1938

    Today Mei came up to me in the market. 'Be ready. I will contact you soon,' was all she said in passing, out of range of most people's hearing. She was gone before I had the chance to ask her a thing. Now I am terrified Richard has been hurt, and I am barely able to get through the day since that is all that occupies my mind.

    Tamura telephoned. He had to go away on business unexpectedly. He wants to have dinner, but I am afraid of missing Mei. I thought of saying I was unwell, but I am a poor liar. I accepted, thinking if Richard was in the area he could at least wait a few hours until I returned. I was convinced that Mei would come late at night for me, in any case.

Harbin, September 1938

    Tamura sent his car. We had never had a formal dinner and he had never seen me out of my usual beige gabardine suites. I felt, given the circumstances, the skin baring gowns that were so popular not too long ago would be inappropriate. I paired a long black skirt with a closed neck long sleeved black blouse and put Richard's pin at shoulder height. I still had Liu's gold cuffs and those three things were the only ornaments or color I wore. My hair was parted on the side pinned at the nape and softly curling.

    It felt strange to be dressed up once more, almost as if I had forgotten what it had been like. For a moment I had the fleeting thought: what if I just gave up on Richard? What would it be like to have a normal life and not to suffer from constant anxiety or fear? To not wonder if I would be loved one day and rejected the next. I felt my love passing, and it was as if all that had been holding me up drained out of my body. I felt free.

    The car took me to his house. This time, the table was set under the cupola and Tamura had had the entire room illuminated by candelabra. He drew out a chair for me, and I saw a package wrapped in the same blue as the painted cupola next to my plate. I sat down.

    'Should I open it?' I asked.

    'Yes, of course,' he replied.

    I undid the package. Inside was a small but exquisitely carved wooden statue of Kwan Yin, the Buddhist goddess of mercy, who hears the cries of all those who are in pain all over the world.

'It's beautiful,' I said. 'Thank you for this.'

'I thought you would appreciate it,' he said.

'I do. And all the rest of it,' I added, indicating the room.

'I like you Tani-chan, very much,' he said.

'And I you, as well,' I said.

We ate, talked, laughed and when I left, he touched my back very lightly. I only remembered later that it was customary to profess one's liking or love in Japan prior to engaging in an authentic relationship.

Harbin, September 1938

They came for me. First, Mei signaled me in the market. I picked my vegetables out and paid for them. When I was finished, a Chinese dressed as a merchant approached me purporting to have some gold and jade earrings to sell at a good price if I followed him. Walking rapidly, he led me down a maze of alleys that were so dark and narrow that I knew no one could follow - and no one did. We found ourselves on the outskirts of town and then got into a waiting car and drove for almost an hour until we stopped in front of a warehouse. The day was bleak, the atmosphere oppressive and laden with the portent of rain. For a few moments, I was convinced I had made a mistake following this man and would probably pay for it with my life. My heart was beating irregularly and I began to sweat.

The warehouse was dark and seemingly abandoned. The man looked around and feeling for something in the floor, unearthed a trap door. I followed him through a tunnel that led outdoors to a forested area that normally I would have stopped to admire if not for the circumstances. We walked briskly to a nearby village and uphill on narrow steps, chiseled into the earth, to a peasant's house that stood higher on the ridge than the rest of the dwellings. I knew that if this was Richard's hiding place he could see anyone coming from miles off and be able to escape easily into the woods.

I was not able to make myself understood to my guide, and I still did not know whether Richard had been hurt or not. I was terribly anxious about the condition in which I would find him.

The guide ushered me into the house. I could not immediately make anything out in the gloom, but presently my eyes adjusted, and I saw Richard and two Chinese men, one dressed as a worker, the other in fatigues. They were bowed over some maps, Richard sitting at the table, the other two bending over him.

I stood to the side and waited. Richard looked up and my guide and the two other Chinese left immediately. I was so nervous I had once again begun to shake and could not control it.

'Oh Tanya,' he said, coming over to me and holding me by my upper arms. He knew he had to steady me until I stopped trembling, but I could not, and began to sob.

'There, there. Everything is fine now,' he said rubbing my back as if I was a small child.

I don't know what I was expecting, perhaps some grand show of passion, but this was something different, more puppy-like, and more innocent. He held me for a long time. There was nothing sexual to it, only the warm communion of two beings.

'Richard, I've been so scared all these months since you disappeared. You don't know what it is like for me, not knowing. The only thing I had to hold on to was hope and your poem,' I said.

'But in that poem I told you not to follow me, didn't I?' he said very quietly. And now he was holding my chin up between his fingers to raise my head, but I could not look at him and turned my head away.

'You must have known Richard, even when you wrote it, that I would.'

Richard sighed. 'I had hoped not, actually.' We were standing close now, but he was no longer holding me. I should have said something tender and conciliatory but instead I blurted, 'Richard, I'm not stupid, if you called me here now, it isn't because you had a burning desire to see me after all these months. I know what the Resistance does here, blowing up rail tracks, and interrupting supply lines. So you are either going into an extremely dangerous action from which you fear you won't return, or you need me to do something for you.'

'There is nothing like killing the moment, Tanya,' Richard said ruefully.

'Ah, Richard. I know I was always too direct for you, in so many ways. So what is it?'

Richard paused, then walked around to his desk and sat down, very deliberately. 'We know that you are friends with Tamura Nobuaki. This man is the direct liaison between Tanaka and Tokyo. Whatever directives pass from the leadership in Japan to Tanaka go through Tamura.'

'So what are you saying, you expect Tamura to share those secrets with me? He, too, is far from stupid.'

'Women can be extremely persuasive. And Tamura has a weakness for beauty, particularly in women.'

I felt my soul falling away from me, following a long and precipitous drop. 'Ooooh, Richard, my darling, you are so tender and warm. So loving that you would suffer me to become intimate with another man to aid your cause.' I was burning with anger now and longed to shout at him and pummel him with my fists, but I knew that was merely a reaction to the pain he was causing me.

'I never said that, Tanya.'

'But if I had to go that far, you would not be opposed to it.'

'Tanya there are greater considerations than our private lives. The Japanese might conceivably win the war if we don't act.'

'So what is that to you? Those hypocrites in London will strike an alliance with them that will be of mutual benefit to both, eventually, when it is all fought out.'

'I don't think you are seeing the greater picture. New global alliances are being drawn up. The world is in a perilous state, and if we leave it to its own machinations, we will end up with the likes of Hitler and Tojo. I needn't tell you what that would look like. You yourself know how the Japanese have conducted themselves in Korea and in Nanking. And we have reports of terrible goings on in Germany. Concentration camps for dissidents and euthanasia of undesirables are par for the course. No one can afford to sit on the sidelines now. I'm not asking you to sleep with him, but you can be close. And you can keep your eyes and ears open. If you can't, you can't. I will understand that, but anything you may learn or overhear could be of importance to us.'

His words were calm, rational and understanding, but his tone said something else altogether, and I thought, if I don't do what you want, even the little love you have given me will be taken away. I detested myself for my

THE LENS OF DESIRE

weakness, for having given my power away to him in exchange for the crumbs he was willing to throw in my direction, but I knew that horrible feeling of aloneness had returned, and I dreaded the prospect of facing life without him.

'I don't know, Richard. You want an answer now. I can't make that decision on the spot.' I had just realized that he was asking for something even worse than becoming intimate with Tamura, he was asking me to possibly risk my life. True, Tamura was attracted to me, but that would not stop him from dealing harshly with a spy.

'You don't have to decide now. Someone will contact you in a few days. You can give us your answer then.'

I lifted my brows and exhaled. 'What now, Richard?'

'Stay with me.'

'For how long?'

'Tonight and tomorrow.'

I had so little pride when it came to him, and the only thing I wanted was that closeness which had made me feel so alive and connected with the universe. For a moment, I thought, I have felt God in that one act. Something in Richard evoked it. He awakened my heart, but even more than that, he opened me to direct experience of that numen. I have felt it also while creating art, but not as intensely. What if I could fill myself with it and not need him anymore? And is all I really wanted from him? I didn't understand all the jumbled thoughts and feelings that were moving through me.

'Richard, it would only confuse me and afterward I would be so weak, so weak, that I would do anything just to keep your love. I can't afford to be like that now. Please call the guide. I'll have an answer for you when your man contacts me.'

Richard's eyebrows shot up. Clearly, he was surprised by my answer, though he managed to say he understood. There was an awkward silence between us until he rose from the desk to embrace me.

'I won't tell you that I love you, because you would no doubt consider it manipulative,' Richard said.

'Tell me anyway. I enjoy having illusions,' I replied.

Richard laughed, but I could see he was disappointed by my remark.

'Don't worry, Richard. I'm going to let you off the hook.' I placed my hand on his chest and pushed him away slightly.

Richard called for the guide, and we stood awkwardly side by side until he arrived. I could feel Richard's presence in the doorway, watching me, but I walked away without a backward glance.

Harbin, September 1938

Tamura invited me to his house again. He said he had a surprise. I was driven there and taken to the loggia by a servant. Tamura was waiting and showed me the table he had set up with inks and quills. He said he wanted to show me his calligraphy and to see what mine might look like as well.

I don't know why this made me so happy, but it did, and I was able to put Richard out of my mind. I watched Tamura as he demonstrated how it was done. At once, I sensed that which I had felt with Richard was also moving through Tamura as he worked. There was a sense of at-one-ment, which guided his actions, and there was no striving only a state of pure being. The result was incredibly vigorous, even to my untrained eye.

'You try now, Tani-san,' he said.

'I don't know kanji script, Tamura-san,' I explained.

'It is all right. Normally the student learns by copying the teacher until it is done correctly, but you may use Chinese script or draw a picture if you like.'

'I'll try,' I said, laughing, and doubting if I could get it right.

Tamura prepared the ink stone for me, saying I could learn to do it later myself. I thought he seemed extraordinarily keen to see what I would come up with. I remembered the character Yukiko had shown me for 'write'. I took a deep breath in, and exhaling, tried to clear my mind. Though I saw the script in my mind, what emerged from my brush looked more like a stylized ginkgo tree.

'It's actually quite beautiful!' I exclaimed, and Tamura just laughed. I don't know what he must have thought of my childlike enthusiasm or my childish attempts, but he seemed to enjoy himself watching me make a mess.

We spent the afternoon playing and joking. It felt wonderful after the encounter I had had with Richard.

We then sat down to tea and Tamura then told me for the first time he had grown up in the United States and in Brazil where his father had been a diplomat.

'I didn't know that, but it would explain a lot about you and your manner,' I said. 'How did you like it?'

'Ah, I loved Brazil. That's where I acquired all my lazy pleasure loving ways.'

'How old were you then?' I asked

'Six through thirteen in the States. Thirteen through twenty in Brazil,' he said.

'What did you love most about it?'

'I loved Bahia. The lazy sultry days under the sun, the beaches and plantations, the churches and Portuguese tiles, my crazy friends, the mulattas, the gambling parlors, staying up all night to dawn without a care in the world.'

'You had a lot of freedom, much more than you have now,' I commented.

'Yes, I have certain obligations which my family and country have imposed on me,' he said.

'You don't want to be here, do you?'

Tamura laughed. 'I was just thinking how nice it would be for me to show you Brazil.'

'Winter will be coming soon,' I said absently.

'Yes, your first in Harbin. It can get cold here, Tani-chan. Perhaps we can take a boat, go somewhere south, and get away from all this.'

'You make it sound so easy,' I said.

'It can be, if you'd like it to be.'

'Oooooh Tamura-san, you are tempting me,' I joked.

'Are you still thinking about that man?' he asked.

'Sometimes,' I replied, 'but mostly I think I made a grave mistake with him.'

'Ah well, I know all about that. Let's do go away,' he said.

'Tamura-san, there's a war on and you are my enemy,' I said, but couldn't keep myself from smiling.

'Yes, of course,' he laughed. 'I have a meeting tonight, but let's do something tomorrow.'

The weekend was coming up and I agreed.

Harbin, September 1938

Saturday morning, Tamura rang and said he had a surprise for me, but that I needed to wear sturdy trousers and boots. I thought perhaps we were going to go for a hike in the countryside and agreed readily. I enjoyed the tranquil greenness of the north, so different from the muggy heat and horrid smells of Shanghai, but had had no real opportunity to explore the countryside.

When I arrived at his house, Tamura, was waiting in front with two fine horses saddled for riding. I laughed and said, 'Tamura-san, I have not been on a horse since I was a child.'

Tamura smiled and said, 'They say you never really forget. It will all come back to you.'

'I hope so,' I quipped, though I was worried I was not up to it.

I breathed into the horse's nostrils as my grandfather had taught me to do upon making their acquaintance, and waited for his out breath, then patted and nibbled at his mane a bit before Tamura helped me up.

I needn't have worried. My gelding was mild and steady, and Tamura had chosen an easy trail. When we stopped to admire a vista, Tamura said, 'I remembered you said how much you felt at home on your grandfather's estate and how much you said you loved his horses.'

I did not recall saying anything like that, but we had chatted about all sorts of things in a completely aimless way during the course of our friendship, so I thought I had forgotten and thanked him for being so thoughtful and kind.

When we returned to Tamura's, he said he would have a lie down before the evening's festivities. I wasn't sure what he meant by festivities and asked, but he only laughed and said it was another surprise.

'Tamura-san, I have to go home to change,' I said, since I was covered in horse drool and sweat.

'Tani-san, there is a third surprise for you. The servant will show you to your quarters, if you want to stay. Don't worry, it's in a different wing from my own,' he added.

'I'm not worried,' I said, despite myself.

Tamura smiled and said he would see me in ninety minutes or so.

I was led to a separate wing at the end of which was a guest room, equipped with a bath. The room itself was tasteful and done in shades of pale grey and lavender with art deco furniture. Laid out on the bed was a gorgeous kimono of the furisode type in blue, green and white.

Stripping off my soiled clothes, I ran the bath. A robe and slippers had been provided, and afterward, I put them on while I contemplated the kimono.

Japanese women tended to be long waisted and short legged with small busts, and since I was the opposite, I knew that I couldn't possibly wear the outfit the way it was intended. I put on the haneri, which was of a lovely white embossed silk. It fit like a gown, and to it I added white tabi socks and sandals. Then I folded the obi like a sash and tied it once around my waist, leaving it hanging. I put the furisode over it and left it open like a robe. It looked quite regal, and I hoped Tamura would understand that I was not wearing it in any particularly dissolute way but as a modern Western woman would.

I swept my hair half up and left half hanging, and tucked in the hair ornament he had left on the dressing table. I put on lipstick and perfume, and checking the time, went downstairs. I stopped on the landing in front of a looking glass to admire the robe, and I couldn't help feel both happy to be dressing up again, remembering how it used to please me, and completely frivolous for harboring such thoughts in such terrible times.

Tamura was dressed in a silver grey kimono. He smiled and nodded his head, 'Very creative, Tani-chan.' He took my arm and we went into room that was arranged in the Japanese style with shoji screens and tatami mats. A Japanese hostess in full kimono greeted us, and slid open the door. As we sipped saki, a range of female entertainers danced and played various instruments for our entertainment. It was lovely, and memorable, and the sound of the koto was quite haunting.

While a dance was in progress, Tamura, who was sitting quite close, quietly said, 'Tani-chan, spend the night.'

'I'm not ready yet, Tamura-san. I'm sorry,' I added.

He seemed to have anticipated my answer because it did not at all spoil *his mood. We continued to talk and laugh. When the evening ended, I said I would go upstairs to change, but he said the kimono was a gift, and there was no need. A servant brought my clothes, wrapped in a cloth bundle, along with my handbag and the driver took me home.*

It was quite the most wonderful evening I had spent in a very long time.

Harbin, September 1938

That glow did not last long. One of Richard's men approached me at the market, pretending to have duck eggs for sale. I looked over the eggs in his basket, and said I was not interested. He understood my answer well.

I don't know what Richard will make of it. I am sure he will write me off as a frivolous woman who cares more for dresses and parties than she does about the state of the world. Perhaps he would see me as a collaborator with the Japanese occupation, or as one of those women who has sold her services in exchange for good times without a second thought. Yet how can I do what he asks? Tamura is good to me, though I realize that he may be merely bored in Manchuria and see me as a challenge. If he wanted a woman, he is certainly rich and handsome enough to attract any number of beauties.

I don't want to be in this position at all!

Harbin, September 1938

A most unexpected thing has occurred. I was asleep when drunken revelers came down the street, an entire lot of them, despite the curfew. I peered out the window, but the police were nowhere to be seen, and I went back to bed, unable to get back to sleep.

I then heard a clicking at the back door and the sound of floorboards creaking in the corridor. I jumped out of bed at once, grabbing a candle stick, which was an absurd choice of weapon, now that I look back on it.

The bedroom door opened and even before I saw the outline of the silhouette, I recognized Richard's distinctive scent, something between fur and herb that I had only been dimly aware of before. I put down the candle stick and threw a shawl over my shoulders. Richard quickly crossed the room and taking my hand, guided me to sit on the bed. He sat very close to me and whispered, 'I had to see you again.'

'Those men, the revelers in the street, they came with you? There's going to be an action of some kind, isn't there?'

'They are causing a diversion but you need not know the rest. I wanted to say, Tanya- because I may never get the chance to say it again- I do love you, and I am sorry for having asked you to spy on Tamura. It was foolish and selfish for me even to consider asking you to endanger yourself. You were quite right to react as you did.'

'Richard, I did not refuse because of the danger but because Tamura has been good to me. Sometimes human considerations should be put above those of borders.'

Richard raised his brows and contemplated this for a moment before exhaling. 'They'll be coming back this way soon, Tanya, and I'll have to go.'

'What should I say, Richard? To say, don't go will exasperate you, and to say be careful is absurd.'

'Don't say anything.' He put his arm around my shoulders and buried his face in my hair, as if he was inhaling the entirety of my being. Somehow, the intimacy of this tender gesture seemed more imbued with meaning than anything that had passed between us before. He kissed the top of my head several times in succession, and then my face.

The revelers were back in the street now, and he rose to leave. I went with him to the rear entrance. Even in the narrow corridor, he did not let go of me, nor did he remove his arm from my waist. Before the door, he kissed me fully on the mouth, pressing his whole body into mine. And then he was gone, disappearing into the night.

I had not wanted my feelings for him to reawaken, yet now that he was gone, I felt that a vital part of me had been removed.

Harbin, September 1938

The resistance has blown one of the main supply lines leading out of Harbin. There are rumors all over town about it. Some say the Japanese have arrested all the saboteurs, some say they got away, and some say they were shot dead. I don't know what to believe. I don't know if Richard is alive or not. The Japanese have not reported it in their newspapers. Soon they will repair the track. I wonder what the point was. Japanese morale is as good as it ever was. And supplies get to their troops in various other ways each day.

Harbin, September 1938

I've had news at the marketplace. Richard is alive and safe in the countryside.

Harbin, September 1938

After the incident, I did not hear from Tamura for days. I assumed he was busy with his duties whatever they might have been at this time. And yet this was terrible for me to contemplate. Tamura has been the kindest of men and yet he and Richard are enemies. I have great difficulty accepting this.

Tamura called today and asked me to come to dinner this weekend. He said he missed me.

Harbin, September 1938

When I arrived, Tamura seemed unusually subdued. He had dark shadows under his eyes, and I knew that the week had taken its toll on him. I said I had heard about the incident and had assumed he, like all the other Japanese in the administration, were preoccupied with it.

'Tani-chan, please never ask me about my work. My home is my haven, and you are a lovely break from the world and its madness.'

'I understand Tamura-san. I really do,' I replied.

'Come see what I've done in here,' he said a little more cheerfully and led me to a little octagonal room that he must have transformed in the interim, since it was filled with mirrors and gilded brackets for blue and white pottery. It was very Russian in feel and reminiscent, in a very small and most charming way, of some of Catherine the Great's rooms.

The servant came in with chilled champagne, and we sat on a settee that once had been gilded but was now flaking. The whole room was nostalgic and evocative for me and I said so.

'I thought it would be when I had it done up,' Tamura said.

'Tamura, you're taking a lot of trouble with me, but...' I struggled to finish my sentence.

'I enjoy it, Tani-chan. Really.'

'I do too. The time I have spent with you has been the best part of my life in Harbin,' I said.

'And yet, you still hesitate,' he said.

'It's the times, and it's our respective positions,' I said, thinking aloud.

'So it's not personal, Tani?' he was laughing now.

Before I could reply, there was a knock on the door. I could see Tamura was irritated by the intrusion, but knew that if it occurred it must be important. He rose and opened the door. The servant was agitated but before he could prevent it, a Chinese man strode past him. I knew from his army uniform and his manner that he was part of the collaborationist government. The man was clearly nervous and in a rush. Before Tamura could take him to a separate chamber, he blurted that the plans were set for the capture of the saboteurs. Tamura drew him away to a corner of the room, but I could make out the fact that an enormous supply of materiel was being moved the following Thursday. I did not however hear the destination nor where the trap would be set. Tamura's Chinese was passable, and he made himself readily understood. The man withdrew and Tamura came back to finish his drink.

'I'm sorry for the interruption,' he said.

'Quite all right. It can't be helped under the circumstances.'

'Tani-san, I don't know what you heard, but it can't go past this room. For all our sakes,' he emphasized.

'I know that. I didn't know you spoke Chinese,' I added.

'Badly. It was traditional in my family to learn it. And now it has gotten me appointed to some additional duties.'

'Which you don't relish,' I said.

'No. I wish the whole damned thing was over and you and I could sail away.'

'Do you, Tamura? Do you really?'

'Yes.'

In a completely spontaneous gesture, I leaned closer and he kissed me. It was a warm and tender kiss, and I lingered for a moment before drawing away.

He refilled our glasses.

'We'll have dinner in here,' he said.

When we were finished with our drinks, he called the servant, who set up a table. Cold zakuski were served Russian style, followed by salmon coulibiac.

'A Russian dinner in a Russian room,' I commented.

'Yes. Next time, we will have French.'

'All right. I look forward to it.'

He was warm and reassuring and there was part of me that wanted to stay with him. I think he could tell by my manner that I was softening my stance because he said, 'I'm so very tired tonight, and I want it all to be perfect for you.'

We briefly kissed goodnight and I went back home. But of course, I could not sleep, having heard what I had.

Harbin, September 1938

I went to the market for three days in succession until I was spotted by the egg man. I bought his eggs and then I told him about the trap. I went home, knowing I would have hated myself if I had not said anything, knowing I hated myself for having betrayed my word to Tamura. I called in sick the next day and slept for almost twenty hours straight.

Friday

Tamura called to say he had been looking so forward to this weekend, but had come down with a cold. I asked if I he wanted me to come look after him, and he said that was absolutely out of the question and he would be well in a few days. He sounded happy aside from his cold, and I felt reassured that he did not suspect the terrible thing I had done.

. . .

Harbin, September 1938

Finally Tamura telephoned! I had terrible anxiety all week and have developed a fear of keeping this diary. I should tear out the last couple of pages, really.

I am so anxious to see Tamura. My feeling toward him is a mix of attraction, curiosity, fear, loneliness and guilt. I don't know what to expect.

Harbin, September 1938

I cannot say it went well with Tamura. It was nothing like what I expected after such a long build-up. He had none of Richard's intensity nor did he have Sasha's imagination.

I think it was his utter lack of feeling that perplexed me so. It was as if he was watching the entire event, somehow observing it from without. I kept thinking how he had said that he wanted it to be good for me not too long before, and I now wonder what he could have meant in light of the events that transpired. I keep wondering if he knew of my betrayal or if this was always the way he interacted with women.

As usual, his car came to pick me up. The white dress I had worn in Hong Kong that had caused such a sensation was not appropriate, yet I had no other, and so I dyed it black earlier in the week. It was still as form fitting but now looked even more alluring and sophisticated. I parted my hair low on the side and left it long and subtly waved. I only wore a dark red lipstick and Liu's bracelets with it.

Tamura was waiting, dressed in a silk robe over his shirt and trousers, and led me into a room with a deep sofa. He opened a bottle of champagne and then asked me if I liked ukiyo-e, Japanese wood block prints. I replied that I adored them, particularly the ones depicting women in their intricate robes. He said he wanted to show me another form of ukiyo-e that was erotic in nature. He said it was called shunga.

He pulled out a few prints and we sat side by side. I cannot say they were particularly stirring to me, though they were of a very fine artistic quality. I cannot fathom why he showed me these things, perhaps to gauge my reaction to certain acts, but in the long run this overture had an alienating effect on me, and I thought it a poor place to start.

He then pressed his body against mine and brought my hand to his erection. I did not withdraw my hand, but neither did I respond. He began to kiss my neck, but unfortunately, those kisses only hearkened back to the print he had shown me of an octopus ravishing a woman and felt as cold a marine creature's. Really, it was the way he was looking at me with glassy fish eyes that disturbed me so. He had his hands about my waist before I pushed him away.

'Tamura-san, it's not right- between us. I think perhaps we are better off as friends,' I said.

'I don't understand, Tani,' he said in a thick voice.

'Neither do I,' I said. 'Perhaps it is those prints. I am not used to anything like that.' I tried to articulate my thoughts, but it was his manner and not the prints I found objectionable.

'Please, Tani-san, forgive me. I had no idea you would feel that way,' he said. He sounded more like the Tamura I had known until then, and I felt reassured. Yet the evening had been spoiled, and I knew staying would be utterly wrong.

'I need to go. Please call the car for me, Tamura-san.'

I think he wanted to say something more but his pride prevented him and he rang the servant. When the car was ready, he walked me to the door and said, 'Please forgive my thoughtlessness. I did not consider that you would not be used to such a thing.'

'I'm sorry as well. We will remain friends, won't we?' I asked.

'Of course. Always,' he replied.

He put me in the car, and I went home in the darkness.

Thinking back on it, I can't logically explain why the whole experience left me feeling so repulsed, but I don't know if I want to see him again.

Harbin, October 1938

Flowers from Tamura each day with notes saying how much he missed me.

Harbin, October 1938

Tamura came here today. He had never been to see me at my flat. He seemed tired and drained. I had not written or called to thank him for the flowers. I ushered him into the main reception room, and he sat down heavily.

'Tani-san, please allow me to explain,' he said.

'Please, there is no need,' I said, feeling embarrassed.

'No, there is need, for me especially. I have gotten so used to you, to speaking to you and to spending time with you. These days without you, thinking that I would never see you again have been difficult.'

I could see he was sincere and I sat down next to him.

'When a man is not a youth any longer, when he has had many experiences,' Tamura searched for words.

'Jaded,' I said.

'Yes, jaded. Then he, at times, needs a certain amount of extra stimulation,' Tamura explained.

'I realize that Tamura-san. It was not the shunga, but something that had altered in your manner that put me off,' I said, perhaps too plainly.

'Tani. I understand you. You are of a different nature. You desire tenderness, emotion, even passion. Emotion is not easy for me.'

'Then how would it work between us, if we are so different?' I asked.

Tamura considered. 'Let us try again. I think that sometimes I am afraid of you, though I am drawn to you. You fulfill the things that are missing in my life.'

'Like emotion?' I joked.

'Please, let's try again,' he said. He was holding my hands now, and his were warm and dry, and his touch felt reassuring.

'I must think it through, Tamura-san.'

'All right. But promise that you will.'

'I promise,' I said.

Harbin, October 1938

I did not go to Tamura's on Saturday and spending the weekend alone was nearly unbearable. The hours dragged, the weather turned, and I could not focus on doing anything productive. I sketched a bit, but my mind was constantly preoccupied with thoughts of Richard, Tamura and Sasha. I tried to sort out my feelings but found them to be confused and incomprehensible. Richard had captured my heart through physical love, Sasha my creativity and imagination- yet Tamura was the one I enjoyed spending time with most.

Mostly I berated myself for being weak, too lonely, and always needing a man in my life, and yet when there was no man present, I felt like a withered stalk. Perhaps I had been different before they had come into my life. I remembered my younger self, and thought -I had been enough for myself before the craving for another had been awakened. But, I suppose it is normal to desire love and companionship, and not to be so alone.

I thought of the three men who had impacted my life: Sasha, who had compromised his own unique vision in the service of a dogmatic political illusion; Richard, who blew hot and cold, one minute loving me the next pushing me away. What did he serve aside from his own sense of adventure? And now Tamura, who was part of a grotesquely cruel imperialistic power, though he took great pains to deny that he was in accordance with its aims, was the one human being to whom I was closest. I was neither faithful to Richard, nor honest with Tamura, and I despised myself for it. Perhaps it was what I deserved for being so careless with Sasha.

Harbin, October 1938

I went to Tamura, as ashamed as I was to do so. I cannot say Tamura was completely emotionally open, but at least that feeling of warmth and camaraderie had returned to our relationship. We talked, and laughed, and drank wine, and what developed next was frank and mature without the awkwardness we had experienced earlier. We did not undress, but rather in a spontaneous moment, I sat on his lap, facing him. Tamura is a tall man, well built, and so it was easy for him to contain me this way.

To me, it was utterly different, a connection that was strangely silent and still. He did not move inside me, and yet we must have remained that way for a long time. He touched me with his hands and mouth and the feeling was one of floating, and of time slowing down as if in a dream, languorous, and without intensity but with a certain joy and harmony of its own.

The room was close and quiet with a muffled elegance, pale grey and white, and the silk velvet sofa caressed our skin when we finally undressed. Tamura and I lay side by side, my back to him, and he embraced my entire body and moved so slowly that I found myself feeling completely tranquil and protected. It was not vigorous or violent with the goal of satisfaction but a flow of being, just as I had witnessed in his manner during tea ceremony or while practicing calligraphy.

Afterward we dozed, just as we were, until we were woken by a telephone call. It was official and Tamura knew he would be tied up for the rest of the weekend with administrative duties. We kissed goodbye, and I went home feeling happy and relaxed.

Harbin, October 1938

Something has awakened in me again, and I have begun to make ink drawings that are purely products of my imagination. They are geometric, circles within circles, sometimes bisected with lines, mostly black and white with touches of red. I have pasted the initial few at the back of this diary, since they are small and easily transported.

I miss designing jewelry for Sirdar Singh, and this is a bit in the same vein. I wonder how they have fared in Shanghai? I miss Anya and Liu particularly. It would be so nice to have another woman to talk to and help sort myself out. It's funny that I have avoided making friends here for fear of answering questions about Richard, and yet Tamura is now my closest confidant. I don't know what is happening to me or where I am headed. Surely, I am being foolish and incautious.

I will show the new work to Tamura. I find it to be beautiful.

Harbin, October 1938

Tamura tomorrow. I made a new evening dress, draped, Grecian with a halter top and a beaded waistband with matching cuffs. I also made a cape edged with a gold fabric to offset the beading. I know I am foolish but it kept me from over thinking things.

. . .

Harbin, October 1938

Lord, lord, the strangest happenings! I have been awake trying to understand and put them all together. The evening began as I expected, a new romance, the thrill of discovery, and after the initial foreplay, we moved to Tamura's bedroom where things became more vigorous and intense. I could see Tamura was fully engaged this time with the aim of catering to my pleasure. We made love for hours, stopping, talking, resting, and starting again. He lay on top of me with his full weight yet felt curiously light as I ran my hands over his smooth golden body that was clean and odorless. He did not orgasm but kept himself inside me, even as we paused to nap for a while, and I wondered how that was possible for him, but it was. Toward morning, we awoke and began again, and lay like snakes, flat with his body covering mine, and then reverted to face to face. When we fell apart, finally sated, he fell into a drowsy state, and I stroked his hair and face until he was asleep.

I rose and tiptoed to the bathroom, so as not to wake him. After I had washed, I walked back into the bedroom. Tamura was still asleep, but I was wide awake. The room was spacious with French doors leading to a balcony. Though the curtains were drawn, I could see the day was beginning to dawn. I pulled them back and looked at the garden. The leaves had fallen off the trees and it looked forlorn, abandoned, pale sepia, and winter green. I then took a turn around the room, looking at the paintings, which were intimate, impressionistic, and reminiscent of Renoir and Monet. There were a few note cards on the fireplace mantle, and I looked them over as well as the photographs in the silver frames. I assumed the children were his, though they did not favor him. I don't suppose I had anything general in mind, other than killing time, as I ran my hands over the sofa, admiring the lavender grey velvet and looking at the pillows that were made of old kimono. I opened the shagreen boxes on the small glass table, containing cigarettes, a lighter, and some notebook paper. Next to his desk was a curio cabinet, and I walked over to it and admired the netsuke, tiny intricate carvings done in wood and ivory, depicting animals and people. They were charming, and I was transported. It was only when I finished going over them that I happened to glace at his desk. I knew immediately that I was looking at train timetables and scheduled transport of materiel and personnel. I don't think I had anything in mind really, certainly I felt severed of my obligations to Richard, and that other betrayal had occurred as I had reasoned the information I had given over might have potentially saved lives. This was different, it was another category entirely, and yet I looked, like the young bride in the Bluebeard story who was allowed everything except access to the one forbidden thing. It did not occur to me to wonder why these things were in open view, and so I perused them, knowing I could not commit all to memory. I was absorbed at the desk yet became suddenly aware that Tamura's breathing had shifted. I looked over at the bed and saw he had woken and was looking at me intently. A shock ran through me, and I knew at once he had known everything, about me and Richard and what I had done.

I must have had a stricken look on my face that confirmed all of his suspicions, but from his expression I knew he was not angry, nor did he mean to harm me.

'Don't do it, Tani,' he said.

'I have done, Nobuaki. I have already done it.'

'I suspected as much, though I hoped it was not so,' he said resignedly.

'What now?' I asked.

'Come here. I won't hurt you,' he answered.

I knew that was true, and walking to the bed, sat on the edge.

'I know how you feel about us, Japan, but Tani, you must never see that man again. He is a death sentence for you.'

I said nothing. I was too afraid to say anything.

'He's clever, that one, but we will catch him and his communist band soon enough. They have been most disruptive and will be punished accordingly.'

He could see that I had not taken in the full weight of his meaning. The only thing I was thinking of was the punishment: a firing squad, no doubt.

'He's a Soviet agent and has been since his student days in Paris. He and Liu Liqiu. Though she is of the domestic variety.'

He could see me plummeting though I shook my head in denial.

'Oh yes. I am telling you the whole truth, though your friends never have,' he said.

I thought back to my conversation with Mei, and I knew he was not lying, and suddenly all the pieces fell into place.

'You're such a light girl, so thoughtless, so unsuspecting,' Tamura continued. 'You think because you are the way you are, everyone is that way.'

'Please Tamura, don't go on. I know what I am.'

He sat forward and gripped my arm, as if to press his point.

'All this,' I looked around the room, 'was it a lie?'

'What do you think? They wanted to use you. Can you understand that?'

'And you wanted to use me too to trap them.'

'No. I really liked you Tani. I had hoped it wasn't true.'

'But it is. And now you see what I am.'

'You must never see them again. Do you understand me?'

'And the train schedules?'

'They are falsified. I could be damaged for telling you that, but I am telling you, in any case. Get dressed. I'll call the car for you.'

'And what about this, Nobuaki?' I said, indicating the things that had happened between us.

'I never want to see you again, Tani. And I can't afford to. Your life is your own from now on, but remember what I said if you value it.'

He got up and left the room, and I did not see him again. I dressed and went outside where the car was waiting to take me home.

Harbin, October 1938

It was hard for me to accept what had happened between Tamura and myself, and just as hard was my new knowledge of what Richard was and had been. I thought that I could not and should not remain in Harbin and decided to look into returning to Shanghai. It would not be easy, and I did have a job and a flat here, unlike in Shanghai, but I reasoned I had landed on my feet before. I wrote to Natalia and Anya describing in a very general way that I thought my time in Harbin was over. I hoped that the letters would reach their destination, since I had not been in touch for some time with either woman and knew nothing of their circumstances. I felt more than a bit awkward, since it seemed that I only looked to them when I needed their help.

In the back of my mind was the fear that Tamura would change his mind and betray me to the police who would arrest me, and of course the knowledge that I would never see him again which weighed on me terribly.

. . .

Harbin, November 1938

I teach, I clean the flat, I sew, and nothing changes. No word yet from Shanghai. It's too soon. I might not get anything for weeks or months even. Natalia was right, it was a mistake to come here.

It's so cold. Winter has set in. I could never get used to the heat and humidity in Shanghai, but I think this is even worse. Although the sun is shining still, I can't help recalling those awful days after my mother died when I thought I would be trapped in that far Russian wasteland forever. I have a similar feeling now, and it is further depressing me and causing me to feel ill at ease.

I am vacillating between making a winter coat and just picking up and leaving.

Harbin, November 1938

Mei was on the street corner looking intently at me as I came out of my apartment building. She began following me as I walked to school. I stopped at the tobacconist, so that she could catch up. I was pretending to look inside the window display, as if wondering what I should buy. She walked up to me, with her palm outstretched, and she was dressed in patched rags, so there could be no mistaking her intention if anyone was watching us.

'Be ready tonight,' she said.

I rummaged around in my hand bag for coins. 'I can't. Tamura knows about me. They might be watching now,' I said.

Before I could ask what had happened to Richard she grabbed the coins and rushed off. It was purely survival instinct on her part. I went to school, taught my classes, but my mind was elsewhere the whole time, and I was worried that something awful had happened to Richard, but then perhaps it had been just another of his whims, a desire to see me again.

Harbin, November 1938

The newspapers have reported that the band of rebels responsible for the sabotage that took place last month has been captured. Their names are listed, all Chinese, Mei's included. The word is that there was an engagement and some of the group were killed. I don't know if Richard was among their number. If he wasn't, they will torture the others until they reveal everything they know. I assume that if he got away, he his ability to operate here will be severely hampered. In any case, he will follow the directive of his handlers.

Even in Shanghai, we had heard of the purges Stalin has been conducting. God help Richard if he survived the Japanese, because there might be even worse things awaiting him at the hands of the Soviets.

I think of Mei often, the girl she was when I first knew her, then the wife, and then I can't help but think of all the women who were driven into the arms of the party by cruelty, and by archaic notions, and their dreams of liberation. To be thought of and treated as human being, of equal rank and responsibility, that is a heady goal and a worthy aspiration, but what a price there is to be paid for it!

If I was brave, if I was in the ranks of that New Woman, I would beg Tamura for her life, to intervene somehow, even if it meant prison for her. But I am a coward and a weakling, and in my heart, I know it would be of no use.

Harbin, November 1938

I went to Tamura's house. I waited to be admitted to his office. He did not come around the desk to greet me, but looked at me coldly. He thought he knew why I had come.

'Tamura-san, I have come most humbly to ask-' but he cut me off.

'He's dead.'

I felt as if I had been cut off at the knees, and I lost my balance and stumbled. My heart was thundering violently, and I could not logically grasp what Tamura had just said even though I had understood him.

'Sit down,' Tamura said coming around the desk to help me. He went to the bar and poured me a glass of whiskey and made me drink it down. It had a calming effect on me.

'I'm sorry Tamura-san. I am quite foolish and behaving badly,' I apologized in the Japanese way.

'No, I understand it's a shock. It was cruel of me to tell you that way.'

'I read there was a skirmish, I assume he was shot then?'

'Yes. I'm sorry. We had hoped to capture them alive, but they fired upon us and we fired back. And truthfully, perhaps it is better that way.'

'The body?'

'A mass grave.'

'I see.' I said. I don't know how I was able to manage the next part of the conversation, but perhaps I still had not grasped the idea that Richard was gone. 'Tamura-san, the reason I came was to ask about the woman called Mei. She was one of my seamstresses in Shanghai. Is there any hope of her release?'

'In a word, no.'

I had already known this would be his answer, but I pressed him. 'Will she suffer much?'

'That is up to her and the answers she gives, but I hope that won't be the case.'

'I see,' I said with resignation. 'Well, then I'll leave.' I rose to go.

'Good-bye, Tani,' Tamura said.

Good-bye Tamura-san.'

When I reached the door I turned around and looked back. His former coldness had vanished and his expression was one of great sadness.

'Tamura-san. I'm returning to Shanghai, and since we will probably never see each other again, I do want to say that the time I spent with you was among the happiest of my life. I'll always treasure it and remember you with affection.'

'I as well,' he replied.

'All right then, good-bye,' I repeated. I don't know what I expected. I know I hesitated for a moment before I left. Tamura made no move to stop me.

Harbin, November 1938

How could I feel nothing for Richard, knowing he is dead? I have no sorrow or tears. It is as if he had meant nothing to me at all. Perhaps I am in shock, perhaps it all has a feeling of unreality to me still, as if I have not absorbed the full meaning of Tamura's words.

I always thought I would keep loving Richard, no matter what. I wonder if that love has been illusory; merely wishful thinking on my part, or a love *that had been born of the body, of loneliness, of a wish to expand my horizons past the limitations I had known prior to meeting him?*

It was Tamura that was on my mind now, though I berated myself for being a feather in the wind, landing here and there, thoughtlessly, without purpose. Perhaps in time I would lose all feeling for him too.

Harbin, December 1938

A letter from Natalia, finally, urging me to return. She says the Russians are faring well in Shanghai, and as the British and Americans leave, they are able to rent property for a song and that the Japanese look upon them benignly.

There is no building going on now and spending and frivolity have been restricted, but she is certain I could find work in a dress shop or teaching. It won't be much, but at least I'll be away from Harbin and back among my friends. She says she is still happy with her Igor Andreyevich and they are making marriage plans. She also writes that a few of Shi-shi's businesses have been taken over by the Japanese, but that he and Anya are still holding out in their apartment and Anya is carrying on as if nothing has altered at all. Perhaps it is better to have happy, positive thoughts. I am beginning to have them as well. My life feels like it will be my own again, at last, after Richard, after Sasha, after Nobuaki. I hope I will be able to create beautiful things again after this is all over and Sirdar Singh, and Yevgeny Borisovitch, and Mr. Isfahani, and Ladislav will once again commission my work.

I have given my notice at school. They were disappointed and wanted to keep me on until a replacement could be found. I lied to them and told them my aunt was ill in Shanghai and I had to go back as soon as possible. I wrote the same letter to my landlady. I don't even feel guilty about it and have started to pack. The only thing left to do is to book my ticket. I can hardly wait to leave.

The Director put down the book. It was the end of Tanya's diaries and the end of Tanya. How he had wondered all these years what had become of her. And now he knew.

PART VI

SHANGHAI, 1986

The land was plain, bare, and never ending. A white sky spread over the yellow hills where the rain had not fallen and would not fall. A procession appeared; tiny dots on the horizon, a funeral, along with a cacophony of sound that reverberated for a short while before silence reigned once again. Human life, it seemed, amounted to nothing of great consequence on the limitless and eternal land.

Withered and sunburned, peasants suffered in relation to the land, hard toil and hard luck were their lot. They had no expectations, they knew of nothing beyond their small part of the world until the Japanese war reached them and destroyed their way of life. Li Kong watched the story unfold on the screen, watched as the good communists came to aid the villagers, and watched the devastation the Japanese left in their wake.

It was not the story he had wanted to tell. His own script had been closer to his heart and told of the hardships his own generation had faced when they had been sent to the countryside for re-education. But that story had been turned down by the censors, and he and his cinematographer, working from the provincial film studio where they had been assigned after graduation from the Beijing Film Academy, had been given the chance to make the film that was premiering that night.

His depiction of nature as all-encompassing was so different from what he had experienced watching the wholesale destruction of forests as eager former Red Guards leveled mountains for wood. He had experienced so much wretchedness and stupidity and still chafed at the memory of the long months when he had scarred his shoulders carrying night soil from public toilets to fertilize the fields. Despite the beauty that had been around him, he had often been hungry and exhausted.

Still, he and his cinematographer had been able to impose their sensibilities on the script, and he felt a rush of happiness remembering their months on the shoot, their joy at being able to overcome the obstacles they were faced with, and the camaraderie they had shared with their tiny cast and crew.

After the closing credits, the lights went on and he was greeted with applause. His professors, his actors, crew, and classmates were all present, reveling in his victory, and analyzed his work, discussing their own films and the films they intended to make in the future. They insisted on taking him to a restaurant to celebrate and he let himself be swept away.

Li Kong had been flushed with wine and happiness all evening. When he came home and undressed that warm glow stayed with him. He sat on the sofa and pulled out his still photography books, leafing through them. There were photos of the shoot, and of his friends and teachers over the years they had worked so hard to learn their craft at the Beijing Film Academy.

He felt grateful to his teachers, who had made marvelous speeches in praise of their students that evening, and now he recalled their dedication. After the desert that had been the Cultural Revolution, they had taken up their tasks with such enthusiasm and seriousness. They had deemed the class of 1983 very special. It had consisted of those still young people who had missed out on formal education, but had either had the drive to educate themselves or had shown exceptional talent in the arts when they were tested for entry. Though he, like some, were over the age of admittance, special dispensation had been made for them after their skills were taken into consideration.

Li Kong remembered how he had been reconciled to failing, thinking he would never get out of the factory he was working in, just as earlier, he had believed he would never leave the countryside for the factory. But he had gotten in by the skin of his teeth, and it was his photographs which had saved him.

He owed his training to Fang Shirong, the Director, the man he had known as Sun Mu. They had read Tanya's diaries, including the last one after the Director discovered how Tanya had died. Then, he had broken down and told Li Kong everything about his past.

Li Kong had not been angry, just surprised by the subterfuge until he reasoned that there were aspects of his life the Director might not have wanted openly to discuss. Our relationship changed then, Li Kong thought, we became closer and more authentic with each other. The Director had shown Li Kong his hidden books and began to teach him how to discern what made art good and which elements made it great. In time, the Director taught Li Kong photography and particularly about light and composition.

It had taken Li Kong some time and effort to master apertures, lenses, the metering of light, and to understand film speed, exposure time, blurring, and the power of cropping. But from the beginning, he had had an innate sense of composition and an eye for drama. And there had been much drama in those days, he thought. Ironically, it had been easy for him, wearing the protection of his red armband to take the thirty -five millimeter hand held Leica the Director had given him and shoot the scenes he saw unfolding before him. He showed the good revolutionary photos to his school friends and made sure the Red Guards noticed his fervor. But he hid the bad photos under the floorboards in his loft. Even now as he looked at them, they were terrible to behold. The damage inflicted to human beings, the rabid devotion to Mao, and the malicious joy on some of the Red Guards' faces were both revelatory and sickening.

Li Kong had been proud of his work until the Director had shown him his own photos. Li Kong had been struck silent by their beauty and elegance and marveled at the Director's strong use of light and shadow. And now, reflecting back, he thought, it was not my time in the countryside that taught me about the relationship of human beings to space, but the Director's own photos, in which people were reduced to geometry, small and embedded, in the long shadows that surrounded them. They featured the city, high rises, staircases, construction sites, and empty streets echoed the Director's own solitary life and mandated silence. Then there were the Director's portraits, which stripped their subjects bare and caught the uncertainty and despair behind the glamour of the 1930's and early forties. He had even saved some of his early work from Paris, where his introspective mood had been born before it was sharpened and refined.

Later, in the countryside, Li Kong tried to do with the peasants what the Director had done with his subjects, and it was those plain and withered faces, which reflected a lifetime of suffering and disappointments, that had won him a place in the academy.

He had continued shooting stills the entire time at film school while he was learning his new craft and reading books which were a revelation to his generation, books by Camus and Kafka, Faulkner, and his favorite, Garcia-Marquez, and watching the films of Bergman, Truffaut, Resnais, Godard, Tarkovsky, Ozu, and the Italian neo-Realists.

And it was there that had he seen the Directors post -war masterpiece which had been banned, that was humanistic and dealt with the personal life of a family in decline, and which came to him as a blow because he understood its greatness, and understood how far he was from crafting his own vision to the standard developed by Fang Shirong.

But just as he had hidden his own frightening work bearing on the Cultural Revolution, he had kept to himself the Director's photos he had been given to inspire him. The photos had come along with books and one film reel of the Director's late unfinished work. Everything the Director had kept safe passed to Li Kong in 1968 as he was being sent to the countryside along with the rest of his generation for reeducation. The Director had suspected that he would be harassed once again, given his involvement in Anita's case, but that was not how things had transpired. Don't think, Li Kong said to himself, or else you won't be able to sleep.

At the academy, Li Kong had projected that film repeatedly, vowing one day to remake it, exactly as the Director intended as a tribute to him. Perhaps he would frame the Director's own film within a documentary about his life and work and so the public would know who Fang Shirong had been and remember him. Yes, that was what he would do. He closed the albums, cleaned his teeth, urinated, and fell into bed after stripping off his clothes.

He felt enervated and yet his mind was racing as scenes from that evening flashed before him, and then he began to think about the next film he had been slated to make which was to be set near the Tibetan border about a family of nomads. He thought about the land, and how he would tell the story, though he only had a rough script and would have to refine it with the woman he had been working with, Lin Hua.

She was a gifted writer and he would only have to come up with a vague idea or a picture he had in his mind for her to be able to run with it. But although she was capable of depicting his ideas with an economy of means which kept them from becoming overly sentimentalized, she herself was not austere in any sense. Instead, when not working, she was full of laughter and fun. Odd, he thought, since she had suffered so much in her life. Her parents had both been sent to work camps in 1958, then later they were harassed and tortured during the Cultural Revolution. She had taken care of her old grandmother and younger siblings but had learned to take life as it comes. She was pretty, tall, and broad shouldered, and she had been a model worker on her collective farm where she had planted rice in the paddies along with the women of the village. He thought he might be in love with her. It was not a grand passion but a quiet love that had grown from their friendship. Perhaps it is best that way, he thought remembering the scenes from the Director's unfinished film. I want to sleep, he thought, but he was restless and dozed lightly before falling into a dreamless void.

Shanghai, 1968

'They are sending my entire class to the countryside,' Li Kong said.

The Director looked at him blearily, uncomprehending. 'The entire class?' he asked.

'Not just our school. It is to take place all over the country. Our whole generation. Mao has decreed it. We are now to learn from the peasants.'

'He was always distrustful of intellectuals, and now he will destroy all the progress that has been made since the war,' the Director said.

'I really think it's a move to diffuse the different factions which are fighting each other. I heard they are using guns in some parts of Manchuria.'

'Perhaps, but do not mistake the power of envy, however unconscious. It's insidious, and in a megalomaniac like Mao, it has always been a destructive force. He knew he made grave economic mistakes during the Great Leap Forward, but he did not acknowledge them, and he is further pressing his point now. He won't listen to moderate voices. I fear your generation will never regain what it has lost. Time, least of all.'

Li Kong sighed. 'If you have relatives in villages, you can get assigned to them. Otherwise, they will send you were they will.'

'Do you have such a situation?'

'Yes, thankfully. I have already been in contact with them and they have agreed. It's beautiful there and it will not be as difficult as in remote places.'

'I remember it from your poems. When are you slated to go?'

'Soon.'

'I want you to take the camera and the books I'll select for you. It may be beautiful and you may be exhausted from the work they'll give you, but sooner or later, you'll need to stimulate your brain and your eye again. You've been making great progress with your photos and you need to continue.'

'I think they'll give us leave to visit occasionally. At least that was the rumor.'

'Then you must come back and show me your work.' The Director made his voice as even as possible. He did not want to make a show of sentiment or to depress the boy, but he knew he would miss Li Kong terribly. The diaries had introduced them to each other, but more than that, they had put him in touch with his past and his true self. And then, he had gotten a new lease on life teaching the boy his craft.

'There's something else,' the Director said, rising. He pushed aside his bed and opened the hidden cabinet, taking out a portfolio and a container of film. 'If anything should happen to me -'

'What could happen?' Li Kong interrupted, though he had long feared that the Red Guards would single out the Director because of his status.

'I'm an old man and my health is not good,' the Director said, giving the most plausible explanation.

Li Kong breathed with relief. 'Oh, is it that? I don't think it's quite as bad as you think.'

'Yes, perhaps I am exaggerating all my little aches and pains. It's like old bachelors to do so. In any case, I'd like you to keep these for me. I am vain enough to think they will inspire you.'

'And the film?'

'Ah. It was something that I never finished. Perhaps you'll find a way to view it. Projectionists come to villages occasionally, you know. I think you'll find its lessons useful in terms of composition, but I think it might be the only remaining copy.'

'I'll be careful with it, don't worry.'

'I am not worried. It's irrelevant to me, in any case,' the Director said, though, in truth, he was not indifferent to the work. His late and acknowledged masterpiece, *Within a Yellow House*, had taken him in a completely different direction than his previous work had done. The film, itself, had been contained and elegiac, with long, still shots, chronicling the demise of a small family after the war. It told story of the death of the son from wounds he sustained in the war, and of the old ailing father who could not recover from it, and the lonely life of the older daughter, who, though sensitive and intelligent, developed a passionate but unrequited love for her brother's much younger comrade in arms. The regime had found it bourgeois and far too personal. And yet, disregarding their opinion, he had gone on with his next project, which had pushed him to his limit artistically.

'What is it about?' Li Kong asked.

'About? Hmmm, I suppose human obsession.'

'Oh, I see,' Li Kong replied, though he did not know what that could possibly entail.

'Yes, I think you will when you view it.'

'No hints?' Li Kong asked, but the Director only laughed.

When Li Kong finally had the chance to see the film, he had been stunned. *The Death of Flowers in Late Afternoon* began with a still silent shot of the afternoon sun moving over a table. In a vase, flowers past their bloom wilted, their petals dropping off. No explanation was given, no back story, just the unfolding of a series of unrelated images with little dialogue depicting the lonely, sensual, almost animalistic, existence of a concubine who had been left to her own devices in a provincial backwater. Her house took on a life of its own and the long shots of empty spaces, the deep silences, the solitude of the garden spoke to her profound isolation. There was a suggestion that she had once been well kept there, but now everything was faded and run down. One old servant, a deaf woman, remained to look after things.

Rain dropped slowly on the leaves of the foliage in the garden, and then a wind swept through the empty streets of the town, bringing a torrent of rain. The rain fell up the sheaves of the house, the eternal silence broken by its patterned sound. The woman watched the rain, her skin was moist, the air was warm, her despair beyond anything that could be remedied. She had given herself up to endless nothingness, her few memories of the once happy past were faded and rendered meaningless.

A straggler arrived with the storm, a young man from the city, swept in by the wind, who beat upon the door along with the pounding rain. The servant let him in; the rain sluiced off his clothes as he stood in the dark hall. The stillness was broken by the woman's bound feet as she walked across the floorboards. She welcomed him, she was afraid of him, though there was no one to inform her lord, who had disappeared, and perhaps had even died, long before. She was shy of the young man as she studied his face surreptitiously when she thought he was not looking at her. She served him dinner and looked after him.

Just as suddenly as he had come, they knew, in one moment, they would be lovers, and not even the pain of death would stop them, for that was the punishment for women who were unfaithful in those days. And then their dance began, the dance of love and desire, of pain and destruction. He took her in a harsh and violent way. The camera lingered on her face, while her expression changed as she grew to love it, as much as he did. She was limp in his hold, the light illuminating her pale still face, her long black hair spilling down the length of his bare arm. They lived for each other in the small moments, in the silence of the house, in the long afternoons, as crickets sang in the garden, and as shadows fell in the cool of the evening. Every gesture spoke of love and mutual understanding. They needed no verbal language. They fitted one another well.

Even as he watched, Li Kong knew their happiness would not last, that something would change and the world would spill within the confines of the house. He did not yet know that people themselves changed, that their desires shifted, that no paradise would, or could remain, uncontaminated.

One day the young man grew weary of the woman and looking around him and saw that China was changing, and he made a decision to join Sun Yat-sen, though he promised he would return. He was fired with a new passion and he spoke new words that she did not understand since she was constant in her desire and love for him.

The scene shifted forward to the future. The man was older and looked at a small portrait with nostalgia and regret. His expression suggested he would have lived his life differently had he had the chance to do it over. The camera shifted to the portrait. It was of her, the woman, and she was still young. Li Kong did not know how they had parted and why they were not reunited. Perhaps history had come between them. Perhaps she had died young. He knew it was, to a certain extent, the story of the Director and inspired by his feeling for Tatiana Zhukova. She had been the one woman he had loved, but he had not loved her enough, though he was able to turn his regret into a higher art form.

He had often wondered how he would finish the story and created dozens of scenarios in his mind. Perhaps, he finally thought when he awoke the following morning, it was better left undone, just as life was never explained, and often remained inexplicable to those who lived it.

PART VII

HONG KONG, SEPTEMBER 2003

Li Kong held catalogue of art deco jewelry that would be auctioned the following week in London. He had bought several pieces before, loving it as he did, for his mistress who was also his leading lady. He had met her, cast her in a historical breakthrough film that had been internationally celebrated. They had gone on to make eight renowned films together, and finally he had known passion and had left his wife whom he still worked with.

He thought he might want to go to London with his mistress and make a trip of it. He was going on to Hollywood to discuss a new film that would be made in conjunction with the Americans and would be on location for months. He thought it would be a nice surprise and perhaps they could go to Paris as well, a city she loved. He had learned English, and preferred London for that reason, but it had always seemed somehow friendlier to him in any case.

October 2003, Cotswolds

Li Kong waited politely while the old lady served tea the English way. She must be ninety-one he reckoned though she did not look it. Her skin was only lightly wrinkled, her figure was trim but sturdy,

241

and her dark eyes were still lively. He had not expected her to be alive, and he had been shocked when he was introduced to her before the auction. Tatiana Zhukova. It was she. She had been invited as the creator of those sublime jewels, of which he had managed to acquire exactly one.

The cottage in the Cotswolds he found himself in was odd in a sense, conventionally charming from the outside, thatched roof and multitudes of roses, which were spilling over the stone fence and onto the road. He had not anticipated what he would find once he crossed the threshold. Apart from the striking black and white photos, it was decorated with many artifacts and furniture from the Far East, and looked in a sense colonial.

He now found himself in a small conservatory amidst flowering plants and placed his cup on a blue and white Chinese garden stool.

'I am familiar with your work and admire it,' the old lady said, forthrightly, 'but I don't quite understand why you wanted to see me.'

Li Kong reached for his brief case and pulled out the five slim diaries his assistant had brought with her from Hong Kong while he had been waiting for this interview. He handed them to her and watched her smiling incomprehension change to a look of recognition.

'But how?' She cried out softly.

'Madam Liu. On a raid during the cultural revolution.'

'Liu!' she exclaimed. 'I don't understand. Why did you save them? What happened then and what became of her?' It came out in a torrent as if she could not organize her thoughts at all.

'I was a Red Guard. It was in the very first months of the Cultural Revolution before my eyes were opened. They were ransacking her house, and when one of the diaries fell open, I saw your drawings. I kept the dairies from going into the bonfire.'

'I can hardly believe it!' The old lady shook her head.

'She thought you had died in Harbin in Unit 731. She saved those to remember you by. I think she felt terribly guilty and responsible.'

The old lady seemed lost in her memories and Li Kong worried that she had lost the thread of the conversation, but then she brightly said, 'In a sense Tanya Zhukova did die, but Dara Moore was resurrected. But I can't believe you kept them all these years! What prompted that?'

He wanted to say they had been his brightest spot and a source of inspiration during those awful years, but something entirely different formed in his mind before he had a chance to think it through. 'You see, Fang Shirong lived in the courtyard opposite and we read them together.'

'Fang Shirong! But it's too much of a coincidence. How can that be?'

Li Kong shook his head. 'I don't really believe in coincidence any more. Sometimes life is more intelligent than we believe it to be and our course is plotted by an unknown force. Or perhaps it really was coincidence,' he added, and they both started laughing.

'Oh the things I wrote about him. He must have been mortified,' she said playfully, and then, 'You must tell me what happened to him afterward.'

'He fell on hard times after he was purged as a Rightist. His films were banned.'

Tanya's eyes moistened, 'I saw Within a Yellow House when it was released. It was a beautiful film, though it had a very short run in France before it disappeared. I thought it had been banned, but I knew he had fulfilled his promise brilliantly. Then I knew nothing more. You knew him during the Cultural Revolution, you said. I hope things were not too terrible for him then.'

'Until I was sent to the countryside, he kept his head down. Then he became involved in Anita Cheng's arrest and trial. I'm sorry to say I found out that he died of a heart attack after trying to visit her in prison one day.' He left out that the Director's heart had been weakened by hunger and that his loneliness had led him to take on Anita's case. Sun Mu had fallen on the street and died alone without anyone to hold or help him. 'I wish he would not have gotten involved, but he did.'

'He didn't live long enough to see your success,' the old lady said astutely.

'Yes, he was my teacher and the source of all I have done since, but your diaries were the catalyst for all that, you know.'

'Oh,' it was a self-deprecating dismissive sound. 'I'm so sorry he died alone. I'm so sorry for everything,' she said softly, shaking her head.

'We all have regrets,' Li Kong replied. 'Everyone who has lived through troubled times. There is no help for that.'

'I can imagine,' she replied sadly. 'And Liu?'

'She was arrested and died in prison toward the end of 1970.'

'Terrible.'

'She told me Richard finished in the Soviet Union. He did very well for himself it seems.'

'Well, it was in his nature to do so, wasn't it?' she said sharply.

They sipped their tea quietly before he asked, 'You know, when I first opened those diaries and I saw your photograph alongside his, I thought that would be a great love story, but it wasn't, was it? How do you look back on that, on him?'

'I've had a happy and full life since, so I can look back with little bitterness. It was a learning experience,' she paused, 'because no one gives you a handbook when you begin your path down life, do they? But you must know that already.'

'Yes,' he paused, 'I searched the archives, you know, to find out about Tamura and Tanaka.'

'Did you?'

'Yes. They were arrested by the Soviets during the liberation of Manchuria. Tanaka was tried and released on pressure from the Americans. Inexplicable really, when you consider what was done there. But you know so many of them got away with murder since the Americans wanted to get a hold of their documentation on infectious diseases and the results of their cryogenics experiments.'

'Yes, I am aware of that. And Tamura?'

'He committed suicide when he realized the war was lost.'

The old lady's cup came down with a crash. Tea spilled over the carpet. Li Kong rushed to pick it up.

He blotted the stain with his napkin. 'I'm sorry to have shocked you. I'm sorry.'

'No, no, please stand up. Don't worry,' she said. 'Perhaps, he was a good man after all,' she said.

'Or afraid of the consequences of Japanese policy?' Li Kong said sharply.

'Perhaps. I was never able to judge.'

'What happened to you afterward? I thought surely you were dead. You never came back to Shanghai, did you?'

'There's a final diary. I translated it into English when I was practicing the language. Actually, I think I was hoping to make sense of things, of my life and all that had happened during those turbulent years. Now, I must leave for a bit. You can stay and read it if you like. It will answer all your questions. It won't take long, and I won't be long.

'You wouldn't mind?'

'Not at all, we can talk more when I get back, if you are not in a rush.'

'No, I'm not.'

'I'll bring it from the study. Won't be a moment.'

6TH DIARY

Harbin, July 1939

It is late and quiet in the house. The servants are asleep and so is Nobuaki. I am in my room alone with the silence, and though I have not written for months I think I shall go mad if I do not pick up my pen once more.

I am like a prisoner here, though I know it is for my own safety. I am confined to the house and Nobuaki has the servants watch over me when he is not here. He allows me into the park when he accompanies me, and that is often the best part of my day, at least psychologically. He has given me the run of the house, except when officials come over and then I must confine myself to my rooms.

He brings me books to read and art supplies, though I am not able to

245

produce anything. Nobuaki is so patient, even when I screamed and screamed when he tried to come near me initially.

I've been under the care of a doctor these past few months. He is silent, Japanese, and, I think, terrified of what Nobuaki would do to him if he ever revealed my whereabouts to anyone. He is, I think, not particularly sympathetic to our situation though he does not know what really happened. He does know I have suffered a trauma, and he has kept me sedated for weeks and given me injections of all sorts of things, vitamins he claims, but who would know the truth of it.

I have begun this because I want to expel the events from my mind once and for all and cannot seem to do so since they play over and over in my thoughts like a film reel that someone is projecting but is not bothering to turn off. I will describe them as I see them in my mind's eye on that terrible night and then in that place afterward.

I was almost ready to leave for Shanghai when a message from Richard arrived through a contact. I do not know if this was the same man who betrayed us to the Kempeitai. I told him I thought I was being watched, but he said it would be all right, that Richard's people had been watching me as well, and that I would be safe. I don't know why I consented. Mei had been right, I was still harboring girlish romantic notions then. I was walking back from the pharmacist's when they approached me, and again I was led through a maze of backstreets to a horse cart on the outskirts of town and hidden in back under blankets and straw. I do not know where we drove, only that the journey was long and that I was stiff by the time we got there. We were in the woods and had to hike in the dusk until we reached Richard, this time hiding in a cave, or rather a stony depression in the landscape. Of course, I should have known it was not sentiment that had made him call me there but necessity. His network had been broken, and he wanted me to carry a message to Shanghai to his contacts. I do not recall what was said in its entirety, though I think much of it was quite ugly on my part. Richard really thought I would want to help his important mission. He once again failed to see how his request would affect me. He only knew that his work against the Japanese must continue by any means. I suppose he considered it somehow inevitable that I would see that, see beyond the personal aspect, and consent to help him. He was aware that I despised him for it but was still aiming to *play on my guilt and the feelings of revulsion I had toward the Japanese occupation. We were hashing it out, and perhaps he would have convinced me in the end, though I will never know for certain.*

I turned away and started rapidly walking through the woods in the near darkness, sensing my way back. He came after me and wrenched my arm to stop me. I tore away and began to run. I hurried toward the clearing where the cart was still waiting. I was blind to what was ahead. Richard had a torch and was following me. It all happened too quickly to register the sequence of events, but when I see it played over in my mind, I think he saw they were there. He didn't warn me. He turned and ran. And then the tape slows, and I hear the voices of the Kempeitai ordering me to halt. I am blinded by the headlights of their vehicles. They are shouting, there are gunshots, I am raising my arms in the air, and they take me captive.

They are rough and crude, and I think they will probably rape me then take me to one of their prisons where I will be interrogated, but as they are driving toward town in the dark they come across a convoy. It is more Kempeitai, taking a truck load of people somewhere. Why they gave me up to them, I'll never know. Perhaps the others had quotas to meet, perhaps bribes were exchanged, perhaps they were feeling lazy that night, or wanted to leave off work early to get drunk and meet their whores. I can't understand it. Surely, they would have known I had some valuable information to impart regarding Richard. I was frightened. I could not understand what they were saying, and, in truth, I thought, perhaps it will be better to be shot along with these other people and have it done with quickly than to be tortured in prison. But I did not know what they had in mind and that where I was going was worse than any jail imaginable.

I cannot think about it now. I still cannot face that part of my story. I will save it for another time, when I am stronger. It is shrouded in darkness in any case, and I cannot seem to retrieve a complete memory, only the dreadful sounds of screaming and pleading for mercy that I heard, in Chinese and Russian, that I can't seem to obliterate no matter how hard I try. Sometimes, I dream of men in white suits reaching for me, their white gloved hands sticky on my body. It's too horrible. Then Nobuaki calls the Doctor who gives his soothing injections, because he does not know what to do with me, or how to stop my teeth from chattering, or how to get me to come out of the corner where I sometimes sit facing the wall, or how to get rid of the claw marks I have made there though the doctor has bandaged my hands with their broken nails.

I do not know what Nobuaki's intentions are. I have no news of the outside world; I know only what he tells me. I do not know how long I will remain in this house or how long the Japanese occupation will continue. Perhaps forever and I'll be locked in my own secret prison for the duration of my life. He won't say anything about Richard. He lied to me on that subject before. He'll lie to me again. He does not know that I hope Richard is suffering the torments of the damned, that I curse Richard and myself for ever becoming involved, that I burn with hatred and loathing whenever I think of his flesh pressed against mine.

Harbin, September 1939

More injections. How I love them. Afterwards I lie here, obliterated. It's only matter of seconds before I can go to my secret world under the sea. That's where I prefer to live, in my jellyfish body, without human legs. It's only a matter of minutes before that blue-green jeweled sea opens its arms and I sink into purple seaweed beds where pale pink shells beckon. I pick through them searching for pearls. There are seals and dolphins that come and stare, and when they see my melancholy and despair, they wrap themselves around me and try to comfort me.

Shall I make a diadem of pearls? I am the only human here.

No date

Mother, oh mother, oh you are shrouded in darkness and beyond the sea. Which land do you reside in now? Will you live in the dark with the limbless white ghosts, forever? Shades in a cave. Now where was that from? I seem to have been there long ago. I can almost remember it. I can't get to the water any more. Just dry land.

Harbin, April 1940

I'm quite well now. I sit in the loggia each day, watching pale green spring and new shoots unfold. At first when I couldn't get up I thought they had cut off my legs, but it's only because I am so weak that I have trouble walking. At first, I couldn't at all, but now I have a cane. Nobuaki looks at me with sad eyes and tries to smile when I show him how far I've come along.

It's no fun for him caring for a pathetic invalid. But what is he to do with me now, after all that has happened? He can't very well turn me out, even though he is tired of me. I try to be unobtrusive and not get in his way.

The Japanese doctor has done something to my head. I've read the previous entries over, but I can't remember a thing.

The sky is pale and pink, blue-golden, and purple clouds sail above the horizon. I'm like those clouds, gossamer and silk. The sun is an orange orb, setting, falling into the lilac mountains that are only clouds. An orange orb, so like the flag of Japan, only it has no rays, no clinging tentacles. It is soft and soon will disappear.

Harbin, September 1940

I wasn't quite as well as I thought. Another relapse, another recovery. I was trying to paint but my hands we shaking too much to hold a brush. Nobuaki gave me a camera. At first, the photos were quite blurry since I couldn't hold the camera steady but now they are better. Such strange things I see, pebbles and stalks of grass, changing leaves, details of the house that take on shadowy meanings, when you take them out of context. He won't let me take photos of him or anyone who works in the house. It's all right, they don't mean a thing to me, just eyes and ears that are always watching. One day I'll run away and they won't have any power over me anymore.

Harbin, November 1940

I'm starting to remember. God help me. I don't want to know.

Entry date unknown:

A body can be so heavy when it's lifeless and limp. The scene from above:

a woman's body, naked, lying in the bath. Her hair is limp and wet, her eyes are closed. Her fingers are shriveled though the bathwater has gown cold. A man bursts in. He's had the prescience to remove the locks long ago. He hauls her out of the tub, but it's a struggle. Laying her on the cold marble floor, he pumps life into her blue-white body. She hasn't had the guts to cut her wrists. She thought a death by drowning would be easier.

Harbin, January 1941

'How did you get me out?' I ask Nobuaki. This is may not be the first time we have discussed that horrible place, but it is the first time I am completely lucid.

'Not I, Tani. Really, it was a fluke. Tanaka-san's driver came to pick up some materials, recognized you and informed Tanaka. It is only because you were kind to his daughter that you are alive today. He called me right away. You were in no fit state and in any case, he could not chance you talking about it.'

'Tamura, how can you live knowing this place exists?'

Tamura does not like this question, and he says, 'Tani, you are the only person to have ever been there and was allowed to leave the way they came. Do you understand me?'

I understand him very well. It means the discussion is closed and there will be no more talk of it. I do not know the extent of what goes on at that facility, but I know enough to suspect the worst. When they processed me, a full exam followed. They were brutal. I do not know if I was infected with anything, I just know I was bleeding afterward. I do not know if the Japanese doctor has given me medicine for that or if I have spontaneously healed. There seems to be no after affect. Perhaps I was there too short a time for any real damage to be done. I remember two exams, some shots and waiting in that cell for them to come again. When they did it was with a man in uniform who put me in a car and took me here. I know I am fortunate, but each day I think I must leave this house.

'Tamura, I would like to get back to Shanghai. Can you arrange this for me?' I ask.

'You are unfit to travel,' he says.

'I won't talk about it, ever. I know it would be dangerous to me to do so. Please let me go.' But no matter how I beg, his answer is always the same.

I have no papers and no money, and I wonder how I could manage my escape. I cannot separate the Japanese from their deeds. I know logically Tamura is keeping me alive, but I cannot get over this and cannot accept him for what he is.

Harbin, April 1941

Each day when I go to the garden, now alone, I reach the tea house and go beyond to the round gate that leads to the alley and outside world. It's taken me months to put my hand on the gate. Now I can step into the alley, but no further. I am paralyzed by fear and dither there, unable to take even a few steps forward. I am certain those who watch me are well aware of this, and make no move to stop me going where I will.

May 1941

Tamura is taking me on an excursion to the Thousand Lotus Flower Mountains south of Anshan. He says it will be good for me and there are things there that I need to see.

'What is there?' I ask, curiously.

'Ah Tani, it will be a surprise,' he answers.

What sort of surprise? I wonder. The town itself is a hub of Japanese activity. The province is mineral rich and they have built their plants and steel works using slave labor there. There really is no end to these peoples' insanity and greed.

'I'd rather stay at home,' I say, wondering why I would use that word after it slips out of my mouth.

'No, I think not. This is something you must experience.' Tamura is quite firm, but he can see I have a fear of the unknown and that makes me grow agitated.

'Don't be afraid, Tani. It is a beautiful, green place in the mountains that is dotted with Buddhist and Taoist temples and shrines. It is a place of great spiritual value and tranquility.'

I calm down at once. 'Promise we won't go near the city,' I say.
'Yes, I promise.'

Thousand Lotus Flower Mountain, June 1941

It was as Tamura said it would be. The green of these mountain peaks,
the jade Buddha, the Taoist and Buddhist temples nestled within them, the
feeling of peace that overwhelms you as you climb winding stone stairs and
get glimpses of pagoda roofs at arch toward the sky is all encompassing.

There's a monk here, an older man who is so -I don't know how to say
this-true to himself- true to what he is that in his presence I can feel all the
angst drain out of my body and utter calmness come over me. I would like to
speak to him, but I think though he is aware of my presence, he is waiting for
me to approach him.

Thousand Lotus Flower Mountain, June 1941

I have spoken to the monk who is called Master Zhao. Master Zhao
appears as one would picture someone of an acetic nature, thin with
prominent cheekbones and deep set eyes in a long face with a wispy beard. He
listens to me carefully and smiles. I am tongue tied and inarticulate, and I
never broach the questions that I really want to ask.

We walk along the paths under blooming trees while I trip myself up in
all sorts of ways. After a while, he asks me to remain for a time. I am not my
own person and I tell him that I hope Tamura will consent.

Thousand Lotus Flower Mountain, July 1941

I am staying here now. I have told Master Zhao some of the things that
have happened to me. He speaks of a world of delusion. It is greed, aversion
and delusion which reign in the world today, he says. He teaches the way of
the Buddha and the Noble Eightfold Path: right views, right thought, right
speech, right action, right livelihood, right effort, right mindfulness, and right
concentration.

I have lived in delusion. My passion for Richard was one such. I was not mindful of the myriad warnings I had before that fateful night. And I was awakened in a most brutal manner.

What about evil in the world, I ask. He speaks of suffering, which is at the core of this teaching and says all beings are subject to the turning of the great wheel of Karma, that deeds follow us, and that one must abstain from taking lives. This karmic retribution gives him great peace of mind, but I do not believe in such things. I think those who are powerful, who are brutal, who see themselves as superior will vibrate with that energy throughout space and time. The victims will cower and bow down eternally. How can it be otherwise? One day a torturer, the next a peon? I do not believe in this just as I do not believe in the great day of Christian Judgment.

There is no wisdom to be found here for me. They speak of enlightenment, but what is the purpose of being at one with the source of all things when the source allows things of this nature to occur in the world? And to become so, one must already be living a righteous life. Perhaps if everyone were enlightened all would be well, but that is clearly not the case. I am in a state of utter confusion. I think I will never find a satisfactory explanation for the things that happened and are still happening in that terrible place.

Thousand Lotus Flower Mountain, July 1941

I think the greatest healing is to be found in nature and away from all of mankind's thoughts and deeds.

This place is magical, the thousand mountain peaks of pink granite, and the rock pines, so old, that grow from them. The moss on the stones, the grasses growing between the pagoda roofs, the purple skies, the morning mist, the winding footpaths through the forest, the birds that sing -that is the true nature of creation. It is all good and harmonious. I walk every day, and I sit in meditation, which slows the tape in my mind. Afterward, I feel my anger has drained away. Who is it that I am angry with? Richard, the Japanese? I think mostly I am disappointed in myself and the choices I have made. What a stupid, silly, shallow girl I have been.

Thousand Lotus Flower Mountain, July 1941

It is warm, almost subtropical in these mountains. I still love my early morning walks. I found something else here. It is the way of Tao, the harmonious path of the universe. It is the energy that flows through all things, that moves throughout all life, that is both a balance between opposites and contains all opposites, that regulates our bodies, that aligns us with life as it should be lived. I can sense this life, this true path when I am alone in nature, and when I sit breathing quietly, emptying my mind of its chatter. It is then that I can see that the Japanese who tortured us are the ones who are tortured and out of alignment with the harmony that is the true way of things.

Thousand Lotus Flower Mountain, August 1941

Torpor and heat. I sit in mediation much of the time now. It's strange but when I do, I seem to be able to see realms of light that are not beyond this earth but overlying it. I see my own body, a network of bright blue electrical channels that pulsate. I see the pointed rose, white or gold colored energy that surrounds the monks. Sometimes, I, too, am infused with light of various colors, sometimes I feel that I am no longer respiring through my nose and lungs but that every cell in my body is aware and breathing. Occasionally I hear music coming through the ether, though oddly it is not Chinese but sounds like a baroque quartet. Neither the Buddhists nor the Taoists pay much attention to these things. Master Zhao says these things happen, but it is wise to not get carried away, or think one has special powers, because of them.

Thousand Lotus Flower Mountain, September 1941

Tamura came for a visit. He asks if I want to remain, and I say yes. It is good, he says, he can see I am getting well. It's odd, but I can see him as separate from the Imperial machine now, a human being who is caught up in events beyond his control. He seems tired and perhaps is uncertain of the things that I am telling him-things that I am experiencing in these mountains. Perhaps he thinks I am hallucinating or the monks have told me of their experiences and I am making it all up. It doesn't matter what he thinks. I take him on hikes and show him my favorite places. He seems to enjoy that. We part as good friends. No mention is made of my papers of or me returning to his house or going back to Shanghai. It's just as well.

Thousand Lotus Flower Mountain, December 1941

Nobuaki has come to visit quite often. Though normally he rarely talks about the war, he mentions the Japanese attack on Pearl Harbor. It seems that once again I have been leading a completely insular life, utterly unaware of current events. The Americans are in the Pacific war now and fighting against Germany and Italy as well. Despite this, Japan is expanding.

'What else?' I ask. They have occupied Hong Kong. Manila is an open city. But Nobuaki does not want to speak of this. He reminisces about Brazil and the things that he loves. I ask about his children. He has seen them on a brief visit. He says they are perfect little Japanese. I know he doesn't like what they have become from the way he says it.

'What will happen?' I ask him.

'Oh, they'll be fine,' he says, brushing it off.

'No. I mean about all this.'

Then he understands that I am speaking of the war and the occupation. 'We are expanding,' he says and rattles off: Wake and Guam, the Philippines, Malaysia, Thailand and Burma.

'America and Britain are against you,' I say, as if defeat against those two mighty powers should be self-evident.

'Tani, please do not speak of things you do not understand,' he says.

Suddenly I think, Richard was right, and all the calming wisdom I have accumulated here rushes right out the door as if on an evil wind. I say nothing to Tamura, but we are, once again, enemies.

Shanghai, June 1942

Since Kristallnacht, Jewish refugees have spilled into Shanghai from Germany and the rest of Europe. This is the only place in the world that welcomed them without visas. The Japanese look upon them differently, as they do us Russians. We are not white lords, and they have no need to humiliate us as they do the British and Dutch, to prove their own superiority.

I seem to be safe here under false identity papers, and not even Anya recognized me when I came to the door, I am so changed. My hair is a silvery white and my clothes hang upon my body. I look quite old now, and no would mistake me for the girl I was when I left. I'm certain Nobuaki could trace me if he choose to, but perhaps he finally realized it would be best to leave me to my own devices.

It took some time to reach Shanghai, but I was determined. The monks put me in touch with people who helped me. In the end, I made it back overland, partly by train, partly by truck and animal cart, since so much of the track had been blown by bombing. I walked part of the way, following columns of refugees, but if you asked me now to recall those events, I couldn't. The details are blurred and I really don't have the strength to sort them out in my mind, nor do I desire to.

When I came back, I contacted Mister Isfahani who immediately got me a job in the Jewish relief organization. He was happy to help as usual. I do not know how to thank this good and kind man for everything he has done for me over the years without any expectation of repayment. He knows something terrible has happened to me but does not ask and uses my new name, Darya Mikhailovna Morozova.

Life is hard for the Jews in Shanghai. The old arrivals from Russia had long settled and done well, but there are twenty thousand new arrivals from Germany and Austria who live in squalor, and the ones from Poland are even worse off. Still compared to the way Chinese refugees live on the streets, they are blessed to have the support of their community, which gives them financial help and has opened soup kitchens. The Poles have terrible stories to tell about the Nazis. It is not that I do not want to listen to them but that I can't bear to. They all know something is wrong with me and after a while, they don't bother. There are a few men here who are kindhearted and some who are opportunistic who would like to get to know me. When I don't respond to them, they give up.

Britain and France went to war with Germany in 1939, after the invasion of Poland. Did I forget to mention that? I might have done. The Battle of Britain, the Tripartite pact between Germany, Japan and Italy, the invasion of Greece, the dismemberment and occupation of Yugoslavia, the siege of Leningrad, the surrender of Singapore, the invasion of Burma, the fighting in the Pacific theatre, these are the events that are rocking the world while I have had my eyes closed on my mountain, locked into my own sorrows.

Shanghai, October 1942

Shi-shi is dead. The Japanese took over his businesses. I suppose they did not need him to run things and prefer to do it themselves. He was just an inconvenience so they took him out of the way. There are other businessmen who have learned to get along. I wouldn't call them collaborators exactly, but they do what needs to be done. This war has made for odd bedfellows: communists and capitalists, gangsters and Japanese. They all rub along.

I live with Anya now. The Japanese confiscated her apartment and we moved to the building where I had lived before. Anya is strange though. She did not wallow mourning Shi-shi. She gets up each day and collects funds from rich Chinese to help the orphans of the streets. Her Chinese language skills are atrocious, and so, she takes me along to do the talking. I've gotten quite good at bullying people into parting with their money. Anya makes it all seem chic and modern. They know she was Shi-shi's mistress, but she wears her black like a widow and holds her head high. They all compete to be like her and suddenly find themselves feeling very generous.

Mister Isfahani understood why I couldn't work with the relief fund any more. It atmosphere was so heavy and it just reinforced my depression. He wanted to put me in the office filing paper work, but I told him I needed to breathe.

The British have defeated the Germans at Al-alamein, scattering them over North Africa.

Shanghai, February 1943

The British and Dutch have been interned into concentration camps and the Jews are being herded into a ghetto at the insistence of the Germans who are Japan's allies. The Japanese occupied the International Settlement where the British lived their safe luxurious lives all the way back in December of 1941, after Pearl Harbor. The prescient left when they could but there were those who stayed, preferring their comforts, and closing their eyes to reality, hoping the war would leave them unscathed. And truly, when you consider the options, war with Germany in Europe, perhaps there is no difference at all. I don't know how they will survive the camps. They are unused to hardship. It was terrible to see them being rounded up in trucks, carrying their suitcases, their women often dressed in furs, looking completely bewildered. They used to be so proud. I couldn't stand looking at this grotesque parade. I realized how much I had looked up to them, despite my criticisms. They were everything that was right with the world: their nobility and sense of fair play, their notions of civilization and what constituted it; their civil law, which they brought to places that had no sense of justice, far outweighed the wrongs they had done. And now I remember the tennis and swimming parties in Hong Kong, the races and dinner parties, the clubs, and dressing for dinner, and dancing. How beautiful life once was, how barbarous it is now. What could make people long for chaos and destruction? Why can't we just live and love one another with a human, brotherly kindness?

In Europe, the Germans have surrendered at Stalingrad. When I heard this news, I cried. Whatever I may think of Stalin and his cohort, I cannot help but feel pride and sorrow for my people, who have suffered so terribly and fought so bravely.

Shanghai, April 1943

I'm a teacher now at a Catholic school. Anya liaised with them through her fundraising efforts and dragged me along to meet them. I was prepared for the worst, having always found the members of that religion to have a strange blend of naivety and self-righteousness. But Father Ignatius, a French Jesuit, is as wise and shrewd a man as I have ever met, and the young Pole he has working with him, Father Paul is, I think, a holy saint, who thinks of everyone but himself and brings light to the world. The school barely functions as that really, the number of children is too overwhelming, and resources are limited and very strained. There are rich dioceses in Shanghai where orphanages and schools were staffed by nuns, but they have been closed by the Japanese, and the American nuns and priests have been confined to their convents and houses. Through Anya, Ignatius hired me to teach several subjects but ran out of money shortly thereafter. It's uncertain when they will receive more funding. Given the wealth of the Catholic Church, this makes me quite upset, but Father Paul says to be patient, that God will provide.

I wish I had his faith. We are living off Anya's jewels, the two of us. Sirdar Singh has joined the army, so we are not even getting what they are worth, or would be worth, even in these circumstances. I do all of our negotiating and Anya sometimes jokes that I'm so tough I must have some Jewish ancestry. I take this as a compliment, of course, though she does not mean it that way. Old prejudices die hard, it seems, even in these times.

Shanghai, May 1943

I've just had a meeting with Father Ignatius. I was quite forward with him, saying, 'God helps those who help themselves.'

'Father,' I said, 'You need a fixer to get you what you need in terms of supplies. You need food, medicine, and a doctor to see to these children. You need nurses for the babies and someone to hold them. They are not thriving and while all your theories about God's will and Heavenly Peace and Him calling the little children unto Himself are well and good, we are living in the real world here.' It was quite a speech and the result was unexpected. He started laughing. He did not deter me at all, though he knows it might prove dangerous to me. I can see the sadness behind his laughter when he looks at me, and I know he knows it will give me as much a purpose for living as it might bring something of value to them. I know he is afraid they will be placed under house arrest like the American Jesuits here and that he worries so about the children.

Ignatius is a tall, stooped grey haired man in his sixties with thick glasses and a bird -like profile. He has huge hands and powerful arms and shoulders. I wonder what his life has been like. I know nothing about him, except that he is from Brittany originally. The Pole grew up in abject misery, in the poorest part of Warsaw, a place of beggars and thieves. I suppose that environment can create saints as well. They sent him to France for his schooling. I suppose his fine mind and his piety distinguished him greatly. Saints make poor fixers, and I am no saint. Not at all.

'All right, Miss Morozova. Do what you can. The children and I are depending on it,' Ignatius said, clasping his hands together, as if already in prayer.

Shanghai, July 1943

Anya and I began to raise funds the old way, thinking we would inject a bit of glamour into this now drab city. Yevgeny Borisovitch agreed to participate, lending us the space in his club and donating his profits, and we got all his old showgirls, and Russian violinists, and an orchestra to work for free.

The Vichy Government will surrender the French Concession to the Wang Ching-wei collaborationist regime, it seems. We rushed to put on the show beforehand, so that we would not need the permission of the Japanese nor to invite them. Instead, we asked rich Chinese and some Russians, those who have now taken over good positions in the absence of the British and can afford to spend money, though like the Chinese, and recalling bad times, they tend to be frugal. Still, when the iced vodka and champagne begin to flow pocketbooks tend to open.

Later, I will call on the Princess and through her get to her German contacts and through them perhaps the Japanese. Anya has colored my grey hair blond. It gives me a sweetly generic appearance that makes me indistinguishable from any other Russian. Yevegeny Borisovich doesn't recognize me at all and thinks I am a friend of Anya's. I say nothing, rarely make appearances, and let her put forth all my ideas. It's better this way.

The Americans and the British have landed in Sicily.

Shanghai, July 1943

The show was a success and I took the money, though Anya and I argued about it, to procure rice supplies. She thinks the Catholics should do more for themselves and that a certain amount should be diverted for the street orphans who have no one to look after them at all. I didn't disagree with her *but had to point out that she couldn't save everyone, it was an impossibility to do so. Then she said something terrible to me.*

'The only reason you are doing this at all, Tanya, is that you can't look life squarely in the face. You ran away from those orphans as soon as you could and are just appeasing your conscience now.'

I wanted to say that I had seen life as she calls it, and I was horrified by what I saw and what I am still am seeing. I opened my mouth to say so, but then, upon reflection, I realized she was right.

'Anya, I can't look at them. Every day more children are coming in and the youngest ones are in such poor condition, I know they won't make it. I can look at death, it's a form of peace, but I cannot look at suffering.'

'You haven't seen anyone since you got back. You don't even ask about them. Natalia, Sasha, don't you care? They were your good friends.'

'Well, then, how are they?' I asked, though I felt myself to be completely detached from the past and from my former relations with everyone but Anya, and that attachment, if I cared to admit it, was a form of survival.

'Natalia and her husband are thriving. Sasha, I suppose, is still with the Communists wherever they are now. I could make inquiries at the studio for you.'

'No, don't. I'm past desiring any relations with men, and as long as he is well it is good enough for me.'

'All right, Tanya, whatever you think is best,' she says with finality, but I can see her looking at me sometimes and wondering what happened in Harbin. Initially, she believed the journey back caused me so much hardship that I was completely exhausted by it in every way possible, but now she suspects something deeper, though I have made it very clear that I will not tolerate her probing.

We hashed it out about the money and finally made a compromise. It won't be enough in any case, either way.

Shanghai, August 1943

I'm negotiating with a Communist agent now. He gave me his name, but of course, it is not real. They are undercover here in Shanghai deploying their networks. I didn't want to see him, but after trying to secure a steady flow of rice into our coffers from several mill owners, I discovered they were hedging their bets by supplying both the Communists and Kuomintang. You can't give Chang's forces any money in this country, they are so corrupted. They'll steal what they can and you'll end up with nothing in the end. The Communists, for the moment, are eager to make a good impression and will deal honestly.

This man is a dedicated party cadre, but I had to pay numerous bribes and wait for him to consent to see me. He received me in a dingy back street house and listened carefully to what I had to say. These people have a very good spy network, but if he knew who I was, or of my association with Richard, he never mentioned it. He merely said he would look into it and inform me when they came to a decision. I thanked him for receiving me. As I was leaving, he said he would send his doctor to the mission. I thanked him profusely.

Shanghai, September 1943

The communist doctor finally came. He has been educated in America and speaks good English, though I could see he had a profound distaste for the Fathers. He says we need quinine. This is only available on the black market, and I might have to see some very unsavory people to obtain it. Chinese crime rings run the drug trade but there are Russians who are affiliated with them whom I can prevail upon. He also says he that the Americans have developed a powerful strain of penicillin that they are reserving for their troops in the Pacific.

When Anya and I discuss this, she says she will deal with it. She has American friends she and has been practicing English ever since she hoped to catch an Englishman before she met Shi-shi. Through them, she's met several journalists and businessmen who she thinks might have contacts within the American command which is centered in Burma and Calcutta.

'What do you think the likelihood of success is, Anya?' I ask, shaking my head.

Anya shrugs as she puts on her finery. 'It can never hurt to ask,' she says, 'and it can never hurt to make solid connections. Tanya, maybe we're going to have to leave Shanghai after the war. America is as good a place as any to *go to.' She puts on her make-up carefully and dabs perfume on her wrists and neck.*

'Anya, you're assuming the allies will win the war, but what if they don't?'

'Oh, they'll certainly win against the Japanese. We have the numbers; the Brits, the Amis, the Soviets, and many millions of Chinese to call upon. The Japanese will capitulate in time, you'll see.' She rolls up her stockings and pins them to her girdle with a wink. She's up to her old tricks. She might not get us any penicillin, but she'll find a way to make this request work for her, I know.

In the meantime, I'll find a traditional Chinese doctor who can perhaps help us with herbal medicines. At the very least, he might be able to boost the immune systems of some of the children in the orphanage.

The Allies are in Naples.

Shanghai, September 1943

We've secured a supply of rice though there is no guarantee how long it will last or how much can be diverted to us. I am looking into other grains. Millet is no good for human consumption.

Shanghai, October 1943

An American journalist friend of Anya's has been placed under arrest in Bridge House by the Japanese. This is a terrible and notorious place where hideous tortures have been deployed. Apparently, he had been blacklisted by the Japanese. They do that to journalists and editors who have the guts to speak out against them. Anya has been campaigning all over town to have him released. She has made many contacts among the Americans, but still we have no penicillin.

Shanghai, October 1943

I went to see the Rajni. She is married to a German diplomat now and lives in high style, though she seemed bored to death of everything around her. When I announced myself, she seemed delighted until she got a look at me. I could see the shock on her face though she tried to conceal it. I know I'm taking a risk but in the end, I decided to tell her I was arrested by the Kempeitai in Harbin. Foolish of me. I think I might have made a mistake. She listened to me ask for help, made some vague promise of looking into it and could barely conceal the fact that she was anxious to be rid of me.

I must look ghastly, and even worse than that, I am surrounded by the odor of despair that frightens people who live for good times and pleasures.

There's still pleasure of a sort to be found here in this city. The Japanese frequent the clubs and brothels and there are just as many sex workers as there ever were, only now, they cater to them. There are terrible things on the streets as well. The Chinese have poured into the former French Concession and the International Settlement. It's a continual horror show walking these streets. The beggars are in rags and covered in sores. The stench of unwashed human filth fills the air, and it's all I can do to keep from gagging, or crying, or wanting to run away somewhere far away. Sometimes my mind slips back to Nobuaki and how he wanted to take a slow boat to some unspoiled place in the world where we would be safe and away from this madness.

I wonder if the Rajni will tell her husband about me. I wonder if he will mention me to one of his Japanese friends who will look me up and have me arrested. It will be the end of me. Still, I'm just hanging on. What for, I wonder?

Shanghai, November 1943

Anya's journalist has been released. He's staying here with us. There's no one else to look after him, and I can tell she wants to. She loves him, I think, even though he is a ruin now. She thinks she can make him well and so we try, taking turns feeding him. He's soft, sensitive, and kind. It's not this recent suffering that's made him so, but something much deeper than that. I can see his eyes when he looks at Anya and watches her moving around the room. He loves her. He's a few years younger than she is, I think, though now he looks older. His name is Palmer Endicott Phillips, but everyone calls him Mike. He's tall and used to be lanky like Gary Cooper. Now he's skeletal.

British troops have re-entered Burma.

. . .

Shanghai, December 1943

Mike sometimes talks to me when Anya is out and about. It's not that he doesn't tell her things, but I think he would consider himself less of a man if he confided in her the way he does in me. I sit silently holding his hand while he recounts the things he lived through, the things they did to him there. The filth and lack of food, just watery rice gruel each day that made him lose so much weight, and the cigarette burns over his body speak for themselves. Anya washes him with a smile on her face but when she leaves his room, she whispers to me that there are burns on his genitals and starts to cry. He tells me about the water torture, a rag stuffed in his mouth, while they poured dirty water down his throat and can hardly get the words out.

'Were you afraid?' I ask.

'Were you?' he replies. I must have looked surprised but he says, 'I can see it on you, you have that look.' And then I tell him everything, about Richard and Nobuaki, about Harbin and that terrible place, and everything that has happened to me. He cries for me and kisses my hands. It's like a Russian novel, really.

'You won't tell Anya, will you?' I ask. He shakes his head no. It's our secret he promises, everything that's happened. Normal people should never have to think about such things.

Shanghai, January 1944

Mike is up, walking around the apartment. Anya won't let him out yet, but yesterday he had a friend bring him some things.

'Come here, Tanya,' he said, 'there's something I want you to have.' He handed me a Leica.

'What for Mike?' I asked.

'You need this Tanya. You're dying on the vine as you are.'

'I have my work for the orphans to attend to,' I said.

'Take this camera and take photographs of the orphans and everything you see around you. I'll make sure they're seen by people back home in the States. You can do far more good with that than you can as a fixer,' he was laughing at me now.

Anya was listening, and she stood next to him and put her arm across his shoulder. They had evidently discussed this beforehand. 'I'll handle everything you've been doing Tanya,' she says, 'but I need you to do what Mike says.'

'All right,' I agree, taking the camera into my hands.

Shanghai, February 1944

There so much freedom to be found in life, so much joy. This camera has brought it back to me, but maybe I was ready to recover. I have taken thousands of photos and the best ones have been published in Life Magazine in the United States, bringing an outpouring of donations for the orphans. Mike has arranged everything. Evidently, he is from a prominent family from the east coast of America, though his branch seems to be an eccentric offshoot that has always been interested in esoteric strains of Protestantism. I think he called this line of thought, Transcendentalism. He mentioned an author named Thoreau, and promised to get me a copy of his most famous book. We talked a bit about this after I mentioned how peaceful I had felt on Thousand Lotus Mountain. He really understood what I was saying and said he could relate to it.

In the beginning, I worried that Anya might not think kindly of my friendship with Mike, but that is not the case. When his letters come, she says, 'A letter from your best friend' and waves the envelope in the air. She keeps the things he writes to her to herself, though she often cries over them. She is still very hands on with the orphans, but I am not. Each day I take my camera and shoot scenes of streets and objects that take my fancy. Mike has made connections for me in the States, and although my first photos were published under 'A Russian Stringer,' they are now using the name Dara Moore to accompany them.

Mike has recovered so well that he has started reporting from various regions in the Far East now. Anya is terrified each time he enters a war zone. She's set up icons all over the apartment and prays in front of them daily.

'You really love him, don't you?' I ask, and she is bewildered that I could even ask such a question. Later when she has a chance to think about it, she says, 'Just because I love Mike now, doesn't mean I loved Shi-shi any less. Perhaps I love Mike in a better, more mature, way because I am older, and

since I have experienced loss I can cherish small moments and simple things rather than taking everything for granted.'

I nod. I can understand that. 'Yes,' I say, though my own thoughts on the subject are completely muddled.

Shanghai, February 1944

Anya and Mike were married. It's the only way he can get her out. She'll be staying with his family in Boston. I have never seen Anya so terrified of anything. It really is quite funny to watch her worrying about the impression she will make on them. She now stands in front of the mirror pulling up the corners of her face to see if she looks younger that way.

'He's told me about them,' she confides. 'They're quite cold and they prize individualism and self-reliance above all things.'

'Well, you're nothing if not self-reliant,' I assure her.

'They'll hate me,' she says. 'I'm older, I'm Russian. I won't fit in.'

'Anya, you're the biggest snob I ever met, and once you stop acting like a worm, you'll intimidate the hell out of all those Boston Brahmins.' I prattle on and on. I know she has deeper worries. She is terrified Mike will be killed in action. I know she wants to have a child by him, to keep part of him if that should happen, but she is also terrified of having a child to care for should that happen, and terrified of being alone in the end, otherwise. And now comes the lamenting and nagging, she wants me to come with her and for him to take me out of China as well. It would be wise, she says, under the circumstances.

London, April 1944

We are out. Anya is in Boston. I've been hired as an official photographer by Mike's news agency. Anya didn't want to let me go. She couldn't believe they would want a woman, but Mike told her about Martha Gelhorn, Ernest Hemingway's wife, and Margaret Bourke-White, and Dickey Chapelle, and Lee Miller, and showed us their work.

'She's just as good as they are,' he said, and she finally stopped her wailing when she understood that having an official job was the only way out for me.

I'm in London now. Mike brought me here and introduced me to his contacts, some of whom are American journalists. I spent a bit of time with them. They are hard drinking, hard living, full of themselves, and occasionally can get tiresome. There's no glory in war but to hear them talk, you would think the story, the thrill, is all that counts. They are billeted at the Savoy, and I have seen the life that goes on at these grand hotels, unabated. The rich have shut up their grand houses in Belgravia and Mayfair and either gone to their country houses or taken up residence in hotels. The Luftwaffe, flying sorties during the Blitz, have destroyed hundreds of buildings and so many have been in the East End, amidst the poor who have had nowhere to go. The government has been slow to build adequate air raid shelters and so thousands slept in the underground, even on the tracks at night. Apparently, eight deep shelters were planned, but underground shelters, trench shelters, corrugated iron Anderson shelters, and basements are still being used.

Even so, I love it here. There is something so civilized about this city and its people. Though they are exhausted, they have kept their humanity despite everything they've been through these past few years. Since January, the Germans have been bombing in retaliation for the night sorties that have destroyed their cities. The English call it the Baby Blitz. Apparently it's nothing compared to what they experienced before. The Blitz, the heaviest bombing, took place between nineteen -forty and nineteen forty-one, and I have heard people speak of it with deep emotion. I don't think anyone who has lived through it could or will ever forget it.

Mike has put me up with a friend of his, an older, dour woman name Sarah Forsythe - Jones, who has a house in Kensington. Though she has the title of Mrs. I have not seen evidence of a husband. There are no photographs or references to any other creature, aside from a small dachshund named Teddy who died some years ago. Mrs. Forsythe-Jones has a short mannish hairstyle and wears no cosmetics save a red smear crookedly applied across her thin lips. She dresses in sharply tailored suits in dull muddy colors. The house reflects her pale, empty life aside from the garden where hundreds of plants are beginning bloom. It will be lush by late summer, I'm sure.

Mrs. Forsythe-Jones is employed at some ministry but does not speak of her work, and so I gather it has to do with intelligence. Indeed, we speak very little since she spends long hours away, but when her maid, Mary, got over her initial shyness, she became quite chatty and told me in English I can barely understand, 'Ow, you should 'ave seen it, Miss. Fires burning into the night one mile square. All we could see when it dawned was Saint Paul's still standin' like.' From her awed expression, I can tell this was a symbol of her city, of the resilience of her people, and of what they were prepared to endure.

Once she gets going, Mary talks a lot about the Blitz and her neighbors who were killed. While she carries out her duties, she tells me of an entire family buried under the rubble. She's not matter of fact about it, just reconciled that things are the way they are. Sometimes, I follow her around like a child, although she is far younger than I am, just to listen to her stories. I wonder what she would make of communism when we talk about the middle classes and common people who are left to carry the brunt of the destruction while the rich retain their comforts.

I wonder if she knows how beautiful she is with her slim figure, dark hair, and blue eyes. In Shanghai, her looks would have taken her far. Here, she'll be a worker for the rest of her life and that beauty will fade, so quickly, I'm afraid.

This time, they've suffered too, those in the West End. I've gone out afterward and taken photos, of the fire brigades, the air raid wardens, the rescue crews, and of people who are simply trying to maintain their dignity and go about their daily lives.

The Germans haven't been back for some time, occupied as they were on the Eastern Front, but now when the air sirens begin we all run to take shelter. You dread those sounds- the sharp intake of air and then the whistle of bombs hurtling through space. You can never guess where they will land, and that sets your adrenaline pumping. The noise is deafening. The RAF, too, fly their 'mosquitoes' and the Germans have to make their way through them. So many have been shot down. I'm glad of it.

I never think about being killed and yet am always pleasantly surprised to find myself still alive. I suppose I'm almost back to normal again. Mostly, I feel the camaraderie between the British and their conviction that they are upholding Western Civilization. It's true in a way.

Sometimes, I think the Germans are as barbaric as the Japanese. When I read what they have done in Poland, Byelorussia, and Russia, I'm filled with rage. *I feel happy when their civilians are suffering as they have made us suffer and are still making us suffer.*

London, April 1944

The bombs seem to have stopped for now.

At the Savoy, over drinks with the boys, as grown American men refer to themselves, I saw Margaret Bourke-White's photos of the Italian campaign. The US Army hires and pays journalists to work for them. The British do too. I'm envious of her and of other women photojournalists who have made their own way. I'm here solely because of Mike, but I have no real purpose. He's taken a desk job at the paper, stateside. Anya is pregnant and he does it to appease her, though I know he wants to be where the action is.

The boys say there are going to be landings on the coast of France, the allied forces in concert, to drive back the Germans on the Western front. I doubt whether they will allow women to photograph it. Even with the combat training that they give to journalists and photographers, it is deemed too dangerous.

The Allies are driving northward towards Rome. There were terrible losses at Anzio, but finally the Germans are being beaten back. The Red Army is moving west. I feel optimistic that the end is in sight and yet I'm afraid I'll miss everything. I must write to Mike and have him get me into the real stream of things instead of just leaving me to hang in Kensington as if I was a replacement for Teddy.

London, April 1944

I have secured accreditation as a war correspondent! I have an assignment, but it is not what I expected. Mike's brother, Dean, has an intelligence role here in London, and through him, I was asked to meet with the British. Mrs. Forsythe - Jones was present as well and, I think, instrumental vouching for my character and abilities. She thought quite highly of my photos of London when I showed them to her.

In short, I have been asked to photograph Tito's partisans in Yugoslavia. But, I should backtrack a bit.

According to my brief, in early April of 1941 the Germans dismembered Yugoslavia after a quick military victory and surrounded it on all sides. Hungary, Bulgaria and Italy invaded alongside Germany. The Croats established a pro-Axis government in Croatia and a large part of Bosnia-Hercegovina, where they have systematically been persecuting Serbs, Jews and Gypsies along ethnic lines. Initially, the Yugoslav government desired neutrality and were going to sign an agreement with the Axis powers, but their air force staged a coup. After the bombing of Belgrade by the Germans, and the surrender of the Yugoslav armed forces, the first resistance movement was initiated by the Serbian Nationalists or Chetniks, as they are commonly known, led by General Draza Mihailovic.

Mihailovic had the backing of his government in exile in London, and consequently, the British. However, reports from the ground and from Cairo where the British have headquartered the Balkan office, deem that Mihailovic's forces were not engaging the Germans frequently enough, It is said they fear the sort of terrible reprisals like the massacre in Kragujevac when every man between sixteen and sixty was killed, and instead prefer to save their resources for D-day, engaging in battles with the communist dominated partisans in the meantime.

In 1943, at the Tehran conference, Churchill switched his backing from Mihailovic's Chetniks to Tito's partisan forces, claiming that they were doing all the fighting against the Germans. Yet there seems to be some uneasiness about this in certain quarters since Britain is, after all, a capitalistic country and uncomfortable with a Soviet trained partisan resistance movement in the Balkans.

The British and Americans at the meeting seem to think that Serbo-Croatian and Russian are mutually intelligible, and that I will be just the girl for the job. It's true there are many similar words but they are accented differently, so I am cramming lessons to learn as much of it as I can.

On the surface, the British say they want human interest stories. My instinct tells me what they really want is to see photographic proof of actions conducted on the ground, since often intelligence reports have been contrary and radio contact sporadic. Additionally, I am told that neither Mihailovic nor Tito have been particularly cooperative with the British. Perhaps it suited them to be initially to garner British aid, and now not much, since they are furthering their own interests in terms of consolidating their respective power bases. Everyone is already thinking what will happen after the war, and yet it is hardly won.

After dinner out, Dean invited me to his flat, which resembles a men's club with lots of books and clubby leather chairs. Everything is upholstered in brown and deep red with paisley fabrics on the walls. You wouldn't expect a man like him to have taste but he does. He is brusque and I can see he won't respond to feminine wiles, so I am always correct with him.

I tried to probe him for more information, but he twists the conversation somehow and never answers me directly. I cannot quite grasp what he is intimating, since he seems to have a pattern of not saying what he thinks but rather observing with his cold grey eyes everything that goes around him. He only resembles Mike around the mouth and is much shorter and more powerfully built. He would almost look common were it not for his impeccable tailoring.

After a few scotches he seemed to have sunk into a torpor, but I soon realized he is like a sleeping dragon guarding his lair and has his pulse on everything transpiring around him. I asked about his books, since there was so many on the shelves but he merely grunts out monosyllabic answers. I then asked him about his Transcendentalist ancestors.

'Romantics, dreamers,' he looked uncomfortable to be associated with such foolishness. 'It was a different age. They believed in the inherent goodness of people,' he snorted and stared into his drink before taking a huge swig. 'I'm a pragmatist and have no time for nonsense.'

I want to open my mouth to affirm the sense I had of a united consciousness on Thousand Lotus Flower Mountain but thought better of it and replied, 'We're living in troubled times.'

He only thawed after I started to ask questions about Mike and their childhood. He seemed almost human then, though I can hardly imagine him as a child.

Earlier, he asked me very difficult questions pertaining to my thoughts on Russia, communism and the Soviet Union and seemed pleased with my answers. And yet, he understands neither the nuances nor the subtleties of our history. Men like him will rule our world when the war is finished. I am terrified of him.

. . .

London, May 1944

Nothing but delays. Mrs. Forsythe - Jones informs me that all of a sudden the prevailing thought is I won't be able to handle riding or crossing the mountains on foot. They want to send a man instead. We were in her pale green sitting room near a bay window having tea and I had to concentrate on holding my cup steady as my hand started to shake. Maybe it was rage, maybe nerves. I can't quite control my impulses since Harbin.

'I crossed China from Harbin to Shanghai, mostly on foot,' I said, trying to convince her of my suitability.

'Why would you take such risks, my dear?' she asked, in that cold, analytical manner she has when she is weighing your every word.

I was at a loss for a moment before the lie came to my lips. 'There were rumors that the Japanese were rounding up women for their brothels and medical experimentation.'

She looked very serious and asked me if I knew anything specific. Apparently, the people who make decisions here have an idea what has happened to British prisoners of war at the hands of the Japanese.

'I left Shanghai for a job in Harbin, but I was terrified of them. They control everything in Manchuria. I had many influential friends in Shanghai, and I thought I could depend on their help if anything untoward were to occur,' I explained carefully.

She nodded. 'I shouldn't wonder you were afraid,' she said gravely. 'Men have become bestial during this war.'

We continued to drink tea and I turned the conversation to the garden, which is her passion.

I was afraid that if I told her the truth I would never be able to leave. They would want to debrief me. God knows how long those sessions would take. And what would they make of my association with Tamura or Richard? Would they see me as a collaborator or as a double agent? I'd never be able to explain myself. At best, they might label me as a stupid and naïve girl who couldn't be trusted to make sound decisions. The only thing that is protecting me is my association with Mike.

I can see she analyzes everything I say. Her hooded eyes dart back and forth while I am speaking as if she was a computing machine. She purses her small mouth when anything strikes her as being incongruous and her stare then goes flat. She's sharp, and if she doesn't think I'm trustworthy, I'll be finished.

We'll see what happens. Dean may yet be influential, if he hasn't forgotten about me, or changed his mind. Perhaps, I somehow appear frivolous or unable to handle hardship.

I'm still sending my photos of London to the magazine. They run them occasionally, but I want so much more for myself.

London, May 1944

The male photojournalist broke his leg while on assignment. I tried not to smile when I heard the news, but there you have it. So, I'm waiting for my orders.

I've met the team that processes Robert Capa's photos and sends them on to New York where they are published. Well, that is, if they are not censored first. They're waiting for the invasion on the continent. D-day. They don't know when it's going to happen. I've been studying Capa's work. He'll do anything to get the shot. His images of the Spanish Civil War leave me breathless. The despair and determination he caught-there's nothing quite like it. I'll never be that good. I just listen when I'm in the presence of good photographers and try to learn all that I can. The rest are a bunch of blowhards. I still look like a dried up shell and that suits me because they don't bother with me. They chase the young, beautiful women in uniform.

In any case, I am to go in by boat to Montenegro and travel overland to document Tito's resistance. Earlier reporters and intelligence officers had to parachute in, so I suppose in that sense I am fortunate.

Vis, July 1944

The British command has confiscated my photos and reports. I don't know what is to become of them. I took careful notes but they are no longer in front of me, and so I am writing from memory mainly for my own benefit.

The Americans and the British are divided on the question of what will or should happen to the country of Yugoslavia after the war. Churchill is adamant in his support for Tito's partisans, but the American officers and intelligence agents I have encountered are uncertain, say that the British receive partisan propaganda as truth, and believe it, but what they have discovered in the field interviewing the populace indicates an altogether different situation. But I am getting ahead of myself as usual.

D-day, the planned invasion of Normandy, occurred on June 6, 1944. One hundred sixty allied troops were dropped on the beaches with the support of aircraft and ships to fight the Germans on the Western Front. Robert Capa was there and took the most incredible action photos of the landing, made even more poignant by the fact that most of his film was destroyed in the processing. The women reporters weren't allowed to go, but Martha Gelhorn managed to sneak aboard a carrier disguised as a stretcher bearer and hid in the toilet until the landing. She got her story.

Initially, I was supposed to go inland but our plans were altered for the Island of Vis off the Dalmatian coast. The British have their command and a submarine base there. We landed a few days prior to the signing of the Treaty of Vis, on June 16, 1944. The island is beautiful in itself, a paradise really, the furthest west in the Adriatic and unoccupied by the Germans. It is small, about ninety square kilometers and surrounded by turquoise waters that are so clear you can see all the way to the bottom. There is a natural harbor, and the old town is comprised of stone houses with red clay tiled roofs. The beaches and hidden coves are unspoiled by fighting, but I heard someone say though there were no sharks in these waters prior to the British arrival, the fish had followed their ships in.

The land, itself, is green but scrubby, with the occasional planted pine. I turned brown in a few days, waiting for my official work to begin, and it looked strange with my white hair.

The best part of day is in the mornings when I would go down to the sea alone and swim for a while, just looking outward at the blue expanse before me. David taught me to swim. I had thought of him only sporadically these last few years, but memories of those heady times returned, and I recalled how kind he had been. Was he was interned when the Japanese invaded Hong Kong, I wonder, or did he join the fighting? Where is he now? Is he still alive? I'll probably never know.

I try not to think about China or the past. It seems that I was always immersed in my own life, my own struggles, but an exile, who did not belong to the land nor the culture. I was unmoored; waiting for my life to begin and always with the expectation of something happening that would secure it. I now feel myself to be living in the stream of history, which is rapidly moving forward. I feel more real, more conscious. I don't know how to explain what I mean, really.

There's an airstrip here, with spitfires landing and taking off. The British are camped in the hills. The Partizan forces are also stationed here, about two thousand strong, women as well, leaving for raids on the mainland and other islands at night. Lots of camaraderie among them, dancing and singing. They are convinced that victory is at hand. The British ferry them and support them with artillery against their battles with the Germans.

I expected to go out with them, but instead, I was taken to meet Tito who speaks Russian and clearly enjoys the company of women. He is a man of about fifty years of age, not tall, but rather robust with heavy features and a full head of hair. He has an odd syntax and pronunciation relative to his countrymen, whether Serb or Croat, but he explains this by saying he spent many years in the USSR. There are rumors that he is really a Ukrainian sent by Stalin to assume the identity of the real Josip Broz, who was killed many years ago. I'm inclined to believe it. People don't lose their mother tongue in their twenties, which is how old he supposedly was when he left his homeland.

Tito was helped by Fitzroy McLean to escape the mainland where fighting took a heavy toll on his troops. This McLean is as an interesting man as I have ever met. He is rather good looking and reminds me of Richard. He has been everywhere, all across Russia, as well. He says he's a conservative, but he seems rather enamored of Tito. I can't determine if he is quite trustworthy, but perhaps it's because he reminds me of Richard that I am projecting my feelings of ill will onto him. He was a bit cavalier about the Allied carpet bombing of Belgrade (and other towns) which were supposed to have hit German depots and rail lines but which killed many civilians. I don't really know what to make of people like him, at all.

I took photos of the island, the partisans, and of course many of Tito, looking quite presidential. Ivan Subasic, the Prime Minister of the Yugoslav government in exile, arrived to sign the agreement that would merge the

Royal government in exile with Tito's communist forces until elections could be held after the war. Subasic posed for photos as well, but I had no introduction to him. All in all, a dull commonplace assignment on the surface. I still can't understand why the British didn't let me out with the Partizans. Maybe they aren't quite the fighters they portray themselves as being. I don't trust them.

Finally, I was allowed to accompany the American fact finding mission inland. At first, everyone was against it, but I had a month to persuade them that I was one of the guys, as they put it. This involved a lot of drinking on my part and not complaining, particularly when they took me on hikes over rough terrain. I toughened my feet by going barefoot as often as I could.

In the end, they consented mainly due to the influence of three Yugoslav-Americans who were with the mission. They were specially selected, by a Major Donovan, to bring back intelligence. We left by ship and were dropped somewhere south of Dubrovnik. We were met by peasants and what struck me were their bare feet and tattered clothes, and the fact that they carried rifles that were old and probably useless. They had horses waiting for us and we rode up into the mountains, roughing it the whole way on the steep and rocky terrain. I had my equipment with me and, of course, I didn't want to ask for anyone's help carrying it, but the men who met us insisted. We stayed at a small village and everyone who met us was so terribly helpful and generous with their food supplies, even though they were terribly poor. I was so touched and made photos of them and promised I would send them when I could. I don't think that will ever happen now.

My sense was that the people are war weary, and despite British claims, none of them particularly favors the partisans or communism except the poorest of the poor who have no other way of making a better life for themselves. These people seem proud and independent, but the way they live within their villages and their generosity and hospitality made me feel that they were already living in the true spirit of brotherhood with each other despite the bitter fighting and civil war between the Chetnik royalists and the communist Partizans.

We interviewed some wounded men in a makeshift hospital, and they said they were not afraid to die but that their greatest regret had been fighting their brothers on the opposite side of the ideological divide. I inquired into their politics and as to that of the other side and they told us that really Tito's partisans were from regions where Serbs were being persecuted by Croat fascists, the Ustashe, and had no one to turn to but the partisans for protection.

Then they said something that disturbed me greatly but that I could not confirm-and that was that the Ustashe, believing German victory was inevitable, joined the Axis, but when they saw the tide of war turning, they defected to the Partizans believing the Allies would win the war. Now their main mission was to secure enough territory contra Serbs and free it for Croatia. Certainly, the Chetniks believe it is true though my British friends assured me that Tito is the only leader who gathers men to himself not along ethnic or religious lines but their willingness to fight the Germans. Some believe that he is the only person who could hold the country together afterward.

I asked why Croatia and Slovenia and Serbia wouldn't be free to create their own countries as they willed, since animosity runs high between them, but I have no concrete answers. Regional stability and British interests were mentioned, and again I think this land, falling as it does between the crossroads of Europe and Asia, is of strategic importance, and what its own populace desires for itself will be negated. However, I discovered that the Red Army is getting closer to the eastern border of Yugoslavia, and I wondered if they wouldn't back Tito in a power play of some sort against the government in exile when the time comes.

I took photos of the wounded, and the most terrible of all was the day I took photos of amputations without anesthetic because the Americans and the British funnel all the supplies to the Partizans who hold on to them, but give nothing to the Chetnik royalists who they want to eliminate as a source of rivalry. It was horrible, the worst thing I have ever seen, and I thought I had seen it all in China. But I thought that if the people who are making these decisions in Washington and London saw evidence perhaps they would be moved to help these people, at least with medical supplies. The whole time I kept thinking, I don't know what will happen here. I don't know why these decisions have been made, what is the truth, what is propaganda. It's all so murky and confusing.

Something happened at the hospital that I'll never forget; a man called

Jovan who had lost contact with his platoon was left alone in the woods. He kept flicking an invisible radio on and off and calling, 'Hallo veza'. He was calling for his connection and his terror went unabated. I don't know if he will ever recover and be in his right mind. I don't know how long a trauma like that can last. That night, I had terrible dreams of Harbin again and that place, only this time I could not get out of my cell. No matter how hard I tried to crawl up the walls, I couldn't make headway. I woke up soaking wet and was afraid to go back to sleep. I dread evening, and I dread night even more.

Afterward, the American mission continued inland to Bosnia and Serbia. I was taken down to the coast. The consensus was that I should go back to Vis to get the film processed, because it is imperative for the two sides to stop fighting each other and drive the Germans out of the Balkans once and for all. I consented, having little choice.

Italy, August 1944

I'm on the other side of the Adriatic now and photographing the British Eighth Army as they are about to march up the coast in their attempt to capture the so- called Gothic line. These men have been fighting steadily since the North African campaign. They have such dreadful losses. At Anzio, the Allies sustained forty-four thousand casualties, and fifty five thousand at Monte Casino. The statistics are horrific. Aside from death and the fear it instills, I don't know how they have stood the everyday struggles they have to contend with: the heat, the lice, the mosquitoes, and the constant barrage of guns. Sometimes the fighting has been as bad as it was in the trenches of the First World War, they tell me, and they had to dig pits to sleep in and to protect themselves. The Germans are ferocious fighters and some say it we are winning only because of superior American fire power.

I've met someone. His name is John Harrison. Lieutenant. He makes me laugh all the time. He has a fine mind and appears to be quite sensitive and thoughtful, though he is awfully witty and often irreverent. He fought in North Africa before Italy.

They call me D. here, and that's fine. I haven't told him my whole history or my real name. We talk a lot, mostly through his grammatical French because he want to practice, though he speaks it like an Englishman, keeping his jaw rigid and never once opening his teeth. He is well educated and knows an awful lot about history, art and literature, though mostly we keep it light. I think the men are so worn out, it's best to focus on the positive and not discuss serious things.

John is very tall, very slender, very English looking, horse faced and beaky nosed with prominent teeth and mouse colored hair. His hairline is receding a bit, though I think he is about the same age as I am or maybe even younger. I'm thirty -two now, though I often feel a hundred and thirty-two.

John sort of hovers around while I am taking pictures and then says something so absurd, I start to laugh and lose my concentration. His personality is the main attraction. Even so, I like the look of him though he is not conventionally handsome.

I thought I never wanted another man in my life, but perhaps I was wrong in thinking so. I don't know why, but I seem to light up when he is around, and I so look forward to seeing him. He dispels my gloom and makes everything seem so much brighter. God knows if he'll survive. After my assignment is finished, I probably won't see him again. I pray that he will live through it. I am terrified that he won't, so perhaps it would be wise not to be carried away. Nevertheless, we promised to write each other.

The Allies are in Paris. The Romanians have overthrown their pro-Axis regime. Bulgaria surrendered. The Germans are pulling out and retreating from Greece and Southern Yugoslavia! I am headed to Rome where it is relatively safe.

Rome, September 1944

On 12 September, the Battle of Rimini began. A letter from John beforehand. I was so excited to receive it that my hands were shaking. Like most of the English, he politely speaks of the weather first. Endless rain is making the terrain impenetrable to heavy machinery and difficult to cross. I don't have to read between the lines to understand the pressure he is being subjected to or the direction of his thoughts: the Germans have fortified the line, digging deep anti-tank trenches. They have mined and booby trapped this whole country, it seems. I can't breathe thinking about it. I feel I should be there, photographing the battle, but they won't let me return.

I am billeted in a private house with rooms to let, though I am the only one here. The room is austere with cracked plaster across the walls and rough linen sheets on the iron bed. My landlady, Signora Lina, is an older woman, friendly enough but not too friendly, seeing how she has nothing but Italian and I am just beginning to learn a few words. She has sharp birdlike features and mispronounces my name.

Food shortages, coal shortages, and bullying by the Germans have left her as demoralized as the rest of the population. The Allied command have tried to instill order and deal with the situation, but find the Romans self-serving and unconcerned about the sacrifices the Allies have made to liberate their country. The Romans, on the other hand, find the GIs' habits appalling. The men are well fed, have cigarettes and money to throw around while on leave, and don't hesitate to take up with the local girls.

Lina complains about them constantly. I cluck sympathetically but privately think the Romans forget that they were allied to the Germans and that these soldiers have been fighting and making great sacrifices for years. Nevertheless, it's making for bad feelings.

I share my rations with Lina, but she is invariably displeased. Whatever I give her is never enough. Shaking her head, she mutters incomprehensibly and looks at me as if I were the enemy. I can't take her too seriously, though. There are too many horrible things in the world. Maybe she's been spared from them or maybe it's in her nature to be perpetually dissatisfied.

Signora Lina cooks for me, but mostly we eat starches. At least we have food. It's terrible in the south, particularly in Naples, which was heavily bombarded. Lina tells me that hunger is prevalent there, despite the presence of the Allies, and that the black market is making it all worse. Most people are starving on less than six hundred calories per day, and many of the women have had to go into prostitution to feed themselves and their families. Lina despairs of the morality of this and wonders if the entire country won't go to hell because of it.

In any case, Roman cultural life continues, and the bright part is that the Germans pulled out without a fight, making Rome an open, or undefended, city and so sparing it from more Allied bombing. I missed the heavy bombing in '43, when the Americans destroyed the entire San Lorenzo district. Three thousand civilians died in those sorties. The Vatican made a stink over it, citing the' churches and cultural treasures that need to be preserved. They have remained neutral throughout the war. I can't fathom why they wouldn't take a moral stance on fascism, other than that they fear communism even more. Still, one would think they would have had more to say about Hitler invading their 'poor, dear Poland' but all they seem to care about is their own institutional longevity.

Nevertheless, life goes on. The cinemas are open and the opera season will feature Turandot, La Boheme, Tosca, Le Nozze de Figaro, Lucia di Lammermoor among others. I have never been to the opera before and am I am excited by the thought. The Baths of Caracalla will feature opera in the summer too. We have ballet as well, and I am looking forward to it, not having seen any dance for years.

Of course, for me, the art is the most alluring part of this city- glorious works, which I know only from books. Exhibits are being organized and it's incredible to see works by Botticelli, Raphael, Giorgione, Titian and others. I spend a lot of my time gawping at paintings, sculpture, and architecture. I feel so fortunate to be here, even if it is a bit lonely. These days, I'm better about having only myself for company. Perhaps it's the thrill of discovery that makes me feel all right about it, that, and the fact that I like the quiet that allows me to think about what I am seeing.

Of course, Lina complains about how awful it all is, but I think, my God, the things you have here: The Spanish Steps, the Vatican, the Sistine Chapel, the Piazza Navona, the Fontana di Trevi, the Colosseum (even though now it's mostly an open air whorehouse), the Pantheon, the Forum, the churches and basilicas, the Borghese gardens! To me it really is the eternal city. Perhaps Venice is more beautiful. I don't know. I hope to see it one day when the war is over.

Rome, September 1944

I'm still waiting for my next assignment and fearing I won't get anything. I don't know if I have been forgotten or perhaps blacklisted for my report on Yugoslavia. I didn't really deliver what they wanted.

I am worried about John and can't stop thinking about him. When I walk through the city, I fantasize about the things he might say to me if he were *present. But my pleasant reveries are often obscured by thoughts of death, his in particular. I need work to pull myself out of this dark mood. At a cafe, I met a reporter, who after hearing me complain, said Martha Gelhorn had attached herself to the Polish troops here and was reporting their activities and history. She's a fearless woman who always takes the initiative, and perhaps, I should do the same.*

Rome, October 1944

John is alive! Lots of things of a personal nature in his letters that take my breath away. I suppose it's normal to think of being with a woman after surviving hell. You just want to live again.

I think back to my old diaries that were left behind in China and how I recorded every detail of my love affairs. But this seems so personal, so intimate, and I am so enervated that I couldn't bear to repeat the things he writes, even here. Maybe it's that I am older and I have more understanding, and understanding of him too-and know though perhaps he says those things now, he doesn't really mean them and it will all come to nothing in the end.

Rome, October 1944

I was introduced to some movie people at a café. Two of them are working on a script about anti-fascist forces in Rome. I hate to sound cynical, but I'm sure the Italians would like to be remembered by history as anti-German, as forming Partisan brigades, as opposed to fascism. But the fact is that the Italian Social Republic is still headed by Mussolini, and though they are headquartered in Salo, they have proclaimed Rome their capitol. Maybe these people are sincere, but maybe like the Yugoslav fascists, they see which way the tide has turned.

In Warsaw, the Polish Home Army rose up against the Germans but were defeated. The Red Army did nothing to help them. They stopped on the banks of the Vistula leaving the Poles to their fate. I will never recover from this. Somehow, I have always been a Pan-Slavicist, and I think it's because Western Europeans have always thought of us as less than they are in terms of both human value and culture. But now my heart is breaking for the

Polish people. How brave they are and how terrible their defeat! Hitler has ordered the wholescale destruction of the city. According to some sources, Stalin desired to crush the Polish opposition and insert his own people into positions of power and ordered the Red Army not to intervene. Some scant air drops were made by the Allies but for the most part the Poles were completely abandoned. The Polish troops that have fought so bravely here and suffered such dreadful losses must be horrified.

Rome, October 1944

I had an amazing day. I met a most incredible woman, an actress named Anna Magnani. She's not conventionally beautiful, but she is so intense, like a force of nature. She's going to star in that film I mentioned. My fatigues carry a sort of credibility here, so I asked if I could photograph her. I explained my war photos are seen in the United States. I'm picking up Italian, by the way. It's not so hard when you have French, and she agreed. I told her not to get fixed up; I wanted her as she was-raw and earthy. She laughed, and her laugh scatters doves. I couldn't stop shooting. I think she was sick of me at the end of it.

'Basta!' she said, but she kept laughing the whole time.

I wrote to John about it and about the opera. Perhaps I had been expecting too much, or perhaps it's that I don't appreciate music, but I didn't think it was all that-too much melodrama, too many dull passages between the beautiful ones. I am a philistine in many ways.

The British soldiers in attendance were awed. Perhaps their own music hall traditions have prepared them for the spectacle. In my letter to John, I described everything, the atmosphere, the events, the reaction of his fellow countrymen, and my own. I don't know if this is the right thing to do. On the one hand, it seems very frivolous to be talking of urbane and civilized things to a man on the front lines who has just survived a battle, as if nothing out of the ordinary was happening, as if the war was not ongoing. On the other hand, I think perhaps it will be a good diversion for him, to get his mind off what he has been through and what he still must endure.

. . .

Rome, October 1944

I showed the photos to Magnani. She said, 'Bah, I'm so ugly.' But really, she is beautiful and so unusual with her messy hair and dark under eye circles. I discovered she is the mistress of a director named Roberto Rossellini. He's one of the men working on the movie script I mentioned.

When I gave her the copies, I told her I used to work on film sets in Shanghai.

'We have no sets here', she said, 'and hardly any film. Rossellini is reduced to begging for money.'

I said I was sorry artists of their caliber had to resort to that. She sighed and looked sorry for me as if she thought I must be awfully naive and privileged. A part of me wanted to explain, but then I thought better of it and better of promising I would beg film off my few contacts. I think the Italians are resourceful and will find their way without me.

I took a long walk and thought about Sasha and our work together. What has happened to him? Is he still alive and making movies? Later at home, I sat down and thought deeply about what I was doing and where I should go from here.

Rome, October 1944

I still don't have an assignment, so I hang around with photographers and movie people, but I don't belong and it depresses me. I'm drifting. When I got home, I was excited to see a letter from John. I feel better believing I have someone in my life even if it will prove to be another illusion.

He writes that there will be a spring offensive. He was hoping for leave but is not sure when he can get it. He has started to write of his experiences without sparing me. Maybe he feels more comfortable or maybe he just needs to get things off his chest. Maybe I'm a woman with special traits he has conjured that have nothing to do with reality. I can't know for sure.

This is what he writes:

Taylor, Wilson, Lewis and I were separated from our unit and spent the night in the woods. We knew the Germans were nearby. From our previous position, we had seen them driving through the scattered farmhouses in the tiny village below the hills. There was a stillness in the autumnal air, the stillness that pervades everything with the coming of that sad season which hearkens death, the death of the earth before its renewal. It was cold during the night, but we kept still and silent. I felt my limbs growing numb, yet it was eerie and beautiful, the black trees against the grey sky. Somewhere beyond the cloud cover, the moon was shining, enveloping the earth in a milky glow.

When light dawned, a mist obscured the valley then slowly dissipated, and we saw the Germans had gone. And yet we were cautious approaching the farmhouses. There was no movement, no sign of peasants beginning their day. We drew nearer. The carcass of a cow was lying in our path. Perhaps birds had begun singing, but all I can recall was the sound of my own blood coursing through my veins. I had experienced it before and I knew what it portended. Lewis felt it too. He looked terribly young and helpless, his pinched features those of a child. Wilson was first in. We covered him, but there was no need. When he came out of the farmhouse, he stooped to be sick. Inside, when my eyes adjusted to the darkness, I saw an entire family had been shot. Two little girls as well. There was no need for that. No need, at all.

Later when we located the other villagers, who were hiding, we discovered the father had been a partisan. The Germans had known it, as well. From his wounds, we could see he had been tortured. The killings were a reprisal, and yet so unnecessary.

Rome, November 1944

I sent my photographs of Magnani and Rosellini in to the magazine. I wrote a short article about the way they envisioned making the film, sort of like a documentary, raw and visceral. I don't think anyone in America is interested in the creativity going on here yet. But something good came of it, money from Anya and Mike, along with letters. I'm almost rich now.

Anya hates Boston and thinks Mike's family is made of stone. At least she is safe. I didn't mention John to them, though now I think of him all the time and read and reread his letters. I'm writing crazy things back to him too. I think he understands what I am trying to say about this film and the ideas they have about it, even though he doesn't know about my background. Mainly I'm excited that creativity is being renewed after all the horror and destruction that we have gone through. John wrote back with some amusing anecdotes about the plays he was in at school. I think he must have been very funny, and from the sound of it, very good, though he says he was terrible.

I dyed my hair back to dark brown yesterday. I've started thinking about what I look like and worrying what will happen when we see each other again. I look like my old self again and a maybe a little bit pretty.

The British are in Athens. There is famine there, and the Greeks are suffering terribly. I feel guilty for my frivolity but perhaps it is normal to think of one's appearance, despite the war and all the suffering.

Rome, November 1944

John can get leave. He asks me to meet him in Florence. The Allies liberated it in August after heavy fighting in the streets. There was shelling and the bridges over the Arno were blown. Apparently, the Germans took a great many art treasures with them when they retreated, yet the men go on leave there, perhaps heedless of what Florence has meant to Western civilization. They are after good times, and since the war is not over yet who can blame them?

John writes how anxious he is to see me, but I am suddenly afraid of going there and seeing him and of everything going wrong. After everything that has been said in our letters, after all the words of affection and desire that have passed between us, I think perhaps it will be a terrible disappointment to him. It's been five years since Harbin and Tamura and I think I might be useless to men now, but I do have feelings for him and he gives me something to look forward to.

Rome, November 1944

All my worries backfired. There have been such heavy rains that John has had a mishap, twisting his ankle in the mud. Leave is postponed. He thinks that he will be taken to a field hospital. The worst thing is that until last September the Thirty-third Hospital was headquartered in Rome. He probably would have been sent there and we could have easily seen each other. Now they have packed it all up and taken it to Livorno. I am worried

287

but he says it is nothing, particularly compared to the shrapnel wound he sustained in North Africa. He says fighting will be postponed until spring, and that old timers are being transferred from the front lines in any case. He says I shouldn't worry and we will see each other soon. The entire time I was reading his letter I thought, perhaps it's a lie and he doesn't want to see me. He will go to Florence with his friends, and they will find female companionship that involves no emotions and no commitments. I have gotten carried away and perhaps it would be wiser to concentrate on finding work instead.

Marshall Tito's troops liberated Belgrade in October, although some say the Red Army did all the heavy fighting. Perhaps I should go back there and see what is happening of my own accord. The Americans will be interested, if not the British.

Dubrovnik November 1944

I have attached myself to Floyd Force, under the command of Brigadier Sir Henry Floyd here in Dalmatia. For whatever reason there has been a blackout on news in Belgrade and foreign journalists have been asked to leave. However, Floyd Force is an artillery brigade that has been here since September on Tito's request. The Partizans have occupied areas in Montenegro and Dalmatia and the British intent is to launch a substantial force in the drive northward. The Germans are pulling back and are now going over the back roads through difficult terrain since British artillery is driving them. Floyd Force has been very successful last month routing the Germans here.

Dubrovnik is an incredible place. It is ancient, built on a peninsula jutting out into the Adriatic Sea, and is girded by medieval stone walls. Some say it was founded before the Byzantine Empire took hold here, but in any case, it came under the sway of Venice after the crusades and was the main port of trade between the Serbian Empire and the Venetians. Once inside its walls, you walk down narrow stone streets worn smooth by generations of feet. Private houses and public buildings are made of white stone and there are red clay tiles on the roofs. Sometimes you head down tiny streets and upstairs, only to find green vines growing out of the stone. The sea is beyond the walls, blue-green and clear. Sometimes, I think how nice it would be to come back after the war, have a studio, and make art in this white city on the sea, so serene, so lovely. I think how wonderful it would be to be able to go down the stairs to the sea and swim, in the morning, and then again in the afternoon in the heat of the day when all is sleepy and quiet and the work has been done. And I think what it might be like to have friends again, real friends, and not be so isolated - and how I would set the table in the garden and invite them for a fish dinner. We would drink wine under the stars and talk about all kinds of things. Then I remember why I am here and that I must concentrate on the work and the world because the war is not yet won.

I am taking photos, but none is exceptional since I have missed the heavy fighting. I don't think of John very much except in the still of the day, in that lonely quiet hour before dusk falls, when the full force of my solitude hits me, and I become afraid, and afraid of being alone the rest of my life.

The word around here is that the Eighth Army will sit out the winter and prepare for a spring drive against the Germans in the north of Italy, just as John said. I wrote to him to say I was going over but have not heard from him since. Even if he decided he wants nothing more to do with me, I wish him well. I wish him all that he desires for himself, and mostly I wish that he survive this stupid endless war.

Dubrovnik, December 1944

Difficulties here. The Partizans are not as cooperative with the British and there are tensions between them. I think some of this attitude comes from British imperiousness and their desire to win the war. They want the Partizans to take orders from them, while the Partizans are consolidating their power base for what will come after the war and need to aggrandize themselves and take full credit for all the gains that have been made against the Germans. Floyd Force was asked to pull back to Dubrovnik since the Partizans claimed an attack on the city was imminent. None materialized, thank God. Now they have had made a broadcast that there has been no signed agreement between them and the Brits authorizing British entry inland. Floyd Force is feeling thwarted at every turn. I have been speaking to the men here and the word is that there will be no large British invasionary force in the Balkans, since they cannot divert manpower away from the Western Front. Once again, it's difficult to say who is to blame, the Allies, or Tito, who keeps rejecting all their suggestions.

Dubrovnik, December 1944

    There are women fighters among the Partizans and I have taken their photos and written down their stories. It's incredible to see, really, how young and brave they are, and some of them are really good looking. Regardless of their ideology, I can't help but admire them. They did what they thought was necessary and took up arms to fight, sometimes in the heaviest battles that took place in this country. Sometimes I think of Mei and how she died, and how she lived, hoping for a better world. You think that perhaps these women are writing their own mythology, and yet some of them seem so open and sincere. Sometimes they came from pro-Partizan villages; sometimes from areas in Bosnia-Hercegovina that were being terrorized by the Ustashe.

    I was taking photos of them and they began to speak about their experiences. We kept talking for a long time. It was so pleasant, like having real girlfriends, even though they are so much younger than I am. I didn't want this feeling to end and so I invited them to dinner at a restaurant and Dragana, Stanka, Rosa, Manya and Biljana turned up. I could see that they were excited and had taken the trouble to make themselves look pretty.

    They are so full of life and hope and I wondered what they will do after the war is over. 'When you've taken up arms and actually had combat experience, can you settle for being wives and mothers afterward?' I asked.

    In unison, they reply that there will be a new era after the war, and they will have the opportunity to become educated and enter professions. They're so excited at the prospect.

    They think I am worldly and sophisticated and will understand them. I am none of those things, feel as though I am unanchored, and belong nowhere. I didn't dispel their notions. They asked me a bit about myself, and I said I had been a designer in Shanghai, leaving out Harbin altogether, and that through my contacts I came to Europe as a war correspondent.

    I then asked them about their experiences. They often spoke with wonder at their fate, sometimes so strange that a chance occurrence, a mere twist on a path meant the difference between life and death. At one point, they talked about a girl named Lepa who escaped from an Ustasha prison and took up arms. She fought in the bloody Battle of the Neretva, in Bosnia, which took place between January and March in 1943, when the Partizans fought the combined Axis troops, which sought to annihilate them and succeeded in killing about twelve thousand fighters. She was caught by the S.S. Prince Eugene Division, which hung her. She died with the word freedom on her lips. She was seventeen years old. It is very hard for me to control myself when I hear stories like that. The loss of life is too terrible, especially in one so young and brave. They tell me there are one hundred thousand women in the ranks, and some have even commanded units of fighting men. Who knows whether to believe them or not? Perhaps I am over cautious and too prejudiced due to my own experiences. Regardless, I liked them so very much.

Rome, January end 1945

Floyd Force has been recalled. I have no idea how my now positive reports of the Partizans will be received. It seems I am always a little out of touch with the prevailing wind. The Red Army has 'liberated' Warsaw and Krakow. The siege of Budapest has begun. The Battle of the Ardennes has been won. I am back in Rome. Cold this year all over Europe.

Letters from John. It seems he didn't know I had gone over again. My letter was delayed. He was worried and thought that either something had happened to me or that I didn't want to see him gain. I started crying when I saw how very sad he felt at having me gone from his life. I don't know why we care for each other so much, having only seen each other for a few days in real life. And yet I feel I know him so much better than I have anyone else. Perhaps all the words upon words we have exchanged are more revealing than those relations which begin on a physical basis, that depend on the eyes and chemical attraction, and on some combination of childhood fears, fantasies and projections. Once again, Florence might be on.

Rome, February 1945

I have another assignment and this one is probably the most important thing I have ever done aside from photographing the orphans in Shanghai. I am working with the Monuments, Fine Arts and Archives division which was formed initially to protect historical monuments as the Allies fight their way through Europe. Now a few art historians, archivists, scholars, archaeologists, and artists have joined the ranks to preserve and restore important buildings. Some are even trying to recapture the hundreds of thousands of artworks and manuscripts that the Nazis have stolen from all over Europe. There are negotiations in progress for their return apparently, though I am not privy to that kind of information.

My job is photographic documentation and though some would find it dull, it soothes me considerably. It's not only the work of cataloging, which in itself, I find, takes me away from the insanity around me but the fact that I am exposed to the most incredible constructs the human race has ever produced. What, if not art, can lift us above the horrors of the things that have transpired in the last century: two world wars, the barbarity of the Germans and the Japanese, the brutality of both fascism and communism? It is unthinkable to contemplate all that has transpired in this war, yet working with these dedicated people reminds me of what I used to call the good and the true-the things that mankind is capable of producing-culture and beauty rather than murder and destruction.

The Americans among them are nothing like the ones I have met so far. They are quite erudite and passionate about art and history. I love hanging around and listening to them.

John read archaeology at Oxford, I wonder if he couldn't get transferred and work with us instead? He told me that the archeologists had an informal role in North Africa. They were soldiers first but when something needed their attention, they would handle it. I gathered that their primary function was to stop the looting. The men like to take home souvenirs and don't hesitate to write graffiti on the walls of buildings that are of historic significance.

February, Florence 1945

Florence is drab and dark, as are my emotions. John has left and I am alone. Who could have guessed that things of such an intense and intimate nature could pass between two people who barely knew each other? Perhaps it is the thought of death that precipitates such ideas and stimulates sexuality, but everything I had experienced up until now seemed to pale by comparison, and my obsession with Richard seemed such a childish thing.

We had the top floor of a private house and the owners stayed out of our way, since, like many Catholics, they have gotten used to the ways of the world, as it is constituted now. The room has a sloping roof and large windows that looked out onto the Duomo. There's a walkway and stairs with wrought iron balusters down to a courtyard. I could picture it lined with flowers and trees but now it's empty and forlorn.

John met me and took me for quite a nice dinner since he has been promoted to the rank of captain and officers have special places that cater exclusively to them and are not subject to the kinds of shortages found throughout the cities and towns here. I filled in the lacuna with conversation of what I had witnessed in Yugoslavia while he listened to me chatter on and on with a smile on his face. I think we both knew that I was nervous and was trying to hide the fact that I had drunk far too much wine. Afterward we walked for a long while, silently, side by side before returning to the place we would call home for the week.

Once we arrived, my nervousness dissipated. There was an old phonograph and some pre-war records that someone had left behind. Later, I found out that this annex had belonged to the eldest son of the house who had been killed in a partisan action. John put one on and we danced, slowly, to the music and kept dancing when the record was done. I thought of his letters and the things he had written, impressions of the war and Italy which were eloquent and which had moved me, often to tears. Yet now there was no room for words and the closeness of having him present, knowing he was made of flesh, shocked me as I tried to reconcile the man I had envisioned from his words to the man who stood in front of me.

We hadn't really touched before. I was out of practice, and I didn't know anything about his life experience. John was holding me, my hand was in his, and his other hand was on the small of my back. I kept getting flashes of Richard dancing with me, holding me. How smooth and perfect his touch had been, and how strange John's was. His scent was unfamiliar and akin to that of paper.

He kissed me, a hard unpleasant kiss, all teeth, and I thought I couldn't possibly go through with it. It had been a mistake, one that was easily rectified. I could tell him to stop and go on my way the next morning, but he kept kissing me. Suddenly, I understood that John had need of me and that I could comfort him. At least that was my initial thought as we slipped into bed.

I worried that I would recall that place in Harbin and not be able to respond to him. But as he warmed up, his kisses became more sensual, tenderer. I sensed that he was going to be a good lover, once he got over his initial shyness.

Then real desire took hold of me, as it did him. At first, it seemed like the coming together of two human beings who had been starved for a long time, for affection, and sex as well, but then it mutated into something deeper, a true longing for one another.

In the end, I do not think it was the pleasure which counted as much as the feelings behind it. I suddenly realized how incredibly childish I had been in my relations to men, always looking for someone to take care of me, to give to me. Since Harbin, I had grown up, albeit in an ugly way, and I understood everything would be different from now on.

We spent the entire week eating, drinking wine, making love, and sightseeing, that is, seeing what is left of Florence. The Germans blew all the bridges but the Ponte Vecchio during their retreat. The Arno is as a sluggish mud puddle, so much rubble has been pushed into it by our engineers. There was heavy fighting here between here Allies and the Germans, sometimes door to door. The horrid thing besides the loss of lives has been the destruction of some of the finest cultural monuments mankind has ever produced. The Germans have absconded with so many paintings from museums, and the rest have been hidden in various villas throughout Tuscany, though no one knows where they are.

Though our backgrounds are dissimilar, we hold many of the same things close and find the devastation of Florence's cultural treasures to be terribly distressing. He thinks my work is important and encourages me.

'How did you come to love such things?' I asked one morning as we are lying in bed. We've been woken by a pair of doves cooing at the window.

Superstitiously, I took it as a positive sign that somehow our relationship has divine approval.

'My father was a teacher,' John replied. 'My first and best, but he died young.' His tone was even but his brows dipped and gave him away. He still feels the loss keenly, despite the passage of time. I'm tougher than he is. I miss no one.

John frequently talks about people he knew at boarding school and Oxford, but my feeling is that he is lonely, as are most people who are different, who feel things intensely, and who don't quite fit in because of it. Though we are compatible in most things, I didn't take offense when we differed as I had with Sasha when I was younger, and the only time we came close to having words was near the end.

'I thought you said you would be taken off the front lines.' I was peevish when we sat down to breakfast the morning before our last day together.

John looked at me with a measure of understanding and before he said, 'There are not enough experienced men to lead the troops.'

'And so you have to do it? The war is effectively over. The Germans know they can't win, so why do they keep fighting?' I was outraged and sounded it.

'Hitler wants to sue for a separate peace with the Allies. He is holding out for that agreement,' he explained.

'What do you mean?' I asked.

'He wants to keep fighting the Russians in the East.'

I could understand the feeling against communism that was building in the West, of course, in light of what had happened in Poland and what was transpiring in Yugoslavia, and yet I could hardly believe that anyone who had experienced the consequences of Hitler's blitzkrieg would or could take him seriously. 'And Churchill is considering this?' I asked.

'Many things are being considered. The world will be a different place now that fascism is waning and the specter of communism is rearing its head.'

'What's the difference?' I snapped, and then recalled that when the fighting was over with the Japanese in the Far East, the communists and Chang's forces would no doubt be battling it out for supremacy. There were enormous ideological divides there and it would affect the lives of millions.

John just smiled. He knew why I was upset. 'We'll be together when it's over,' he said.

'Will we be? I mean there are no guarantees, are there?' I was close to tears.

'There never are in life and you know that.'

'But statistically the chances are worse,' I said.

He took a bite of his bread, seemingly lost in thought.

'I could come with,' I said.

'No.' he shook his head.

'You have no right to say that to me,' I said.

'No right, but I am asking you not to.'

I would have argued with him or resorted to crying in the past, now I said, 'It's almost our last day, let's not let anything spoil it.'

'Agreed. What should we do, take a walk?'

'We could, if you want.'

'What do you want?'

'I want to stay in and make love to you all day long. I want to hold you close and not let go. This might be the last time.' I really was crying now, but not for myself. I wiped my eyes with the back of my hand.

'Yes. All right.' John agreed, and we did.

The parting was awful, and though I tried to be stoic, we both shed tears in the end.

Florence, March 1945

Two things: Dresden and Yalta, last month, though I was only aware of them in the vaguest sense. The Allies firebombed the German baroque city of Dresden. They claimed they were aiming for industrial facilities and transportation routes but in some quarters, it is said civilians were deliberately targeted in an effort to demoralize the German populace. The effects of firebombing are dreadful. Rather than the sudden impact of the bomb itself, the entire city rages with fires. Goebbels has released the numbers of victims and photos of incinerated bodies. Even if he exaggerated, this is a horrendous way to die. There was a terrible backlash and criticism of the

Allied offensive in cultivated circles. Dresden, they claimed, was a center of German high culture.

I have seen the results of their culture, and I have spoken to Poles in London who have given me accounts of the ghettos, labor, and death camps in their country. They said the Polish underground have gone into such places and documented the systematic and deliberate torture and murder of the Slavs and the Jews there. They also said that they were not believed and that such things are dismissed as propaganda in the west. And yet knowing what the Germans have done in the eastern front, I believe all that the Poles have claimed. No one is insane enough to dream such things up, and yet, German violence and insanity know no bounds. I suppose I should pity civilians, but those masses supported Hitler and his plain spoken ambitions concerning Slavic sub-humans who were to be slaves in the New World Order, as well as his plans for the annihilation of the Jews.

Is there a moral equivalence and should we allow ourselves to sink to their level? I ask those questions of myself. But now as John is waiting for the final push to begin, I would like to see their armies ground to dust and disappear from the face of the earth. I have no pity and the fact that I have none makes me as barbaric as they are.

The Americans are doing the same in Japanese cities. When I heard that, I remembered Nanking and what the Japanese had done there and in Manchuria. I can't help but recall their awful sense of superiority and their monstrous behavior towards the Chinese and the people of Shanghai. But do common people deserve to suffer for what their armies and their leaders have done in their name? I should not believe in collective guilt, but sometimes I do and cannot help myself.

There is the other thing as well: Yalta. Eastern Poland is to be given to Stalin. John writes that General Anders' forces are desolate.

After their release from Soviet camps, a number of these brave Poles came overland through Iran and Palestine. Since, they have been fighting alongside the Allies with devastating results. They captured Monte Cassino, and they have been fighting northward up the boot of Italy all along. This is how they have been repaid. Some wonder what it has all been for, since their sacrifices have amounted to nothing but betrayal. There is another thing that perturbs me greatly: all Yugoslavs and Russians are to be repatriated to their respective countries. This means prisoners of war, refugees, and slave laborers, people who have fled in the wake of the communist drive west and do not want to return. These things are horrible to contemplate, and I am beside myself.

I have stayed on to work with the Fine Arts and Monuments people here providing photographic documentation of anything they may recover. I'm ashamed to say that some other photographers have been careless in the way they have laid out paintings in all sorts of weather. They don't have the culture or finesse of the curators.

I'm not in the annex anymore. The owners need the rental income and officers will pay more. I have small room in the back of the house that belonged to a maiden aunt who passed away last year. It smells of death. Sometimes, I wonder if that's how I'll end up in my old age, in some tiny room, unloved and unwanted, a burden to anyone who might know me.

Florence April 10, 1945

The Spring Offensive began on the 6th of April. I can barely function. My thoughts are dark though I am trying to control them. I think of John night and day. In the morning when I wake after a fitful sleep, he is the first thing on my mind. Although I try to think positive thoughts, they are soon superseded by the bleakest of fantasies. I find that prayer is useless. It's like begging a punitive parent for favors. Still, I say aloud, 'Just let him live and I will do whatever you want me to do.'

Then I think what if he is maimed? Of course, I will want to be with him and take care of him, but will he want me? Men can become cruel when they consider themselves less than whole, and I wonder if he would reject me out of bitterness or from the nobility of his heart. He probably would not want me to sacrifice myself. Yet he willingly makes sacrifices, knowing that the Red Army is fighting the Germans at the outskirts of Vienna and is pushing towards Berlin, that they will force capitulation, and that the Italian campaign is considered almost irrelevant by all sides at this point.

I should get out after work, see people, and step out of my solitude and my mindset. It is no good like this. Although my obsessiveness has become less *intense over the past few years, I still harbor under the strain of it. It must be an illness of a sort, I imagine.*

I wonder why I love John as much as I do and sometimes still compare him to Richard. There is no comparison, of course. Richard kept me at arm's length always. John is kind and tender. He seeks out my companionship and enjoys it.

Then I try to think back to the very beginning with Richard and why I fell for him. Was he not warm, did he not want to be with me? Did he change toward me because I was so eager and so in need of him to take care of me? I wonder if John tire of me as well? I recall how eager Nobuaki and Sasha were, how desirous of my presence. Is it because my ambivalence acted as a stimulant and they had to strive to attain me? I hope John is more developed, more mature. I hope our time in Florence was not just an anomaly.

Perhaps such thoughts are just a diversion to keep my mind off death, because once you've lived through a war, everything else should be easy-and all the striving -for adventure, and career, and achievement gets put in perspective-and you realize what might really be important in life.

Florence, April 15 1945

I'm only thinking of John and nothing but John. Images will come to me when I least expect them, flashes, memories of our time together. When I wake up-sometimes in the dead of night, sweaty from bad dreams, he is at the forefront of my mind. It is then that I remember things that were so unexpected. I think back on all his permutations, the wit that attracted me initially, and his irreverence. Although he can be quite serious, he lacks that annoying self-delusion that makes men go to the top as if they really believe in the world, as it is constituted. And yet he is disciplined and accomplished.

In the beginning when I first met him, I liked that he made me laugh. After his letters began, he tugged at my heartstrings because I could see how alone he was and how lonely. There are few people he can really share his thoughts with-because when men are that intelligent and sensitive-well, they tend not to expose themselves, do they? And yet he needed to be heard and to know that someone had understood him during the short passage that we call life. Then when we were together in Florence, I loved the way he seemed to make everything seem all right, as if it really would be. I never second guessed his motives, because he was guileless. And that, too, is what I remember when I awaken.

But then there is something else:

I've woken up from a fitful dream and can't sleep, and I toss and turn until I am afraid of disturbing John, who is asleep next to me. He doesn't register my movements, or if he does, they don't seem to bother him. But when I get up and glide across the floor as soundlessly as I can, and go down the half landing to a water closet, he comes to look for me. He has noticed I am missing and he is concerned. Perhaps he is half asleep as well.

'Where are you?' he asks.

I don't laugh or answer sarcastically, 'Well, where could I possibly be? I understand him and his need for connection. He is like me, so I reply that I won't be a minute. And when I climb back in the feather bed, he wraps his entire body around mine and folds my legs over his. He can sleep like that and is comforted. I marvel watching him and think I could easily spend the rest of my life like this, doing nothing but loving him.

I've told him bits about Shanghai but not the whole thing. It didn't seem right to bring it up and spoil things. It is also strange to me that I could respond so readily to him in a sexual sense, but whatever I experienced in Harbin seems to be not related to this, to John, or the way I think about him.

Florence, End April 1945

Marshall Zhukov and the First Belorussian Front are at the outskirts of Berlin! Partisan activity in the north of Italy. Will we see a civil war here as well? Mussolini is dead after being captured by partisans.

Florence, May 1 1945.

Dachau has been liberated. I will not invoke the name of God, who cannot possibly exist, having allowed such horrors to be perpetrated in this world.

Today I have seen the worst of humanity and everything the Soviets and Poles claimed about the world of the German concentration camps will now be witnessed by the Western public who have been so dismissive of the reports that came from the east.

When Majdanek was liberated by the Red Army in July 1944, the true horrors of the death camps were revealed for the first time. The BBC reported the news, but it was considered by most people to be Soviet propaganda. Now they will know and not doubt because there is a visceral immediacy to a photograph that no words, no matter how well chosen, can convey.

I joined some journalists in café that I often frequent when I am feeling lonely. There was a group of them hovering around a table. They were uncharacteristically somber and my curiosity was piqued. I wish I had never looked. The shots were taken by an earnest young photographer who was there with the American troops, and I think he is still in a state of shock. He was fine one moment, talking normally, but then his eyes glazed over, as if he was looking at something in the distance. It took a few minutes for him to come back to the present and afterward he seemed lost and confused. I shouldn't wonder. No one who has seen those starved and naked bodies, thrown away, dead and dying, as if they were driftwood, can register the true horror of the suffering that went on, sometimes for months and years, nor the mentality of those who conceived those horrors.

What will become of the inmates who have been through this? How will they be able to live their lives, having witnessed and experienced what they have? I came out alive as well but what I experienced was minor, yes, I say, minor by comparison, and yet I could barely cope with the knowledge of what had been done in Manchuria, let alone the reality of having been there.

How will the world understand the level of depravity that the Nazis have created? How will it react? What will happen to the Germans once they surrender? No punishment can be equal to what they have done. Firing squads and hangings are the easy way out.

Florence, May 3, 1945

Hitler is dead! The battle has been won. Yesterday the Germans surrendered in Italy. I am waiting to hear from John.

.   .   .

Florence, May 8, 1945
  Germany has surrendered!

Florence, May 18, 1945
  John is alive! All is well. I knew it would be, despite the fact that I wrung myself out with worry. I had an almost supernatural sensation that he would come through this and contact me once more. Maybe it is wishful thinking, or maybe there is a real connection between human beings who feel close to one another that is not dependent on proximity. Two nights before his letter arrived, I dreamt I was walking up a hill. To my right was a basilica, to my left, a great body of water. Sparks of light fell all around me creating a rainbow colored dome. John was not there, but I sensed his presence, and when I awoke, I felt peaceful for the first time since the campaign began.

Florence. June 1945
  The team is working hard to recover and catalogue treasure that has purportedly been set aside by the Germans for safe keeping, away from Allied bombardment. In San Lorenzo, they have found three hundred works, including Caravaggio's Bacchus and Botticelli's Minerva stored in damp jail cells. The truth of it is that Hitler and Goring were stealing it all. Goring for himself, Hitler for his Fuhrermuseum.
  On the fourth of April, thousands of artworks and gold bricks were found in the Merkers Mine in Austria. Also in April, paintings by Michelangelo, Durer, Rubens, and Vermeer, among six thousand other works, were found in the Altaussee Salt Mines.
  It's strange to think about Hitler's relationship to art. He was a failed painter after all. My colleagues claim despite his often questionable taste, he did appreciate the arts. Still, men who deem themselves important and who are rich enough to purchase great art, or appropriate it, have always aggrandized themselves with their collections. Perhaps it is a path toward social acceptance, of showing the world their level of sophistication and culture. Mussolini never did appreciate Italy's patrimony, and in the

beginning of the Axis alliance, he sold treasure troves to the Germans at bargain prices.

Hitler gave the order for everything he confiscated to be destroyed if Germany fell, but mercifully he was ignored and these priceless art treasures have survived. It is not surprising considering his outrageous egomania that he would order everything to go up in a conflagration with him, a Valhalla of sorts. But we too, the Allies, destroyed the sixth century Abbey of Monte Cassino with our bombs. Had it not been for the Germans who took the contents of the abbey itself and those of the Naples Museum, which had been removed to the abbey for safekeeping, I dread to think what would have happened.

Florence, Mid-June 1945

Michelangelo's David and his Slaves were entombed in brick to guard them from destruction during the Allied push northward. Today those bricks were removed. I have never felt so elated, so thrilled, as I was when I saw the colossal David revealed. What wondrous talent, what a glorious work! There will never be anything like it again.

My elation was short lived when one of our people was killed afterward. We had been told a few paintings of minor importance were hidden in the villa. A couple of men went inside, despite knowing the Germans have booby trapped and mined so many places that anything can happen. I was standing outside the villa chatting and smoking with a group of GI's. It was an ordinary day. Until it wasn't. I was laughing at a joke. There was an explosion. We all ran towards it, but it was too late. You never get used to death. It's so random and unjust. The sappers came afterward to demine the place. I don't know how they can stand it. I would have lost my nerve long ago.

I ask myself what value a painting has. Is it worth more than a human life? Perhaps one painting does not, but what about the Sistine Chapel, or a single masterpiece like the Laocoon, or any number of great buildings or churches and their contents. And what if we consider the wholescale destruction the Germans engaged in the Soviet Union and in Poland, where the cultural patrimony and national identity of those nations were slated for obliteration?

In Leningrad, people starved and froze before they would destroy one stick of wood fencing, let alone a building. It is about more than saving a work of art or a pile of bricks, it is about sending a message-this is who we are, this is who we have been, this is what we have produced and you with your marching bands, bombs, and beer gardens could never achieve what we have, despite your claims of racial superiority.

Despite the fact that I did not know the man who was killed, I was so sad and so filled with rage. I wrote to John, pouring out all my bile.

You have to give them Bach, Mozart, Beethoven and Brahms at least, John wrote back. Fine, I replied, but then there's Chopin, Tchaikovsky, Rachmaninoff, Mussorgsky, Rimsky –Korsakov, Stravinsky, Prokofiev, Shostakovich, Dvorzak, Janacek... and then I am reminded of that long ago party in Shanghai when Natalia debated Russian culture and the superiority of Russian writers with Frau Hrbek and laugh at myself. It's vulgar, this tribalism, isn't it?

Rome, mid -July 1945

Joy! The Florentine works have been restored to the Uffizi, the Pitti Palace, the Bargello Museum and the Palatine Gallery. One hundred nine crates at San Lorenzo, forty-six at Campo Tores, all loaded on a train headed back home. The arrival of the art was celebrated throughout the city and thousands of Florentines came out to cheer while the bells were ringing and the trumpeters at the Piazza della Signora heralded the parade of cars. A tremendous effort on the part of the team who toiled ceaselessly to make it happen. I took photos of the entire event. I was so elated. It was like riding a wave of energy and excitement. Afterward, I felt depleted and, once again, very alone. I felt the need to get back to Rome.

When I got back the first thing I heard at the cafes was that Rossellini wrapped up his film a few weeks ago. There's a lot of speculation about what it is going to be like. I can hardly wait until the premiere.

Sadly, there are darker things in this world. A letter from John about an extraordinary Polish officer named Witold Pilecki, who was recently released from a German POW camp, and who has joined General Anders here in Italy. Pilecki was captured in the Warsaw Uprising, but even before, his work underground was exceptional. Apparently, he volunteered to infiltrate Auschwitz and set up resistance cells to prepare for a general uprising. Information is emerging about those places now, but Pilecki was there from the beginning, chronicling the brutal deaths of Poles and Red Army Prisoners of War, who were the first to be interned and killed. Pilecki not only managed to organize resistance but also escaped with two others to get word out of what was happening. He is writing up an account for his superiors that will be shared by the Allies since the Nazis who ran the camps and committed atrocities will, no doubt, stand trial. Certainly, the Soviets will insist on trials, since they have suffered so horribly at German hands.

John wants to spare me the details of the camps, but today I have read something as dreadful that will not leave me. I had a letter from one of the girl Partizans I met last December. Her name is Manya and her mother is a White Russian, and so she writes to me, in Russian, though I can't say why. Manya is a lovely girl with dark hair and eyes, and ideologically divided from her mother who she deems frivolous.

Manya is an ardent anti-fascist. She and her comrades have fought their way into Croatia routing the last remnants of the fascist Ustashe, with the Second Army under General Koca Popovic. What she has witnessed upon the liberation of the Ustasha concentration camps has shaken her to her core. Trials of the war criminals, who committed such bestial acts that the German command complained to their superiors in Berlin, are now being conducted by the Partizans.

What is so terribly distressing is that among all the innocents, women and children were killed as well, clubbed, burned or buried alive, tortured, cut with knives, raped, and that these crimes are unprecedented for having had been committed by Catholic priests. What crimes did the victims stand accused of? None, other than belonging to the Orthodox or Jewish faiths in the Independent State of Croatia.

Manya writes that all this was done with the complicity of the Vatican, that the go ahead was given for forcible conversions and that whatever the Vatican's claims of innocence are, their Papal legate was present in Zagreb and well aware of the archipelago of camps- where the most heinous of acts were committed against Serbs, Jews, Roma, and Croatian resisters. The world will never know the extent of it, she writes, due to the power of the Vatican, unlike the Nazi concentration camps, which were run by a defeated Germany, and whose horrors will be broadcast all over the world.

Why does Manya write this to me? Perhaps I am the only journalist she knows, and Orthodox as well, perhaps couched in her child-like Russian she believes I can use my influence to broadcast this news, but I, too, know that it will go nowhere. The Catholic element too powerful and entrenched-and I think few will believe the extent of Vatican involvement with the fascist leaders in the now defunct Independent State of Croatia. They will dismiss this as communist propaganda, or perhaps even Serbian propaganda, though Tito is a Croat as are many of his Partizans.

Manya writes of the Spanish Civil War, of fascist clergy, who blessed the guns of the militia, and of Croat nuns who ran the children's camp in Sisak, starved, and poisoned the children with caustic soda. She equates religion with fascism and fanaticism, and a mindset, which is opposed to democracy and liberalism. I have not looked at the world this way, but only in terms of my own opposition to the effacing of the individual in favor of the collective under the communist despoilers of my own land. What is the difference, I wonder, in the final analysis, when the result is the same? Death, torment, and fear. Nothing more.

Rome, August 1945

Japan has declared it will surrender. The war is effectively over, but at what cost? The Americans dropped powerful atomic bombs on the civilian population of Hiroshima and Nagasaki. The Vatican newspaper has strongly condemned this action and these types of weapons, noting their threat to all of humanity, but I am told the American public has welcomed it. I have such mixed emotions, it is hard to separate and make sense of them.

I haven't wanted to think about China or the Japanese for so long, and I still don't want to, but I keep remembering my pupil, Yukiko, a young and innocent girl, who had nothing to do with what transpired in the Far East. Harder to reconcile are the feelings that arise when I think about Tamura. He was kind to me, he rescued me, and yet he was complicit in the actions his country undertook. He knew about that dreadful place and the things that went on there, yet he could turn a blind eye to it. He focused on the pursuit of pleasure, on creating beautiful scenarios, of pursuing me, but one in a long line of women. Was that the way he escaped from reality or was he able to live with those dichotomies and somehow accept them? Or perhaps like his fellows, he looked at the rest of humanity as less worthy, less important- as expendable.

What face did he show to me? Was that the real Tamura or just a portion of himself? How difficult it is to know.

I've seen some dreadful sights on the streets. Women who consorted with German are being publicly humiliated, beaten, and tormented by the mob. A while ago, I was walking down a street when I heard a commotion. I turned around and saw an unruly group of Romans. I couldn't see what they were up to at first and pushed my way forward through the throng of bystanders. Men were dragging a woman who once must have been pretty, although now her head was shaved. It had been done in a brutal fashion and rivulets of blood from the gashes on her scalp pooled down her face. She was whimpering and her tears were mingling with snot as she tried to cover her modesty, but her clothes had been ripped and her breasts were exposed. Her attackers were shouting all sorts of ugly words at her. I wanted to tell them to stop, that what they were doing was inhumane but I was pushed back. A woman with compassionate dark eyes met mine and she simply shook her head, as if to say that nothing could be done.

I turned away, though I felt a sensation of shame arise in the pit of my stomach and spread over my body, stinging like fire ants. I might have so easily been in her shoes. Why did I let myself be sucked up by events, why did I not have the sensibility to understand what was transpiring around me and behave accordingly? I have to wonder about my morality. I feel guilt, dreadful guilt, at having had an intimate relationship with Tamura. I can excuse my youth, my frailties, my endless loneliness, and the kind of manipulation that Richard subjected me to, or rather, that I allowed myself to be subjected to. I can claim I was weak, but, in the end, I must take responsibility for my own actions.

People have done terrible things to each other during this war, there has been such brutality, so many betrayals, but they seem to be able to cope, to

brush things off, and not recriminate themselves. I don't understand it at all.
I don't understand myself either.

Rome, September 1945

    I feel a bit better. My work is winding down, and I am content that I have
made a small contribution to the incredible accomplishments of the
Monuments people in Italy. But that's not why I'm feeling happy. John wants
to see me.

    Sometimes, I feel almost girlish again and find myself anticipating
meeting him -almost in the same spirit as I did in the old days in Shanghai. I
plan the outfits I will wear once we are reunited. There are wonderful
shoemakers here, of course, and all you have to do is bring the materials,
which aren't always easy to get. I've been going to a hairdresser who has
made me look quite glamorous again. I do all this not because I am so
enamored of my own image or the impression I might make but because it
passes the time, and because I am counting the days until I can see him.

    It's all quite pathetic when I think about it, really, but, in a sense,
concentrating on life again is holding back the bad, that profound sense of
nausea and disgust when I regard the human race and what they are capable
of doing and what they have done during this war.

    It takes a concentrated effort to focus on the good things, and I do each
day. You have to be grateful for the tiniest things- sunshine, a flower, a kind
gesture, good work done well, and not fall back on brooding because that is so
easy to do. I think back on my time with the monks and the things I learned
there, like the notion that the evil on earth is perpetrated by those who are not
aligned with the flow of the universe, who live far from the light, and whose
souls are weighted with their deeds.

    I cannot think what could have motivated the Germans to feel such
hatred as to seek a final solution and exterminate the Jews, or attempt to
expropriate Slavic lands for their own use and enslave the populations there.
No amount of economic analysis could account for such behavior. Yes, they
were defeated in the First World War. Yes, they had to pay heavy and
unreasonable reparations. Yes, they lived through dreadful inflation, but the
Great Depression was global and few sunk to their level. Like the Japanese

military's perversion of Bushido, the S.S was built upon a culture of racial superiority and violence. Violence for the sake of violence and the glorification of permanent military readiness and the necessity for brutality. Certainly, they believed and still believe because most of them will not be rounded up and punished. They will not consider what they have done and repent. They will instead merely rationalize it, if they think about it at all.

How do these traits manifest in the first place and in otherwise normal human beings who supported these monsters? I have read the accounts of Red Army officers who claimed Auschwitz came as no shock because they had already witnessed such gruesome deeds on the Eastern Front, entire villages destroyed, children maimed, women raped, and whole populations exterminated.

It is true that Lenin developed labor camps in Siberia to quell political opposition and even in Shanghai, we had heard tales about deportations and deaths under Stalin. I have to wonder if there is a moral equivalent. The Russian people do not support this, nor is violence glorified there, nor is there a plan to exterminate whole populations on a racial basis. And what about the Americans who have fought for freedom in Europe? They suppress their own people of African origin and they have exterminated the Indian tribes.

What is it about the other, those outside of our own tribal units that causes us to disregard them? And what about the way humanity brutalizes animals every day- from the peasant to the cart driver to the laboratory scientist?

When I spoke to Polish soldiers who recognized the dangers inherent in the collectivist mentality be it communist or fascist, they knew that individualism, intellectual freedom, and spirituality would suffer as a result in their own country. But many of these men are Catholics and devoted to their church. In their lands, it has been a boon, but how would they account for the Vatican's complicity in exterminating Orthodox Serbs in such horrendous camps as Jasenovac? How could they account for a hatred such as the Catholic Croats had towards their neighbors the Serbs, who look and sound like them and who did nothing to merit that kind of brutality whatsoever? Ostensibly religions have been the source of so much slaughter historically, but what is at the bottom of that- greed, envy, desire for appropriation of goods, economics, and the drive to enrich oneself and one's own group? The Crusades, the extermination of New World Indians, and colonialism could be seen in such a light.

There must be something more to it, something wicked, or, at least, destructive, that lies within the heart of men. I keep thinking about Nobuaki and still can't explain how he could knowingly serve evil.

Perhaps my focus on survival, my little bits of cloth, my need for love and to make things pretty were not so horrible, not so selfishly wrong, because what is there in a life that matters but love and beauty and kindness? And those who abuse it, regardless of ideology, regardless of their intent to right or wrong the world have caused more hardship and pain than anyone has.

Rome, October 1945

I waited for John on the Spanish Steps, and when he didn't arrive at the appointed time I thought he had changed his mind, and all the months I had waited, and worried, and pined for him would come to nothing at all. It was hot, but it was a dry sun and the heat felt as if it was burning the collective weight of the past off my body.

I was thinking I would go up the steps to the hotel, run a bath, get beneath the linens, and have a long afternoon sleep, listening to the noise of the street to compensate for my loneliness. It was a strange idea, but I didn't feel like going back to my own dingy place after I had told my landlady I would be meeting my sweetheart.

The flower sellers had their wares out. One of them began talking to me and I thought, yes I'll have a bunch of red flowers. As I handed over some coins into her outstretched palm, I looked up and saw a tall man striding toward me, his head characteristically cocked to one side. I would have known him anywhere, and I waved before shielding my eyes from the sun, holding the flowers, and waving with them, once again.

I went down the steps to meet him halfway. He looked at me with warmth and kindness in his eyes and bent down to kiss me, though there was a moment of confusion, and instead of kissing him fully I merely grazed his lips. And then I thought, how foolish that was of me, but I was suddenly shy. I realized that the one week we had spent had been isolated and magical -as an enchanted, sheltered oasis in the midst of chaos- but I wondered what things would look like between us now that the war was over and we had returned to civilian life.

'I thought you might have changed your mind,' I said suddenly.

'Ah, I was afraid you might think that, but the train was running late. I would have found you, by the way, had you gone up to the hotel.'

'Yes, of course,' I said. 'Let's unpack and see the city, shall we?'

He looked a bit wistful before agreeing. I was still nervous around him and he could sense it and my hesitation. I sensed he felt rejected, but instead of taking him by the hand, I fumbled with my bag before he took it up.

'Look,' he said as we reached the top of the steps, and I turned to look at the city, the golden light falling upon the dome of St Peter's, the birds flying overhead, at the people who were going about their lives and thought, we're alive, we made it out alive, and we are together. I took his free hand as we walked up the street and through the doors of the lobby.

The hotel was owned by a friend of his. It had been closed to the public after the Americans had used it as their headquarters, but John had convinced him to allow us to stay there. The proprietor, a short dark man with a slim mustache, greeted us with such a profuse show of affection for John that I knew there had been a history between them, though no one bothered to tell me about it. Then he took us to a suite overlooking the city. John put our bags down and drew the curtains.

'Come,' he beckoned. I stood at his side, and when he looked at me to gauge my reaction I stood on my toes to kiss him, and he bent toward me, knowing my intent.

I wanted to remember every moment of that day, the kisses that followed and everything that passed between us afterward that seemed so natural and unconstrained as if we had never been apart, but I didn't write anything down because it seemed a waste to be away from him for even an instant.

Now, that time seems blurred when I recall our walks and the things we showed each other, the narrow streets, and plazas, the flowers hanging from windows, the statues, and fountains. We ate when we were hungry, stopping at small unknown places, and we made love in the afternoons that led into night.

There were details that will always be part of me: his long body in the bath as I washed his hair, the way he wrapped himself around me when I felt restless and wakeful in the darkness. Most of all, I recall his patience and forbearance, and how comfortable and comforted I felt in his presence. There was no anxiety, no sense of rejection, or that I was somehow cutting into his time. There was no desire to be away from him and no second guessing as to who he was as a human being.

We were friends; we were lovers. There seemed to be no ideological barriers between us and no condescension, but honest speech that made us love one another, openly and dearly. We were walking down the Corso when he suggested we take a picnic basket into the countryside the following day. He could get a car from his friend, he said, and I agreed.

We set out in late morning, provisioned, and when we arrived at the spot, which John had known about beforehand, I asked why he had chosen it.

'I don't know. When I saw it the first time, I thought it would be a nice spot to have a picnic after the war was done. I assumed I would live through it,' he added wryly.

'And you did. What now?'

'What do you mean?'

'I mean what are you going to do with the rest of your life?'

He thought for a moment. 'Not sure. Teach, probably.'

I shrugged slightly. It was inevitable. I thought then that this interlude would be our last since he had said nothing at all about the future, so I hurriedly interjected, 'I'm thinking about making a proposal to the magazine when my work here winds down.'

'What's that?' he asked, spreading the cloth and pouring wine.

'The fight for China will begin now. I speak Chinese, and the American public is interested in China and the specter of communism falling there. I never really made an impact with my European photos, but they remember my work in Shanghai.'

'Is this what you really want?' he asked.

I shrugged. 'What choice do I have? I have no home of my own and maybe this is how I am meant to live.'

He looked thoughtful and a bit sly, 'Why not make a home with me?'

'How do you mean?'

'As my wife.'

I suppose a part of me had always been hopeful, but I asked, 'Do you think we could adapt to a conventional life after this?'

He laughed, 'Our life can be as unconventional as you want it to be. You needn't stop working, you know, if that's what you want.'

'I don't know what I want aside from you. However, I have an alternate proposal. Many of the monuments officers have moved northward and will be demobbed shortly. I have made friends among the Italians and still I think I can get some work. They could use an archaeologist, though the pay will be next to nothing, I'm sure.

'I think I'd like that,' he said thoughtfully, 'but then what?'

'I don't know. Let's see where the road takes us.'

'All right,' he said, 'Let's.'

Oxfordshire October, 2003

Li Kong put down the diary. Tanya had not returned. He stood, stretching his legs. Surely, they must have married and returned to England, or else she would not be living here, he reasoned. He took a turn around the room and then took the liberty of walking through the rest of the ground floor to examine the photographs that were arranged on the walls.

He recognized the beaches of California where he had been himself, and those of the American desert, though the shots were long and curiously devoid of human presence. He saw that she had been in Mexico from the stark images of Indian women weavers and pyramids which cast their dark shadows under the blazing the sun. Later there were photos of Hong Kong, which must have dated to the 1950's and were almost unrecognizable, and many of Italy, from the rubble of the war to the lush and hedonistic resorts of the seventies. Here too were shots of London through time, beginning with the Blitz to the present, favorite places, revisited again and again. And finally, there were monuments of Egypt, Italy and Greece. In one prominent photo, a tall slender man stood by a desert dig. He had put his hand up to tilt back his hat, as if he was contemplating what was before him. Li Kong moved closer to have a look, thinking the image must be of John when he heard the door opening. He snapped to attention like a small boy who had been caught trespassing.

'Ah, there you are,' the old lady said. She was accompanied by a tall man who was stooped and walked with shuffling, hesitant steps, while leaning on a cane.

'John, this is the young man I told you about. Li Kong, John Harrison, my husband.'

Li Kong rushed forward to shake John's hand but realized it was difficult for the old man to transfer the cane to his left.

'How do you do?' John mouthed with difficulty, and Li Kong guessed that he must have had a stroke at some point.

'Let's go in, shall we? It's easier for John if we sit,' Tanya said.

Li Kong followed them as she helped John maneuver the step down to the conservatory. The afternoon sun was low in the sky, and she asked if it bothered Li Kong.

'No, actually, I love it. When I was sent to the countryside, I shot images of the sunrise and the sunset each day. I know it was a foolish thing to do, wasting film like that, but...' he stopped short.

'You were moved by the beauty of it,' she finished his sentence for him.

'Yes. And there was little beauty in those days.'

'But you managed to transform your experiences into art. We've seen your films, John and I,' but she did not go into detail, though Li Kong found himself longing to hear her opinion of them.

'What was it really like?' she asked, referring to the time he had spent in the farms.

'Then I thought it was like immolation, a slow death of the mind that I would never be able to transcend. Later, I realized it was beautiful in its own way, and the loneliness I experienced was transformative. It was a period when my ideas began to coalesce.'

John nodded his assent. 'I felt the same in the desert,' he said.

Li Kong strained to understand him. He saw that Tanya was anxious, and he knew that it would be more convenient for her to speak for John but she restrained herself and allowed him to finish his sentence.

314

'Sometimes, after the war, I needed to be alone with my own thoughts, particularly when I was writing. She never left me to brood for too long though,' he smiled lopsidedly. 'She won't let go of me even now.'

'Oh, you're far from that,' she said, though it was obvious from the way her voice dropped she did not think so. 'So many of our friends are gone. Anya and Mike, and Natalia, oh, so long ago now. Change is the one constant in life, and death is an inevitability.' She paused for a while, lost in thought. 'It's strange how art is made, isn't it? Sometimes the best things grow from the pain and suffering we have experienced.'

'Yes,' Li Kong agreed.

'I never did anything really important like you and Sasha did, but I'm glad my diaries brought you together. It makes me feel that in a small way, I also contributed. You found some meaning in them, and that is good.' she said.

'But your jewelry designs were lovely and important. They give people pleasure,' Li Kong said.

'That is so, but they do not say anything about the human condition or leave people with the experience of having glimpsed at something truly profound.'

'Your photographs have done that.'

'Perhaps, but only very occasionally.'

'I have something else for you,' Li Kong said, taking out a disk from his briefcase. 'I made a print that you can have. It's Fang Shirong's last unfinished film. I think when you see it, you'll know he achieved what we in the creative arts aspire to, but rarely can fulfill.'

'I'll treasure it,' she said, taking it from his hand.

'No, just watch. That's all.' He stood to go. 'Good-bye, and thank you for everything,' he said.

In the last dying hour of the afternoon as the flowers were fading on the windowsill, an old man took out a small portrait of a woman from

315

a drawer and looked at it. His face was etched with regret, and Tanya knew at once that Sasha had understood that few mistakes were rectifiable and that love is rarely accepted by those who are fated to be alone, despite their best intentions.

She remembered their last time together when she had thought they had come to a deep understanding and when she believed it would last. Then she remembered the day he had come to send her away. He had captured the essence of that moment perfectly, as the young man told the concubine he was leaving her for the great world.

She thought of love in all its permutations, of the kind that is never allowed to develop, and that which ends in betrayal and animosity. All love alters over time, she thought. Often and most sadly, it merely ends.

Despite the fact, she had told Li Kong she had had a happy life with John, she had often wondered if giving so fully and unconditionally of herself had been a choice well made. Perhaps, she mused, had she been capable of producing genuine art, she would not have chosen a life that revolved around another, no matter how deeply loved. She recalled how she had prioritized his career, had followed him, and adopted his enthusiasms until she genuinely shared them. True, she had designed and illustrated covers for children's books, and there had been that stint the sixties and early seventies when she had opened a boutique and imported Carnaby Street fashions to California while John was teaching there. But overall, she regarded herself an artistic failure.

'He captured you well,' John said.

'What makes you think that's me?' she asked.

John laughed. 'Being able to love like that is a gift, as great as any art. Though I haven't always shown it, don't think it has gone unnoticed or has not been reciprocated.'

That was the thing about John, she thought. Whatever her doubts, he always managed to dispel them.

She reached for his hand, and he squeezed hers lightly before bringing it to his lips.

. . .

Shanghai 1969

Sun Mu had been to the prison gates once more, hoping to bribe the new guard for word of Anita. He had made friends with the previous guard who was friendly and sympathetic. She had gotten him news of Anita, who was being interrogated regularly. Once he had even brought soap and a pot of face cream, and the woman had sworn she had given them to Anita on the sly. He was not certain she was telling the truth, and even if she had taken them for herself, he would not have begrudged her. But now she had been replaced, perhaps sanctioned for her friendliness, or her thievery. The new guard was of a different sort and had heaped abuse both upon him, a stupid old man, in her words, and that spoiled degenerate actress. She had chased him away from the prison gates all too easily.

Perhaps it was just as well, and he wouldn't have to be the one to bring the message that Gong Wei had committed suicide after his final public humiliation. It might break her, he thought.

Once, the friendly guard had mentioned how clever Anita had been in fielding the questions posed to her.

'Who told you that?' Sun Mu had asked, not trusting her level of intelligence or ability to ascertain what was clever or not.

'I heard the interrogators speaking among themselves. Clever, but they don't think she'll be able to get away with it for long. She's tough, you know. You wouldn't expect it from a woman like that, so pampered and spoiled.'

'Yes, she's tough,' he had agreed. But would she be tough enough to withstand the news of Gong Wei's death? He had been foolish to think that by bringing the news himself he could mitigate its impact. If the interrogators believed it would influence her confession to the imaginary crimes she had been accused of, perhaps they would use that knowledge, but perhaps they were as ignorant as the guard and wouldn't make the connection between Gong Wei and Anita.

For a few moments, he thought that perhaps he and Anita might keep each other company in old age after she was released from prison. Then he chastised himself for being a sentimental old fool. She'll never leave that cell, he said to himself, and knew it was true. He

317

suddenly realized he was terribly hungry and felt weak and dizzy as his heart began to beat erratically.

'I must remember to eat,' he said aloud, thinking how depressed he had been since Li Kong had been sent to the countryside. He had had something to do when Li Kong had been with him, something to aspire to, teaching the boy as he had done. Now, his days were empty and there was little to fill them. I didn't want people around taxing me emotionally when I was young, he thought. Now I miss them.

He felt a sharp pain shooting down his arm, so sharp he fell to his knees. He was conscious in his last moments, aware he was having a heart attack, through the layers of cold sweat and nausea he was experiencing. The street seemed strangely deserted, and he did not know that it had been closed off for a late afternoon rally. He opened his mouth to call out but almost laughed at the futility of it. No help was coming, and even if it had been, he would not want it.

An image of a woman's hand with a jeweled cuff and painted half-moon nails reached for a cooked lobster and pried it apart. What an absurd thing to think about, he thought. And then he was dead.

Shanghai, September 2014

Li Kong was directing his actress. She was French, slight and dark, and twenty-seven years old. She wore a lightweight bone colored gabardine suit that recalled the silhouette of the Shanghai of the nineteen -thirties. A section of the Bund had been closed for the filming and they were shooting around new construction.

The actress held the hat closely to her head as a slight wind blew it upward. She walked hurriedly, an expression of anxiety marring her lovely face. Her steps were hobbled by her too tight skirt, and the portfolio she carried was unwieldy. Letting go of the hat for a brief moment, she raised her hand, and hailing a cab, got in.

'And cut,' he said.

He did not know if the film would be any good. He knew he could never match Fang Shirong's delicate, and subtle, late output. His own films were cruder, rawer, and sometimes powerful, often containing a political subtext. In the past decade since his Hollywood breakthrough, he had directed large scale historic epics for mass consumption. This film would signal a return to his smaller, more intimate films.

He had begun the story with the day the Japanese invaded Shanghai and Tanya had found Richard's villa empty and her hopes dashed. He had decided he would compress the story, leaving himself out of it and ending it with Tanya's fictitious death in Unit 731. It would be a tale of thwarted passion and betrayal set against the turbulent backdrop of the city in the 1930's and the early war years. He had often thought how much to reveal about his own part in Tanya's story, and over time he and his ex-wife had transformed the script from the original, paring it down considerably.

He fretted over this version and had even resorted to calling his ex-wife in the middle of the night to run new ideas by her. Finally, weary of him, she had said, 'Li Kong, you can only do what you are capable of doing at the moment, and then you must move forward to the next project, regardless.'

She was right, as she had always been, and now that he had long broken with his mistress and had had a multitude of inconsequential relationships with young actresses, she had remained stalwart; his closest collaborator and best friend. Sometimes, life was oddly circular, he thought.

'Let's try it one more time,' he said to the actress, 'and this time, I want to see you really sweat with anxiety over seeing Richard again, knowing he has always rejected your love.'

The actress nodded and with an uncanny instinct transformed herself into Tatiana Zhukova, a woman who had thrown away all her opportunities and who would come to a desperate and tragic end.

ABOUT THE AUTHOR

Lily Temmer is the author of four novels and four books of short stories. Her prose has been deemed 'perfect' by Kirkus reviews. Lily is a trained anthropologist but has worked in various professions, including website design, editing, and advertising. She is widely traveled and has climbed Machu Picchu, survived a jaguar attack in the Petén, danced in Parisian nightclubs, and sailed the five seas.

Lily lives in Evanston, Illinois with her three controlling black cats, hundreds of books, and tons of plants that friends leave behind to be nurtured. Aside from spiritual development, writing has been her consuming passion.

Independent authors do depend on reader reviews. If you enjoyed this book, please leave a review at Amazon.com.

If you would like to receive news about upcoming books and specials, please use the sign up form at lstemmer.com to sign up.

You can also find all of my published works available on Amazon under the name L.S. Temmer.

ALSO BY L.S. TEMMER

Meridian

Death of an Activist

End Game

Children of the Sun and Other Stories

Mr. Heathcliff's Fortune and Other Short Stories

The God of Rock and Other Stories

Throw Granny off the Balcony and Other Short Stories